# LIZZIE'S DEVIL

By the soft light of the candle's flame, Li's taut skin gleamed gold, the aching line of his neck, the fine arch of his alien brow—strange untouchable beauty.

She was dying in this room, secret with the intimate scent of a musk that lingered like sighs on Li's rosy sheets. Lizzie's heart beat slowly in her white throat; her white skin shivered under black velvet. A part of Lizzie Stafford was fading away like a whisper, forgotten in the wind. She had not come to tell this mysterious man she was sorry. Nor to warn him about James. She came to Li because—she had to.

Some struggling something in her mind put up one last fight. "I came to tell you that James is going to hurt you, you and your people, he's the one behind—"

Stepping quickly away from the bed with the rose sheets, Li put his hand on the back of Lizzie's pale neck. She gasped. His touch was no longer tender; it was a harsh grip, possessive. He was hurting her.

"You should not be telling me this. You and I must not be on the same side."

His hand was burning her skin.

Roughly, Li pulled Lizzie toward him. He dug his fingers deep into the soft black geometry of her hair, pulling her head back until the green eyes were forced to look up into his beautiful Chinese face. His alien eyes burned with a copper light.

"Damn you, white ghost," he murmured.

Her heart slipped sideways.

"Then tell me to go away. Tell me to get the hell out of here."

"I can't. This is a game we shall both lose." Li's hand twisted in her hair. "The devil will take it all." He bent her backward, kissing her long white neck. "But we will play."

Lizzie, with a sob, set her sights on Satan. . . .

# CHINA BLUES

## Pamela Longfellow

**BANTAM BOOKS**
NEW YORK · TORONTO · LONDON · SYDNEY · AUCKLAND

*This edition contains the complete text
of the original hardcover edition.*
NOT ONE WORD HAS BEEN OMITTED.

CHINA BLUES

*A Bantam Book / published by arrangement with
Doubleday*

*PRINTING HISTORY*

*Doubleday edition published June 1989
Bantam edition / July 1990*

ISBN 0-553-28529-7

*Published simultaneously in the United States and Canada*

Bantam Books are published by Bantam Books, a division of
Bantam Doubleday Dell Publishing Group, Inc. Its trademark,
consisting of the words "Bantam Books" and the portrayal of
a rooster, is Registered in U.S. Patent and Trademark Office
and in other countries. Marca Registrada. Bantam Books,
666 Fifth Avenue, New York, New York 10103.

PRINTED IN THE UNITED STATES OF AMERICA

RAD                                    0  9  8  7  6  5  4  3  2  1

To Sydney

# CHINA
# BLUES

# Prologue

In the early hours of the eighteenth of April 1906—one of those first sweet years of the twentieth century when America still thought it was young and had a good grip on things—half the world, as usual, was asleep.

Ancient China, mysterious and patient, wearing the tenacious Manchurian yoke of its Dragon Empress, Tz'u-hsi, yawned and snuffed the candle. Hawaii, its islands liquid green tips of fiery underwater mountains, murmured under a blanket of dreams. And California, a long fat crescent of continental coast, booty for a thousand robber barons in its high Sierras, the makings of a hundred cities in its shadowed forests, vast valleys heavy with pumpkin, orange blossom, and artichoke, the westernmost thrust of an arrogance called the United States, was just about to wake up.

When Los Angeles was a sun-blown pueblo waiting for the movie to begin, San Francisco was *the city,* a fabulous metropolis by the bay—straight streets driven reckless up her seven steep hills of yellow sand; tall buildings perched on the turbulent slopes like exclamation marks; humming docks and bursting warehouses nestled on landfill like smug frogs on a lily pad. She held back the ocean with a sieve. San Francisco, dancing on her hilltops for less than sixty years, was Queen of the West. Her people, immigrants from all nations of the world, were drawn to her by gold and silver, by adventure and open space, by the trade of a deepwater port second only to New York—by easy pickings, by land grabs, and by greed.

It was the end of the line, the edge of the world; it was as far as a man could go without falling off.

The hustling bawdy city by the western sea opened an eye on the April dawn, totted up the odds on a new day, snuggled back against her soft sand hills, and then fell out of bed with a bang.

San Francisco *was* surprised.

The boy never understood what woke him. Birds? Rats in the walls? He only remembered a sudden jolt from soft white dreams into a deep, waiting, wide-awake dark. Hot with sleep, his little sister, Su Yin, was wedged between him and his elder brother, Chang. The even breathing of his family, shallow and slow, told him their souls were out wandering, spinning circles of eternal light, away from the room that was all they had, all he had ever known. It was home. He listened. There was nothing else.

Outside the tenement building there was no sound of creaking carts, no sleepy voices in singsong complaint pushing back stiff store shutters. The air was cold and clear; Chinatown's daytime haze of cooking fat came with the sun. It was too late for the drunken sailors looking for Chinese girls or opium, too early for the babble of tradesmen, the workers, the women and children. Inside, the plumbing had yet to groan, rumbling with the visits of neighbors. For the first time in his short cramped crowded life the boy felt alone—and afraid of being alone. The dark air brooded over Chinatown, alive with something coiled and waiting. It was very quiet and very wrong.

His heart shuddered in his chest, skipped, and slowed. How long before the light came? When would his mother awaken to lead him back home from fear? Rocking him, chanting his descent line, the list of ancestors that was the Chinese link to reality. His skin, stiff with goose bumps, tingled. The soles of his feet ached. To keep away the fear, he played a game with himself, a game he'd discovered when he was seven. His father, the best tailor on the Barbary Coast, had taken him into the world outside Chinatown. With pride he'd led his son through the white streets, bowing to the white faces, moving deferentially out of the white way.

"This is my son," his father told the *baak gwai lo*—white ghosts, people he knew on his rounds. "This is Li Kwan Won. He will help me now with my work. He will be a tailor like his father."

Li's father flushed with pleasure when the strange faces smiled, looked humbly away when they did not, moved on quickly when any of the ghosts grunted in contempt. Li was terrified. He couldn't understand what his own father was saying; the words were alien, hostile, white. He couldn't understand what the white demons said to his father. He watched the wet red mouths moving, overwhelmed by their thick meaty smell, mesmerized by the bristling mustaches and fierce beards, red, yellow, black, standing away from the moving mouths. Outside Chinatown the world was so big, so quick and nervy. There were no comforting yellow faces, no soft Chinese words.

Li learned his game to protect himself from all the darting, staring whiteness. He held his breath. As long as he could hold his breath, nothing bad could happen to him. When you weren't breathing, you weren't really alive, and if you weren't really alive, you weren't really there. No one could hurt him then, not even ghosts who shook the land of the living—*baak gwai lo,* white devils.

Now Li held his breath in the dark, his hopeful eyes on the room's one window. Uncurtained, it looked out onto a small balcony and a painted brick wall. Faded on the brick was a once gaudy sign: JIMMY LAU'S HAND-ROLLED CIGARS. The cigar factory would wake soon and add the smell of roasting tobacco to Chinatown's exotic perfumes—spices, herbs, incense, nut oil, opium.

Gray light began to leak into the room as the bells of

Old St. Mary's tolled. Five o'clock. The light inched across the bare floor, crawled over the still bodies of his parents on their thin mattress near the window, and then, leaning up like a cobra, struck at the rest of the room. Startled colors from yards and yards of filmy material stacked against the far wall caught the snaking light. He could see the red paper on the family altar and the brass bowl with its punk sticks, the peacock feathers and silk flowers. Yellowing pictures of Li's grandparents hung above the altar, people from the north of China who had fled south to Canton, people he had never met, the mouths his father still fed—the ancestors. Li's father had been one of the fortunate few. He had brought his young bride with him when he came to the Gold Mountain to seek his fortune, fleeing the famine in China. In San Francisco he was a happy man; he had his sewing machine, his sons, and his wife, her face once sweet as a blossom. But the woman lay beside him, dry now as husk, longing for moon doors and village gossip and the first tender shoots of rice. Over the altar was the Chinese sign for the new year, 1906, the Year of the Fire Horse. Li's mother said it would be a year of dread; bad things happened in such a year. Li's father had laughed. Bad things in China maybe; bad things always happened in China, but not in California—not to the white ghosts who lived on the Gold Mountain.

Crawling out of bed, the boy struggled into his blue denim tunic and trousers and stood up. Trembling, he crept into the hall, passing a big brick chimney that pressed its cold back into the room. Still black, the air in the hall pushed at him. Li's stomach lurched; on bare feet he sprinted for the toilet at the far end, holding his breath. Somewhere inside the building a dog howled, ending on a low anguished moan. Li yanked open the bathroom door, held back his thick black pigtail, and heaved into the gaping mouth of the toilet. Engulfed in the smell of his own vomit and the dreadful odors of the hundreds who shared this dank room, Li's stomach lurched again. The boy's mind stalled, his senses pinched and outraged. He turned back into the long dark hall, trying to play his game—but the air was gone. Suddenly

Li couldn't breathe. The sky had inhaled first, sucking the air away from Chinatown. Shocked, Li leaned toward the wall—and it leapt at him, buckled, and cracked. He screamed, running for his own door, a long long way away, back into the raging dark.

As Li woke in Chinatown, Rose St. Lorraine was sitting arrow-upright on the wine-red upholstery of her big black Peerless car. The car was parked in the court-yard of the Palace Hotel, and her chauffeur, who had been waiting for three hours, was slumped snoring over the wheel.

Rose, swanning serenely through the last years of her madcap youth, was the grande dame of San Francis-co's notorious Barbary Coast. Rose wasn't beautiful. She wasn't even pretty. What she was was magnificent. She had a *fin de siècle* face. No matter what the new century might bring, halcyon or holocaust, her face would always reflect sumptuousness, a sense of late afternoon, drowsy and languid. Old-gold hair, piled up loose in a Gibson Girl roll, succulent flesh ample and white as cow's milk, her waist reduced to nothing by whalebone, dressed in jade green velvet smothered in apple green feathers, gloved to above the dimpled elbows in hot pink, booted in green lace-up leather, she was topped off by the slanted sweeping fuss of a huge Lillian Russell hat. Now she leaned forward and rapped smartly on the head of her chauffeur with a closed fan.

"Dammit, Ike, wake up! It's dawn. Me and Addy want to go home." Rose had a voice with grit in it, low and musical and penetrating.

Appetite Ike, Rose's driver, also her bodyguard, her handyman, and her head barkeep at Silver Street, came to with a snort, swallowing his plug of sodden tobacco. "Right," he said, and jammed his chauffeur's cap back on his grizzled head. He cranked the Peerless into life, slammed it into gear, and the great car lurched back-ward, almost catapulting Rose and her dapper escort, Addy Chase, into the front seat.

Rose smacked Ike harder with her fan. "You crazy old coot, you're killing my goddam car!"

The back of Ike's neck, crosshatched with age, bristled at her as he yanked away at the gearshift, the Peerless screeching in protest. "I likes horses. Cars, I hate."

Ike, once a sailor, had a permanent squint from staring at the sea and, once a miner, three fingers missing on his left hand from frostbite up in the snow of the Klondike. At the age of fifteen, he had been a soldier in the Civil War; one leg was shorter than the other from blowing up his own foot. Aside from that, he'd been anything he'd ever thought of being, but none of *them* had left a mark on him. Ike, built like a chicken wing, was thin as a pickax, short as a pegleg, and ugly as a vampire bat. He stuck to Rose like tar, fierce in his loyalty.

The Peerless jerked forward, plastering Rose and Addy back against the padded seat, roared across the galleried Grand Court of the snooty Palace Hotel, barely missed one of its decorative palm trees, shot under the hotel's towering main archway and out onto the cobblestones of Market Street. Ike bore down on the Ferry Building, scaring the horsecars and scattering a clutch of late-night pedestrians.

Addy Chase sat calmly beside Rose in his soft gray suit, dove-gray spats, and stiff white collar. The creases of his trousers were anglicized—creased at the front, not the sides. His canary-yellow gloved hands were folded neatly over the silver top of his cane as he fondly regarded Rose and Ike. Addy Chase was the doyen of San Francisco society. He was old money, the inheritor of a steamship line that did a nice trade in sugar from Hawaii and exotica from the Orient, and had reached the age of thirty-five unwed. For four years he had loved Rose St. Lorraine, the city's most spectacular madam, like a dog loves: a very high-bred dog, but a dog nevertheless. A man great in length of both frame and feature—even seated, he was looking down at Rose—Addy had mild brown eyes in deep sockets on either side of the bony bridge of his tremendous nose. The pearl stickpin in his subdued tie gleamed as he surveyed the wide sweep of Market Street with a sense of quiet possession. Today he had determined to ask Rose to marry him.

Rose was whacking Ike on the back of his head with the fan.

"For Christ's sake, Appetite, left, turn left, *left* on Montgomery, now! That's the way to the Coast, you damn fool!"

Instead, Ike turned completely around from the driver's seat and faced her, the Peerless bumping its way furiously down the street.

"Ike!" screamed Rose. "Watch where you're going!"

"You wanna drive, missus," said Ike, chewing hard on his new plug, *"you* drive. You don't wanna drive, then shut up!"

Rose's painted generosity of a mouth thinned. Her words stopped, but her thoughts made her deep blue eyes swim.

Addy smiled and offered her a cigarette from his chased silver case. "Here, sweetheart," he said in his soft Ivy League drawl, "take one of these. It'll calm your nerves."

"Nerves?" snapped Rose. "Who's got nerves? I'm *mad.* Nerves is for ladies. I need my roll-ups." She dug around in her green velvet bag, found the Bull Durham and her works, and deftly rolled her own while the Peerless did a bump and grind up Montgomery Street.

Ike clipped a car coming the other way. Addy politely doffed his gray homburg at the man with the staring eyes and the huge mustaches in the back seat. Addy's smile faded faster than rain in Death Valley. "There goes Boss Ruef," he said. "Not long now before Sam and I nail the little shyster."

With his good friend the fat Samuel Jenkins, Addy was the driving force behind a campaign to clean up San Francisco's City Hall. With Eugene Schmitz as mayor and his puppetmaster, Abe Ruef, behind the scenes, City Hall stank like the Augean stables. Addy wasn't Hercules —he'd been sweeping like mad for a year—but Addy had the fervor of youth. He thought that once two bad apples were gone, the city would flower like the Garden of Eden. He'd yet to see that what Ruef had done, he had done as easily as playing triangle on "Strike Up the Band."

But Rose saw. It didn't take vision—she'd been paying weekly graft to Ruef's City Hall ever since she hit town. She patted Addy's knee. "Rose doesn't doubt it for a moment, sugar."

Addy grabbed her hand. "Let's not go back to Silver Street. Come home with me and sleep the whole day away."

"Sleep, Addy Chase? You know I never get a wink of sleep at your place."

For a man who looked like Abe Lincoln's brother, Addy blushed easily. This wasn't how he'd planned it, but the words came out anyway. "Marry me, Rose."

"Don't spoil things, sugar."

"Spoil things?"

"Not for me, for you. What'll become of your society with *me* in it?"

Ike twisted around in his seat. "You tell 'im, Rose." Then he shot a steaming bolt of black tobacco juice out of the car window. When the mess hit the ground, the Peerless jumped sideways, shivering. Addy fell over Rose, crushing her velvet and feathers. Bells all over the city clanged in formless fury.

"Ike!" screamed Rose from under a dismayed Addy. "That's it! That's the worst driving you've ever done!"

"Me?" he screamed back. "I ain't done nuthin'. The car done it!"

"Car, my ass. Cars don't drive themselves, and they sure as hell don't jump. Get off me, Addy, you're mussing up my hair."

"This car does," said Ike, as the Peerless jumped the other way, throwing Rose onto Addy.

The buildings on both sides of Montgomery Street were swaying like long grass in a fickle wind, and the whole of the stone pavement sank down beneath the Peerless with a sickening *whumpf!*

"It's an earthquake!" shouted Addy. "Hold on to me, Rose!"

"What do you think I'm doing, sugar?"

The ships off the East Street piers rose and fell against one another like horses on a rampant carousel. From one moment to the next, San Francisco changed its tune—from a slow old-fashioned waltz to a hot shimmy.

It had taken fifty-nine years to build the golden Mecca, a fabled city of wealth and style and beauty. It took a single twitch of the earth's irritated hide to knock it all down.

Li was sobbing aloud by the time he reached the end of the bucking, roaring hallway. All thoughts of breath-holding had fled from his mind; his consciousness of self shrank to a pinpoint, like eyes at the back of a cave. He stumbled back into the room, took one barefooted step in, then another—to stand rigid and still.

What had the Fire Horse done? The big heavy brick chimney was gone, the window, his mother's cooking balcony, the entire far wall empty, gaping, open. In wonder, Li found himself gazing at the whole of Jimmy Lau's cigar factory, seeing it through swirling red-brick dust, blinking bewildered at the tons of rubble that lay against the wall. The floor beneath his feet sagged, swaying down to the outer edge that hung over Beckett Alley two stories below.

The Fire Horse reared up again on its great hind legs. The building came alive with people wailing, screaming, cursing; the streets outside rang with the shouts of men, the keening of women. Horses stumbled on the shivering stone streets. Li threw himself on the rubble, digging at the broken bricks, dug until his hands were scraped and bloody, dug in a fever of fear. His raw fingers found his father's face. The eyes were open, filled with brick dust. Dark blood bubbled up and spilled out of the slack mouth, ran down the chin and into the neck of his father's sleeping shirt. Silently, Li turned away. His mother's blossom face was crushed beyond bitterness and futile longing. Li gagged, but his stomach was empty.

Elder brother Chang would never draw another deft Chinese character, his thin face tight with concentration. Only Su Yin, the little sister, was alive. As Li pushed away the bricks that had crushed her tiny chest, she smiled at him—a shy smile, faint and fleet as a whisper in the dark. Li remembered what his mother had said about girl children, said even after Su Yin was old enough to understand her mother's hard words.

"When fishing for treasures in the sea, be careful not to pull in girls. There is no profit in raising girls."

But Little Sister was all there was. There is profit in that, Mother, thought Li. Su Yin is my family now, and I will be the one to chant our descent line and blow away demons in the night.

Li carried Su Yin to the door and the earth convulsed again. In terror, Li rode the Fire Horse down the dark staircase and out onto Dupont Street. Han people were everywhere, pushing, jostling, many weighted down by children rescued from the tarpaper shacks, hovels of tin, flimsy tenements of ten to a room. Li struggled through them, cutting his bare feet on broken glass, crossing the chaos of Dupont, heading blindly down to the docks. Su Yin was quiet in his arms, light as his mother's turkey-feather quilts.

Li picked his way through morning vegetables, flecked with blood and scattered among the fallen masonry, stepping carefully over the body of an old man. The man, his skinny arm twisted under him, whimpered; with his good hand he snatched back the coins that had fallen from his pockets. The boy turned onto Washington Street. Su Yin was heavier now, her eyes closed.

Halfway down Washington, a swarm of battered bleeding people were emerging like rats from a cellar. They were climbing over each other to get up the rickety ladders, poking at eyes, digging into backs. Hundreds lived in the cellar: men, women, children. Hundreds were trying to get out at the same time. Li kept going. He didn't know where, just down and down San Francisco's steep sides, toward the sea. The Fire Horse wouldn't touch the *baak gwai lo.* They were always safe. Li was taking Su Yin to where the white ghosts lived.

A tall man dashed by them, howling. He held his arms away from his body like the ghost Jesus—the skin of his arms and his chest and his neck was charred, dropping away like roast duck. There were more people ahead, rolling on the ground, driven insane by fear. Li dodged into China Alley to keep away from the crazy people. His mother had said the spirits of the mad could bite his soul.

Dancing in a ruined doorway was a horribly painted old woman, laughing. Li knew her. It was Mon Op, the woman who owned many girls, girls to sell to the white ghosts. Mon Op had a huge black mole on her chin. When she saw Li, she stopped laughing, fixed him with a cocked eye, and yelled, "I am safe. Aiiii! I have lived!" Her mouth was a hateful red O in her fat creased face. The mole was like another eye. "You hear me, boy? Mon Op is blessed. She will live forever! You want to sell that girl, boy? Mon Op pays well!"

Li turned away from the old woman, her laughter a din in his head. Mon Op's girls were still locked in their tiny cribs, small connected shacks tumbled one against the other. Holding their arms through the barred windows in their doors, they cried pitifully. Some were no older than Li, a few no older than Su Yin. Tiny licks of orange flame flickered from the tarpaper roof of the last wooden crib like the tongue of a curious snake, tasting, searching.

Li left China Alley behind. "Do not worry, Little Sister," he whispered into Su Yin's tiny ear, "I won't sell you. We will go where the Fire Horse cannot reach us."

Ten-year-old Li Kwan Won ran, away from the Chinatown that the ancestors so hated they shook it apart like a terrier shakes a rat, shakes it until the neck snaps and it dies.

"Look out for the kids, Ike! Lord, don't hit them!"

Appetite Ike jerked hard on the steering wheel of the Peerless. The huge car jumped a cracked granite curb and crunched its gleaming bumper against a gas street-lamp. The reverberating *bong!* echoed down the ruptured street.

Rose was out of the back seat as soon as the car came to a jarring halt, dragging Addy with her. They were outside the Miner's Exchange building. The doors of the once solid bank had been wrenched open, yawning in free invitation. For now, no one bothered. The looters would come later. Ten-story buildings leaned drunkenly down into Montgomery Street. Crazy-quilt fissures steamed in the cobblestones. The body of a dead horse lay a few feet away. Ike eyed it all gloomily.

"Get a move on. I don't like the look of things."

Rose took off her hat of green feathers and threw it into the back of the Peerless, then walked slowly toward the tired boy with the bloody bundle in his arms. The air was choked with dust.

"It's that boy of Uncle's, Addy, you know who I mean. The Chinese guy that sews for my girls."

Addy stepped around Rose, holding out his gloved hand to Li. "Here, son. Let's see the little one." Addy had stooped his long angular body, softened his already soft voice, but Li backed away.

Rose kept her distance. "Let me talk to him, sugar. The kid's in shock." Rose smiled at Li, but she didn't move. "Now, honey, you know me. I'm Rose St. Lorraine. And your name's Li Kwan Won, ain't it? See, I know you." She took one step forward. Li stared at her. "Bring the little one to Rose. Rose can help, honest, kid. Let Rose help."

Li stood rooted to the spot, his ten-year-old arms aching from the weight of Su Yin. He heard the golden ghost speak to him, caught his own name and hers. Rose. Li remembered Rose. His father had liked this woman with the sun in her hair. He said she wasn't a real *baak gwai lo;* she laughed like a Cantonese woman—you could trust a woman like that. Was this the ghost who would keep the Fire Horse away from Su Yin? Was she where he was running to?

Rose came closer. "My God, Addy! The baby's bleeding to death!"

Ike was waiting, his squint so bad that his unshaven face looked like a cave-in. "Get them kids in the car. Lookit over there. South of the Slot looks like an inferno. That's them warehouses. An' there goes the waterfront! Sheee-it!"

"Hold your horses, Ike. Can't you see the boy's scared to death?"

Ike spat. "We'll all be scared to death, that fire gets any closer." But he sat back, folding his arms across his scrawny chest, chewing.

Rose had reached Li. "Poor child, poor baby," she crooned. "Christ, Addy, she's hurt so bad, real bad. We've got to get to Silver Street and find us a doctor awful fast."

Addy didn't say anything. He quietly wrapped Su Yin in a blanket, got everyone back into the Peerless, and shut the doors.

"Go like hell, Ike," Rose urged.

The Peerless leapt up what remained of Montgomery Street.

"Go like hell?" muttered Ike. "Damn road's half tore up—more like go *to* hell."

"Ike," said Rose, "shut up."

San Francisco's underworld was unlike anywhere else in the world. The merchant, the miner, the sailor, and the Barbary Coast—everyone showed up at the same time.

From the moment the word "gold" echoed down from the wild Sacramento Valley, a siren song that galvanized the needy and the greedy from New York to Canton, the Coast dug deep under the skin of the town like a battening tick. To glittering California came buzzing swarms of gamblers and thieves, harlots and heavies, politicians and parasites to feed on the blood of the gold seekers. The new town became a bedlam of vice overnight. A sleepy Spanish outpost, Yerba Buena, turned into a carnival of tents and mud and hasty shacks, suddenly American territory: San Francisco! Daughter of the itching palm. Ships from the seven seas piled into her bay in a wilderness of mast and rigging and sail, each deserted by every man jack of her crew, all headed for the hills of gold.

What the miner labored months for, ripping out of California's soil in a frenzy of unlimited gain, he lost on one throw of the dice at the El Dorado, the Mazourka, the Alhambra, the Aquila de Oro, or his pants in the tents that straggled up and down Telegraph Hill, squirming with Chilenos, ladies from the southern hemisphere. Staggering away, he was beaten and robbed of whatever he had left by the Hounds, ruffians who preyed in gangs;

conned and shanghaied by the Sydney Ducks, citizens that England had thrown away—convicts out from Australia. It was worse than New York's vicious Five Points or London's St. Giles. From the waterfront to old Dupont Street, from Morton Street to Telegraph Hill, it was the Barbary Coast and it was as glamorous as hell.

By the April dawn of 1906, it was even better. The tents had grown into great ornate barns, dance halls, parlor houses, concert saloons, and hundreds of low dives where a man could still have a fine old time. Getting fleeced, flummoxed, and filleted, straying, if he wanted, into neighboring Chinatown where his dreams went up in smoke.

Rose St. Lorraine's Silver Street was the pride of the Coast. Standing back from Washington Street, it was brazen in its three stories of weathervaned turrets, Gothic cupolas, spanking new electric light, and gay bunting. Unlike Spanish Kitty's raucous Strassburg, the venerable Bella Union, or the fly-by-night saloons that clotted the Coast, Rose's "Street" was first class, from the acts on her stage to the unloaded dice, from her wing-collared orchestra that could play anything from Strauss to ragtime to her girls. Rose's girls were the very best, from fox-faced Ninx, a coppery-haired Jewess who wore nothing but red down to the single garter on her creamy leg, to the very young Dido, Rose's latest find.

Dido was a tall strapping black whore whose skin shone in candlelight like bittersweet chocolate, the imported kind: Dido, who strode rather than walked, and whose pride was like a second coating. No one got close to Dido unless the price was right, and even then the visit was short-lived and chilly. Next to Ninx, Dido was the most popular girl in Silver Street. Rose, who was always a quick study, shrugged and said, "Some like them hot, some like them cold. Men? They're easy."

Silver Street, with its high vaulted ceilings, massive marble columns, crystal chandeliers, gilt mirrors, and stained glass depicting the rape of the Sabine women, was the talk of California. "Should be," said Rose, "it's vulgar enough. Besides, it cost plenty."

Just inside the glittering entrance Rose put up a sign:

NO THUGS. NO DRUGS. NO SWEARING. At five in the morning Silver Street had been going strong. Thirteen minutes later, nothing had changed—except San Francisco.

When the Peerless pulled up outside Rose's gaudy landmark, most of the Coast was still standing—or running. Gamblers, pimps, late-night swells, sailors on a spree, carousing longshoremen—Washington Street was thick with flushed-out lowlife.

A kid not much older than Li jumped onto the car's running board. He was as wiry as a monkey, most of the "boy" already gone from his dark darting eyes; a baseball cap on backward and a cigarette dangling from his wide mouth confused anyone trying to pin him down. The kid stuck his head through the car window and said, "Holy Cow! Ain't this something!"

"Get out of the way, Kit," snapped Rose. "Do something useful for a change, instead of hanging around Dido all night long. Find me a doctor. We've got a child in here dying."

"Yeah? Wow! Let's see!" Kit Dowie spat out his cigarette and pushed his eager head farther into the car. He gaped at Su Yin, noted all the blood seeping into Rose's grand green dress, then looked at Li. The two boys stared at each other. Li didn't lower his eyes.

Kit let out a slow whistle. "Jeez! That your blood, kid?" He glanced sidelong at Rose. "Chinks, ain't they?"

"Kit," warned Rose, "this ain't a news story, and you ain't a reporter. Beat it and bring back that doctor."

"I was just asking," the dark boy said, but he scrambled down off the car and was gone, pushing through the confused crowd like a high-tuned bantamweight. Addy left a minute later, pursuing his civic duties. With the whole town down around their ears, Addy Chase would be a busy man.

When the two children were brought into Silver Street's private back parlor, Rose's girls pressed around the plush sofa.

"Get back!" hissed Rose. "And if I hear one more word about Chinks, I'll send the lot of you packing, and I mean *you,* Dido."

Dido snapped perfect white teeth, turned up her fine Ethiopian nose, and left the parlor, sashaying her pert ass.

Su Yin lay on the gold velvet sofa, now stained almost black with her blood. Her breathing came shallow and seldom. Li had curled himself by her small head—all his tears cried out—surrounded by ghosts, white, brown, red, black. It was the black ghost, the *haak gwai,* who scared him the most. The *haak gwai* had stood back from the others when the old man, Ike, had carried Little Sister through the glitter of Silver Street, hitching away her skirts when Li passed. Her eyes were the eyes of a snake: flat, unforgiving, venomous.

Now all the ghosts were gibbering at one another, pushing forward to watch Little Sister die. Su Yin was going to die, soon and without complaint. Li saw it as clearly as he saw Rose. Su Yin was real to Rose. His father had been right about the loud woman, even if he was mistaken about the white ghosts of Gold Mountain. The Fire Horse had come for them too. If the Fire Horse saw no difference between the Han people and the white ghosts, why should he? Li's young mind felt the first tender gasp of freedom, while Rose paced her carpet. Rose would know when Su Yin's spirit left.

"Where the hell is that damn Dowie? Where's Addy?" Rose was heedless of the loss of her sofa, the blood on her thick rugs, the destruction of her green gown. She strode the length of the parlor, a room stuffed with potted palms, painted screens, dead wildlife under glass domes, oil paintings of naked women in massive gold frames—pink and fat and coy—and one whole wall glutted with books. The room was hot. It smelled of face powder, feminine sweat, and waiting. Without warning, Rose lifted her head and hollered, "Where is that doctor?"

Li jumped. At the instant Rose yelled, Su Yin died. Her soul fled like a small gray bird rising on powdery wings. No one noticed but Li and Rose. The others had lost interest, were staring out of the windows at the burning city and the passing melee, yawning, fidgeting, whispering, all with sly sidelong looks at Rose. It must be time to be moving on. What was Rose doing?

Rose stopped in mid-stride. "Oh, hell," she said. "Oh, goddammit to hell."

Struggling with the strangeness, Li's mouth formed a white word. "Rose," he said. That was all, but it was enough.

Kit Dowie, sharp face flushed, his youth betrayed by his excitement, ran back through Silver Street like he was going for his first major-league home run. He burst into the parlor, setting the quiet scene into turmoil. "We gotta get out! Oh, boy, what I'd give to be workin' for the *Call* or the *Examiner* now! This is gonna be the biggest thing in Frisco since gold!"

Ninx, her pointed face freshly painted, said, "Take off that cap, boy. Can't you see what's what here?"

"What? Oh. Shit. Sorry." Kit's clever eyes flicked over the two children on the sofa. He kept his baseball cap off for five seconds, then slapped it back on. "Listen, Rose, I just saw Addy talking to some of them city officials. Everything below Market Street is on fire. We ain't got much time. Wowie! You should see the flames! They're something fierce, shootin' straight up into the sky like a blast furnace. The fire department's going to blow up buildings to keep the fire South of the Slot, but I bet it ain't gonna work. The Call building's burning now; I saw it. They'll be starting on the financial district first, then the Coast. Addy says they ain't got enough water to fight it. So Addy's off getting his carriage to come for you and the girls. Ike's out front in the car waiting. Jeez! The militia is clearing everybody out of their homes, and the water mains are busted, and the cable-car tracks are all twisted like stuff caught in a mangle. Nothing's working anymore. Where's Dido?" Kit ended his speech on a dead run and panting.

"Where's the doctor?" said Rose, no longer interested in explosions and a young boy's sex drive.

"Doctor! You got to be kidding! Every doctor in town's got his hands full. I couldn't get any of the ones I saw to come here just for a Chink kid. Pardon, Rose, but it's the truth. Cross my heart."

Rose shook her head, her golden hair hanging in wet tendrils, her feathers drooping in the weighted air. "Doesn't matter now, does it? Go get me Ike and a clean blanket. I want this baby wrapped up proper. No one's going to say Rose St. Lorraine didn't give her tailor's daughter a damn good funeral."

The interior of the Peerless was jammed with Ninx, Dido, and every other Street girl who could cram herself in. Ike gunned the big engine.

"Move yer butt, Rose," he said. "We got everything we can take an' then some."

Rose lingered. With a shrewd eye, she looked over the Barbary Coast for the last time. "They'll build all this back, Addy. They'll do it as fast as they used to build Dawson City every time it burned down—the only difference is this time they won't be sifting the ashes for gold. You watch. Pity, too, because this quake is doing all the things you wanted. Talk about cleaning up Frisco!" She snapped open a white parasol to keep the sparks off her hat, pink now, and frou-frou with lace. The parasol was rapidly littered with black ash; sparks ate tiny red-edged holes through the white silk. "But it won't. They'll bring back the dives and the cribs and the cow yards faster than you can spit."

Addy, tying on a last bit of luggage, looked up. In spite of the haggard look in his brown eyes and the smears of grime on his craggy face, he was still dapper. "Sweetheart, you might be right, but not if I can help it. Right now, we haven't time to discuss it."

Rose still didn't move. "You know, sugar, I been thinking. Maybe it's best if I just let Silver Street go."

Faint sweat beading his quivering mustache, Addy turned. His long face beamed at her, his nose questing. Hope shone in his eyes like nuggets of gold on the bottom of a slow creek. "You mean that, Rose?"

"I mean that, Addy Chase. I'm through with the Coast. It doesn't suit me anymore." Then she laughed, a full, throaty hoot. "Instead, I think I'll build something better—classier, you know—and move it on uptown. Maybe to the Tenderloin. You've got property on Mason

Street you haven't built on. I could use that. I've got dreams, sugar. And a name: the Blue Canary."

"Yahoo!" Ike was grinning. "That's my girl!"

Addy sighed and went back to his knots.

Li, eyes wide in shock, Su Yin's cold body cocooned in its blanket on his lap, sat next to Ike. He no longer knew where he was going or why. There was mercy after all; his mind was empty. Unlike the Peerless. Everything the girls and Rose could take was piled higgledy-piggledy anywhere they could get it.

As the Peerless began to pull off, Kit jumped off the running board. "I'm not going with you guys!" he yelled above the tumult, squinting as he lit another cigarette, cupping his hands around the flame of the match he'd lit with a flick of his thumbnail—posing for all he was worth for the proud departing Dido. Firemen were busy setting dynamite charges against Silver Street's foundations. "I got business here."

"You're eleven years old," snapped Rose, "and you ain't got any business anywhere. Get back on this running board with Addy right now and cut the crap."

"Yeah?" was all Kit could counter that with. "Says who?" He sauntered casually off while the girls watched, got around the side of the doomed Silver Street, and then ran for it. This was his big chance. He was going to be a Hearst reporter if he fell down a hole doing it.

Dido smiled after him. It was almost warm.

Rose snapped open her fan. "Giddyap, Ike. In a minute they're blowing my Silver Street clear to hell. And I'm damned if I'll be here to see it."

The clouds over San Francisco boiled black, blotting out the April sun; smoke rose like mad prairie twisters, lit up from inside with a fierce ruby glow. The air tasted like sulfur and the sky rained fire. It was the noisiest, busiest morning Frisco had ever been thrown out of bed for. With a racket of clanging bells, fire engines raced by, the heavy horses lathered in a white sweat, huge hooves ringing on the cobblestones. A jumble of carts and carriages, wheelbarrows and tall awkward automobiles, overloaded wagons, jittery saddle horses, eyes rolling in their red sockets, hordes of refugees on foot—all fleeing the other way—hindered the desperate engines. Whole families, rich and poor, reduced to carrying what they could scavenge, were headed for the open space of Golden Gate Park, there to hunker down under John McLaren's sand-planted cypresses, eucalyptus, and Monterey pine. Or to the Ferry Building, leaning like the Tower of Pisa, its clock stopped at 5:13 A.M. but holding. All hoping to catch ferries that would take them east or north or south, anywhere but the burning city.

The Peerless, honking through the mad crush, worked its way to Addy Chase's mansion, high and, he hoped, safe above Van Ness Avenue. Its hard wheels juttered over broken trolley-car tracks in tooth-snapping rhythm. Rose's girls hallooed and blew kisses. Even Dido, leaning regally out the window, slowly waved.

"For Christ's sake, you idiots," said Rose. "What do you think this is, a goddam parade?"

The big car came to an enforced halt on Pacific between Stockton and Powell, straining to keep its rubber grip on the steep rise of the buckled street. Rose yelped. "My God! Look!" She reached over the silent Li to poke Ike. "Ain't that Saddle Mary?"

Next to the Nymphia, San Francisco's most notorious cow yard—threatening to collapse under five hundred thundering trollops making their frantic getaway—was a run-down two-story frame house of no distinction whatsoever. It might have stood sober once, but now leaned at a tipsy angle against the Nymphia. Its windows were wide open, and from them frightened girls threw the whole house down into Pacific Street; half the stuff was smashed to pieces on the sidewalk. A middle-aged woman, her soiled negligee open and flapping, exposing a body that made Addy shudder, directed rescue operations from her front door at the top of the stoop. Her voice was like a blunt hatchet cutting through the fire bells and general uproar.

"Murray Blinn! You git your butt back here an' help your mother with this bleedin' piano!" Her graying hair stood out from her painted mask of a face in grizzled shock.

A rough-looking youth in a derby hat, a few years older than Li, with a sly face and big ears, stopped chasing one of the girls down the sidewalk. He turned back reluctantly. "Aw, Ma," he whined.

"Now!" screeched the woman at the top of the stoop, struggling to keep her piano from taking a nosedive down the front steps. "Leave them whores be. I don't want no more cigarette burns on 'em. Git over here!"

Rose, watching all this eagerly from inside the Peerless, said, "That's her all right, that's Saddle Mary. I told you about her, girls. She was the lowdownest bitch ever hit the Klondike. Remember, Ike?"

Ike grimaced, his mouthful of yellow teeth stained brown by tobacco juice. "Yep. Worked on her back in Dawson, down Paradise Alley. Always wondered where she got to."

Rose straightened her hat. "Don't move. I can think of a certain someone who'd give his eye teeth to know where that old bag is now. Get off the car, Addy. I'm getting out to pay my respects."

Addy tipped his homburg and patiently moved aside. Rose flounced out of the car, stepping over a crack in the street a foot wide and as hot and deep as sin.

"Yoohoo!" she called gaily. "Hello there!"

Startled, the slattern looked up from her piano.

"Howdy, Mary." Rose took off her pink lacy hat and waved it. "It's me—Rose. What's cooking, sugar?"

Saddle Mary took one look at Rose St. Lorraine, gave up her struggle with the piano, and scooted back into the drabness of her house. The piano hit the street in a deafening jangle of wrong notes. The wily-looking kid with the big ears and the derby hat stood still, his red lips slack in amazement. "Ma!" Murray Blinn called to the empty doorway. "Oh, Ma. Your piano's busted."

With a hoot and a swish of her skirts, Rose bounced back into the Peerless. "Drive on, Ike dear. That made my day."

A few blocks later the neighborhood had improved, but the fire was on its way just the same. A shrill voice called from behind them, plus the desperate tinkle of a bicycle bell. "Addy! Addy Chase! Hold on a minute! Drat this bicycle."

A fat man in a tattered plaid bathrobe, a pair of baggy tramp's trousers, and a silk opera hat puffed up Pacific toward them.

Politely, Addy made room on the running board. "Rose, this is Samuel Jenkins, a fellow member of the Pacific Club. Sam, this is Rose St. Lorraine and a few of her—ah—friends. Where *did* you get those clothes?"

The fat man laughed, bowing to the ladies, taking them in with a twinkle and a knowing smile for Addy. Addy had the good grace not to blush. "Got everything burnt off me 'cept the hat. A fine *Carmen* last night, wasn't it? Saw you and the lady—Rose—at the opera. Caruso was in damn fine form; his Don José will become history." Sam slapped a thigh thick as a holiday ham. "I saw him running for the St. Francis Hotel after the quake hit. White as chalk, but the fool was practicing scales as the whole blasted city fell down. *Mi-mi-mi!*" the fat man laughed until his moon face turned red. He smacked Addy on his thin back. "Buck up, Chase. If we can't get rid of our respected major and his pal Ruef just yet, we sure as hell got rid of City Hall. Fell in like a house of cards. Damn fine sight. The City Hall and the Opera House, the Emporium and the Call building, and now maybe every mansion on Nob Hill, mine included." Sam wheezed in great good humor. "All 'cept Flood's, of course. Built to last, that one. The Palace Hotel is still standing. You can see its flag from here. I'd like to be there, though, when the Stafford folly goes."

Addy shook his head. "I don't mind any of it, except the libraries, all the books. Are the libraries gone?"

"Going." Sam's jaws wobbled. "But that's not what bothers me. What I mind losing is Dr. Jordan's House of Horrors."

Through all of this, Li sat rigid, clutching the covered body of Su Yin. The world inside his head was private, stunned. When his little sister died, Li stopped thinking, stopped trying to make sense of the babbling of the *baak gwai lo,* retreating to a simple place of gray mist and silence. He didn't know where the ghosts were taking him, didn't care. The only thing Li saw was the old woman Mon Op, dancing in her doorway. The only thing he heard was the cries of her young girls trapped in their burning cribs. Li wished Mon Op would burn too. Burn and twist like red paper in the flames of the white ghosts' hell.

A Chinese boy wandering alone in the land of ghosts was nowhere at all.

As Rose and Addy and Ike were driving away from the Palace Hotel, little Lizzie Stafford, wide-awake and eager, pattered barefoot over her Brussels carpet and scampered up onto a window seat. In her bedroom at the very top of her grandparents' house, it was as dark as soot, but a pale lemon light from the setting moon spread out near an alcoved window. Using the heavy lace curtains, she pulled her little body up, to stand shivering in the moonlight.

Lizzie pressed her button of a nose against the chilled pane. Her city slept below, dropping rooftop by rooftop down the sleek west side of Nob Hill to the cold foggy bay. Foghorns mourned across the black water.

Her grandfather's house imposed itself on San Francisco, a monstrous monument to sudden wealth. Charles Mortimer Stafford, awesome in personal bulk and the weight of shining Comstock silver, had had it erected in 1874 with an exhibitor's eye. He sited it at the corner of Taylor and California streets, smack on top of the roller-coaster city's most exclusive lump, Nob Hill. No one in the raw and pushing town could miss Stafford's statement, even if they wanted to; all they had to do was look up. Now, over thirty years later, it still stood in all its baroque madness against the California sky, proud, unsullied by architectural opinion, and embarrassing. Competing tycoons—gold, silver, railroad, and speculation men—had built around him. Crocker, Stanford, Hopkins, and Huntington, the Big Four of the Central Pacific Railroad, put up their piles, but no one could equal the individual, breathtaking, lunatic vision of Charles Mortimer Stafford.

"Ha!" said Charles, as the houses went up around

him. "Here come the shopkeepers. It's money that talks in this town 'cause nobody's got anything else. Money is nothing but freedom, but they build themselves cages with it."

Lizzie's rooms were at the top of one of the gingerbread towers. The house of over a hundred rooms had three towers, each different and each stuck on somehow —none of them made sense.

The little girl, standing on her window seat in the moonlight, was waiting for the sun. The room that arched back into thick black behind the lemon-lit alcove was stuffed with her possessions. Back there in the darkness was her canopied bed, the fine white sheets already growing cold; her dollhouse from New York; her rocking horse with a real leather saddle from England; her dolls from France. The dollhouse was older than the Stafford mansion and splendid in its symmetry. It had three stories, twenty rooms, and each perfect room was filled with perfect furniture. In Lizzie's room there was a rosewood wardrobe filled with her dresses and coats and capes and muffs and hats. There were Lizzie-sized chairs, bureaus, mirrors. And she didn't give a snap of her little pink fingers for any of it. Today was her sixth birthday.

Possessions didn't matter. What mattered was the party. That's when all the people came. Then Elizabeth Sian Stafford would prance among them, pampered, petted, cooed over. Lizzie was San Francisco's society princess, a six-year-old tyrant.

"Your birthday is the event of the season, Lizzie," Grandfather had said. "Ned Greenway wrote that in the *Argonaut,* and he ought to know. Mr. Greenway makes society."

"What do *you* make, Grandfather?" asked Lizzie.

"Make? Why, nothing, baby. I'm rich."

The bells of Old St. Mary's tolled: one, two, three, four, five. St. Mary's spire was just below her window, a few blocks down the steep street. She could look right over it. From her turret, she could also see into the narrow alleys of Chinatown. Grandmother never let Lizzie set foot there. Dirty place, dirty people, Mary Maud said.

In spite of Charles's money, Mary Maud's prairie soul was intact.

A salmon blush bloomed over the slumbering mountains across the bay, tinting pink the fog that lay over the cold water like soft meringue on a salty pie. "Wake up, city," Lizzie lisped, pressing her forehead on the pane until it ached with the chill. "Today is my party."

Streetlamps all over the city dimmed and went out. The big wardrobe was vibrating. Lizzie backed away as the huge piece of furniture walked toward her, rumbling on its rosewood feet.

"Gosh!" she said, clutching her doll. "You see that, Lolly?"

Lizzie turned. Her grandfather's house was tipping toward the street, Lizzie's tower first. If it fell over, it would tumble right into Chinatown. In an agony of indecision, the great folly on the hill shivered, tilting with crazed wooden shrieks. Lizzie's window bulged—bulged until it burst, spitting glass over the room, nicking Lizzie's face and hands, and air rushed in the broken window, smelling of seasalt and shock.

"Lizzie!" There was a frantic battering at the door. Her maid, Irma, crinkled brown hair in a net, large face smeared with cream, had had to smash the door with an ax to get it open; it had been knocked out of plumb. "Dear God, child! What are you just standing there for? We've got to get out of here!"

"Get out?"

"Lord, yes, girl. The tower is coming down, the whole house!"

Narrowing her green eyes, Lizzie stared at Irma. "But it's my party today." Her pink mouth was set.

"Forget that, you little fool!" Irma pulled on Lizzie's arm. "The city is shaking itself to pieces. There isn't going to be any party."

Lizzie yanked her arm away from Irma and yelled, "But it's my birthday! What about all the people?" Her eyes snapped in fury. "It isn't fair. I want my party. And I want it now!" With Lolly, Lizzie hauled off and hit Irma as hard as she could. Lolly's head caught the maid in the stomach. "You let me go, you!"

Gasping for breath, Irma smacked Lizzie's butt, hard. The look on the child's face was the most satisfying sight Irma had ever seen in three years of working for Charles Mortimer Stafford. Then she slung the kicking brat under her arm and bolted from the collapsing room.

Thirteen-year-old James Alexander Hamilton cowered under his covers. The narrow military-academy bed fidgeted over the floor under him, and the air was racked with the loudest, closest thunder he'd ever heard.

"All right!" shouted the muffled voice outside his blankets. "All out smart, line up on the parade ground, and keep away from the windows as you go. Now!" That was his sergeant. Pompous ass.

From under his blanket, James heard the sounds of the other boys leaping out of their beds, heard the ordered march of bare feet as they filed out of the dorm on the double. His feet refused to march with them, his body stayed where it was, hunkered down in bed. Abruptly, the blankets were jerked away, and the whistle of a riding crop came just before the painful smack on his rump.

"What did I say, Mr. Hamilton? Get up!"

For the first time in his life, James was too afraid to whine. He lay there staring up into the furious face of his sergeant, his blue eyes wet and pleading as the dorm walls shivered and cracked around them. Academy bells clanged without purpose, adding to the thunder. James thought he would go crazy.

The sergeant loomed over him, spittle spoiling his clean-shaven chin. "Officer material, eh? You upstart, you sniveling baby! Get up, boy! Get up before I skin you alive!" The sergeant reached down, gripped James painfully by his ear, and hauled him up from the cot. James found his voice; he howled.

The sergeant stared at him with withering scorn. "Wet? You peed the bed, boy?" He raised his already raised voice. "You all hear that? Because of a little earthquake, Mr. Hamilton has wet his bed!"

From outside the dorm, James could hear his fellows snickering. He'd kill the sergeant; he'd kill them all.

Squeeze their hateful necks until their eyes popped out of their heads, cut them into red dripping—

With the sudden toe of his shining boot, the sergeant kicked James toward the door. "You won't forget this day, Hamilton."

How could James forget? It was the worst day of his life. He stood, thin, tall, and quaking, his stinking pajamas clamped to his legs, at the end of a long line of boys. No one looked at him, but he knew what they were thinking. Christ, he'd show them, the shits. Someday he'd show them *all.* Them, and the sergeant, and his lily-livered father as well. He'd pay his father back for being poor, for being meek, for sending him to this school, for being so *small.* James Alexander Hamilton would get power and money, so much that they'd have to shut up, shut right up and drop dead. They thought they knew what he was made of? They thought shit.

James was so busy feeling sorry for himself, spinning in his tight humiliated circle of fear and revenge, that he forgot about the parade ground trembling and splitting under his feet, so intent on imagined mayhem and future glory that he barely noticed when the low wooden dorm splintered, then twisted in on itself, nails shrieking protest.

# Chapter 1

San Francisco fought back with as much style as she burned down. When the water ran out, she used sewage, and when the sewage ran out, she used wine. The holocaust swept over the city for three days and two nights, until both the city and the fire got tired and called it a truce.

On the fourth day, San Francisco was the "damnedest finest ruins" California or, for that matter, the United States, had ever seen. Twice the size of the Great Fire of Chicago in 1871, six times bigger than the burning of London in 1666, San Francisco was five hundred blocks of spidery black girders against the careless sky, tons of twisted steel and rubble, melted granite—and silence. And then, after it was all over, the rain came. White wistful steam rose from a thick layer of hot ash that covered the devastated hills like a shroud.

The churches, the courts and jails, great buildings of commerce, theaters, libraries, art galleries and museums, hundreds of restaurants and ten thousand gardens, the schools, transport systems—all were gone. The homes of a quarter of a million people were reduced to nothing except the determination to rebuild it all, every brick, every lamppost, every shack, and every mansion that topped the skittish hills—and to do it as fast as possible.

When Addy Chase took stock on the fifth day, he discovered that he was almost penniless. He still had his houseful of colorful refugees on Lafayette Park above Van Ness, but his stocks and bonds, everything that had made him a wealthy man, had burned along with the banks that held them. His ships had sunk at their moorings. The firm that carried his insurance, a German company, turned its back on his claims, as did hundreds of other firms, foreign and domestic, for thousands of other claims.

Rose hugged Addy. "Don't you fret, sugar. I've still got mine. Ike and me buried everything I had under Silver Street. When things cool down we'll go dig it up."

Charles Mortimer Stafford, his great bulk balanced on tiny feet, stood outside his charred mansion and watched the last of its crazy towers crash into California Street. Addy stood next to him with little Lizzie up on his bony shoulders. Charles Mortimer laughed.

"I lived too long in this town to keep much of my money here. I remember when Lucky Baldwin's hotel and theater burned down in '98—that broke the damn skinflint. He lost three million dollars. Then there were the quakes of '68 and '98. A man learns or a man dies. I got all my money back east, and I'm not the only one. Except for Crocker, but that wily old goat put everything on a boat day of the quake and took it all out into the middle of the bay and just sat there with it. Now, Chase, if you'd had your pile in Crocker's bank, or in Giannini's, who kept his accounts in his head, you'd still be a rich man today."

Little Lizzie, high up on Addy's shoulders, said, "Are you still a rich man, Grandfather?" Her black curls were shining in the dizzy sun.

"'Course I am, baby. Couldn't let my princess go without."

Addy had smiled ruefully at that, rubbing his long nose with a long finger.

Not a stick of Chinatown or the Barbary Coast was left. An old Chinese laundryman, squatting in the ruins at the corner of Sacramento and Dupont, the latter yet to be renamed in honor of past-president Ulysses S. Grant, said to no one in particular: "By 'n' by, we build all new." His remark made the papers, and the papers went into a tizzy. San Francisco didn't want to build "all new," not for the Chinese. She wanted her least-loved people, huddled right under the nose of Nob Hill and smack in the middle of her most valuable acreage, the financial district, out—forever. The press raved about the heaven-sent opportunity the city had of finally ridding itself of the little yellow hordes, not to mention acquiring the rich building sites for white interests. But before you could shake a pigtail, the Chinese, first out of the refugee camps and first off the city breadlines, put Chinatown together again, so fast the City Fathers were still at their drawing boards, chewing on their pencil stubs.

Appetite Ike spent weeks in the detested Peerless until they were both famous. The Peerless was an ambulance and a hearse; it hauled food, and medical supplies, and members of Mayor Schmitz's committees of safety and relief. These were cobbled together from the town's most prominent men, Addy and Sam Jenkins and Charles Mortimer among them. The applause of the public through newsprint and magazine for the role of the automobile in bringing San Francisco back to life irked Ike. "It was the horse, not them cars, ought to be remembered. Horses ought to have a statue stuck right on top of Telegraph Hill, a hoppin' big one. They're workin' thousands of 'em to death. Horses are droppin' in their traces cleanin' up this damn mess."

By early 1907, San Francisco was running on all cylinders. The racket of rebuilding was worse than the roar of the quake, but the racket of the politician was, for the moment, quieter. Mayor Schmitz went out on his gorgeous ear, and Boss Ruef would finally be jailed for graft. Addy, using his friend William John Burns, the Sherlock Holmes of San Francisco, to outmaneuver and entrap them, had a large hand in their downfall. He was jubilant. "I told you we'd get them," he said to Rose.

And Rose replied, "It only makes a nice big hole for someone else to crawl into."

Meantime, the Blue Canary on Mason Street was open for business and raking it in.

Seventeen years after the quake San Francisco was bigger and fatter and sassier than ever. In 1923 the quake of 1906 was a story for wide-eyed tourists, an excuse for parades and memorials. To Ike's eternal disgust, everyone forgot the horses. Nothing had really changed in San Francisco, except her heart. It wasn't quite as gay or innocent. But it was gay enough. It was three years into Prohibition, and the city was having a fine time.

In New York and Detroit, Cleveland and St. Louis and Chicago, bootleggers ran riot. The newly forming Mafia had their fingers in everyone's pie. Chicago grew bloodier by the day as John Torrio and his lieutenant, Al Capone, tightened their death grip. But in San Francisco things were wide open. Dozens of small-timers cleaned up the takings. San Francisco had always done things her own way—gold strikes, silver booms, powerful and corrupt tycoons. It was a continuous mad scramble by everyone to take as much as they could get. It was the American dream.

Prohibition didn't make it any different.

Lizzie Stafford had grown into everything she'd ever promised to be: wild and willful, utterly selfish, and utterly charming. Even though he'd been dead for three years, Charles Mortimer had a lot to answer for.

Her shoulder-length blunt-cut hair was as black as the Orient, a blue sheen on bangs cut low over long green eyes as clear and uncomplicated as water. The eyes were deceiving. Lizzie was as complicated as a Chinese box. She had fine wide cheekbones and a small impertinent nose which gave her face an offbeat beauty, but the chin was too strong to make her pretty, her brows too black and too fierce for restraint, and she was a little too tall to be cute. Lizzie's mind was like a high-wire act. It was breathtaking what she could achieve on such slim support. Charles Mortimer had bought her an education, but

Lizzie treated it like the expensive dollhouse she'd had as a child—she played with it until it bored her. Her mind made unexpected and startling leaps at ideas, held on briefly, did chin-ups, and flashed back, instantly poised for the next trapeze.

Right now, Lizzie was a little bit blotto. It was 1923. It was a balmy Sunday evening in July, and it was her second wedding anniversary. She was in the Stafford mansion, which was right where it had always been, quake and fire be damned, and, even though rebuilt, was just as architecturally hopeless. Lizzie was watching her husband, San Francisco's most dashing and youngest-ever district attorney, James Alexander Hamilton, who was leaning languidly against the back of a Regency needlepoint sofa on the far side of the mansion's main ballroom. The ballroom, big enough for all of Mrs. Astor's four hundred and then some, had eighteenth-century Chien Lung wallpaper, salmon-pink moiré curtains, and a French parquet floor. Lizzie's party had cost $40,000— the red roses alone, which were everywhere, set her back $7,000.

Even though the imported parquet was thick with guests and Lizzie's view was distorted by bootleg gin, she could tell that James was pretending that the woman seated bold as beans on Lizzie's priceless sofa wasn't his mistress. Lizzie had found out two months ago. She was wondering who else knew. Esmé Baker, a divorcée in her early thirties, had a certain hard-boiled class and admirable tact, but Lizzie knew. What she didn't know was what to do about it. Did James love the woman? Was it that bad? At twenty-three, this was the first crisis in Lizzie's sheltered life. She was jealous and ashamed, bewildered and frightened, but first and foremost she was angry. So she'd been learning to drink. She'd been doing that for weeks, ignoring the swish and dazzle of café society, hiccuping down from her pedestal as leader of the younger social set.

But tonight the cream of San Francisco society had gathered to celebrate what they saw as little Lizzie's brilliant marriage to the up-and-coming Hamilton: Addy Chase, Adolph and Alma Spreckels, Mary Garden—Chicago's most famous opera singer—Gertrude Atherton, the W. H. Crockers, former Senator Phelan, all four de Young girls, Elinor Glyn, up from Hollywood on the arm of Lord Curzon, the former in crimson lipstick and long purple veils, and the outré Aimee Crocker with her husband of the moment. There was a prominent New York stage actress, another Gertrude, Mrs. Gertie Arlington—a very literary lady—and the senior Hamiltons.

The Stafford mansion didn't suit the Hamiltons. They were the apartment-in-the-basement type. Ever since Lizzie had married their son in a rosy uncomprehending daze, they'd gaped at the house whenever James let them in—which wasn't often. But they were in now, and after Lizzie had politely welcomed them, James had ignored them. They sat together near the food, meek and daunted, talking to no one—and vice versa.

Lizzie's eyes were just the right color for the situation—green—and for her own anniversary she wore black: a long draped number by Erté in crepe-de-chine which suited her long neck, wide shoulders, slim hips, and foul mood. She had as much class as Esmé, at least until she got to her fourth or fifth or sixth orange blossom, but who was counting? Lizzie threw back the drink with a quick flick of her celery-thin wrist, and the square-cut emeralds on her bracelet flashed.

Kit Dowie was counting. "You're getting good at that," he said.

Startled, Lizzie jumped. "Christ! Don't do that!" Then she focused on Kit and frowned. "You're late."

"Late? I wasn't even invited. What is this, a wake?"

"This is my anniversary." Lizzie kissed Kit, leaving a scarlet smear on his cheek. "You weren't invited because even *I* didn't want to come. This isn't a party for friends, but thank God you're here anyway. *He* invited *her!*"

"What? Who?"

"James invited Esmé Baker, the redhead over there on my sofa, that older woman in blue. She showed up with his new friend, Mr. Olemi, but she belongs to James, all right. I need another drink."

Kit waved away the dignified Japanese servant hovering with a full tray. This was Keiko. Everyone knew he ran the Hamilton household.

Lizzie kicked Kit. "Dammit, Kit. I want what *I* want. It's *my* party."

"It'll kill you. What do you think that stuff is made of?"

"Who cares?"

"I care, you idiot, and you know I care."

"Keiko!" Lizzie snatched another orange blossom from the tray. "Look at them ignoring each other over there. It's humiliating."

"Speaking of caring, do you really?"

"Of course I care. What will everybody think?"

"What kind of caring is that?"

"I *do* care about James. Well, I *did* care. Oh, hell, I still care. God, I don't know anymore. I think I care."

"Let me know what you decide." Kit lit another cigarette from his first one and dropped the used butt into a four-foot-tall Ming vase crammed with white carnations.

At twenty-eight, Kit Dowie was exactly what he'd set out to be—a hotshot newspaper reporter on Hearst's *Examiner*. He'd fast-talked himself onto the staff by the time he was sixteen. Kit was as out of place at the Stafford mansion as a bobcat in a litter of Siamese. They lived on their names; Kit lived on his nerves. He hadn't dressed for Lizzie's swank affair. The other men were in white tie and tails, the ladies in the latest and the best from Paris. Kit wore a gray pin-striped suit with a snap-brim hat pushed back on his sleek dark head. The tie was black and the shoes two-tone. He hadn't changed much over the years. He was as quick and intense as the boy in the back-to-front baseball cap running wild-eyed through the great fire. Though he was only three inches taller than Lizzie, he was built like a prizefighter, with all the fighter's explosive grace. His cynicism was skin-deep and the wisecrack his ace in the hole. Kit Dowie was full of questions; in his late twenties he thought there were answers. Lizzie Stafford Hamilton was the only one of her crowd Kit could stomach. A kind of unquenchable optimism made him believe in pearls, which meant he had to believe in sand. For Lizzie, he had hope—and, more than that, passion. Neither Lizzie nor Kit knew how much. Arriving to find the huge house full of society wasn't his idea of a good time. He'd just got off the train from Montana, where he'd covered the dismal Dempsey fight, moseyed on over to say hello, and now—he wished he hadn't.

Lizzie was talking to him. "I've been to parties like this all my life, Kit. Lordy, I *gave* this one. Do you know how long it took me to realize that the only point is so everyone who got invited could read about what a swell time they had in the society pages the next day? I think I'm getting depressed." Lizzie quietly hiccuped. "What do you think they'd say if they knew about Esmé Baker and James? Would they pity me?"

"They'd probably say you drove him to it." Kit put an arm under Lizzie's elbow; she was beginning to droop. "All they can see is the hooch."

"Really! But why? She's over thirty and I'm only twenty-three. Why's he doing this to me? We've only been married two years. It's too soon—I mean, things like this aren't supposed to happen to you when you're only twenty-three."

"Ever think of writing for the movies, Lizzie?" Kit removed his hold on Lizzie's elbow, and she began a slow slide down a marble pillar.

Stung, Lizzie snapped out of it and clambered back up. "Why're you so mean? I just want things to be nice. You're the wise guy, what do *you* want?"

"Truth?"

Lizzie's eyes widened in horror. "I thought we were friends, but we don't want the same things at all."

Kit's dark eyes danced in his tomcat face. "I know. Isn't it interesting?" He took Lizzie's drink away from her and walked away. "I'll go check out the opposition. You stay here and behave yourself."

A full orchestra had just finished Jerome Kern's "They Didn't Believe Me" and now cranked into a diluted white man's jazz. Precisely balancing his loaded tray on one hand, Keiko, followed closely by Kit, eased his way through what had become a frantic bunny hug by fifty of the younger guests on the parquet floor—led by Elinor Glyn and Aimee Crocker, competing in enthusiasm. When Keiko left Lizzie's side of the ballroom, the tray had nine glasses on it; when he reached the other side, it had one.

By a subtle lift of his brow, Keiko drew James away from Esmé and the crowd around the needlepoint sofa.

"Mr. Blinn is here," he said quietly when he got James alone by an immense pier table. The anniversary guests had scarcely touched the guinea hens stuffed with wild rice, the lemon sorbet kirsch, or the cheese straws, but the imported caviar in its big silver bowl was a memory, and the homemade champagne was running like Niagara. Kit was helping himself to a cheese straw and, like any reporter worth his byline, eavesdropping.

"Here?" said James.

"Yes," said Keiko.

"He brought the stuff?"

"No, not come, Mr. Hamilton."

"What!"

"Only Mr. Blinn. He asks to speak to you in kitchens." Keiko bowed and slid back across the busy sprung floor. Kit chewed his cheese straw and watched Hamilton.

Judging solely by appearances, James Alexander Hamilton beat all competition hands down. Without "background," his achievement was a matter of will. His awkward years behind him, James was slim as liana, with an easy, almost southern grace. His voice was low and slow and soft, and he used it like a hypnotist uses a bauble on the end of a silver chain. When Hamilton spoke, he was listened to. He spoke a lot: in courtrooms and smokers, in private clubs, for committees—wherever he was asked. James had ambition, but he was wise enough to keep it from showing, and no opinions; for a politician, opinions were not an asset. He was just tall enough to be imposing but not tall enough to intimidate. All the parts —ash-blond hair, a firm jaw with a hint of a cleft in the chin, sober blue eyes, and the voice—made a whole that seemed as natural and assured as an aristocrat. To look at, Kit realized James had only one fault, but even that came up trumps. His teeth weren't good, so he rarely smiled. People mistook it for seriousness; he must be a sound man since he reinforced what they already believed; he must have a lofty mind, perhaps even a visionary one, since he told them things would get better and better. This, of course, thought Kit, was with the tacit assumption that it was Hamilton who could make it better. San Francisco was impressed with her district attorney. Men found him manly, women delicious. Only Lizzie was beginning to get the whole picture. That's if you didn't count Kit's opinion. For the moment, not many did.

But Kit had to give the fellow credit. James had pulled it off. From nowhere—namely, the city's Western Addition, a neat suburb of anonymous houses, and a father who worked as a clerk at Levi Strauss—to Harvard, and then its law school, an officer in the Great War, a hero's return, a marriage to Elizabeth Sian Stafford, society's horribly rich darling, and, now, high public office. Barely thirty, James would only go up. There were plenty who intended to go with him. Hamilton knew what he was doing, and he was doing it well. Lizzie was only part of the plan; she was the "right" marriage and, of course, money. Kit had watched James single her out when she was seventeen. That was easy—black-haired, green-eyed, headstrong, Lizzie was highly visible. Hamilton had waited to propose, gambling on his charm and good looks to hold her, until Charles Mortimer died. With the Staffords both gone and Lizzie's parents dead just after her birth, she was worth a fortune. Kit Dowie almost admired Hamilton's sense of single-minded purpose. It was chilling, but it was effective. Little Lizzie hadn't known what hit her and she wasn't listening to Kit, not then and not now. Propped up by the pier table, Kit watched James thinking. The little metallic cogs and wheels of Hamilton's sharp mind were no doubt dealing with running out of booze at his own party. Hell, thought Kit, the guy could probably handle that as easily as he could sum up a stacked murder case.

James started moving, Kit right behind. Taking the arm of a flattered fat lady in ostrich feathers and beads and talking his head off, Kit propelled her after James. They all got to the far side of the room around the same time. James found who he was looking for near a massive arrangement of red roses and fern banked around a more than life-size ice sculpture. The sculpture was of two swans necking; it was Lizzie's idea. Now it was melting. The man James sought, Leo Olemi, was talking to a clutch of characters Kit knew well. Isaac Arnold was the federal Prohibition administrator for California, Jack Albright was an assistant state's attorney, and Robert Bent was San Francisco's police commissioner. Leo Olemi himself was Italian and called himself a businessman, which, in a way, he was. Leo was San Francisco's Syndicate boss, newly appointed by the big boys back in New York. In intent, all four were as alike as a precision dance team, though nothing like in capability. Kit got rid of the fat woman and stationed himself by the lump of ice.

Nice guys to have at a society do, thought Kit. Hamilton was racing a little close to the wind here. Arnold and Albright, two distinguished silver-haired gentlemen holding key government positions, got there by the usual time-honored means—backhanding and a certain lax attitude toward the law, especially the Eighteenth Amendment. Robert Bent was neither distinguished nor a gentleman. His skin was sallow, pitted, almost parchment in texture. Sniffling and sneezing, he seemed to have a perpetual cold, his small eyes watered, and he yawned at the oddest times. The stiff rented tails sat badly on his uneasy frame, but it was his hands that gave the state of his nerves away—they were always moving, and he talked too much. The police commissioner was loyal to Leo. He had to be; his vices, awesome in their eclecticism, consumed him. A man with so many bad habits would never bite the hand that fed them.

But it was the presence of Olemi that surprised and intrigued Kit. What was a member of the East Coast Syndicate doing with the swells? Olemi was as devious as the Sphinx and just as quiet—he never took bows. In his early forties, with a face as bland as bread and most of it below his nose, he wouldn't stand out in a crowd, unless you looked at his eyes. Kit was looking. They were sad, mud-colored, and ruthless. Arnold, Albright, and Bent were Leo's men, and he played them like Chaliapin sang basso. With the addition of James Hamilton, Dowie knew, Olemi would have a full score to read from. Pleased with the thought, Kit composed an opening line for an article that would probably never see print: "San Francisco's crime could be a symphony; Leo Olemi has been sent west to conduct."

"What's up?" Kit heard Leo say as James passed, cutting Bent off abruptly in the sneezing man's retelling of another dirty joke.

By way of reply, James said, "Trouble."

Without a word, Leo shrugged and followed James. Robert Bent, aside from everything else he wasn't, wasn't bright. He misread his relationship to Olemi and Hamilton and tagged along after them. Arnold and Albright were smarter; they stayed with the party. And Kit, who couldn't think of any reason to explain his tagging along as well, was left on the wrong side of the kitchen door. Little Lizzie's husband fascinated him. What was clear as rain to Kit seemed to be mud to San Francisco. But then, San Francisco didn't know who Leo Olemi was. And Lizzie didn't know who James was. If it weren't for hurting Lizzie, Kit would have been happy to clear away the debris for his fellow citizens. Right now, for instance: he understood why Olemi would woo Hamilton, but why was the DA palling around with someone who could give Al Capone a run for his money? There weren't any answers on Kit's side of the door.

Murray Blinn was waiting for James in the Stafford kitchens, which were vast, domed and white-tiled like the inside of a mammoth icebox. Standing by the servants' entrance, hat in hand, gat in pocket, he was watching the kitchen staff as they worked the Hamilton anniversary. Envy was all over his face. Saddle Mary's little boy had grown into a jovial, pudgy, eager hustler, and his ears were still too big. Raised in a two-bit whorehouse, Murray had lost his taste for women early, replacing it with a taste for himself. He plastered his scant yellow hair down with paste and plucked his eyebrows. The paste made him smell odd, and the eyebrows made him look odder.

Murray had a loose smile, his eyes were lopsided, and his mother had taught him everything he knew, which wasn't much. He wasn't the best bootlegger in town, but he was trying.

Before James or Leo could say a word, Murray held up a delicate palm. If he'd had a ring on his thumb, he'd have had a full hand. "Don't start on me, Mr. Hamilton. I know you told me not to ever come here, but I got a good reason. You wanna hear my reason?"

"No," said James. His "no" was coiled. "I merely want to know why I'm running out of alcohol."

"The booze!" Blinn was laughing, but it didn't sound like it. It sounded like something bit him. "It's on its way, I swear. Blinn always delivers. But you gotta listen to why it's late. It was the dirty yellow guys, them rat-eatin' Chinks, that's the reason. They hijacked our boat off Hunter's Point—from a shrimper, for Pete's sake. Why can't they stick to dope and leave the hooch to decent white men?"

Bent had pushed his way in front of James and Leo. He grabbed Murray by his too-wide lapels, which were attached to a loud checked jacket. "You stupid pansy! You mean you let the bastards get away with it, a bunch of Fu Manchus?"

Murray squirmed. "You told me you didn't want no wars. You didn't want Frisco gettin' a name like Chicago. And I ain't no pansy." Murray turned a pleading eye on Leo. "We run a clean town here, don't we, fellas?"

Leo, casually sampling a bit of anniversary icing on a cake waiting to be presented in the ballroom, said, "Let Murray go, Robert."

Bent grudgingly complied, but he pushed as he stepped back. Blinn staggered. "No need to play rough." He straightened his jacket and slapped on his hat. "I coulda got them Chinks, me an' the boys, but I ain't makin' waves till I get told. That's right, ain't it, Leo?"

"That's right, Murray," said Leo, licking his fingers.

Blinn, encouraged, continued. "An' if we didn't have to run our stuff in from Canada, an' we didn't have to off-load it in Half Moon Bay, where the harbor master is earnin' more'n me, an' if we didn't have to sneak it over to Sausalito with the Coast Guard breathin' down our backs, we'd all be in clover. An' if we didn't have to compete with the stuff they're makin' in Amador County, if we had us our own operation, a still right here in Frisco —now, *that* would be pretty, wouldn't—"

"Excuse me," said James, his anger growing by the second. "Do you think you could have this conversation elsewhere? This is my home. I have important guests here." Hamilton wasn't a fool. His intelligence, though limited, was profound. What he did not know, he was blind to; what he knew, he knew well. He understood Leo Olemi as he understood himself and was content to use him as he was to be used—for now. Someone had to do the dirty work. Leo's ambitions extended to San Francisco and eventually to all of California. But James had his eye on the entire United States of America, from sea to shining sea. The White House called to him like Circe. James knew his American history. He was as treacherous as Jefferson, as opportunistic as his namesake, Alexander Hamilton, and as vain as George Washington. As long as he could keep his head, he would fit in. And keeping his head in more ways than one. A cheap bootlegger in his house wasn't helping.

One second later, Kit Dowie walked into the kitchen.

Grinning, hands shoved in his pockets, Kit crossed the vast kitchen. "What's up, boys? Running out of booze? If you need a quick supply of anything, a friend of mine would be happy to oblige. The Blue Canary has a very reliable source. You want me to call Rose St. Lorraine?"

Before James could stop him, Bent snorted. "More talk about Chinks! The Canary is crawling with Chinks!" Frustrated in his efforts to bully Blinn, Bent went for Kit, shaking off Leo's restraining hand. Kit and Bent were both thin, but Kit was the taller by over a head. Bent had to scream upward. "If we got something from the Canary, it'd be those slit-eyed geeks that gave it, and it'd probably be our own stuff anyway!" Then he sneezed, spraying fine phlegm over Kit's gray suit.

"You don't say," said Kit, peering down at the little man through laughing eyes. "Anyone got a hanky?"

James quickly stepped between them. Things were not going well at all. What was Kit Dowie doing in his kitchen? Dowie was a pain in the ass, a friend of Lizzie's, though God alone knew why, but he was a reporter, and what he wrote hit the front page. Bent was a pawn, and a damn stupid and temporary pawn at that. "I'm sure your friend Rose's Chinese supplier is doing well enough without my small business, Dowie. But I thank you for the offer." James was using his voice on Kit, asking him to excuse the company: namely, Robert Bent. After all, James was trying to tell him, he hadn't elected the man; as district attorney, he was merely stuck with him. "Things are under control here, aren't they, Mr. Bent? I suggest we all go back to the party and let Mr. Blinn handle things."

Blinn took his cue, ingratiating himself out. Kit smiled at James and Leo, ignored Bent, and left. He understood what James had tried to tell him—mainly, shove off. But he'd seen what he wanted to see and heard what he knew he would hear. Mr. Hamilton was getting into bed with a nice new crowd. Kit was delighted.

James and Leo watched Kit go. Then they stood silently until Bent finally got the hint and left as well.

When the kitchen door swung shut on the police commissioner, Leo chuckled. "Close, eh, Hamilton?"

James was shaking. "What was that idiot Bent doing here? I didn't invite him."

Leo looked at James, his muddy eyes hooded, picking a speck of icing off his white cuff. "Gate-crashing? Aside from whatever else he is, our police commissioner doesn't know when he isn't wanted. He is also a paid-up Klansman and a smoke. A very odd combination."

James understood what the Ku Klux Klan was—who didn't? The Klan was rapidly becoming a power in California, which was a nasty surprise for reasonable Westerners who thought it was only a southern affliction. For Hamilton it was just another power base. But a smoke? He'd never heard the word. What the hell was that?

Leo saw the question before James asked it. "An opium addict, a smoke."

"Christ." James whistled.

"Robert spends a lot of his valuable time in Chinatown. He might go to sleep on me someday and wake up with his wires crossed. We wouldn't like that. But it's not your problem, Mr. DA, it's mine. I'll deal with it when the time comes."

That was just what James wanted to hear. His shaking stopped. The booze was on its way, the snooping reporter had been mollified, Esmé and his guests were waiting for him, and this was as good a time as any to mention a little problem he had to his friend Leo. He knew he was allowing the Italian a hold on him, but it was a small hold and a small risk for a big gain.

"I've bought a stretch of useless sand south of the city in San Mateo," James began. Leo listened, but his listening was like the way he looked, flat. "I got it for practically nothing. The word's out in high places that an airfield's been included in the new city budget, a very big budget. They're thinking way ahead for a change. Naturally, I suggested they site it at Mills Field."

"Your sand?" Leo tapped a cigarette on his gold case.

"Of course. But the title deeds are so complicated by now even *I'd* have some trouble getting to the bottom of them if I didn't know better. I stand to make a fortune."

"That's nice," Leo said, and stuck the cigarette in his mouth, though he didn't light it. "Why tell me?"

"Because I have a little problem I'd like you to handle. Addy Chase's lady friend, Rose St. Lorraine, owns a damn great plot right in the middle of mine. Hers is on record. She's had it for years; why, I can't imagine. Maybe she's farsighted, who knows? I need hers to put the deal over. But for some reason, my sources tell me she won't sell. Nobody knows about the city's interest. Hell, I only put the idea into their minds today. I want to know what's up. I need that sand, no matter how I get it. But I can't be seen to do anything about it."

"Suits me." *Now,* Leo lit his cigarette. "Cut me in, and I'll take care of that problem as well." Something stirred the mud in Leo's eyes. After this, the DA owed him one. Leo tucked the card away where he kept all his aces. "I'm told your famous Rose has a Chinese connection, and it isn't just her bootlegger." Leo smiled. It was about as friendly as a slammed door. "Maybe the time will come to let Blinn and his boys loose on the Celestials after all?"

The two men looked at each other. What else did they need to say? It was as good as done.

When James and Leo got back to the party, Lizzie was creating a stir in the middle of the dance floor. She was trying to do the bunny hug on her silken knees—without benefit of a partner.

The crowd, including Addy Chase, prudent to a man, drew back to let the beleaguered husband past. He had all their sympathy. What did they know? Not about Esmé, certainly. If they had, it might have changed things.

Kit saw him coming, saw the look on his face.

"I think the party's over, kid. Maybe you ought to get up?"

Lizzie wasn't sober enough to get up alone. "Screw James," she said.

Her husband helped her up. He didn't do it gently.

Kit kept out of the way. But in one brief hiatus when no one was listening, busy as they were gathering up fur coats and sequined wraps, dodging the departing orchestra, and pretending they were all going home because they wanted to, Kit tapped James on his cold shoulder.

"Remember Paris, 1919?" he said. From the look he got, which wasn't nice, James did.

Kit was right. The party was over.


Lizzie and James stood facing each other in the middle of the ballroom, with only the debris of vanished guests, thousands of wilted red roses, and a lot of melted ice for company. Keiko was calculating the amount of staff he'd need to clean up the mess, but for the moment he didn't count.

James listened while Lizzie screamed, swamping him in the frustration of two months of jealous rage.

When she'd finished, worn out and shaking, James knew just where he stood. Lizzie had found out about Esmé, and she didn't like it. So much for her drinking and sulking. What a party! Blinn, Bent, that newspaper reporter, Kit Dowie, whom Lizzie had strangely befriended, and now Lizzie. James looked at his wife and considered the odds. He was respected; *she* was drinking too much, and publicly. He would be believed or, if not, forgiven. What was a man to do with a wife like Lizzie? Who would know which had come first, her drinking or his mistress? James was on to a winner. Her behavior had given him carte blanche with Esmé, but if it went further it might spoil his chances for the future. It was time to put a rein on little Lizzie.

When James finally spoke, it was with Olympian calm. "You, my little golden goose, are a decoration. Whatever you think about anything adds up to zero. Conversely, whatever I think and whatever I do counts for a great deal in this town. It will eventually count for a lot outside this town as well. I suggest you sober up, gather your wits, and make the best of things as they are. I'm fond of you, but your light is beginning to dim. Think about it. And please remember that you are the wife of James Hamilton."

He kissed his wife's clenched hand and left the ballroom, switching off the lights as he went. Nine blazing chandeliers blinked out. Lizzie stood there in the dark and seethed—for exactly three seconds. Then she turned on her high heels and left as well. Only she went out. The last thing she remembered about her second wedding anniversary happened about one o'clock in the morning. That was when her car hit a fire hydrant on Powell Street.

# Chapter 2

Lizzie Stafford Hamilton opened her wide seagreen eyes. The surprise at waking shot a bullet of pain through the exact center of her head. She was lying, curled up and hot, on a small and messy bed. But whose bed? So far so bad.

Hung over and dismayed, she carefully lifted the gray blanket and peered under it. Gray blanket, gray sheets. "Oh, God," she groaned aloud, and dropped the blanket. At least there was no one in bed with her—not now, anyway. Aside from that sole comforting fact, she was naked. Unless she counted her emerald bracelet. Lizzie pulled the covers up to her chin and sat up.

She was in a room, and the room was large. But that's all it was—a big room. There were two windows, but their tobacco-brown shades were drawn tight against the late-morning light. What sun was left to filter through gave the room a deep caramel glow. No pictures on the walls; they couldn't have stood it. The walls were covered, all four of them, with some indeterminately colored wallpaper of overblown cabbage roses. The roses were determined enough—they were squat, one-dimensional, and dead. Aside from the bed, there was one scuffed dresser, two of its three drawers gaping open with someone's clothes spilling out of them, a man's clothes. There was a table held up by old varnish and held down by dirty dishes and two smeared glasses. There was a Pathé windup gramophone, gramophone records stacked against it, and an upright piano, its keys orange, pulled out into the room. There was a mirror above the dresser. Its glass, dim with mottling, was framed in florid gold with two smirking chipped-nosed cupids hanging on grimly.

The only piece of furniture that impressed her was the rolltop desk. It was enormous. And the books. They were everywhere. Piled on the floor and up the walls, sliding over themselves in tumbled heaps. There were stacks of newspapers from all over the country, but a New York paper, the *World,* and the *Emporia Gazette* from Kansas made up the bulk of them.

Lizzie leaned over the side of the bed as she followed the march of books. Just below her was *archy and mehitabel, Main Street, Spoon River Anthology, The Beautiful and the Damned, Huckleberry Finn, The Waste Land,* and back issues of *The Smart Set.* Lizzie straightened up. She hadn't read any of them. Who needed to, when *Harper's Bazar* and *Vogue* were around?

The room reeked of stale butts, booze, and the printed word. It made her headache worse.

"Gah," said Lizzie, and got up, gray blanket and all. Once on her feet she swayed, fighting down nausea. Maybe she'd know where she was if she could remember what she did to get there. Clues? Her black Erté and slipper satin chemise had been tossed over a big walnut radio cabinet in what might have been, at the time, gay abandon. Her ankle-strap shoes and sheer stockings could only have ended up in far corners of the room by being tossed there. Lizzie staggered over to the mirror of cupids. Taking courage, she lifted her head. In the butterscotch light, things weren't so bad. Smudged makeup made her look older, which made her look interesting. The cheekbones, high and wide, never let her down, but

Mildred, the woman who did her hair, would not be pleased. It was as tangled as a gypsy's. She still had her dimple and the sweeping flash of black-lashed green eyes. Lizzie smiled. She liked the whole effect—until she ran her tongue over her teeth. With an addict's need, Lizzie thought of coffee. Surely, she could make something as simple as a cup of coffee? All she had to do was heat it up. She found a kind of kitchen crammed into a kind of closet; one look and she slammed the door. Forget coffee.

There was no bathroom. No bathroom? Stumbling on her trailing blanket, Lizzie found the front door. Three letters were on her side of the mat. Sinking, rather than bending, to save her throbbing head, Lizzie picked them up. Now was the moment when Mrs. James A. Hamilton, wife of the DA and well-publicized rich girl, would find out who she'd spent the night with. It wasn't much, but it was everything.

Mr. Dowie. Kit Dowie. Mr. K. D. Dowie. Kit! Dear God, she was in Kit's room. To be precise, Lizzie had slept at the Crawford Apartments, 620 Eddy Street, number 27. Although she'd never been there before, she knew the address. Lizzie saw the room in a new light. This was Kit's home, one crummy room? In her house up on the Hill there were rooms she hadn't seen in years.

Kit had told her he lived above a couple of cheap bootleggers and just down the hall from a few very busy ladies of the night. The Crawford was the home of newspapermen, artists, and assorted lowlife. Lizzie was thrilled, briefly. But where was the bathroom? Where did Kit pee? She thought of the stained kitchen *cum* closet and shuddered.

Dropping the envelopes on the already littered rolltop, she cracked open the front door far enough to stick her tousled head out. A long caked-mustard-colored hallway stretched before her, smeared with the fingerprints of anonymous men. The fingerprints led to and from number 29. Halfway along there was a wall pay phone with a three-legged stool next to it. At the far end a door stood open. It was not inviting. There was the hard gleam of a once-white tub on its clawed feet, and . . . aha! The bathroom! Three mysteries solved. Where?

Who with? What about a girl's toilette? None of the answers cheered her up, but if she was careful they could all be lived down. The aged Mr. Ned Greenway, cocooned in a turn-of-the-century daze and still puffing out copy pinked with French phrases for the *Argonaut,* San Francisco's society paper, was her biggest fan. Lizzie Stafford Hamilton made news. But, oh, brother, not with this.

There was one problem left and it was a doozy. Did she or didn't she? Everything pointed to a big fat yes. Inside her blanket, Lizzie flushed. Dropping it, she looked down the golden flat-bellied length of her body. It looked the same. Moderately unused. The scene after her party washed over her. James! He didn't give a fig what Lizzie thought about his affair with Esmé Baker. That hurt. But in the light of day, what hurt most was not Esmé. It was what James thought of Lizzie. Other than as his wife, she was nothing but a decoration, someone whose thoughts didn't count. Was that true? Did everyone think that? What would they say if they could see her now? They wouldn't blame James.

Using one careful finger, Lizzie felt herself: warm and moist. But not wet. Not wet? She lifted one long muscled leg onto Kit's bed to get a better look. No telltale signs, wet or dry. The bed itself, then? Kit's small bed had seen many things, the sheets stretched under better days, but nothing noticeably new. Had she or hadn't she?

"Oh, hell," said Lizzie. "What did I do last night?"

But whatever it was, thank God it was with Kit. Funny, sharp, irritating Kit. If she'd been bad, it might as well have been with her best friend. Yes? No! A complete stranger would have been better than Kit Dowie. Now he could do more than tease her about her money and her friends, he could torment her. Kit was right about bathtub gin. It was poison. She must remember to change her bootlegger.

Lizzie shoved piles of paper around on the rolltop, found her evening bag, and in it her cigarettes and lighter. She lit one, flopping naked onto the desk chair. How dare Kit take advantage of a girl when she was not quite herself! The thought made her gulp smoke. Kit hadn't taken advantage of her in the six years she'd known him, and lately she'd been blotto around him plenty. If anything had gone on between them, *she* must have started it. Double damn.

Whatever happened after she'd hit the hydrant was so far back in her mind, it might as well not have happened at all. Lizzie sat up. *That* was a thought! It didn't happen. Does a tree fall if no one's looking? Or a girl, if no one knows? There was only one bug in this fine idea— Kit must remember it. She sank back. So it did happen. How utterly humiliating to have to ask Dowie for details.

And where was Kit? He must have left a note. Lizzie focused her aching eyes on the mess of paper on his desk. There it was, on top of his typewriter. "If you're still here —back around five. Spare key under the typewriter." Five? That was hours away. What was she going to do with herself until then—without coffee?

On top of the Remington and everywhere else on the desk was a stationer's dream. Envelopes, carbons, letters —to Kit and from Kit. The amount of his correspondence amazed her. Who was he writing to? Who was writing back? Hadn't he heard of the telephone? Lizzie went through a few short stories and scraps of verse. She read one that was attached to an acceptance slip from a New York paper, the *World,* signed by a Franklin Pierce Adams. It welcomed him to The Conning Tower, whatever that was. The poem was cynical, punchy, and terse. She almost liked it. Even better, she understood it. Which wasn't good news for Kit. It couldn't be poetry if someone could understand it.

Kit, the man she thought she knew, her only real friend, had so many secrets. Letters from Chicago and New York and Los Angeles. How many people did he know? Lizzie assumed they were secrets because in six years she'd never thought to ask Kit about Kit. When they were together, she told him about Lizzie. Kit was a good listener. For the first time, Lizzie wondered what he thought of her. Her friends thought her charming and fun and even a little bit daring. But where were her friends when she needed them? She needed someone.

And the awful truth was—there was really only Kit. He was still there, whether she was married or not. He neglected her for months at a time, but he kept coming back at the oddest moments—like last night. He was the only person she knew who wasn't from her world—except James. But James wanted to be, and he was getting what he wanted. Kit didn't. He mocked Lizzie's society. Perhaps that's why she liked him. He made her look at things the way he looked at them. He made her laugh.

But not when he talked about what interested him: politics, literature, sports, history—things she knew nothing about. And if you did know, what were you supposed to do about it? Some of what he said filtered through. But as far as Lizzie could tell, it hadn't done her any good at all.

There were steel-gray filing cabinets next to the rolltop. Lizzie pulled open the drawers. Unlike the rest of the room, the stuff in these files was as neat as an audit. Hundreds and hundreds of clippings, all written by Kit. Twelve years of newspaper print. Dowie in the Mexican Revolution, at the Johnson-Willard fight, at political conventions, interviewing Teddy Roosevelt, Charles Evans Hughes, Pancho Villa and Babe Ruth, Theodore Dreiser and Maude Adams, Pershing and that new bald man in Italy, the blustering Mussolini. Lizzie flipped through the folders until she came to 1917—America's proud entry into the European War. That was interesting; in fact, it was riveting. Looking back, with Kit's front-page stories on her naked lap, Lizzie suddenly realized that the war had been the best time of her life—*her* war.

That was when she'd met James Hamilton and Kit Dowie. Both on the same day. But before running headlong into them, Lizzie Stafford had been seventeen, rich, and without doubt the most popular girl in San Francisco. The city had been swept with patriotic fervor. Everyone vied to find cute places to hang little American flags. Charity balls and society hunts, polo games, fund drives, yacht races, and grand dinners at the great houses to honor old heroes or new: Lizzie had been queen of them all. Charles Mortimer bought her a Paris gown a day. Mary Maud in brown, the only color she wore for the duration, beavered away with the other matrons making things to send to our boys "over there," but little Lizzie had dressed up in her changing gowns and smiled. She'd danced and flirted, skated and sailed on the choppy bay with ribbons in her hair and, oh, Lord, it had been a wonderful war. Lizzie had had few girlfriends, but who needed girls when one girl had all the boys?

If she didn't count right now, the end of the war was the worst thing that had ever happened to her. But in the beginning, when her days were spent in a rush to get ready for her heady nights, nothing spoiled the splendor of being Lizzie Stafford.

Then came Phoebe Hearst's—Mrs. George Hearst, mother of William Randolph Hearst—1917 Fourth of July Military Ball, held down south in her Pleasanton mansion. Lizzie wore white chiffon, her black hair swept up and dressed with white silk butterflies. Mobbed by the best young blades, all smelling of Russian Leather, Lizzie was doing what she did best—flirting—when she'd looked up, and there he was: James Alexander Hamilton. Tall and soldier straight, his silvery blond hair falling over a high pure brow, his pants, his cuffs, his shirtfront perfect, just perfect. From across the ballroom he'd smiled, a lazy lingering look that made her heart flop over. Lizzie had fallen in love, fallen into *something,* the minute ice-blue eyes met green. Just at that moment, that precious moment, she'd turned, breathless—and found herself face-to-face with a muscular young man. He had snapping black eyes, thick black hair, and was only a little taller than she was. What he was wearing wasn't perfect, it was absurd: a salt-and-pepper three-piece suit with brown shoes. It took what was left of Lizzie's breath away. He wasn't smiling, but out of sheer habit, Lizzie did. One of her best, the sweet dimpled smile with lowered eyes where her sooty lashes just brushed her soft pink cheeks. It had always done the trick. The dark young man had clicked his heels, kissed her hand, and said, "You're cute, kid—but not *that* cute." Then he had walked away. Dowie hadn't changed; he was still like that.

Coming back to the present, Lizzie sighed and put the folder away.

She read Kit's coverage of the 1919 World Series. In black-inked outrage Dowie had practically called for a federal investigation. The Series, he wrote, had been fixed. Lizzie remembered Charles Mortimer saying the same thing. The old man, multiple chins wobbling and a great hurt in his fading eyes, had gone around buttonholing everyone he knew, man, woman, and child, asking them all where the world was going to if America's favorite game, "Good God, man, baseball!" could be sold down the river for a few measly bucks? As far as Lizzie could recall, no one had answered him. But Kit's article did. Kit said, briefly: to hell, that's where it was going, straight to hell in the back pocket of greed.

There were files on national scandals and lurid murders. Lizzie devoured every word of one of them, chain-smoking, her elbows propped on the rolltop, her long legs tucked under the chair, her bare behind on the edge of the seat. Fatty Arbuckle had been big news—the case began right in the St. Francis Hotel on Union Square. Publicity had been national, and James's name went with it. Fatty was the real beginning of his meteoric career. It was 1921 and he was the prosecuting attorney, young, fresh, and eager. Lizzie had been Mrs. Hamilton for almost five months; her crush on James was in full flower. With her husband, Fatty hadn't stood a chance. Fat men who rape young girls deserved what they got. Virginia Rappe, poor thing, had died. James had been brilliant.

But as she read Kit's coverage, Lizzie grew confused. The coroner, Kit wrote, said the Rappe girl's insides had burst not from the weight of Fatty but from a social disease. Virginia was someone who got paid to be the life of the party, not an innocent young thing seduced by an overfed, overfeted movie star. The only crime Arbuckle had committed was to be there when life ran out for Miss Rappe. It was just one party too many. Kit had a lot to say about James and his handling of the case. Summed up: Famous people had to be careful when they had fun, ought to think twice about who they had fun with, and never do it under the nose of ambition.

Now, two years later and for the first time, Lizzie saw Fatty as Kit had seen him: hounded, disgraced, a scapegoat. Was Kit right? All she knew was that James had become district attorney on the strength of the Arbuckle case. The prosecution hadn't convicted the comic, the public did. Hamilton came out of it, silver in voice and charisma—and Fatty might as well be dead.

Lizzie was more than confused by Kit's writing; she was stirred. What a job he had, chasing around the world getting angry! As the years passed, Kit's name got bigger until everything he did was on the front page. What a circus the world was, and Kit had his nose right in it. Twelve years of murder and intrigue and fixes and fights and wars and famous people doing famous things—but he lived in one room, and he didn't own a thing worth having.

She found his private files: letters from people named Ben Hecht, William Allen White, Robert Benchley, Dorothy Parker, Anita Loos. Anita? Dorothy? Lizzie glanced through those, then put them back. They weren't love letters. Sometimes she surprised herself. Why should she care if they were? But she did care. She hadn't recognized it before, and it surprised her now. Lizzie wanted Kit to *like* her, to save her letters as he saved Dorothy's and Anita's. Lizzie wanted his respect.

The telephone out in the hall rang. Lizzie sat waiting for it to be answered or to stop. Neither one happened. The phone rang and rang and rang and . . . just as Lizzie was about to scream, it stopped ringing. Her left foot was asleep. Gritting her teeth, massaging the pins and needles away, she rifled through the last of the files. This one contained song lyrics. Kit wrote songs? That explained the piano. But did anyone sing them? They seemed a little too wordy to her, too clever to be successful. They must be a hobby, like the poems and short stories.

Lizzie was hungry. No food, no coffee. But the worst thing about her afternoon in Kit's room, apart from the problem of last night's sleeping arrangements, was that there wasn't one word about Lizzie in all this paper. She'd spent hours reading about everything else. It made her feel restless. Something long dormant in her mind was struggling to awaken. A critical sense? Judgment? Curiosity? Whatever it was, Lizzie shrugged it away, shutting the last of Kit's files. She noted two thin folders way in the back. The first was marked LS. With a shiver, she reached for it and found every letter she'd ever written him while he was in Europe batting out the war on his typewriter.

How sweet, she thought, gratified. She hadn't kept any of his. Every scrap James had sent her was tied with an unfaded scarlet ribbon, but Kit's had been thrown away upon reading. James's letters were big backward sloping sprawls that called her "dearest" and "my heart," laughing off the danger at the front, talking about honor and glory and ultimate victory. Hers to him, her gallant young Harvard lawyer fighting in France, were all the outpourings of her teenage heart, spiced with a spoon-fed imagination and imagery from romantic novels.

But what she wrote to Kit she remembered as witty, even literate. Hard going for a girl who'd majored in sport at the University of California—all extracurricular: smoking her first cigarette, drinking from flasks with a fast crowd she'd met at Berkeley, betting with illegal bookies on the races at Tanforan, cakewalking, necking in rumble seats, and shopping.

Kit's letters to her were about war, the real war. The best of us won't be coming back, he'd said; the youth of the world is dying. He wrote of boredom and fear, fleas and filth and the lack of supplies, the lies he heard from the important mouths of important people well back of the front lines. There was confusion and tears, loss and futility, but most of all there was death "over there."

"I type in a night," one went, dated in late November 1917, "lit with German star shells, a fresh crater for an office, breathing in kerosene and what the boys call mackabby, meaning the stench of mud and blood, flesh putrifying off living bones, and the unburied dead. How's your French? The soldiers all say, *A quoi bon la guerre?* Good question. No answer."

What kind of letters were they to write to a girl? She'd skimmed over them as she was skimming now. Lizzie hadn't liked his letters and hadn't believed them. He called the Great War "Europe's gothic scrape." What did he mean by that? They were men he was talking about, brave men, and their cause was just. Everyone said so. And what about James? Risking his life while Kit wandered around with his Remington criticizing everything. No wonder she'd never kept his letters. When they'd arrived, she'd sneaked them up to her rooms and blushed over them. But there was a little pride—after all, he'd written them to her. Lizzie'd read enough of her assigned lists at Berkeley to know what he wrote was impassioned, organized, and strong. He was wrong, but his wrongness was so well written. Kit pulled no punches. She saw the trenches slick with blood, *smelled* them, heard the screams of the dying and the thin whistle of bullets. Could almost touch the caked mud on the empty faces of the dead, shoo away the fat droning flies in the long still wait for the glare and the whine and the crash of more mortar and more bombs and more gas, more fear, and always more death. Like Kit's songs, no one wanted to hear it—but he told Lizzie. There was something in that.

Kit was a strange man. If he didn't love her, why had he written so often? There was no romance in his letters to Lizzie. At the time he wrote them, they hardly knew each other. The meeting at the Military Ball, two or three times afterward, and then, like James, like all the young men, he was gone. She'd been surprised when the letters started coming. Now, of course, she knew him. He was a writer, and a writer writes. Lizzie Stafford had been his diary.

One letter, though, she'd kept. In it Kit mentioned meeting James in Paris just after the Armistice—only a few words. It said nothing, but it thrilled her. Her next letter back had been full of questions. What did James look like? What had he said? Had he talked about her? How many medals had he won? What for? Was he well? Kit wrote of nothing but the war; James barely mentioned it. When Kit wrote again he didn't answer one of her questions, not in the next letter or the next. The omission drove her crazy. James never spoke of meeting Kit, and now Kit never . . . it made her spit. When Kit came home—long after James, who arrived to ticker-tape parades and banquets—even then, Kit wouldn't say a thing. She remembered how she'd greeted him. "Well, Mr. Dowie, James denies ever meeting you in Paris. What do you think of that?"

"Does he?" said Kit, and then dropped the subject.

Lizzie thumbed through the LS folder until she found the letter she remembered, her best effort. She'd spent hours on it. It was a detailed, racy account of a skating party at Sutro's Cliff House where all her friends had done such funny things.

As she read her own handwriting, Lizzie's spirits sank, dimmed, and then clenched into a dark fist. It was schoolgirl writing. What she'd thought was funny was tiresome. The antics of her friends made her cringe. How could she think they were clever? On paper, they were all foolish, thoughtless children. Her descriptions of clothes, ice, pranks—life itself—gushed and simpered. In horror, Lizzie crumpled the letter, all twelve pages of it. It was the work of a spoiled brat. It was *her* work. Through it, Lizzie saw herself as Kit saw her. What *he* must have seen as he sat in the bloody mud of Flanders field or wherever he was when he'd read it. Compared to Dorothy and Anita, it was drivel.

Lizzie squirmed in her chair. Damn Kit. Why did he have to save things? What did she have to prove to Kit Dowie anyway? Aside from being an amusing friend who had traitorous ideas about his own country, who was he? A newspaper reporter, a songwriter. A person who lived in one room on Eddy Street, and what a room! He made Lizzie laugh, but he had no money. Who was anybody without money? What was worse, it didn't look like he was ever going to get any. Where would that leave him? Kit had been all over the world, seen what seemed to her like everything, written it all down for throwaway newspapers, and what did he have to show for it? Bylines, that's what—and that's all, as Grandfather used to say. A room with a rolltop desk full of worthless paper.

But Kit hadn't written the letter, Lizzie had. Kit

hadn't scribbled those silly words, thought those silly thoughts, Lizzie had. No wonder he talked to her the way he did, brushed aside her pouts and rages. The miracle was that he put up with her at all. Perhaps she had grown since the letter. She was twenty-three now; she was married; her husband was fooling around with a woman older than Lizzie. That ought to make one grow.

Lizzie reached for the last folder. It was marked JAH. JAH? Surely James never wrote to Kit? Just as her fingertips touched the stiff manila paper, she saw something that would change her life. Lizzie couldn't know that what she didn't do now would alter everything past this moment, and not knowing made the dazzling choice much like any other, unremarkable. She snatched her hand away from the folder.

Smeared makeup, no coffee, and a certain nagging worry about the night before were one thing—well, three, actually—her nails were another. The bathtub waited for her at the end of the grim and very public hallway. Never mind that it was used by people she'd never met. Never mind. Dirty nails were the last straw.

There was a sharp knock on Kit's door. It wasn't just any kind of a "hello there" knock, it was a demanding pound with the side of a balled fist. Whoever was out there wanted in—bad. The pounding got louder. Lizzie jumped for the blanket and crept to the door. On her side, she crouched down, waiting for the pounding to go away. This time she wasn't in luck. The pounding got really determined.

"Yes?" she finally said. The word was forced out of her like a blown egg.

"Who's that?" demanded a low throaty voice from the other side of the door. It was a woman.

"Who's that?" said Lizzie, feeling scared but, worse than that, foolish.

"Never mind me, honey. Open this door." There was menacing music in the dark voice. "I got to see Kit. Kit, you in there?" The doorknob rattled.

"Kit's gone out."

"Listen, you. Let me in and let me in now. You don't

open this door, I'll bust it down." The pounding became a steady hammer.

Lizzie had no choice. If she didn't let the woman in, her pounding would do worse than her presence in Kit's room; it might bring the police. Lizzie opened the door and was almost flattened by a tall woman, an Amazon, head up, nostrils flaring, practically sniffing the room for Kit.

"Where is he?" she said.

"Work?" offered Lizzie.

"Says you."

In her blanket, Lizzie watched the woman stride around the room on long legs, opening the kitchen door and then slamming it as Lizzie had done earlier. She snorted in disgust. "Men! They take some beatin'!"

Lizzie was stunned. It couldn't be more than one o'clock in the afternoon, but the woman was dressed like someone who expected to win the big prize at a *bal masqué*. She was all in silver, crystal bangles and bugle beads, shoes, stockings; her earrings were thin silver wings that swept back over her ears. But it wasn't the dress or the jewelry that shone, it was the woman. Tall? My God, she was over six feet tall, and that was without the silver heels. She was as lithe and alert as a greyhound; the face was smooth, exotic, and fierce. Her hair was cropped within an inch of her proud head. But all that was nothing compared to the fact that her skin, every square inch of it, was as black as Lizzie's hair was black.

The woman noticed the open filing cabinet. "How long you been here, sweet stuff?"

Lizzie was shocked and she was naked, but she wasn't down. "None of your business."

"Well, honey, looks like you been here long enough to do yourself some snoopin'."

Lizzie had had enough. She pulled her sagging blanket up; her spirits followed. "I don't snoop."

"What you call it, then?"

"I don't call it anything. Kit and I are old friends."

"That so?" The black woman ran a silver nail over the curved case of the radio, hooked Lizzie's Erté dress, didn't bother to look at it, and flicked it off. The dress landed at Lizzie's feet. "You tell the man, you see him first, that Dido came by. Tell him to come see me over the Blue Canary. I got something he should know—you say it's about Miss Violet Louise; he'll know what you mean. Tell him I phoned, but that his *old* friend wouldn't stir herself enough to answer and save Dido the trip here." Dido kicked one of Lizzie's shoes out of her way and strode to the door. Before she left she looked back at Lizzie and smiled, a great big hungry smile that had as much warmth in it as Baked Alaska. All it took was a slow lift of her damp black beautiful upper lip. "Ain't it time you got dressed, Mrs. Hamilton?" Dido left with the swish and click of a thousand silver beads, leaving a shaken Lizzie and the overpowering smell of gardenias.

When the door slammed, Lizzie came to. How did that woman, a woman of color, know who she was? Kit, of course! Dowie, the skunk, had told her. Lizzie snapped on the radio. It took a minute to hum into life while she tumbled into her chemise, and when it did, it blared. "Yes, We Have No Bananas" vibrated through Kit's room. "Not that song again!" Lizzie cried, twisting the knob off to get the volume down. How dare Kit go round telling a colored woman, *any* woman, about her? Too angry to worry about niceties, she bathed down the hall, used Kit's toothbrush on her teeth, and dressed. She took the spare key from under the typewriter and left. She looked great; she felt murderous.

# Chapter 3

The afternoon sun hit Lizzie like a mallet. Right in front of the Crawford, slewed up onto the curb where she'd obviously left it the night before, was her 1922 Cadillac V8, a pearl gray sports cabriolet, one tire up on the sidewalk, the top down, and a gem of a dent in the front bumper. Lizzie glared at it. She'd walk. She was too shaken to drive. Tripping on down Eddy Street, she was looking for coffee—anywhere she could get it would do. Around her swirled a mass of city people wonderful in their similarity. Gray suits, brown suits, derby hats, little summer cloth coats and little summer dresses—most printed with that season's fashion rage, the Egyptian look. Cloche hats, handbags, brown, brown, brown. Shoulder to shoulder with Monday-afternoon telephone operators, dictaphone typists, manicurists, department store salesgirls, usherettes, coffee-shop waitresses; all their feather-bobbed heads as full of dreams as Scheherazade. Lizzie Stafford, in a black Paris evening gown and a furious soul, felt like strong-arming them all.

The buildings on either side of Eddy, all tiny look-alike hotels full of nameless look-alike men, leered down on her with a thousand blank eyes. Wind freshened and snapped down the natural funnel of Eddy, and what sky there was above the buildings was changing from a cold blue to the colder slate of a city sidewalk. A sheet of newspaper wound itself around her silken legs when she got to the triangular intersection where Eddy met Market and Powell. The racket of the cable cars on their turntable brought back her hangover. There was a small coffee shop across the traffic snarl of Market. Lizzie ran for it, dodging streetcars.

Other than the sullen chit of a girl standing guard over the coffee pots, Lizzie had the place to herself.

Elizabeth Sian Hamilton née Stafford was a lady. She knew who she was and she knew who her people were—at least unto the third generation. Before Charles Mortimer Stafford, with his self-cornered millions, and Mary Maud, the tight-lipped pioneer who stood behind him and added it all up, things didn't count. That kind of knowledge gave one a comforting sense of security, a rightness about time and place. Normally, she knew where she was and, better, that she belonged there. Lizzie belonged to San Francisco, or the other way around. On top of that, she had pots of money. It bought her whatever she wanted. At times, it had the nasty habit of buying Lizzie the wrong thing, but James wasn't something to think of just now. Always having money meant that she didn't even think about it. She had no idea what it was like not to. In her ramblings with him, Kit had shown her examples of poverty. She'd dutifully looked and, while looking, had the feeling that she was observing freaks, aberrations, things flung up now and again by nature to put the fear of God into a person. Lizzie had brains, but she used her charm. It worked better. So far. Except for Kit, and now, maybe, James. Finding herself in a crepe-de-chine ball gown, black pumps, and an emerald bracelet in the middle of the afternoon in a cheap Market Street coffee shop, Lizzie showed her mettle. She felt out of place but welcome. Like linen in a truck stop.

She carried two pieces of toast and a cup of strong coffee back to a table facing Market. And there she sat, fuming. She had her coffee, two slices of toast getting cold, a pack of gold-tipped cigarettes, the window on the busy street to herself—and lots of free time.

The ash trembled on the end of her cigarette, then fell with a brief zzt into the coffee. Lizzie didn't notice. Absently stirring the ash in her cup, Lizzie was talking to herself.

I'm not going home. To hell with James and his crap. At least not for a few days, I'm not. It's *my* house. Grandfather left it to me. This isn't merrie olde England where what's the wife's becomes the husband's, thank God. I'll go back when I'm ready.

Lizzie shoved a fly off her toast. It went and sat on the other piece. She looked down at her dress. Two days in the same dress is one and a half days too long, at the very least. Lizzie searched through her evening bag. Three sticks of gum, a compact, lipstick, and rouge, blood-red Cutex nail polish, and a packet of Bayer aspirin. She took four. There was also nine dollars and change. Who cared? She'd simply go on up to Union Square. I. Magnin would put everything on credit, her old friend, Mary Ann Magnin, would send the bill to James, and Lizzie would pay it. And maybe Mary Anne's grandson, Cyril Magnin, would be there. That silly young man would be thrilled to see her; Cyril had asked Lizzie to marry him yearly since they were both seventeen. She drank the rest of her coffee, ash and all.

The lone waitress, a small harried number, stood over Lizzie with one of her pots. "Want some more, lady?" The girl's hair was a soft blond bob, but her eyes were down to their last dime.

"No, thanks." Lizzie noticed the girl's frayed cuffs, the sad little watch on her wrist. It probably didn't even keep the right time. With unending credit, Lizzie didn't need cash; she left the waitress a five-dollar tip.

A girl needs things; a rich girl gets them. With the thought of shopping, Lizzie found purpose. Her dark head came up, and her shoulders straightened.

Outside, the sun was gone and the sky cracked open. Out fell drops of rain as big as silver dollars, ringing change on the sidewalk. The air smelled of gasoline and dust and the sea.

By the time Lizzie walked up Powell to Union Square, she was soaked. Two frantic hours later, the rain had stopped and San Francisco wore its usual summer frock—fog. Lizzie wore a white wool suit trimmed in black mink. The mink ran over one shoulder and followed the slim white wool to her ankle-length hem. The suit had a matching round mink muffler and a cute white wool hat. Lizzie also carried enough boxes, bags, and bundles to make a camel spit. It was still more than an hour before Kit's note said he'd be home. The idea of going back to that room alone made Lizzie practice her breathing.

Right in front of her on O'Farrell Street was the Orpheum, one of the last holdouts on the vanishing vaudeville circuit. The front of the old red brick building was plastered with posters, some new, most old. Comics and girls, novelty acts, song-and-dance teams, magicians and jugglers—names she remembered from her childhood when Grandfather used to take her to the Orpheum every Saturday afternoon. But what caught her eye, and held it, was across the street. A brand new picture palace picked out in colored lights, and on the flagrant marquee the name of a new movie: Colleen Moore in *Flaming Youth*. Vaudeville was taking a nose dive, but a movie— what fun! Lizzie loved Keaton and Valentino, Gish and Nazimova, who was all fashionable sin.

The lady in the box office, wearing loop earrings a couple of parrots could have perched in, crooked a fat finger at Lizzie in invitation. "Come on in, dearie. Rest your weary dogs. It don't rain in here, no sirree."

Lizzie shrugged. It was a day of firsts. Why buck the tide? She paid her nickel and went in, sitting way in the back with a bag of hot buttered popcorn and some saltwater taffy.

Three stories above her head the house lights, stabbing down from the ceiling like giant cookie cutters, dimmed.

For the next hour, Lizzie, shaken by silence, experienced a kind of ecstasy, a delirium in the dark. After the newsreel and Felix the Cat, the black-and-white screen brought brilliant dreams, dreams brought revelation. That girl up there, Colleen Moore, was free. She was young and fun and couldn't give a damn for the kind of world James knew, or Lizzie, for that matter. James would hate Colleen, just like he hated Aimee Crocker. A flapper in the White House? Fat chance. All the Esmés in the world couldn't touch her. Lizzie's brain cartwheeled. What did she need? A few dresses that shimmied and shook. And a visit to Mildred for her hair. James said her light was beginning to dim? Well, watch her crank the wattage up!

The age of the Jazz Baby had finally dawned for the rich girl from Nob Hill.

"Oh, God," Kit said when Lizzie stumbled back into his room at the Crawford. It was six-thirty.

Lizzie was a jumble of packages, a blur of hatboxes, and all sorts of surprises in tissue paper.

"What now?" Kit had been lying back on his unmade bed, hat and shoes still on—though he'd loosened his polka-dot tie. He was smoking a cigarette and reading *archy and mehitabel*. Now he was just staring.

Lizzie dropped everything in the middle of his floor.

"What have you done to yourself?"

Lizzie posed. Her green eyes glared at Kit's tomcat face, daring him to laugh. "What do you think?"

Kit took the dare. "You mean, besides *eeek?*"

"Isn't it the cat's pajamas?"

"Christ. You'll also be learning 'whoopie water,' 'party pooper,' and my all-time favorite, 'vo-do-dee-o,' won't you?"

Kit got up, still smoking, and walked around Lizzie, looking her up and down.

"To tell you the truth, if I didn't know how you used to look, I'd say you looked swell. It's not a class act anymore, but it sure as hell is a sight. As Coué tells us, 'Day by day, in every way, you are getting curiouser and curiouser.' "

Lizzie had marceled her blue-black hair, rolled down the stockings on her long coltish legs, and her ban-

gled amber skirt barely covered her knees. She watched
Kit with a wary eye.

"You mean I look cheap?"

"Cheap but tasty."

She put her hands on her slim hips and, swaying,
batted her eyelashes. She lisped, "Like this?"

"For Pete's sake, don't overdo it. What happened to
your eyelashes?"

"They're beaded. Mildred did it with a toothpick
and some hot black goo. Wax, I hope."

"Jeez." Kit whistled, pushing his hat to the back of
his head.

"Isn't it something? What do you think James'll
say?"

"He won't say anything. He'll biff you one."

"That bad? Perfect."

"You want him to biff you one?"

"I want to make him mad, mad as he's ever been,
especially about something he can't do a damn thing
about."

"You will. Trust me."

"What do you think, Kit—I mean, really think?"

"If you were my wife, _I'd_ biff you one. As it is, I can
only laugh."

"Thank heavens, I'm not your wife."

"You said it."

"What kind of a crack is that?"

"A cheap shot, but accurate."

"If you mean what I think you mean, and I think I
do, you can soak your head. Why can't you just once say
something nice to me, you bastard?"

"Why, Elizabeth, my dear. Your language! But to
answer the question, when do you ever deserve it? You
get crocko at your own party, insult your guests, walk
out on your husband, spend the night with a member of
the lower order, not to mention a _male_ member, crinkle
your hair, put enough goo on your eyelashes to make you
look like Theda Bara in a La Brea tar pit, spend even
more of somebody else's money—"

"Mine!"

"The late Charles Mortimer's, once he'd stolen it

from everyone else who was around at the time, not counting the native Americans, but then, nobody counts *them*—and you still haven't gone home."

"You want me to leave?"

"What do you want to do?"

"Well, I thought—well, of course, I can't stay here," Lizzie ended lamely, pointing at the one small bed.

"In a nutshell, lady."

"But I'm not going back to James, not yet I'm not."

"He'll kick himself if he misses the new you."

"He won't miss me. He'll get the full show, but it won't be up there." Lizzie jerked her new marcel in the general direction of Nob Hill. "I'll make it as public as possible."

"So this is all for his benefit?"

"I'm not sure *benefit* is the right word."

Kit laughed, took off his hat, threw it on the desk, strolled back to his bed and lay down again, crossed his legs, and put his hands behind his head. Then he laughed some more. "You know, kid, I've got to hand it to you. When you do something, you *do* something. Why is it, though, I get the creepy feeling that things aren't going to go with a bang?"

Lizzie stood her ground. "What do you mean by that?"

"Well, first of all, *you're* the one who has to walk around the better parts of town looking like something out of a Lon Chaney movie—"

"I can get the marcel—"

"Crinkles."

"—crinkles out whenever I want to."

"Like Chaney in drag, which in your circles will go over like a lead cello."

"But Kit, that's just it, don't you see? My circles are James's circles. My circles make and break politicians. How are they going to take James Hamilton seriously with me for a wife?"

"Ah!" Kit's dark eyes narrowed. "I got it, a plot! You intend to arrest his mad flight to the highest office in the land, to stop him at the very portal of the White House. I suppose you figure he won't even make the governor's mansion in Sacramento. It's a novel way to go about it. But why should you want to do that? Don't you see yourself as First Lady?"

"James doesn't deserve the presidency."

"Because of a little philandering? Don't be silly, lady. *Anyone* is welcome in Washington. Look at the boobs there now, Harding and the boys from Ohio."

"Harding is a fine man."

"Harding is a sap."

"Will you be serious?"

"I am being serious. You're the one playing the fool." Kit leaned over the side of his bed to pick up *archy and mehitabel* again. "But don't you worry, dizzy Lizzie, Kit Dowie's in your corner. And I'll still be there when you fall on your fanny. I know you better than you think." Kit opened the book and began to read.

Lizzie was left blinking. As usual, this wasn't the way things were supposed to go. She could skin Kit. Did he practice being a son of a bitch, or did it just come naturally? She blushed as a memory—or, rather, the lack of a memory—swept through her. "Kit," she said, chewing her lip. "About your knowing me. . . ."

Kit put his book down and laughed. "I was waiting for that. Forget it, kid. You passed out on the bed right after the striptease. I covered you up and left."

"Oh, thank God. Left?"

"You had the bed. I needed one."

"Where?"

"Oh, out somewhere."

"You went to Dido's, didn't you?"

It was Kit's turn to look uneasy. "Dido told you that?"

"Dido didn't tell me anything." Lizzie pressed her advantage. "It's you who tells Dido things. She was here looking for you. I was to tell you it was about Miss Violet somebody or another."

"She found me. You hungry?"

Lizzie could tell a brush-off when she heard one. Kit didn't want to talk about Dido. But he damn well talked about Lizzie *to* Dido. She wasn't having that. This was one of those times that called for brains. Lizzie stuck to her guns; she used her charm. She sat on Kit's bed, gently removed the book from his grip, and smiled her dimpled smile.

Kit grinned at her, a cheeky challenging grimace that almost made her swallow her tongue.

"Stop that, Elizabeth. Last night was a close shave, men being what they are and me being what I am—"

"And what's that, Kit Dowie?"

"Sane. You and me, little Lizzie, weren't cut out to be lovers."

Struggling with the surprise of hearing that someone might not want her, which had nothing to do with whether she wanted him, Lizzie shocked herself.

"We weren't?" she blurted. Then flushed. That was not what she meant to say. What she intended to say was "Of course not!" or "Buzz off" or—God, she could cut her tongue out.

Kit was laughing at her again.

"Not on your life, girl. We're pals. What do pals want to fool around with that kind of grief for?"

"Indeed, but I—"

"Drop it, Lizzie. It didn't happen. It won't happen. You're safe with me."

Lizzie was appalled to find she didn't want to drop it. She wanted—well, what the hell did she want? Nothing. Right? Right. But dammit, she wanted Kit to want it. By *it*, did she mean her? Really, Lizzie! She was getting confused. Damn Kit. He'd had the last word again. But not this time, no, not now. Lizzie pulled herself together.

"Kit, you working tonight?"

"Why?" Kit looked worried.

"Because I want you to take me out. Take me places I've never heard of, real places—*you* know."

"Real places?"

"Don't pretend you don't know what I'm talking about. Dives, holes, speaks. Where a girl like me wouldn't be seen dead."

"What for?"

"So I don't have to be a girl like me."

"I like girls like you, among others."

"I don't."

"Don't get cute. You like no one better."

Lizzie jumped up, pulling on his hands.

"Let's go. I'm thirsty."

"James won't like it."

"How much do you care?"

"Not a lot."

"Neither do I."

Kit put his book down for the last time, got up, and jammed his hat back on. "Follow me. You asked for it, kid."

At the door, Lizzie paused. "You going to wear that tie?"

Kit looked down at his red-and-white polka dots. "You kidding? You wear what you want, I wear what I want."

# Chapter 4

At the very moment Lizzie was making her choice between the folder marked JAH or her nails—seated at Kit's desk stark naked and unconsciously tender (Rembrandt would have swapped every model in Amsterdam for those caramel skin tones)—James Hamilton, fully dressed in a tailor-made suit gray as campfire smoke and a snow-white shirt with ebony studs, was at *his* desk.

The desk was in his office, and his office was in the Hall of Justice on the top floor. On the floors below him were the assistant district attorneys, the judges, the clerks, the courts, the typing pools—all the hustle and bustle of San Francisco's complicated legal system.

The office had been designed and furnished by Abraham Livingston Gump himself. Gump's elegant store had swept away Victoriana, replacing it with everything Gumpish—mostly silver and jade. Clearing away the old clutter, Gump's left a businessman with less fuss, less dust, and an impressive bill. James's desk was a solid expanse of blond oak. On its imposing surface it had two telephones, a silver fountain pen in a jade stand, a smoky jade ashtray, one mushroom-shaped lamp with tassels, two sheets of closely typed paper—and that was it. James himself was reclining in a maroon leather swivel chair, his back to the comfortable room and his feet, shod in oxblood English leather, propped up on the sill of a large window that gave him a nice view of downtown San Francisco. Most of it was less than seventeen years old, but the rambling Montgomery Block, grand survivor of the quake, hunkered down amid the new architecture to give the city a hint of what was gone—almost everything. James wasn't thinking about the past; the future was the only kind of time that held any interest for him, the future he was going to shape. He'd have his name in dictionaries, on dedication plaques, in *Who's Who*. He imagined his own portrait in oils, ten feet tall, painted by someone who really knew his stuff—by that, James meant someone who would flatter, although he thought of it as someone with an eye for detail—hanging in the portrait gallery at the White House. Did the White House *have* a portrait gallery? If it didn't, when James Alexander Hamilton was President, it would.

He was watching the weather make up its mind. Across the black-watered bay, storm clouds were piling up over Oakland, San Francisco's shoddier industrial sister, but in *his* city the clouds were still white and fluffy and kept bumping into each other. It looked like rain, it smelled like rain, but it didn't rain. Typical. James's ash-blond hair shone silver in the shifting light.

James Alexander Hamilton, only son of a sales clerk, hadn't always been as he was now; what he'd become was what he'd made of himself. James was born clever and impatient. Other than that, he was a virtual clean slate on which he wrote at will. It was by observing his father that he made his first discovery: to wit, simple values—honesty, hard work, and deference to one's betters—get a man exactly nowhere. He did remember small early moments of pride in his father: when the man had sat at the head of the table, beaming over the family he'd fed and clothed; a Fourth of July when mother in white and father in black had strolled with their awed little son through Golden Gate Park, pointing out the curve and burst of skyrockets. He also remembered the military academies, logical extensions of his father's lectures, the birch, and the prayers. So far back the memory was like catching at a fleeing dream in daylight, the boy thought his father had some connection to the patriotic colors that exploded over their heads. As James grew, so did his contempt for the father who'd spent half his life behind a counter at Levi Strauss and the other half squeezing the heart out of the only two people in the world he had power over. James concluded that his father was part sucker—duped and used by the kind of person that James would make of himself—and part tyrant. He had early on determined that there would be more than a stout woman in white to bully, a frame house in the suburbs to rule, a little boy who saw that skyrockets were out of a father's reach, and the stoop of sudden age for James Hamilton. He also made another discovery, the most exciting and rewarding of his life. He learned that when a man said, "You can't judge a book by its cover," the man was a fool. You not only could, but everyone did. Men were judged by the cut of their clothes, the pattern of their speech, the schools they attended, their wealth, their wives, by anything and everything but the man himself. So James set about designing his own book cover with all the ardor of a truly ambitious man. And his father, true to his nature, paid for it and was proud. Harvard cost him his modest house in the Western Addition, but the cost was nothing next to the achievement of his brilliant son. James never felt he cheated his father. A man could choose a life for himself; his father had chosen his. James thought he cheated no one. If he had looks and brains and the sense to use them, it was no accident. It meant that if he had them, he deserved them. They were the results, not the causes, of what he'd achieved.

And James found to his pride that he was correct. He *was* judged by his cover. James, on the other hand, did not judge himself at all. Knowing that what he seemed was the result of what people wanted to see, his judgment was reserved for others, and the contempt for his father extended itself to all men. What else could you feel for so shabby a trick that was rewarded so well? If there was loneliness in this, James had yet to feel it.

Dragging his attention from a workman on a nearby building pasting up a new billboard—MURAD, THE GENTLEMAN'S SMOKE—James slowly turned in his chair to face Stringer Bellew, his assistant district attorney, the only one of the many under him he knew he could trust. Stringer knew some of his business, but James knew all of Stringer's. After all, it was James who had taught him how to conduct it.

Stringer Bellew, in no position to lounge, socially or otherwise, stood erect and waiting on the dark blue rug. He was on the customer's side of the big desk, chewing gum and smoking a small cigar at the same time.

"You remember the Arbuckle case, Stringer?"

Made anxious by the long wait, Stringer was too eager. He almost shouted. "Sure, boss!"

"Well, you've got the same thing here, haven't you? Except that this time the young man in question is as guilty as they come."

"So we win?"

"No, we lose."

"Lose?"

"The prosecution—meaning you, Stringer—is going to take a dive. Buddy Le Blond is scum, he's vicious and probably crazy, and in my opinion he ought to get the chair for raping poor Miss Violet Louise, let alone practically killing her, but he is also the son of the president of Western Allied Insurance and Banking, so he won't. That's your job, to make sure he doesn't. With Arbuckle, we put it to the fat man; now we put it to the girl."

Stringer Bellew was all angles, in body and in mind, and he looked like he might blow away in a high wind. There was something very Tom Sawyerish about him— maybe it was the freckles and the red hair. Recently he'd grown a thin red mustache to give his boyish face a little weight, but it hadn't worked. It made him look sly. He scratched his head under its thicket of springy crinkled hair and grinned. "I get it."

"Now, forget it. Le Blond Senior carries a lot of weight. I want it on my side. Harold McNutt is Buddy's defense attorney. Feed him whatever he needs and let him play up the color angle. Miss Louise's daddy was a Negro. If I know the public, that ought to help his side of the case. Meantime, lose a few things the police have dug up. Buddy left a trail a mile wide. The police don't need *all* that evidence, do they?"

"Right, boss." Stringer thought about stubbing his cigar out in the smoky jade ashtray but decided against it. The ashtray was too clean. Everything in James's office was clean, even the pictures on the walls. Mostly photographs, silver framed and hung in straight lines, every one had Hamilton in them: James with his Harvard class; James with his unit in France; with the mayor of Chicago; Jimmy Walker of New York, the dandy who was going to wind up mayor; Al Smith, governor of New York State; Friend Richardson, California's Quaker governor—homely as a dirt farmer next to the tall boyish DA; the King and Queen of Belgium; and with Mr. and Mrs. Wilson in 1919 when they visited San Francisco. James shaking hands with Coolidge; James accepting an award from William Jennings Bryan. Stringer made a point of avoiding the photo of James's war buddies. If James noticed him looking, it started him talking. James talking was a treat, but on the subject of what he went through during the war the treat could get sticky, like eating too many banana splits. And the DA always started the same way. "There are two types of men," he would say, "those who went, and those who didn't." Bellew knew what James thought of those who didn't—they stank. Stringer hadn't gone. He stuck with his cigar; it smoldered hot between his fingers.

Harvey "Stringer" Bellew was thirty-seven years old, and his favorite word was "peppy." For five years he'd worked with James Hamilton. Hamilton was younger and quicker and better-looking, and, as far as Stringer could tell, his bandwagon was going to roll. Bellew intended to roll with it. Ten years of wagging his tail in the ranks had got him nowhere, except for his nickname "Stringer," as in second-stringer, until the day he fell in behind James. Lately, Stringer had taken to imitating the younger man: he tried to keep his high-pitched voice down, his jerky movements controlled, the once-constant smile off his freckled face. He didn't know it, but he hadn't come close. Stringer had merely managed to look more uncomfortable than ever, and a touch more devious. Yet, though he thought James was God, or close enough, now and then James's methods got on his nerves. Stringer's idea of a hero was a *successful* hero, not a moral one, but ideas aren't always enough. Conscience kept creeping up on him. He decided he was close enough to James to express a doubt, but he chewed his gum faster when he did it.

"I feel kinda sorry for the girl."

"Why?"

James hadn't snapped at him. It was a nice "Why?" Stringer took heart. "Miss Louise is getting a raw deal, wouldn't you say?"

"Because Le Blond the younger isn't going to jail? What good is that going to do her? She's already had the worst of it. Buddy Le Blond spending a few years behind bars—and that, by the way, is all he'd get if we won—isn't going to change that."

Stringer allowed himself a frown over the district attorney's logic; his red eyebrows sunk lower. "But he'll do it again. And maybe next time he'll do it to a lady."

"Buddy won't do it again. He won't be doing anything to *anyone* again. Psychopaths aren't wandering loose on my streets, rich man's son or no rich man's son. There are other ways of dealing with young Le Blond. You get him off, and then I'll take care of him."

Stringer took a moment to digest that, and when he did his grin of relief and admiration stretched the thin red mustache as far as it would go. "That's swell! I'll get on it right away. Leave it to me, boss."

"I intend to."

James watched Stringer practically scamper out of his office, sighed happily over the gullibility of mankind, and on second thought decided there might be something to his bluster about Buddy Le Blond after all. Now that he had Leo Olemi as a very silent business partner, who knew what the limits were? On the other hand, what would Leo want in return for taking care of Le Blond?

James wasn't that public-spirited. He shrugged and put Buddy out of his mind. He pushed the two pieces of paper around on his desk, ignoring the enormous backlog of work in his in-basket—Prohibition was glutting the courts with "dry" cases. Robert Bent was having a great time padlocking hundreds of saloons, but only those who wouldn't, or couldn't, pay him enough to stay open. James swiveled back to watch the weather some more and found himself thinking about Lizzie.

What was the idiot up to now? She hadn't come to bed; he'd checked her room. Something was going to have to be done about Mrs. Hamilton. He was fond of her, it was hard not to be, but Lizzie was beginning to make him mad. Maybe he ought to start sleeping with her again. In bed, she didn't know much, but she tried. Perhaps if he had the patience to teach her? James's knowledge of the pleasures to be found between the sheets were varied, tested by France and time. Ever since he was fourteen he'd been learning the art of pleasing women. Life was simple. You talked to men, made love to women. Yes, he could move back into Lizzie's room; that ought to calm her down. As much as he liked sleeping with women, they liked sleeping with him even more. It was also a good way of controlling them. Which made him think of Esmé. Bless Leo for introducing them. She was the latest and the best in a long line of conquests. Still, he had to admit, he shouldn't have had Leo bring her along to Lizzie's anniversary party. That was a mistake. He'd make it up to Lizzie. He wasn't giving Esmé up, but it was clear that little Elizabeth needed some husbandly attention.

Without knocking, James's private secretary, a sharp-faced woman with eyes as hard and flat as a vacant lot and the same shade of baked brown, stuck her head around his door. James hated it when she did that, and Mrs. Heney knew it. Her lead-gray hair was pulled back so severely it almost gave her a face lift.

"Mr. Addy Chase would like a word, Mr. Hamilton. You *are* in?"

Mrs. Heney was a rarity. Of all the women in the typing pool, all the secretaries, the cleaning staff, and the girls in the cafeteria, Mrs. Heney wasn't the least bit in love with James Alexander Hamilton. It went further—she didn't like him at all. Of course, she was past forty, but that never stopped them. Even old Alma, the crone who sold flowers down in the lobby, had a crush on the district attorney. But Mrs. Heney thought he was too good-looking, too smooth, and even though she seldom smiled herself, she didn't trust people who never smiled at all. Mrs. Heney didn't think James was deep; she thought he had something to hide—she didn't know about his teeth.

Mrs. Heney put James off his stride. What was worse, his voice fell on deaf ears. Skipping the cover, she was one of those rare people who judged the whole book. But she was as efficient as a ball bearing, and she came with the job. James made the best of it and never stopped working on her. Like now.

"Indeed, Mrs. Heney. Please show him in."

"Check," snapped the private secretary, and pulled her head back out of his office. All of Addy Chase replaced it.

James rose from his chair, hand extended. Here was someone who would listen to him, and someone he needed to talk to. "Chase! What a surprise. I'm flattered."

At fifty-one, gravity had taken its toll on Addy. His long lanky frame was slightly stooped, and his soft deep-set brown eyes had weakened; now he was required to wear spectacles if he was to see at all. But time had been kind to his spirit. The eternal spring of political corruption had finally turned him away from public life. Once, Addy Chase believed that if evil was cut off at the head, the body would die. Now he knew better. If the head was chopped off, the body would sprout another and yet another. Rose had been wiser from the start. But Addy had a rare gift—he could learn, and unlike men who learned caution, even bitterness, as the years passed, Addy had acquired the art and solace of humor. He had become amused. He thanked Rose St. Lorraine for that.

Addy shook the young man's hand. "It's a madhouse out there. I came to visit Judge Mordden and found him swamped. You're not too busy as well?"

A good start, thought James. He needed Addy Chase. Addy could help him with Lizzie, he was the best entrée into male society on the hoof—James had no trouble with the distaff side—and now, with his relationship to Rose St. Lorraine and James's little problem with his sand lots, Addy was to be smoothed, soothed, and wooed.

"Don't ask me to be polite and lie to you, Addy. Of course I am. The Buddy Le Blond case is not as open-and-shut as the newspapers would have you believe. I've just had word that the police might have been too hasty getting their man. Damn awkward for the prosecution, trying an innocent boy, if that's what he proves to be. But you've met our police commissioner; you know what I'm up against." James was pleased with himself; that was very neat.

James couldn't fault the old man on his taste. The mustache, once a rich chestnut, was silvered now, the hair dense salt-and-pepper gray. The lines in Addy's craggy face cut deep, but the eyes behind spectacles were as mild and bright as ever, and he stood almost as straight. James admired the pink rose in his lapel, the English walking stick and watch fob, but he loved the lavender spats that matched the lavender gloves. The man was a fop. Vanity was a weakness James knew well.

Addy shook his courtly head. "I haven't much time myself, but I was in the building, and I thought I'd drop in and invite you to the club tonight—that is, if you're free. I'd be honored to have you as my guest."

James covered his mouth with his hand, pretending to cough. He had to—he was almost laughing with glee. No need to ask the old man what club. The Pacific Union Club, of course! Addy's club, the one in the old Flood mansion, the one that was right next to the Stafford house on Nob Hill, the one James passed every day and looked into the glowing windows of every night, the one he hadn't been invited to join yet—even though he'd been married to Lizzie Stafford for two years, and Charles Mortimer Stafford had been a charter member. James

was in the Bohemian Club and the Burlingame Country
Club and the so far single-membered James Hamilton for
President of the United States Club, but the Pacific
Union Club! That was the top of the heap, the one that
mattered. James had known they'd make him a member
someday, in spite of his damn father who still stood behind a counter at Levi Strauss in a shiny suit selling
denim jeans to workmen and the occasional dude; they
had to—he was James Hamilton. After all these years, he
was somebody. At Harvard he'd never made the A.D. or
the Porcellian, not even Deke. A few "waiting clubs"
took him, but only after a second or third round. James
Hamilton didn't know the right people, didn't have the
right background, and even if he had, he didn't have
enough money. Membership in the A.D. and the Porcellian was expensive. In the end, it all came down to one
simple fact: Mr. Hamilton wasn't a "young gentleman."
Maybe not, but he wasn't stupid either. He graduated
magna cum laude. Besides that, the only thing he could
really say was that he was in Harvard's Triennial Cata-
logue. James remembered what Edmund Quincy, son of
one of Harvard's presidents, had said. "If a man is in the
book, that's who he is—if he isn't, who is he?" As for the
Pacific Union, they had taken their sweet time getting
around to him. And now, here it was, with Addy Chase
as spokesman. He was as good as in.

"Of course. I'd be delighted."

"Good," said Addy, looking around James's office.
His expression told James nothing about what he thought
of it. James didn't like not being able to read the man's
face. It disturbed him. He prided himself on second-
guessing people.

"Gump's?" said Addy.

James nodded.

All Addy did was nod back and then say, "Hmmm."
It told James as much as Addy's face.

"When Charles Mortimer died," Addy said, breaking into James's unease, "he made Lizzie my ward. Last
night reminded me that I was derelict in my duty, both to
her and to you as her husband. I may no longer be responsible for her welfare, but I thought it was time I got

to know the husband of little Lizzie better—and, of course, that you got to know me." Addy turned to leave. "Eight o'clock?"

"Eight it is." James was impressed. That was about the most subtle way he'd ever been offered help with a woman. He was also gratified. Not only were people noticing that Lizzie was acting up, they assumed it was her fault.

Addy was almost out the door when he checked himself. "Oh, yes, I thought you might like to know that when my old friend Warren Harding arrives in San Francisco in a few weeks"—Addy's eyes flicked over the photographs on James's office walls—"I'm hoping to introduce you."

"The President?"

Addy laughed. "The very man."

"I'd like that very much."

"I'll arrange it. You'll bring your own photographer?"

James wasn't amused, but he pretended to be. He hoped Addy believed him. There were times a politician's lot was onerous. People with a sense of humor made him nervous.

With Addy safely gone, James hurried behind his desk, picked up a phone, and placed a long-distance call to Los Angeles.

"Let me speak to Mr. Doheny. . . . No, not senior, *junior*. . . . Ed? You alone? . . . Hamilton here. You heard about Harding? What's the fool up to? . . . *Who* killed himself? Who's Jess Smith? . . . Justice Department, eh? . . . Harding is on a voyage of understanding, is he? And just what does he expect everyone to understand? That he had nothing to do with selling the leases? Don't make me laugh. . . . But things are that shaky, huh? . . . Damn, it looks bad."

As James listened, a slight sheen bloomed on his upper lip. Other than that, no one would have known from watching him that the district attorney was in a mild panic. His heart was leaping in his chest and the palms of his hands were wet. The more he heard, the worse it got.

"Are they nosing around the California oil leases? . . . What about Elk Hills? . . . Thank God. Listen, Ed, I think you'd better come up here. We need to talk."

James hung up. And sat there. Oakland's clouds had made it to San Francisco. Oakland, Earl Warren's town, where Earl had made a name for himself nine years earlier as a crime-busting district attorney. Earl Warren, the man James had patterned himself after, not in spirit but in style. Two years since his own election, James had gone after an abortion ring with police and political connections, he'd organized a juvenile crime prevention program—anything that gave him a good press and behind-the-scenes friends. The closing of the abortion ring stepped on no toes; they were doomed anyway, and everyone who had to had already washed their hands. Like Earl Warren in Oakland, Hamilton was looked on in San Francisco as a reformer, a crusader.

Suddenly the weather knew what it was doing. It was raining. Hard. His office darkened and so did James, until he thought it all out. Harding coming to San Francisco? But the trip was a campaign to save his own neck, not to put the finger on James. The leases were in the senior Doheny's name. Only Harding and his Ohio cronies, ex-Secretary of the Interior Albert Fall and Attorney General Harry Daugherty, knew James was in with the Dohenys, and then, that only by name. They'd never met. He might think of naming a few names to divert the heat. And James, thanks to an increasingly valuable Addy Chase, was going to meet him. In person. Things got a lot clearer. If everything went well, there'd be no problem at all. In the privacy of his own office, James smiled. It wasn't pretty.

He switched on his tasseled mushroom desk lamp and asked the operator for another number. The Harding trouble was in the future. Right now he had other plots to hatch—sand castles, for instance.

"Leo? It's James."

Before he could say another word, he had to listen to Olemi tell him about a deal in the East Bay. A boarded-up distillery was for sale.

James cut in. "You're telling me you want to get it

going again? How are you going to put that one over?
. . . Oh, Arnold's in on it. Well, what's a federal Prohibition administrator for? How much do you need from me?"

James had to hand it to Leo. Give the loaf-faced man a problem, and less than twenty-four hours later he was coming up with solutions. The idea that Leo outlined was sweet. They needed a still? They bought a government-closed distillery with Arnold's blessing, and probably with some of Arnold's money. They took the immense profits, cut back on the danger of running stuff past the Coast Guard, cut out the middle man up north in Canada, put everything closer to Frisco than the old mining town, Jackson, up in Amador County, could compete with, and put the whole thing in Blinn's name. If anything went wrong, Blinn took the fall. But meantime Murray Blinn would cruise along with the big boys, puff himself up, and take orders. All they had to do now was find out exactly which Chinese to set him on, and that problem was coming along nicely. It shouldn't take long. James had his meeting with Addy in the evening. Not only would he finally get into the Pacific Union Club, he'd find out who was advising Rose St. Lorraine.

James had one other thought, one he didn't intend to share with Leo Olemi. Blinn would take a fall, all right, and when he did James would prosecute. For that, he was happy to help set up Blinn as big as Capone, bigger, *if* he could do it to someone like Murray, with a brain the size of a radish. The bigger Blinn was, the bigger the fall. James would look great to the people of San Francisco, taking him down.

James fished around in his small vest pocket and took out an ornate silver key. The key fitted into a lock that opened a drawer in his desk that James saw only rarely—times when he wanted to feel good. He wanted to feel good now. He didn't need the cocaine, he *liked* it.

James placed one last call. To the Pinkerton detective agency.

"That's correct. Just a quiet tail. Let me know what

she does and who she does it with. Her name is Elizabeth Sian Hamilton. . . . Yes, *the* Lizzie Stafford Hamilton."

It had been a good day at the office. James's blue eyes had a glitter in them—like sun on glass.

He sat back and watched it rain.

# Chapter 5

Kit Dowie led Lizzie, who still thought she was Colleen Moore, through the door of O'Flooty's, the dreariest dive she'd ever seen. It had to be; it was her first. The peep-hole attendant hadn't bothered to ask Kit's name, he just grinned and waved them in.

Kit Dowie was well known in O'Flooty's and O'Flooty's was well known to certain San Franciscans. It was jammed between Pier 17 and Pier 19 on the Embarcadero, once the East Street piers, the city's turbulent waterfront. Though, just then, it was taking a breather from strikes and soapboxes and the marching boots of angry bomb-throwing labor. And padlocks. O'Flooty wouldn't pay Bent. O'Flooty's was a "blind pig," from the outside nothing more than a blank black wall with a door in it. In the door was a smaller door at eye level. There was no name anywhere. The place didn't need one; it got by on its reputation. It was *the* waterfront speak among waterfront speaks for a very good reason: Fearless O'Flooty owned it.

An ex-prizefighter, ex-longshoreman, ex-hobo, and

practicing poet, O'Flooty had named himself Fearless when he was fifteen years old. He'd decided then that if you were named after something, you became that thing. In his case, he was right. He was a Bolsheviǩ, "Bolo" for short, and he was fiercely self-educated. He had giddy demons dancing mad Irish jigs in his mad Irish brain, and being Irish, Fearless O'Flooty's genius lay on his tongue like an unswallowable lozenge. He forced people to listen to the tumult of his obsession but it was an avid audience, an unpaid claque. The man was downright inspiring. Kit wrote a short story about him. "I soaked in his bloody rain," it went, "and bloomed great red flowers." Kit told Lizzie all this as he drove Lizzie's cabriolet from Eddy to the wide Embarcadero. As Kit parked the car, the wind was tearing at the fog like a child playing with spiderwebs. Lizzie actually listened to Kit. Something about her day had changed her. She thought it was the movie.

Inside, O'Flooty's was a long tunnel extending back into purple darkness. There was room for maybe two abreast to walk its length. The bar ran along the left wall, its surface pitted with cigarette burns and glass rings. The walls, painted in a peeling gunmetal gray, were hung with photos of prizefighters, but the ceiling was invisible, curtained in smoke. The place stank of sweat, grain alcohol, tobacco, has-been fighters, bookies, sports promoters, longshoremen, union agitators, newspapermen, and poets.

Kit shouted his way up to the bar, dragging Lizzie with him like one of the blind mice. Everyone knew Kit. He was back-slapped and glad-handed as he elbowed his way between a big blank-eyed man wearing a blue plaid logging jacket, half asleep over an empty beer mug, and a burly character with tattoos, whose great behind swamped his bar stool. The burly man was running to fat, but the muscles were still there. The tattoos were everywhere. Folds in his neck lodged a month's dirt. While Kit ordered, the man's neck watched him with hostile attention.

At the far end of the long bar, next to a scuffed door leading to the toilet, sat two old men, their piping voices cutting through smoke and din. They were swapping tall tales with a vocabulary of less than two hundred words, all of them colorful.

"So I says to him, I says, Who you calling a no-good wop, you greasy spic? In my day, I'da planted him one in the kisser for that kind of crap. In my day, I'da planted 'em all one in the kisser."

The bartender, with a head full of curling yellow hair and tired eyes, wiped a soiled glass with a soiled rag. "Long time no see, Dowie. Nice tie. What'll it be?"

"Thanks," said Kit, loosening the knot in his polka-dot tie. "Beer. Where's O'Flooty?"

The bartender shrugged. "Out. Back soon. He'll be glad to see you. Got some news about Chinese bootleggers. What you been doing?"

"Montana. With Dempsey. Sport once again bites the dust."

"We heard. What'll the lady have?"

Kit turned to Lizzie. "Well, Elizabeth? It's your turn."

Lizzie, who'd kept close to Kit, was floored. She'd never in her money-sheltered life seen people like the people in O'Flooty's—and they were friends of Kit! The more she knew about Dowie, the less she knew about him. She was also unhappily aware that here she was out of place and unwelcome. Lizzie was tongue-tied. The bartender peered at her with a look that she could only call suspicious.

"Any time, lady," he said, spitting on his rag.

"I—ah, I—" she stammered.

Kit was already drinking his beer. His look she could only call mischievous. But she was used to that.

The bartender waited. Kit waited. The whole bar waited. Even the two old men shut up. Lizzie was the only female in the joint.

"Um, give me, could I have . . . ?"

What? What? Every cocktail Lizzie had ever had fled from her mind. It was a skill at which she was lately becoming adept, at least in the right place—home on the Hill. If she kept it up Kit had promised her that soon she'd be able to tell the difference between brands of bootlegger whiskey, dead drunk and blindfolded.

"I'd like a brandy Alexander."

Kit choked on his beer.

"What?" said the bartender.

Lizzie got the gist of his glare. "Well, perhaps a martini, then?"

"Lady, we got beer and we got straight shots. You want a cocktail, you put 'em together and you get a boilermaker. You want a boilermaker?"

"OK," she whispered. "Give me one of those."

"Coming right up."

Everyone in O'Flooty's clapped approval except the tattooed man with the attentive neck. He swiveled his huge ass around on the bar stool.

"Hey, sister," he snarled at Lizzie. "Whaddaya think you're doin' here?" He pushed his fat red face into hers. The stink of his breath almost knocked her out. "This speak is for men only. You come for a good time? I'll give you a good time." He grabbed her thin wrist and pulled. Lizzie stumbled forward, landing in his lap.

Kit tapped the tattooed man on his hulking shoulder. "Excuse me," he said quietly. "The lady is with me."

"You better believe it, bub," added the bartender.

"We'll share her then." The tattooed man grunted, swung his bulk around, and made an awkward but accurate dive for Kit. He picked Dowie up bodily, took five easy steps, and threw him out the barroom door. Kit landed on his back out there, losing a lungful of air.

Everyone froze; the whole room had gone silent. The tattooed man stood beady-eyed, watching the door for signs of Kit. Eyes now awake and deadly, the bartender, with a full bottle of Jack Daniels on the upswing, was coming around the back of the bar, aiming for a good whack on the tattooed man's head. And the guy guarding the peephole was on his way with a pair of brass knuckles.

"Whoopie!" yelled Kit, charging back in through the door. "Try that again, fat man, and you deal with dirty Jake McPug, holder of a world title in pigsticking!"

Red eyes rolling, the tattooed man went for him, and

the bartender's bottle of bourbon missed his thick head by a hair.

Lizzie woke up. This was getting out of hand. Without thinking twice, she jumped on the tattooed man's back, claws dug into his dandruff. The bar floor whirled under her as the fat man spun on furious feet, trying to toss her off. One of the old men beaned him with a bowl of stale peanuts. Lizzie and the tattooed man hit the floor, her teeth snapping together with a sickening crunch. Lizzie had a clear view of smashed cigar butts, spilled beer, sawdust, peanuts, and boots—when the bar came to life. It was no place for a lady. Lizzie wondered if Aimee Crocker had ever been there.

Kit jerked her to her feet.

"You had enough of 'real' places?" He laughed. "Let's get out of here!"

Lizzie and Kit ended up sitting on a damp seaweed-sour pier, Kit with multiple bruises and a beautiful egg forming on his head from his introduction to cement. Lizzie, dandruff under her precious nails, had the bottle of Jack Daniels, the spoils of war for her first barroom brawl. The tattooed man wound up in the hospital—but that was some time after Lizzie and Kit had left O'Flooty's.

Kit caught sight of Lizzie's prize. "Give me a slug of that. That's the real stuff."

"After me, Dowie. I didn't even get my boiler-maker."

"Time to go home," muttered Kit, after he'd watched Lizzie swig straight from the bottle.

"Home? Are you kidding? That was swell! That was great. You were wonderful. I was wonderful. It was the best time I've had for years. You know such interesting people."

"I'm glad you liked it. If O'Flooty had been there, it would've been better."

The irony in Kit's voice went right over Lizzie's dark head.

"Really? Take me back when he's there."

"Oh, fine."

Lizzie's face was smudged with dirt, her bangled

dress torn, and her new marcel matted with beery sawdust. The saltsea fog played in her hair as she sat on the slick wet wood with her feet dangling over the edge of the pier, wiggling her toes. Her shoes were back at O'Flooty's. Fifteen feet below, black bay water oiled against sodden struts. Lizzie's green eyes were lit up like a cat's caught in headlights. Kit was awed. My God, sometimes Lizzie was more than beautiful, she was dangerous. Kit gave up.

"Where to now, kid?" he said, and taking the bourbon from her, he knocked back a healthy swallow.

The old Barbary Coast never really recovered from the earthquake. Like Chinatown, the Coast rose from hot ashes fast enough to dazzle and dismay. Within three months it was cooking. But in spite of the new bagnios and casinos, the saloons and dime-a-dance halls, something was wrong. Times had moved on. Raw sex, nose-thumbing lawlessness, and the hootchy-kootchy suffered a lingering death. It took eleven years, but, like an old whore, it died—worn out and tawdry. San Francisco wasn't a rootin' tootin' overgrown mining camp anymore. The shimmering City by the Sea had grown up just as Addy Chase had hoped she would. She became cosmopolitan. Like her older, more sophisticated, sisters, her high stakes and sex for sale didn't go away—they hid. And became mysterious. What a man truly loves never dies, it just changes its tune. By 1923 that tune was jazz.

With the coming of the roaring twenties San Francisco kissed the wild frontier goodbye and said an eager acquisitive hello to the new America. Now came the fast-talking salesman, the working girl, the trumpeting media, instant fame without merit, Freudian psychology, Bible thumpers, votes for women, and—things. Telephones and toasters, radios and movies, kiss-proof lipsticks and washing machines, and best, or worst, of all, cars for the masses. H. L. Mencken called the people the *booboisie,* and the name stuck. Prohibition came too. After that, where could you get a drink in Frisco? In open saloons, restaurants, nightclubs, dancing academies, drugstores, delicatessens, cigar stores, soda fountains, candy stores, the back rooms of barbershops and shoeshine parlors, from hotel bellhops and headwaiters, from night clerks and day clerks, in motorcycle delivery agencies, in paint stores, malt shops, fruit stands, vegetable markets, grocery stores, athletic clubs, grillrooms, chophouses, importing firms, tearooms, boardinghouses, Republican and Democratic clubs, laundries—and Chinatown, where it was made under cover of a mah-jongg factory. Where couldn't you get a drink in Frisco?

Rose St. Lorraine, shrewd as ever, sang her old song in a lower key. True to her word, she rebuilt, and just where she said she would—on Addy's blasted lot on Mason Street between Bush and Sutter, the uptown Tenderloin. Because he refused a share of the business, she paid Addy top dollar for his land from the sale of what was left of Silver Street—its prime location. Just as the Street had been the city's hottest whorehouse, the Blue Canary became the sleekest, jazziest nightclub.

As usual, Rose knew just what she was doing. The Blue Canary had class. Rose's girls, her supply of fresh faces inexhaustible, ducked down out of sight, but her gaming wheels spun and the prohibition booze flowed; her white wing-collared orchestra became a black band, first ragtime and then jazz. Low-down, dirty, intoxicating jazz. The big-time bands came all the way from New Orleans, later from St. Louis and Chicago. The Blue Canary attracted the best. When the Cotton Club in Harlem was just getting off its knees, the Blue Canary was a high-stepping, heart-stopping legend of San Francisco good times. Rose spent seventeen years reminding Addy that he'd made a bad choice—the profits were staggering.

As Kit Dowie and Lizzie Hamilton walked in under the dark-blue scalloped awning, the black-and-silver-liveried doorman snapped to attention.

"Good evening, Mr. Dowie. Nice egg. What's the other guy look like?"

"Evening, Pete. Bumped into a tattooed wall."

"Some wall."

"You said it."

Lizzie had changed her clothes, rolled up her chiffon

stockings; she had a silver band, Indian-style, around her forehead, but her hair was still marceled.

A dark man in a dark suit came in seconds behind them, slipped Pete, the doorman, a couple of bucks on top of the fifteen-dollar cover charge, asked for a receipt, and then blended into the scenery.

Inside the Blue Canary, everything was first-rate. On a curved foot-lit stage, twenty leggy chorus girls in white ostrich feathers and dimpled knees were tap-dancing their syncopated toes off. Clusters of tiny candle-lit tables edged the sunken dance floor, and slick waiters flitted in and out between them. One couple did a great shimmy, and twenty others stood around and admired their style. Cigarette girls sold smokes for a dollar a pack; flower girls pushed boutonnieres of roses for five bucks on guys eager to impress a date. With the tip making the transaction double, their ladies felt loved. All the women had go-to-hell eyes, and the men looked willing.

By the time Lizzie and Kit got to the s-snaking shine of an ebony bar with chrome footrests, a girl with a nasal voice was singing:

> *"My sister sells snow to the snowbirds,*
> *My father makes bootlegger gin,*
> *My mother, she rents by the hour,*
> *My God, how the money rolls in!"*

At the bar of the Blue Canary, Lizzie got her brandy Alexander. It was served with flair by a dwarf with a squint and three fingers missing on his left hand. He wasn't old, he was ancient. And he wasn't ugly, he was hideous.

Lizzie dug Kit in the ribs. "Get him," she whispered. "The old guy behind the bar."

"Hiya, Appetite," said Kit, ignoring her. "How's things?"

Appetite Ike hadn't changed at all. He still looked like he'd just put down his pickax, even though Rose had forced him into a short black jacket and a red bow tie. She also forbade him to chew tobacco behind the bar. At seventy-seven, Ike was no longer a chauffeur, but his bartending had only improved.

"See for yourself," snapped Appetite.

Kit already had. The place was jumping in a refined sort of way. O'Flooty's regulars wouldn't have felt at home. Rose's clientele were socialites and bankers, theater people from New York touring hit shows, silent stars up from Hollywood, California intellectuals, and, just for the night, Aimee Semple McPherson, taking a break from preaching the word of God to Los Angeles for a fat profit. But Rose had hired the King Oliver Creole Jazz Band, with a kid named Louis Armstrong on cornet, the best you could get. With that kind of music, who cared about the customers? Joe Oliver had gotten rid of the chorus girls and the singer with the nasal problem; he took off into a slow underwater blues. The couple doing the shimmy sat down.

"Makes you sick, don't it?" said Ike. "We even got a room for Ping-Pong an' mah-jongg, an' the walls turn theirselves around for the times we get raided." He went limping off to serve someone else. The old man missed the brash and boisterous Silver Street.

Kit, leaning against the bar, grinned. "That," he said to Lizzie, "is the wisest man I know."

"And the ugliest," said Lizzie.

The Blue Canary didn't make Lizzie sick. It made her heart race. It was right out of a movie, and a better movie than *Flaming Youth*. It was decadent and stylish and everything she was looking for. The floor was silver, the walls black, the tablecloths pure white. Huge baskets of ferns stood out a wet startling green against the black. Lizzie got Kit's point about her idea of a flapper—it wasn't a class act. If she was going to become a regular at the Blue Canary, she'd have to go shopping again.

Gradually the lights dimmed, leaving only warm candle glow; the talk went down to a muted hum, then stopped altogether. A smoky blue spot cut through the dark expectant hush, picking out a round-bellied black man on the stage. He held a cornet in his hand. With a big white smile, the black man leaned forward, wiped his mouth with a handkerchief, and rasped in a broken voice,

"Ladies and gentlemen, for your pleasure the Blue Canary presents her very own, the best there is—she ain't soft and she ain't sweet—Dido!"

Lizzie's green eyes darted to the stage, her drink halfway to her lips. Dido?

Then everything receded—the stage, the band, the Blue Canary itself. When she stepped into the blue spot, there was just Dido, her silver beads sparking back the light, her glossy black head held high, daring the white folks to breathe. The hard black eyes lit on Dowie and stayed there.

A clarinet slid down the register, starting high, ending low, and then Dido sang. Dido sang to Kit and Kit watched her sing and Lizzie watched them both, a fury growing in her soul.

The song was "China Blues." Dido growled it and soared with it and made the hair on the back of Lizzie's neck stand on end with it. Lizzie was in torment. She'd never heard anything like the blues or felt anything like the blues. They reached down under her skin and from there spread like dope into places Lizzie didn't know she had, deep, dark, disturbing places she wasn't sure she wanted to know she had. It made her want to do things, see things, feel things she had no name for. It hurt.

Then it was over. The lights came up. The applause rose to a roar, and Dido was gone. Somehow, that hurt too.

Lizzie turned her face away from the stage and back to the bar. She caught Ike's attention. The time for brandy Alexanders was past. Lizzie needed a drink.

"I'd like a boilermaker—forget the beer."

Kit turned with her. "What d'you think of that?"

"The singer or the song?"

"I know what you think of Dido. It's written all over your face."

"Kit, for God's sake, she's colored."

"You don't miss a thing."

"But she can't be thinking of marriage. That woman devours you."

Kit laughed, a short sharp bark. "You're a pip. What the hell are you talking about? I grew up with

Dido. Also, she's taller than me. Besides, Rose, who owns this joint—she's the oldest friend I have."

"Who isn't your friend?"

"Sometimes, lady, you're not."

"You mean because we don't sleep together. You sleep with Dido, don't you?" Lizzie didn't know why she was talking to Kit as she was. The harsh words had a will of their own. Behind them, she was small and frightened.

Kit looked at Lizzie hard. "If that's what you think my idea of a friend is, God help Fearless O'Flooty. I *mean,* dammit, what about the song?"

"It made me nervous."

"I wrote it."

"You ought to be arrested." Lizzie bolted back her shot of whiskey and tapped on the bar for another.

Kit reached up and held Lizzie's strong chin, twisting until she faced him. "Is that the only answer you've got?"

"Until I find a better one. Let go."

At that moment, Lizzie found a better one. An answer so devastating, so awesome in its implications, that even the whiskey couldn't warm the chill that gripped her spine.

At the far end of the bar was a long, lean, elegant solution. Assured and composed, he stood there, one slim hand in his jacket pocket, a gardenia in his smart black lapel. His brown eyes were uninvolved, as if he were looking at them all running a race he'd already won. Why bother to place a bet?

Lizzie's quick mind did a back flip. The worst thing, the *best* thing, was the color of his skin, the shadow in his eyes. If Kit could have an African, what couldn't Lizzie do with a Chinese? A man from China! Someone so socially unacceptable, James couldn't compete.

Kit followed her gaze and then her thoughts. His slavic face fused into a real anger. "That's not an answer, Lizzie." There wasn't a hint of wisecrack in his tone. Kit became what he seldom was—serious. "Leave it alone."

Lizzie stared him down. Without her knowing why, Kit had suddenly become the enemy. She had so much to learn about herself. "Leave what alone?" Lizzie was determined to do it the hard way.

"Kit Dowie?"

They both jumped, turning at the same time.

"Hammett!" Kit's surprise erased his sudden anger. The man at the end of the bar was forgotten. "Where've you been? I haven't seen you in months. Lizzie, meet Dashiell Hammett, a Pinkerton agent. We worked the Arbuckle case together. Dash was on Fatty's side. He fed me what he could get of the truth, and I tried to get it published. We both failed. Dash, this is Lizzie, wife of our esteemed DA. An assistant when Fatty went down. Christ, you look terrible."

Lizzie found herself staring at a thin man who was swaying on his feet. He looked shy and sweet and lonely and sick. He also looked drunk. The high bony brow, exaggerated by thick swept-back hair, was dead white, but hard spots of angry red burned in his gaunt cheeks. The sad smile he gave her was sloppy, but the eyes were steady. Hammett held out a shaky hand, the one that wasn't clutching a highball. "Beautiful girl, Kit. You're a lucky man."

Lizzie blushed. So did Kit. They both answered Hammett. "No! We're not—"

"Together, eh? But not together. Ought to be." Then Hammett neatly turned the subject, leaving them both protesting to thin air. "I quit the Pinkertons a year ago, Kit. Wasn't good for my health, outside in the cold, peering in. Outside in this town means fog." Hammett coughed, a raking bone-shaking rasp that even hurt Lizzie. "See what I mean? You been fighting again, Kit? The lump. I'm impressed."

Kit rubbed his head. "It's nothing. If you're not snooping on people, what *are* you doing?"

"I'm writing now. That's all I can do. Write and cough and drink and smoke and cough. Short stories. About a little fat guy I call the Continental Op—an idea I had from working for the agency. Maybe you'd like to read a few? *Black Mask:* you've heard of it, the detective magazine? Hell, Kit, they're going to publish!"

"Hear of it! Christ, I'm a fan. 'Shagbark Jones' and

'Pigs Is Pigs'! Read one of *yours?*" Kit's eagerness was close to boyish. "I'll read them all! Remember me? I was the one who told you you had talent. When can I see them? I'm ready any time."

Kit Dowie and Dashiell Hammett forgot Lizzie. The thin man stopped swaying and Kit stopped showing Lizzie "real" life. They were both writers, and writers talking to writers fascinate themselves.

Lizzie listened long enough to get bored. That took her less than a minute. She didn't write; she didn't even read. What she did was order another boilermaker from the old fellow with the leering squint. And drink it.

"I send out my stories like notes in a bottle," Hammett was saying. "I gotta get back east, Kit. That's where the world is—New York City." He put his long arm in its baggy brown jacket around Kit's shoulders and leaned in close. "You're the only other writer I know in this burg. The only other artist."

Kit feigned offense. "I'm not an artist. Shit, I'm a newspaperman."

"You're a goddam artist, Dowie, so shut up. What are you still doing here? Go east, young man, go east. This joint we're in now is the only place in Frisco ever makes me think there's wit west of the Wabash. What the hell have we got here? Edwin Markham? 'The Man with the Hoe'? One poem—did I say poem?—one dirge of sublime porridge, and Markham makes enough dough to keep him in curling irons for life! Or Joaquin Miller? The most barefaced poseur since Nero. How about George Sterling? Our George who thinks he's Dante, whose only claim to fame was getting pie-eyed with Jack London, and who now squats, accepting homage in a baby-blue room, dying of the fear of dying."

The ignoring of Lizzie gave her time to herself. One short second of that and she remembered what was on her mind before the thin man showed up. The answer was still at the far end of the Blue Canary's long classy curved bar. He was still alone, he was oddly attractive, and he was still Chinese.

Lizzie Hamilton was terrified. Making up your mind to vamp a man is one thing, doing it is another. And that wasn't taking into account the possibility that he didn't speak English. Lizzie wasn't afraid she'd fail; she was afraid of what she might get herself into when she succeeded. Twenty-three years of being rich and the cutest thing in San Francisco society made her bold; her natural inclination was for action before thought, but just what, exactly, did a girl say to an Oriental? They couldn't read the same magazines or go to the same movies. All she knew about them she'd learned from the pulps that Keiko read—most thrillingly, the diabolical Wu Fang, arch oriental villain. Of course there was that sweet Chinese boy in D. W. Griffith's *Broken Blossoms* who loved Lillian Gish, but he was played by Richard Barthelmess, a white actor. Maybe they weren't even the same species? There was a chilling thought. What did Chinese men do? Wash clothes, smoke opium, eat rice, carry sharp little hatchets, and sneak around in dark alleys a lot. Who really knew except a Chinese woman? What kind of conversation could you make of that?

The hell with it. Lizzie was good-looking, she was young, she was rich, and she was white. An African or a Chinese or the Dalai Lama would fall over himself to be seen with a white woman; as for being seen with Lizzie Stafford, well, what could possibly be the problem? She was a shoo-in. She only hoped she could stand being seen with *him* until James got wind of the situation. For one split second Lizzie felt a little cold-blooded. Thinking of Esmé stiffened her nerve.

She checked her makeup in the beveled mirror behind the bar, straightened her stockings, took a deep breath, and walked toward him. Slunk, really. She tried the walk she saw Nazimova use in her *Camille,* a kind of aristocratic glide. It got her to his end of the bar fast enough to keep her from changing her mind.

She was two feet away and he still wasn't looking at her. Not good. But having come this far, she'd be damned if she was going back. Lizzie took her cigarette case out of her beaded handbag, opened it, selected one, and very, very slowly put the gold tip into her mouth. Then she looked for her lighter and pretended not to find it. Not finding the lighter gave her the opportunity to look vexed. The little pout suited her dimples. Then, as if she'd never noticed him before, Lizzie looked up and her green eyes locked into the sable, slightly slanted, eyes of the Chinese.

"Would you mind?" she said. Her tone was throaty and low; seduction sang in it. The invitation was enough to bring Valentino to his knees.

The Chinese looked at Lizzie for what seemed forever. Not one expression crossed his pale-tea-colored face. Without a word, he reached into his pocket, took out a black-and-silver enamel lighter, and held it under her waiting cigarette.

The tips of Lizzie's fingers tingled. He was supposed to be responding to *her*. Asking her name. Would she like a drink? Would she like a drink! You bet! Or, Wasn't it a nice night? Anything would do. But nothing? The silence between them made her knees spin. Or was she the one responding? He was tall for a Chinese, he was tall for anybody, and he was graceful. His face was strong, delicate and fine-boned. Lizzie caught a hint of sweet husky cedar as the words of Dido's song spun oriental silk in her head. There was something vital about him, strong and silent and controlled. Had she caught the secret curve of a smile? Was he laughing at her?

The Chinese snapped the lighter and Lizzie bent to the flame. She lit her cigarette for as long as she could, her brain tumbling her emotions together like lottery tickets. Find the right one, Lizzie, choose the winner. When she looked up from under her blue-black bangs, her emerald eyes were sultry, her dimple was dancing, and her heart was in her mouth.

He was looking right over her head.

Lizzie had run out of cards. She'd played them all. Short of stomping on his foot, she'd done everything she knew to get his attention. Lizzie was embarrassed; no, she wasn't embarrassed, she was humiliated.

"Thank you," she said, her voice tight as a lock.

He said nothing. Just bowed and walked away.

It had never occurred to Lizzie that the Chinese wouldn't want her, wouldn't jump at the chance to seduce her. What the hell had happened?

Gathering up what was left of her dignity, Lizzie walked away as well—very slowly. She could see Kit and Hammett still talking at the end of the bar where she'd left them. If nothing else, Kit hadn't seen her little pratfall. That, she couldn't take. She walked right past a dark man in a dark suit who *had* seen it, though—a man paid to report it. She also walked past Dido. *Her,* she could surely do without.

The tall gleaming-black singer smiled as Lizzie passed. The smile was fresh in from the Arctic.

"Didn't work, did it? You come see Dido sometime, white stuff. When you out slummin' again. Dido'll give you a few moves to try on Mr. Li Kwan Won. You don't know the right bait to catch a Chink."

Lizzie wasn't humiliated any more; now she was furious.

"Back off, blackie!"

Lizzie couldn't believe she'd said that. Mary Maud Stafford would have thwacked the back of her bare legs with a hickory switch. Dido couldn't believe it either. They started out with contempt for each other. Now they had hate. Lizzie was surprised. It tasted fine.

# Chapter 6

After his meeting with James Hamilton at the Pacific Union Club, Addy Chase walked from the top of Nob Hill to the Blue Canary. It took no effort at all; simple gravity propelled him down the three steep city blocks. Just before fog covered everything for the night, he had a dizzy view of San Francisco's electric hills, the water of her black bay restless with great swellings like the slick spines of a school of whales, and a black western sky smeared with Van Gogh stars. Few pedestrians bothered to climb up Mason Street through nightchill and low fog; fewer cars dared. Addy pulled the Edwardian collar of his camel-hair coat up and his beaver hat down. It was ten thirty. Fog muffled his brisk footsteps and shortened his spectacled sight, but the cold woke his mind.

He wasn't a happy man. The motive for inviting young James Hamilton to the Pacific Union had been just what it seemed, an older man's concern and regard for the troubled granddaughter of his deceased, irascible, and treasured friend. Eternally taken up with Rose, Addy had neglected Lizzie for the two years since her marriage to

Hamilton. His excuse was exactly that: her married state; with a new husband, Lizzie wouldn't need an old guardian. Seeing her the night before told Addy Chase just how wrong he was.

Lizzie was like his own. From a fond avuncular distance he'd watched her grow. The bright mischievous hellion had acquired a woman's face and a woman's body, but she still had the mind of a spoiled child. He could easily forgive her extravagances, her selfishness, her headstrong headlong rush at life; after all, he had forgiven them for years—and Charles Mortimer Stafford himself had nurtured them. Addy did not demand, expect, or desire placidity in women. If he had, where would he and Rose be? But last night, at what Addy still persisted in thinking of as the Stafford mansion, Lizzie hadn't been childlike; she'd been childish. Elizabeth Sian had disappointed Addy Chase. Two years of marriage hadn't settled her down or made her wiser; they seemed to have set her on a mad flight to destruction.

Addy wanted to talk to James so he could discover why. (If he'd known why James had wanted to talk to him it would have chilled his soft heart.) But Addy came away from their meeting understanding nothing, except that James claimed he didn't really know Lizzie either.

Unknown to Addy, James had left the Pacific Union understanding everything, or at least what he desired to understand. Now, as Addy walked down Mason, James was nipping back into the looming Stafford mansion, pushing through white fog that rolled in from the Pacific and closed his world down to just the top of this small privileged hill. Like an explorer, James had planted his flag on the summit of San Francisco. Now he had new heights to climb. Phoning Olemi, he said, "Leo! I've got the information we've been after. I picked old man Chase's mind like a dog picks bones. I think it's time we turned Blinn loose on some Chinks."

But James's youth and brutal vitality made Addy understand something about himself; he'd seen his comfortable old club as it really was. The Pacific Union had become a hothouse of juiceless old plants, cosseted in unhealthy isolation, rooted deep in depleted soil. Gone were the days when its walls witnessed brash excited men, great wealth newly theirs, wide awake and chewing on the ends of their cigars, spittoons brimming at their feet, giddy and bold with grandiose ideas on how to spend the easy-come fortunes, heady with firebrand politics and fierce frontier independence.

Addy sorely missed Charles Mortimer. If Stafford had been at the club tonight he would have laid about him with a stout stick. Until the day he died, Charles remained marvelously bullheaded, contemptuous of the airs his equally low-bred peers increasingly gave themselves, and as eccentric as an English lord.

Addy Chase's family had style and breeding. Unlike San Francisco's new rough-and-ready would-be socialites, his roots extended back to the American Revolution. But if you dug down among those roots far enough, the family tree would be discovered to have sprung from a very small acorn, one Matthew Clinton Chase, toiling as a lowly clerk somewhere under John Hancock, Esquire, President of the Continental Congress. Like an industrious mole, the first notable Chase had busily undermined the finances of the Revolution, supplying shoddy cloth for Washington's troops to wear as they did what fighting they could—General Washington being what he was, incompetent. Matthew laid aside enough colonial capital to feather a nest for the future Chase family to happily incubate in. A hundred years later, more or less, it hatched out Archibald Chase, a man of ruthless determination. Single-handedly he'd cornered the California market in sugar and ships. When his son, Addy, entered the business at the age of twenty-one, Archibald gave the boy two years to prove himself. Fifteen months later, Archibald gave up and let Addy leave the business and do as he pleased; anything was better than his son's bold leaps into financial ruin. So Addy did what came naturally—he set himself the task of giving San Francisco a sense of elegance and style—until he met Rose St. Lorraine in 1902, fresh off the boat from the Klondike. Since then, Addy's sole effort had been Rose.

When he told Rose about his early departure from the family business, she'd listened carefully, rolled a cigarette, and then said, "Getting out in time takes talent—you're a goddam genius, sugar." That's when Addy Chase fell in love with Rose St. Lorraine.

Only fifty-one, Addy felt the terrible danger of becoming like the Pacific Union, asleep on his feet. For over two hours, he'd found himself under the spell of fine old brandy and a good cigar, the wonderful voice of James Hamilton lulling him into accepting every picture James had spun in the heated air. Now, out in the clarifying cold, Addy discovered that though he was disturbed by nothing James had said, he was damned disturbed by something that had happened just as they were both leaving. Hamilton had received a message from the Pinkerton agency about Lizzie. Over two hours of a deepening wish to believe, and then a sharp slap of doubt. Fancy a man's knowing and trusting his wife so little he was reduced to having her followed by a private detective! Lizzie appeared to be distressed and she *seemed* aimlessly destructive, but something was wrong, and it wasn't just Lizzie. At that moment, Addy recognized what, or rather who, James Hamilton's voice reminded him of: Newton Booth, of course. Booth had been California's greatest orator. His term as governor was before Addy's time, but as a young boy he'd heard the man speak. Ironic, thought Addy, that Newton Booth died of cancer of the tongue.

Private mansions had barely given way to luxury apartment buildings when Addy reached the discreet façade of the Blue Canary. The only difference between the illicit nightclub and the massive dwellings on either side was a short length of rounded awning, a dark blue carpet, and Pete, the sharp-eyed doorman, in his black-and-silver livery. Addy took ten strides from the soft quiet cold fog into the hard loud hot Canary, and Rose St. Lorraine reclaimed her own. King Oliver's band was steaming. Jazz hit Addy full in the face. Ah, Rose, *his* Rose. He was home.

It wasn't hard to spot Lizzie. She was the one making a fool of herself at the bar.

Kit, with the common sense of the seasoned newspaperman in a crisis, was keeping a low but observant profile. He stood some distance away from the restless, excited, chattering Lizzie, sleek head to grizzled head with Appetite Ike. Incensed, still in his camel overcoat, Addy made a beeline for them.

"How did she get like this, Dowie?" he demanded. "I hold you responsible."

"Me? Hey, wait a minute, Addy. I've been trying to stop her all night. Blame Ike; he makes a mean gin fizz." Kit turned to Ike for support. "What did I do?"

Ike grunted. It didn't answer the question.

Addy answered for him. "You, I gather, brought her here. Therefore, *you* had better do something."

"In that case, *we* better do something. Ike too. I'm not doing it alone. Have you seen her? The state she's in, she could do us both some damage. I've taken enough lumps for the night."

Addy thought about that for a minute. "You're right. This calls for a little finesse. I'll get Rose."

Rose St. Lorraine stood at the side of her canopied bed, a bed fashioned in the shape of Cleopatra's barge and just that bit smaller, looking down at the peaceful body of Lizzie Stafford lying sodden in its stern. So this was the girl Kit pretended he wasn't crazy about. There, thought Rose with considerable amusement, am I—or, more like, was I. Young, strong-willed, undisciplined, and making a perfect hash of life. Rose was in her private rooms above the Blue Canary. The apartment was more astounding than the nightclub. Everything was white: the rugs, the furs, the canopied barge of a bed. Her crystal chandeliers were bigger and a hell of a lot more ornate than the ones at the Stafford mansion. Two white Persian cats were lying around yawning, a big white dog with big white teeth was grinning at her, and another dog, some kind of strange miniature that fitted into the sleeve of her powder-blue ostrich-feathered wrap, was complaining about something in high-pitched yips. Little bits of blue feather floated around Rose's golden head.

"Dowie!" said Rose, as she sat down on a chaise longue. There was menace under the amusement.

"What?" Kit was lying on one of Rose's rugs, a flattened polar bear; his dark head, resting on the bear's snarling snout, came up fast.

"What happened to this child?"

"Drink happened."

"Whose drink?"

"O'Flooty's and yours."

Lizzie woke up just in time to hear a woman's voice say, "Drink doesn't look good on woman or man, not when the bottle is bigger than the drinker."

Lizzie raised her aching head to see a blond woman with a dog in her sleeve, stretched out on a chaise longue, smoking a roll-up, her hourglass figure oddly fragile from close up. Addy Chase, sitting on a footstool at Rose's feet, was still taller than everyone else, and Kit, looking sheepish, was lying on a rug made of some kind of angry bear.

The blond woman leaned forward to slap an ice pack on Lizzie's forehead, and the dog growled. "Shut up, Spike. Here, honey, I figure you could use this."

From under her ice pack, Lizzie stared at Rose St. Lorraine and Rose stared back, tendrils of soft gray smoke softening the curious air between them. This was the pink-and-gold woman Lizzie was told was a monster, the skeleton in Addy Chase's closet. Her grandmother, Mary Maud, had set her thin lips whenever the subject of Rose came up, shooing little Lizzie out of the room, though not out of sly earshot. She'd chaired committees to run Rose out of town, and committees to put a stop to prostitution in San Francisco. To Mary Maud's loudly expressed glee the city finally passed its Red Light Abatement Act in the first year of America's involvement in the Great War, 1917. That was the final straw for the dying Barbary Coast, but it didn't touch Rose or the Blue Canary. Somehow, whatever the matrons and good folk of San Francisco did never bothered Rose. Lizzie remembered Mary Maud's fury. The Stafford mansion suffered for days from her grandmother's silence. Charles Mortimer went out a lot. Lizzie noticed Rose's eyes; they were indigo, a deep direct blue.

"It seems you've been making a fool of yourself,

honey, and the men in my life thought I could help. What do you think?"

Lizzie didn't know how to answer that, so she looked at the dog in Rose's sleeve. It had bulging black beady eyes, its nose was pushed deep into its flat brown face, and its mouth was wide enough to swallow a pancake sideways. The big white dog had settled himself near Kit on the polar-bear rug. Lizzie's ice pack made her teeth chatter. Making a fool of herself? The last she remembered was singing a song for some most amusing people down at the bar. At least, she thought they might be amusing. On the other hand, Lizzie thought that *she'd* been terribly amusing. Now she had another of her headaches. This one was a humdinger. It involved more than her head. There was tomcat Kit, stretched out below her, Addy, his long face grim, and that awful old man, Ike, with his missing fingers, scratching himself with the one he had left, chewing something vile. Why was Rose fussing over her? And why did Addy keep looking at her over his spectacles as if she'd done something wrong— no, not wrong, something sorrowful?

Rose adjusted the bag of ice on Lizzie's head and sat back in a flurry of blue feathers. "I knew your grandpa real well, Lizzie Stafford. Last thing he ever said to me, besides booking an hour of Ninx's time, was—"

"Ninx?"

"The best redheaded whore who ever worked for me. A real Jewish spitfire. Owns her own place in LA now. Anyway, he told me how much he thought of you. Dropped dead a day later. We had a party in his memory, lasted two days. Your grandpa would have loved it."

"My grandfather was a friend of yours?"

"Hell, honey. Charles Mortimer and I were the best of friends. Always kept me posted on what your grandma was up to."

"Rose," said Addy, "maybe you shouldn't tell the child these things."

"Don't sell the girl short, sugar. Truth can't harm anyone but a liar. Besides, she's learning. And how in hell do you expect her to do it? Sitting on her fanny in a Nob Hill parlor?"

Addy held up a long hand in mock horror. "Ah, but there are better ways than bootleg hooch."

Rose swatted Addy with her blue ostrich-feather fan. "True. But we all have to learn the hard way. I never knew a soul who took advice, good or bad. It's not human. Human is to go on out and take the licks coming to you and *then* learn. But even so you've got to be able to recognize opportunity when it smacks you in the face. Ike, honey, get us some champagne and something to eat. Spike and Sergeant Huggins too."

Lizzie looked around. Sergeant Huggins? Who was Sergeant Huggins?

Grumbling, the old man left the room, dragging the shorter of his two legs.

Rose leaned back on her white couch and blew smoke rings. She was getting her first close look at little Lizzie Stafford after years of hearing about her from Charles Mortimer, from Addy, from Kit. Elizabeth Sian Stafford Hamilton, the little rich girl whose birthday fell on the day San Francisco burned down, had them all turning circles. Now Rose could see why. Men were so goddam easy. They all saw the pretty face, and they all missed the sharp light behind the green eyes. But Rose saw. She looked through the same light.

"Oh, goody, Ike. Caviar! Spike loves the stuff." Rose took a silver tray from Ike and started spreading thick gobs of caviar on crackers, shooing away the Persian cats. "Beat it. Dammit, Ike. These are your cats. Get them away from the fish."

The old man limped over, scooped a cat up in each hand, and threw them out the door.

Rose handed Lizzie a cracker. "You do what you want, honey, don't let them railroad you. I damn well did what I wanted to do, and I don't regret a thing."

"That's our Rose," said Kit.

"Well, I don't." Rose fed Spike a cracker; the strange flat-faced beast snuffled it up, making a mess in Rose's sleeve. "Over here, Sergeant Huggins, get your cracker too."

Lazy and slow, the white dog rose up from Kit's side, gently took a cracker from Rose's hand, and lay down again. So that was Sergeant Huggins. Lizzie watched, fascinated.

Rose lowered her voice and leaned toward Lizzie. "Listen, honey, if something's troubling you, you come up and talk to me about it any time. What do *men* know? They want you to act the way it makes *them* feel comfortable. I ought to know—I've been making men comfortable all my life. You don't want what someone else wants for you. Wanting things like that is a big mistake. Have some of this champagne. Damned if I know where it came from, but it cost a mint."

Kit hopped up and snatched away Lizzie's ice pack. "I need this more than you do, Elizabeth." He propped it on his own head and lay down again, grinning at Lizzie.

Lizzie had learned caution whenever Kit called her Elizabeth. It meant he was winding up for a low blow. Perhaps she'd better get out of Rose's place while she could. "I really ought to be going. I feel fine now—"

Everyone ignored her. Rose shoved a glass of champagne in her hand, Addy leaned way back in his chair, smiling up at the ceiling with his eyes closed, and Ike made a horrible gurgling in his throat; he was looking for somewhere to spit.

"Ike!" yelled Rose. "You spit that mess on my white rug, I'll make you eat it!"

Lizzie was now wide awake. Except for Kit, no one had ever talked to her as Rose talked. She'd thought Dowie was unique, peculiar and prickly, but since he was male that explained him. Men could get away with anything. But here was Rose St. Lorraine, mentioning things that would usually make Lizzie blush, drinking champagne, swearing, gobbling caviar, and keeping a dog up her sleeve. This wasn't a movie, this was a woman who seemed to have created herself out of her own individual vision, uncompromising and strong. She'd done what she wanted, in the way she wanted, and to hell with the rest. Lizzie's thoughts weren't as clear as that, but that was the gist of them. Swimming frantically in a sea of imitation and celluloid fantasy, grasping at "who to be?" and "whose fault is it if I'm not?" Lizzie decided to stay. So, like Rose, to hell with Kit and his tricks.

"It was the Klondike taught me what I know, Lizzie," Rose was saying. "That was the maddest wingding I ever saw, like Coney Island on the moon." Rose rolled a cigarette, stuck it in her mouth, and lit it with a match she struck on her painted thumbnail. Lighting that match was for Lizzie more of a revelation than Colleen Moore's midnight dive into the icy ocean. *Flaming Youth* was a movie; Rose was here, unwinding right in this white room.

"You think you've got troubles? We've all got troubles. Troubles test you. Without them people would be like jellyfish, no backbone. But I have to admit, you've got it hard. Having money makes things confusing."

Lizzie was interested now. So far, talking about Lizzie had been the point of her life. "Money is a problem?"

"Sure, probably the biggest. People all think if they were rich, everything would be smooth as a baby's butt, but it isn't like that at all. Money blurs the edges of things so the choices aren't obvious. That wasn't a problem of mine until I hit the Klondike. Before that I was so broke there wasn't cream for my coffee. I was in Frisco, working music hall, when the *Excelsior* sailed into the bay with all those horny miners on board. Everybody in town went rip-roaring crazy heading for gold—even my dentist. Also every cardsharp, piker, pimp, saloon dude, bawd, jackass, outlaw—and me. That was back in '98 when I was twenty-one years old. Close to the same age as you, Lizzie. About that time Addy Chase was charging up San Juan Hill behind his hero, Teddy Roosevelt, weren't you, sugar?"

Addy didn't bother to open his eyes. "I certainly was, and I'd still be voting for him if he hadn't decided to die, thereby depriving this nation of its last great spirit, and its—"

"God!" yelped Rose. "Stop him. He's off on Teddy again."

Now Addy opened his mild eyes and fixed them on Rose. "I might remind you that we have all heard about the Klondike before."

"The Klondike's interesting. Roosevelt is dead."

Addy sighed and closed his eyes again.

"Anyway," continued Rose, "up in the Klondike, the other girls did flame dances and snake shimmies and tearjerkers in sausage curls, but I did 'Oh, Dem Golden Slippers' buck naked on roller skates—"

Kit cut in. He now had his feet up on the stuffed head of the polar bear and a glass of champagne balanced on his chest. "Always meant to ask, Rose, were you any good at it?"

"Kid," she said, blowing another smoke ring, "I was so bad, I got a raise."

Addy laughed so hard Kit hopped up and slapped the ice pack on his head. Rose waited patiently until things had settled down before she said, "I made those miners laugh. And they made me rich."

Lizzie, listening intently, said, "So you had money too?"

"Sure, sweetie. But not from the moment I was born. When I got my hands on it, I was *ready* for it. And that's because I knew what it was like without it. I came back to Frisco and opened Silver Street, the best whorehouse this city ever saw, and ran it until the quake knocked the damn thing down; then I built the Blue Canary, and ran that until Frisco got religion and made my girls illegal. The Coast didn't have much life left anyway. That wasn't Mary Maud's doing, though she thought it was. Damn shame, though. It didn't stop a soul, it just took the fun out of it. Like Prohibition is doing now. The law made it a business, and the mobsters started moving in." Rose looked glum for a minute, fed Spike another cracker, then brightened up. "I've got too much grit for them to touch me, and besides, I've got Li."

Li? Lizzie wondered what Rose meant. What had Li Kwan Won got to do with it?

But Rose was still talking and Lizzie couldn't ask, not with Kit in the room. "I got out of the Klondike with all I earned, but you know, there weren't many like me. Girls got knifed and girls got rolled and girls got left flat, but not Rose St. Lorraine. Because I learned the hard way, like Lizzie is doing." Rose brushed crumbs off her blue-feathered bodice.

Kit stirred himself. "Tell the story about Saddle

Mary, Rose. It's better than Robert Service. Someday I'm going to do a piece about that woman."

"Kit," warned Addy, "we'll be here all night if you get her started."

"No, please—I want to hear," said Lizzie. Caught by Rose's bright light, Lizzie wanted to be there for as long as she could: all night, all the next day, all week.

Rose looked into Lizzie's eyes. Maybe she could show the dark girl with the lonely green eyes some short-cuts no one had shown Rose. "Why, sure, Kit. Somebody ought to write it down because it won't be me. I'm a talker, not a writer."

"That's the truth," said Ike.

Rose took a deep breath, a slug of champagne, and started. "There was one girl who got out another way. Saddle Mary, they called her in Dawson, for the obvious reason. Me, I danced and I sang. Of course, I turned a trick now and then, but I had my pick and I picked the best." Rose reached out and stroked Addy's head; the craggy-faced man almost purred. "I hadn't met the best of all, Addy, yet. But Mary, she took what she could over on Paradise Alley, one step up from Louseville across the river from Dawson. First time I saw her she was wearing her own red lace bloomers on her head and parading down Front Street—advertising her wares, so to speak. That was as close as I got to *that* one until the fall of 1901 when I was going south. You could tell the Klondike was played out by then if only you had the wit to see it. Lots didn't. Hell, Ike tells me there's still some old farts up there scratching around."

Ike stuffed a cracker in his mouth. "An' one of 'em me," he said around crumbs and caviar, "if it weren't for Rose."

Rose laughed. "Appetite kind of stuck to me after I'd cleaned him out of his poke the first month I hit town. Probably figured I owed him."

"Still do," said Ike.

"But Lloyd Harper knew when to get out. He was the flashiest gambler in Dawson. Lord, *I* even fell a little. Lloyd went up and down Front Street bragging about how much he was taking with him when he went, buying the best dog team in town to carry it all, and hiring two of the wiliest dog men on the run; *and* he was taking Saddle Mary with him. Nobody could figure that one out. Poor Lloyd turned out to be a fool in the end, believing Mary's hard-luck story, and *his* luck ran out when he did. Anyway, he left Dawson City a clear week before me. I went on down with Appetite. We wanted to beat the snow, but damned if it didn't come early that year. Ike and I got caught at White Horse trying to get to Bennett for the train to Skagway. The both of us were thrashing around in cold snow up to our butts along with a pack of wolves when we come across what was left of Lloyd Harper and his team. They'd been bushwhacked—the two drivers killed outright and Lloyd wounded real bad. He was lying curled up against the wheeler dog—all the poor dogs were still in their traces and starving slow, with Lloyd trying to keep warm but dying all along. There was no sign of Saddle Mary. No sign of Lloyd's gold, either. Ike and I fixed up Lloyd best we could, then Ike took care of the dogs. He cared more about them than Lloyd and his lost gold."

"Saved every one of 'em, too."

"Sure did, honey, and bought them off Lloyd so they could get some rest. Appetite loves his animals. So anyway, Lloyd told us how Mary'd set him up. Friends of hers just appeared out of nowhere third day on the trail and shot everything up. Then they grabbed the gold and Mary and skeedaddled, sure that everyone who could talk was dead. Lloyd sure as hell would've been, too, if Ike hadn't tripped over him in the snow. Lloyd never found Mary, but by God, I never knew a man try harder. He said he'd look for her and her fancy man, Blinn, until hell froze over."

Addy, who'd heard all this before, showed no signs of boredom as he listened again. All of them, Ike and Addy and Kit, faces flushed, were leaning forward, eyes full of snow and gold and history. For Lizzie, it was like coming home. The white room and the gold woman and the *words,* Rose's words, her voice gritty, amused with itself. Long words, fat words, funny words, exploding words, words like boulders, words like jackals, like floods, like dark alleys, like diving bells, like soup, like stars, snowballing Lizzie into a part of herself that couldn't care less about James and Esmé and shopping, that made them seem remote and dim, unimportant— and revenge the least important thing of all.

Lizzie didn't notice, but Kit was watching her, his dark eyes intent and careful.

Addy laughed. "The funny part is that Saddle Mary's right here in San Francisco. Ike and Rose and I saw her in 1906 trying to save her cathouse from the fire. Rose scared the pants off her. She's still here. Now that boy of hers, Murray, is a bootlegger and just like his mother."

Ike spat. "Sure is. Lowdown an' mean."

"Ike!" said Rose. "Watch the rug!"

Like a throwaway line, Kit said lazily, "Baby Blinn was at Lizzie's party." But no one heard him.

Revenge was what Lizzie was thinking about. What of Lloyd Harper's revenge? Certainly he had more reason than she to nurse a grievance. "But why didn't you tell Harper when you found Saddle Mary?"

"Honey," said Rose, "Lloyd wasn't much better. He shot one of his girls in Dawson, shot her right in the back, and the law let him go. They said it wasn't a crime to kill a whore."

"Oh."

The shock of the word "whore" for the fourth or fifth time in Lizzie's presence woke Addy up to his manners. "It's late," he announced, rising from the footstool to his full height. "Lizzie ought to be going home."

Ike yawned. Every tooth in his mouth, three, took the air. "Say, that's right. I gotta get on down an' check the floor. The place is prob'ly fuller now than it was when we left it. Come on, Dowie. I need help."

"You do?"

"Yup."

Lizzie waited a full minute after they'd gone, Sergeant Huggins trotting after Ike; she waited until Addy had sloped off to get her coat. That left her alone with Rose. Quickly, she leaned close. "You mentioned someone called Li. Would that be the tall Chinese man down at the bar?"

"Sure, honey, that's him."

"I was just curious. I'd never met a Chinese before."

Rose stroked Spike, now asleep and snoring in her sleeve. "They aren't much different from the rest of us, though Li might be. Better, if anything. I never had any kids; maybe something's wrong. But I raised a child just the same. That Chinese boy, he's my son, just like Kit Dowie's my son, even though Kit's got a daddy somewhere, just like I did once—but Kit ran off when he was nine because his daddy was mean and because he had newspaper print for blood. So they're both mine—and Addy's. I love my boys. Kit's a newspaperman just like he said he would be, a damn good writer. As for Li—well, there's no one like him. Smarter than a whip. I'd trust him to the ends of the earth, which is a lot more than I can say for most folks, white or black or yellow."

"And Dido? Is she like a daughter?"

"Hell, no! That girl is nobody's child. Don't mess with Dido, honey. The only human in this world Dido loves is herself, and maybe Kit Dowie, and sometimes I'm not so sure about that."

Because she was asking, Lizzie kept asking. "And Kit loves Dido?"

Rose snorted. "Let me put it this way. I wouldn't come between them."

Impulsively, Lizzie hugged Rose like she used to hug Charles Mortimer, hugged her for her exuberance, her daring, her confidence. Rose St. Lorraine smelled like violets and warm feathers.

Rose put her head back and hooted. It wouldn't be easy, but she could get to like this girl. "Look what you've done, sugar, you woke up Spike."

# Chapter 7

Grant Avenue, once Dupont, was the heart of two of San Francisco's most colorful districts, Chinatown and North Beach. Chinatown was vehement with Chinese, North Beach was full of Italians. They all insisted they were Americans, whatever that was.

The Avenue ran without hesitation, straight up from the big-city-newspaper hustle of Market Street in the south to the busy commercial piers—placed like spokes on the slow curve of San Francisco's bay, its deep ocean blue ruffled by white manes of salty foam—in the north. On the way it passed, climbing steadily, through a ritzy area of tall office buildings, fancy scrolled-stone hotels, elegant department stores, fine restaurants, and flower stalls, to narrow and sweep and leave America behind; from there it was ten bumpy blocks or so of yellow faces, odd misshapen vegetables spilling out onto the crowded sidewalks, rusting fire escapes and tiny balconies draped with pot plants, fuchsias, geraniums, cineraria, the colors hot against the drab wooden walls—strange smells, strange signs slashed with bright paint, and stranger sounds. When it crossed Columbus—which ran down and across Grant at a racy slant—it skirted the bottom of abrupt Telegraph Hill, with its hundreds of crazed wooden steps and the houses hanging on for dear life, to become the old world. The faces here were swarthy, the smells recognizable, the signs readable, and the sounds the rattle and rush of rural Italian.

North Beach was the home of Murray Blinn and his mother, Mary. In Murray, Oscar Wilde's dictum, that "all nature imitated art," became hair-raisingly true. If Kit Dowie and Dashiell Hammett and Keiko read lurid pulps, Murray devoured them—lived for them. He believed every word. Ludicrously patterning himself on his reading of the English "hero," Raffles, he threw in an increasing dollop of Chicago's rapidly rising Capone, not yet the Napoleon of crime. It made a jarring mix. Blinn's only actual tribute to the English gentleman thief was his idea of sartorial dash—the loud colors, the hair oil, and the plucked eyebrows. They looked as silly on him as they would on anyone else. Blinn thought they were swell. But if that was all Murray did—dress comically and smell funny—he would have been laughed out of town. People found to their cost that Murray Blinn was not to be laughed at. They could get killed that way. Buried deep in his small mean mind, Murray had an unwelcome and unrecognized suspicion that he wasn't what he thought he was, so the self-delusion became frantic and brittle. Like many small people, his bite was much worse than his bark. He frightened most of his minions, just as his superiors scared *him*—all part of Nature's sweet balance.

Murray and his mother lived two stories above their teashop and bakery. La Pallottola was one of Murray's jokes. Behind its clink of china cups and tinkle of spoons, its butter pats, buns, and crisp white tablecloths, was the Blinn speak, hangout for neighborhood Italians and multiracial hoods.

The Blinn windows looked out over Grant. If they'd been clean, someone looking through them could have seen little Italian kids playing below in the street, Carlo at his newsstand hawking papers, vendors with their carts, mustachioed housewives dickering over pasta and fruit, and dark-haired girls, still juicy and ripe with youth —but the windows, like the apartment, were dim with dust, greasy handprints, and the droppings of flies. Domestically, nothing had changed for Saddle Mary, except that it was no longer she and an assortment of slatternly girls who supported the Blinns, it was Murray, with his speakeasy and La Pallottola and his bootlegging. Not allowed to set foot in the teashop—to cover the slim possibility she'd ask why and get her feelings hurt, Murray told Mary it was beneath her—Mary insisted on doing the upstairs housekeeping and cooking. The Blinns weren't Italian and Mary wasn't a cook. Murray ate out more often than in.

The gold Mary stole from Lloyd Harper had blown away three years after she got her hands on it. Her man Blinn took it with him when he sneaked out one night, leaving behind a little seedling in its place—Murray. The boy couldn't quite replace the cash, but Mary almost liked the kid anyway. He reminded her of herself: greedy —she called it ambitious; mean—she called *that* careful; and vicious—to Mary, that was just common sense. Folks being what they were, it was wisest to stick it to 'em before they stuck it to you. As for how the kid looked, Mary didn't notice. She had no eye for beauty, and no eye for the hideous either. Things looked like they looked. Take it or leave it.

After Blinn the elder went on the lam with all that loot, Mary knuckled down to what she knew best: running a cathouse. Her place kept them alive, but barely. Mary had no style, and on the Barbary Coast she was up against stiff competition; there were four or five low dives on every block. Until Murray got old enough to add to their income with his clever fingers and, later, his brain, Mary was never sure from day to day where her next drink was coming from. But goddammit, if Murray wasn't something now! Rum-running, a speakeasy, even a teashop. And he had people working for him. Murray was taking care of his old ma like she deserved.

Their apartment was decorated with butt-worn overstuffed chairs, empty wine bottles, overflowing ashtrays, and the Blinns' library: movie magazines for Mary, and for Murray tattered dime novels and stacks of dog-eared thriller magazines, Murray's precious collection that gave him all his overworked melodramatic ideas. Also Mary's dirty clothes. Murray's, always fresh from the laundry— as he said, "For Christ's sake, Ma, what are Chinks for?" —were hung smartly in three cheap wardrobes: clean and pressed, the mustard yellow handkerchief with the lime-green plaid jacket, the white tie sporting blue clocks for the brown Harris tweed. He had fifty pairs of shoes, two-tone and correspondents, and two drawers of collars. His choice of outfits was enormous and unerringly terrible. Mary could look around their home and feel pride.

The Blinns were at dinner. They had guests. Murray and three of his boys sat at the big round table under the window waiting for whatever Mary might serve up. They kept their mouths shut, but a good guess about the meal was clear from the expressions on their faces. No one looked happy.

Saddle Mary walked in from a door that also brought smoke and the smell of burning fat. Her hair was grayer and her face was lined, but she still wore soiled wrappers, and her makeup rivaled her son's for a sense of color. At the end of a large raw hand she was carrying a frying pan. The pan made spitting noises. She pointed the angry skillet at Murray.

"You'll eat it," she said, and scooped out the burnt mess fairly onto five plates. Throwing the hot pan on the floor, she sat down, lit a cigar, and dared them to eat. She didn't, but they did, while the weak sun traveled down the dirty window and winked out behind the houses over on Russian Hill.

Murray got through the meal by sneaking most of it to Tommy, his brindle bulldog, who wallowed, drooling, under the table. His boys weren't so lucky.

When Tommy finished whatever it was, Murray pushed his greasy plate away. "Ma, that was awful."

Mary slapped the skinny kid on her right, called Jugs Kelly. "Can't reach Murray," she explained.

Jugs Kelly, up from a small dusty farming town somewhere in the Imperial Valley, was a callow pinch-faced Irish boy, with a taste for the vicious, and a dead shot. Back home he'd practiced on birds, rats, stray cats —anything that moved and wouldn't get him in trouble. He'd come to the big city to practice on something else.

Seated across from him was Whispering Mike, a shambling Hungarian hulk from the boxing rings of Detroit, who was impossible to put down in a stand-up fight. Murray took him everywhere he went—for muscle. Whispering Mike got his name from a hard left to the Adam's apple; he was ten years older than the rest, but no wiser.

The third, Coffee Trujillo, fresh from the Mexican barrio in Los Angeles, had a quick mind, a short fuse, and a slow-burning ambition. Murray's outfit was the first one he joined when he arrived in San Francisco. Now that he'd been in it for three months, soaking up possibilities, city smarts, and contacts, he'd decided to stick around; he had plenty of time to move on to something bigger and classier. The pansy, Murray Blinn, seemed to know a few people that needed to be known. The pansy's mother was just something to tolerate. After that, it was Chicago or New York for Coffee.

These three were the core of Murray Blinn's high hopes. With them, he intended to bust San Francisco wide open. The takings were there, just as they were in every American city in the fat easy times of Prohibition —whoever thought that one up deserved a medal from every hustler in the country—and Frisco was his. With the arrival of Leo Olemi and his successful snuggling up to the DA, a personage Murray himself could never have got close to, his dreams were about to come true. Murray scratched Tommy's massive head. Tommy wagged his stump and farted.

Murray laughed. "Cute, huh?" Standing, he poured rough Italian red into five dubious glasses. "We got something to celebrate here, Ma, and it ain't the shipment coming in tonight. This one should be close to the last runs of the small stuff. I waited to tell you till now. That's why we had this here little dinner party."

Everyone held their breaths, but not because of Murray. Tommy was more than cute, he was disgusting.

"I got plans, big ones. Got my hands on something that's gonna finally get us out of just rum-running and into our own operation." Murray sat down, delighting in the looks of surprise that passed between the boys at the table. He neglected to tell them that it was Olemi's deal. Would Capone have shared his sources? He sure as shit wouldn't. Murray was no dummy.

Mary dropped ash from her cigar onto the cold congealing food, her hard eyes lighting up with the possibility of gratified greed. "What something, Murray?"

"We're gonna own a distillery, Ma, right over in Oakland. We're gonna make our own stuff, and them Chinks ain't gonna be able to touch us."

"You don't say!" said Mary.

"I sure as shit do. Two, three weeks, we'll be running flat out."

"Well, ain't that somethin', boys?"

Coffee's hand went for his pocket. Someone was coming up the stairs from the speakeasy below. Tommy, the bulldog, didn't move. He was trying to scratch something that itched. He groaned and snuffled and missed his own skin with his own leg by three inches.

Murray grinned, his plucked brows rising. "Don't be so damn skittish, Coffee. How would anybody we don't know get past the boys down in the speak? Ma, go see who it is."

Saddle Mary, shuffling in her down-at-heel slippers, went without grace—and came back with a waddling fat man, puffing from his climb up the Blinns' stairs.

"Heart's not so good," he said, smelling of Sen-Sen and sweat.

The four men at the table said nothing, waiting for him to get to the point of whatever it was he'd climbed all those stairs to say.

"Leo sent me. Just a message. He said to tell you, Green light on them Chinese. That's it. Now I gotta climb all the way back down."

An hour later Mary's table was covered with paper, maps, scraps of wrapping, and what was left of Mary's cooking. Murray was scribbling away on a map with a blunt pencil. "We'll do it like this, see, we'll get guys to spot us here and here, imported guys. If the Torrio-Capone mob can do it in Chicago, I can do it in Frisco. And say, I don't even got much competition."

Saddle Mary, grimy elbows on the table, big hands supporting her sagging painted face, cigar butt clamped between her splayed teeth, was studying the arrows and marks on a map of San Francisco. "This ain't the same kind of town, honeybunch. The cops here ain't so cowed as they got 'em back east."

Murray laughed, punching Whispering Mike on the arm. "I'll make it the same kind of town—for *me,* and, of course, the boys here. Us in this room'll control the booze from here to LA, and then the girls and the numbers and the tracks and anything else going. Won't we, boys?"

"Hell, yeah," croaked Whispering Mike.

Jugs giggled.

Coffee just nodded his small brown head on his big fit body. If things were as Murray said, he'd done the right thing picking up with the pixie. Little guys were unpredictable, but they didn't scare easy. Being small, they couldn't afford to. Coffee's quick fingers were playing with a thick rubber band. He worked it around his thumb and forefinger and shot it across the room. It hit an ashtray, spraying butts onto the floor. The butts joined dozens more.

"Ain't we got the East Bay still, Ma?" crowed Murray, his speech spiced with his cheap reading matter. "And ain't we got speaks doing business all over town, and some up north too, and ain't we got the Longshoremen's Union where we want 'em? That labor troublemaker O'Flooty shoots his mouth off one more time, and Jugs here'll have to pay 'im a little visit. . . ."

"I'd like that, Ma," said Jugs.

"Who're you callin' Ma?" said Mary.

". . . And ain't we got soldiers, and can't we get us more, and don't everybody hate Chinks? The little yellow bastards can't operate outside Chinatown. We'll just go in and bust up their works, and then we'll hem 'em in. Who's to stop us? We got Olemi now, and he's got the politicians where they oughta be, in his pocket. What do the Chinks have? Nuthin'! That's what they have. They got the hole in the doughnut."

Mary's strange little eyes gleamed. "The Chinks work with that stuck-up floozy, Rose St. Lorraine, don't they? I got a score to settle with her that's waited ten years. Maybe the plan ain't so bad." Mary scratched something under the table, and it wasn't Tommy. "Well, now, ain't this grand."

Pushing back his chair with a sudden tooth-aching scrape, Murray stood. "OK, now, we had a dinner party and I gave a little speech. Get your coats, boys. I don't know about you but I gotta get me something to eat."

The scramble for the door left Mary talking to herself. "Wait a goddam minute here. Who's gonna clean this mess up?"

*Chapter 8*

Lizzie couldn't sleep. By the dim light of the moon, she stretched long restless limbs in crisp sheets, wriggled her toes, and frowned. She was propped up by satin pillows, chain smoking, eating blackberry jam out of a jar with a gold spoon, and sipping warm champagne straight from the bottle.

Addy had delivered her home as promised; by the time they got to the Stafford mansion, it was closer to dawn than dusk. The house was dark; everyone was asleep. Addy hadn't had much to say on the short ride up the hill. At her door, he'd stammered a little, taken off his spectacles, wiped them, fiddled with his cane, and then said in a very low voice, "You know I love you like a daughter, or a niece, or some blessed relative, Elizabeth. Please, promise me, you'll never doubt it." Then he was off. Lizzie watched him go. Silly old Addy.

She'd turned on her heel, marched the lonely distance to the white-tiled Stafford kitchens for the jam, snapping on lights as she went, passing through a great formal drawing room—it smelled of dead roses and wasted time and looked as if Queen Anne herself had done the decorating—across the enormous dining room seating a hundred, then down God knew how many stairs to Charles Mortimer's extraordinary wine cellars to grab a bottle of champagne, and finally made for her own rooms upstairs. She ignored the grilled elevator Charles Mortimer had used to haul his enormity to higher floors, using instead the main staircase of swirling gilt tritons and sea nymphs lit by cut-glass seashells. The journey took her ages. Sometimes a big house was a *big* house. The ballroom alone was larger than City Hall. She never realized before that a place with so many rooms could make one nervous. She'd lived there all her life and she could still get lost. Meanwhile, the din of her voice chattering in her head sounded foolish, decorative, small, and confused.

Now, safe in her own corner bedroom on the second floor, Lizzie's wide mouth worked as she chewed a bottom lip between well-tended teeth, her dark head busy with dark thoughts, her marcel tangled. Long green eyes snapped at nothing but dim shapes in the quiet room. Dim shapes, dim thoughts—enticing turmoil in her mind. Outside the tall windows, the sky hung close and grainy as newsprint, and shining through high lacy fog was the moon, thin and cold as a dime. A whisper of memory curled itself just beyond her racing thoughts, a distant soft hiss she couldn't shake. Was it something Grandfather had said to her when she was still little Lizzie, serene in herself, sure of her world? "They built themselves cages with their money, baby."

A lady knows how to behave. She's bred for it like a mink is bred for a mink coat. And if a lady has money she also knows what to expect. Another damn day, ticketed and hung on a padded hanger like a limited copy of a designer original. A lady has pastimes, not hobbies. Style, not fashion. Dalliances, not affairs. Sometimes a lady—oh, God, Lizzie!—sometimes a lady lives in a cage.

Her bedroom had muted grisaille walls, Savonnerie rugs, and a ceiling covered in silver tea paper. Over her bed cascaded silvered drapes from a fringed corona. In San Francisco's annual attempt at winter, Keiko kept a fire going in a fireplace Lizzie could roast a boar in. This room, and her private sitting room beyond, opened onto a solarium. The solarium was a glass cathedral, webbed with fine steel braces painted a brilliant white, arching up two stories to the mansion's gabled roof. During the day glorious leafy things stood on tiptoe, holding up eager green palms to catch the light. Conducting arguments on the wing, tiny exotic birds darted through the branching green, all gaudy yellows and flashing reds and blues. The solarium soared like a great Gothic bubble of moist green air and Lizzie hardly ever went near it. It was Keiko's toy. Her Japanese servant gave it life. Lizzie *had* everything—but what did she give?

What did she have to give? After spending a few hours, dazzled, listening to Rose St. Lorraine, Lizzie realized how much she hadn't done, didn't have, hadn't seen. Grandfather left her all his money, which was nice; all she'd done was spend it. And he'd left her his agnosticism, allowing her to choose belief for herself; so far, she hadn't decided. But he'd left her something else she was only just becoming aware of. The fortune she'd inherited was not old money, not hidebound with monied traditions. Grandfather had willed her a kind of freedom, a certain integrity of mind, a pioneering spirit, an honest heart. Lizzie had no discipline, but she had curiosity. Charles Mortimer hadn't left behind rules to break; he'd left her the strength to make some for herself. Lizzie took a long swig from her bottle. The bubbles went right up her nose. Freedom is a scary thing. It's lonely out there on your own. She sneezed like a cat: *Chew!* But Rose St. Lorraine hadn't been scared, not enough, anyway, to stop her. Surely Lizzie could do what she wanted as well? The trouble, she realized, was that she didn't know what that was. Lately, all she'd done was drink, hiding in a daze of daiquiris—only this afternoon she thought she could be Colleen Moore, a free and easy good-time flapper—but these weren't things she *wanted* to do, they were what she thought she *ought* to do to punish James. Now, perhaps, it was time to be Lizzie. Isn't that what Rose meant? Of course, that left her with a problem. Who was Lizzie?

On impulse, Lizzie switched on her lamp, slammed

the bottle of champagne and the jar of jam onto her night table, and hopped out of bed. She'd left all her new clothes at Kit's place; she'd give them away tomorrow— all except the delicious white suit with its black fur. Even a rich girl doesn't throw away an original Erté. But she could still get the goo off her eyelashes and wash the marcel out of her hair. Thank God she hadn't had it cut.

Lizzie, in heady inspiration, had decided to *do* something. With her hair back to its straight and shining black cap, she'd think of something *to* do. She went directly to her black marble bathroom with the gold taps and washed her hair.

For instance, she could travel instead of playing puppet to James, take a long ocean cruise, broaden her mind, or perhaps a train to Chicago, then the Twentieth Century to New York. She'd meet the people Kit knew. That brought her up out of the washbasin fast, head dripping suds. What would she say to them? She didn't read. Well, then, she *would* read. Kit could tell her what to start with. No, she couldn't travel. Not yet. Wouldn't that be running away from her troubles with James? Would Rose do that? Of course not. But then, Rose wouldn't have trouble with James in the first place. She'd bop him on the nose. Thinking of James, maybe Lizzie could spend all her money. Then where would he be? He needed the Stafford millions if he was going to run for all those political offices he craved so dearly. For Pete's sake, Lizzie— she was back to plotting revenge. Besides, nobody could spend all the Stafford money; it kept coming in like a crazed cornucopia, like something from the land of Oz. Charles Mortimer's mining company just kept on giving. Gosh, thought Lizzie, suddenly struck by an idea as she rinsed the suds down the drain. I did read once. I read every Oz book Frank Baum ever wrote. Did that count? She might ask Kit. With a huge bath towel wrapped around her head, Lizzie sat herself in front of her vanity mirror and smeared cold cream on her face.

No, Lizzie wouldn't run away, and she must stop thinking about punishing James. Ah, she knew! Why hadn't she thought of it before? She'd buy acres and acres of land in Marin County, north of the Golden Gate. No one lived there—well, not too many people, certainly no one she knew. Every spring when she was growing up Grandfather had taken her to Marin for picnics, just the two of them. They rode the ferry from San Francisco's wharves across the windy bay to a little fishing village called Sausalito, then took a small train on a small track to Larkspur.

Southern Marin was a wilderness of forest: manzanita, madrone, scrub oak, buckeye, and, most lovely of all —red trees with thick dusty bark, as tall as legends— stately sequoias that lived forever. Larkspur was a sleepy little town tucked into a pleat in a small mountain called Tamalpais, rising from the Pacific like a miniature Fuji. Someone told Charles Mortimer that Tamalpais was Modoc Indian for Sleeping Maiden. He fell in love with the name and the mountain. For a few months, Charles had toyed with the idea of buying the whole damn thing, but the government wouldn't let him. They made the mountain into a public park or something. That made him madder than Mary Maud got when her committees couldn't stop Rose St. Lorraine. But he kept taking Lizzie back every spring to sit on it and pretend it was his.

They bought food in Larkspur's general store, and then they hiked a few miles—when she was old enough and he was fit enough—Grandfather wheezing, gamely following little Lizzie, deep into Madrone Canyon with its wet woods, silent and still. Charles Mortimer always stopped at the same rough picnic table, spreading out his newspapers, his supply of cigars, making sandwiches, drinking from his jug of whatever it was, while Lizzie went off alone for hours. Walking on pine needles as soft as wool under the wet red trees, collecting stones and moss to build islands in the rushing canyon creek, sitting on the damp earth, head propped on her hands, watching the clean cold water break around her mossy rocks, dreaming of South Sea islands. Lizzie hadn't been back since she was fifteen—the spring she'd discovered her interesting effect on boys. When she wouldn't go with him any more, Charles Mortimer stopped going too. It was only at this too-late moment that Lizzie realized how much that must have hurt the old man.

She'd go back to Larkspur now. If she couldn't buy the mountain, she could build a house in Grandfather's canyon, a small sweet rambling house of stone and shingle, with fireplaces, a house that hugged the steep mountainside, where she could paint or write or . . . hold on a minute, Lizzie Stafford. Who was she fooling? Whatever she was, she definitely was not an artist. Oddly, that was a relief; at least she knew something she wasn't. But she could support artists. She had enough money to support them all! She remembered what the thin man, Kit's friend Dashiell Hammett, had said, "No wit west of the Wabash." Lizzie would start an artist's colony like Princess de Polignac's in Paris. Lizzie knew about the arts-mad Princess: she was always in *Vogue*—her parties, her celebrated mingling of odd people, her sense of style, and —enough!

None of this was what Lizzie wanted. She groaned, squeezing her buzzing head between her hands. What the hell *did* Lizzie Stafford want?

If she couldn't buy the answer, dear God, she'd have to learn it, just as Rose had said. How long would that take? Maybe she wasn't as perfect as she'd always assumed. It was even possible that it was her fault James had had to go to someone like Esmé Baker. Stunning thought. Why would a man want a mistress if he had a good wife? Where was that book James had given her for her twenty-third birthday? Emily Post's *Book of Etiquette*. Stuffed in the back of her glove drawer. Emily had a good deal to say on how a lady ought to behave, and Lizzie couldn't stomach any of it. But maybe now? She opened the book at random, read a few of the maxims, and then stuffed it back in her glove drawer again. It still made her shudder. What was the point of having so much money if a lady was supposed to live like a bug on a pin? Come to think of it, what was the point of being a lady at all? Forget Emily. She couldn't help. And bless Charles Mortimer.

Lizzie hadn't seen James since she'd walked out of the house right after their anniversary party. How long ago was that? This was Tuesday morning. Twenty-four hours—the earth had traveled once around the sun, and Lizzie had simply gone along for the ride.

James was so close, asleep in his room. In the Stafford mansion, that meant he was far enough away to be a stranger. Why did they have separate rooms? That had been *her* idea, hadn't it? It seemed so reasonable at the time, but now look where it had got her. She'd wake him up, talk to him, ask him about Esmé. She'd save her marriage. How exciting.

Lizzie dried and brushed her hair until it crackled with electricity, wiped the cream off her face, added a hint of rouge to her wide, slightly Slavic cheekbones, and a dab of Chanel No. 5 to her wrists. The perfume gave her one reason to be thankful for money. Lizzie was a good customer; on her last birthday, Coco Chanel had sent her a bottle of a new perfume all the way from Paris. Coco was a heck of a lot more useful than Emily Post. Slipping an oyster silk kimono over her bare shoulders and jade green slippers onto her feet, Lizzie rustled down the corridor, past her husband's private study, which separated their two bedrooms, and crept into the dark quiet of James's room.

In the gathering dawn, asleep and silent, James looked as he had when they'd first met. Lizzie sat on the edge of his bed, looking down at the smooth face, the strong forehead, the silver-blond hair. She caught the warm smell she associated with men, but mostly with Charles Mortimer, a mingling of faint tobacco, leather, and the sour sweetness of brandy. Outside James's window the same shivering moon hung low, setting. Lizzie studied him, running a gentle finger over one arching blond brow. Poor James. Lizzie could answer Kit's question. Of course she cared. And she'd make *James* care.

What was the matter with them? What was wrong with her? James Hamilton was as handsome as a movie star, as clever as Charles Mortimer, as tender as—not now, but once—as tender as a lover in an old book. Unshed tears salted her green eyes. They felt like love. Or what Lizzie thought of as love—self-pity. She sneezed. Chew! James mumbled something, turned over, but he didn't wake.

She was lost in memories, remembering the man he was when he'd come home from the war: attentive, almost shy in his wooing, never pressing her, taking his time, not wanting to upset Charles Mortimer, making her feel like Grandfather had made her feel when she was little Lizzie—special. When Grandfather had died, Lizzie's world fell apart. But James had been there, talking to her, taking care of her. Mary Maud followed Charles Mortimer a few months later, but by then Lizzie had someone to lean on: James Alexander Hamilton. The leaning felt good. Their wedding was in St. Mary's Cathedral—James was an Episcopalian but let Lizzie choose the church. Everyone had come. James, standing tall and straight and silver at the altar, tipping the hearts of Lizzie's girlfriends over in little flurries of envy. Lizzie had gripped his arm, smiling with fierce pride. The reception at the Fairmont took up two pages in the *Argonaut.* Ned Greenway's pen had almost gibbered in admiration. Why was it, though, that the thing Lizzie remembered with the clarity of a photograph was that damn Kit Dowie goosing her in front of the Persian pavilion? Never mind.

The Hamiltons had gone to Lake Tahoe for their honeymoon. The clear deep mountain lake had recently been rediscovered by the rich of San Francisco. In the summer, it was *the* place to go. James called on the Crockers and the Athertons, the Popes and Drums, Lizzie smoothing his way, amused and delighted by the interest he took in her friends. James fell in love with the place, its lodges and chalets, boating parties, water carnivals. Lizzie fell in love with his joy.

It had been cold, even in July. The frigid grandeur of the high Sierra lake, with its mountain peaks glinting like fangs against the thin blue sky, chilled her blood. It wasn't like Marin. There, the deep forests were soft and moist and dark, the earthy smell of rotting leaves and spongy bark, of evergreen needles dripping with rain, the distant smell of the salt sea enveloped her in a cocoon of maternal quiet. Lake Tahoe had no smell. The cold smooth rocks, glittering with mica, were like paste. She felt apart from the beauty; it was like looking through a pane of glass. Lizzie could see, but she couldn't touch.

Mostly, she stayed by the fire in their mountain lodge, curled up with her *Vogue*s. But James understood. After a few days, he paid his calls alone. Lizzie Stafford had grown up with these people; she could see them any time. But James was like a kid in a new playground. As he understood her, she understood him. And he always came back to Lizzie. Remembering Lake Tahoe brought Lizzie a little revelation. The way she'd seen the lake was the way she saw James ever since Esmé had come along —she could see but she couldn't touch.

James sighed in his sleep. Lizzie felt a renewed surge of pride in his pride, in his confidence and ability and ambition. How could she win him back? Well, first, of course, she'd stop drinking; then there was the matter of the separate bedrooms. She'd have Keiko see to that in the morning. She'd move into James's room—that meant redecorating. Why, it wouldn't be more than a matter of days before Esmé was a memory.

Already idly imagining the room as she would redo it, Lizzie's eyes dropped to the table beside James's bed. He'd been doing some late-night paperwork. Lizzle toyed with the papers on his night table, touching them, barely thinking of them, her heart full of sentiment and her mind full of plans and schemes. One was a draft of a letter to a man named Harry Daugherty in Washington, D.C. The words "Washington, D.C." jumped off the page. Someday her husband was going to be President of the United States! In her frothy mood, Lizzie found the idea thrilling. President! Her James Hamilton. The contents of the letter meant nothing to her. But it amused her when she realized she'd started the day looking through Kit's letters; how apt to end it looking through James's. Under the letter to Daugherty was a note pad covered with doodlings. Rose's name, and over and over; the word "Chinatown." Lizzie put the pad down, for a moment puzzled. Why would James be thinking of Chinatown? For her, the word only brought back a sharp sense of shame over her vamping fiasco at the Blue Canary. How silly that seemed now, in the gray dawn light. Of course, she could never go back there. Kit hadn't witnessed her flop, but that creature Dido had—and Li

Kwan Won, naturally. She must have been mad. Or drinking too much. Rose knew what she was talking about. Stick to champagne. What a pity, though, that she'd shamed herself in the Blue Canary. How was she ever going to see Rose again? Never mind. She'd figure out a way around that. There was one last letter. To Esmé. As with Kit's articles about Fatty Arbuckle, Lizzie read every awful word.

In horror, Lizzie dropped an unfinished page like a scarlet letter, jumping away from his bed. The pages of James's handwriting, still large and sloping, fluttered to the floor like paper airplanes.

All her outrage flooded back. Damn James! Damn him to hell! While she was thinking of him, *he* was thinking of Esmé. And what thoughts! The letter was filthy, describing what he wanted Esmé to do to him—clearly, clinically. Things that Lizzie had never done to anyone, *would* never do to anyone. Reading the letter made even her black hair blush. It wasn't a love letter, though perhaps James had meant it to be; it was pornography. The words he used were abrupt and graphic. And he'd mentioned Lizzie. Writing about his wife with scorn, ridiculing her in stiff correct prose. Whatever tremulous growing Lizzie had managed in her long day, groping painfully toward herself, whatever common sense Rose had planted in her mind, was lost, swept away in jealousy, self-pity, wounded pride—and disgust. Mostly the last.

There was a pitcher of water on the night table. Lizzie pulled her husband's bedcovers down to his knees. One leg was drawn up; the other hung over the edge of the bed. His naked feet were white and bony in the thin light of dawn. She reached for the pitcher.

Lizzie would go back to the Blue Canary. She'd go back, and this time she wouldn't fail. Who was Li Kwan Won to turn Elizabeth Sian Stafford Hamilton down? James wouldn't laugh *that* off; he'd choke on it!

With the dedicated patience of the vengeful, Lizzie very slowly and very carefully poured the tepid contents of the pitcher into her husband's bed. Then she pulled the covers back up.

*Chapter 9*

Esmé Baker seemed fragile and tender and sweet. Esmé was none of these things. She was tough and practical and seasoned. But Esmé knew where those qualities would get her—nowhere. Not with men. Her thirty-one years had etched tiny lines around her eyes and cut angles in her cheeks, but few noticed. What they noticed, because Esmé made sure they would look, was the mass of flaming red hair, the big brown eyes where her thoughts seemed to swim like bright fish, the voice with little bells in it, vague and breathless, the porcelain skin. She made men melt like candles in a hot oven.

Unlike Lizzie Stafford Hamilton, Esmé Baker knew what it was like not to have money; she knew hard times and hard men. James, whether he knew it or not, was going to change all that. Good times were coming; Esmé had earned them.

From an Irish kid's orphanage on the Lower East Side of New York, to slinging hash on Fourteenth Street, to the chorus lines of countless Broadway revues, Esmé learned the ropes. Slogging as a waitress in places that smelled of sour boiled cabbage and exhausted breath paid the bills; Esmé paid with her body to get into the shows, hanging around with out-of-work vaudevillians across from the Palace Theatre to pick up casting tips and trade dance steps. Everybody called the triangular patch of city turf where Forty-seventh Street met Seventh Avenue and Broadway "Panic Beach." It was the right name for it. Hopeful kids from all over the States, hoofers, specialty acts, song-and-dance teams, wasted their youth waiting for the call that never came.

Esmé was one of the losers. She was still dancing in the back of the third row—one-two-three, kick!—when she met the first guy who said he'd help her out. That took her to Chicago's South Side and a load of broken promises. It was two years before she wised up and found another guy with different promises—a traveling salesman. She wound up in a hotel in Atlanta, Georgia, waiting for him between business trips. Somewhere during one of those empty-bed nights, Esmé decided if the salesman could hit the road, so could she—to Reno, Nevada, and from Reno to the little town of Hollywood. They were cranking out two- and three-reelers down there, three or four or five a week, to feed the growing demand for dumb "movies." A girlfriend in Reno told her she could get a job as one of Mack Sennett's bathing beauties. Esmé believed her. One cardboard suitcase and a long-distance bus fare later, Esmé met Sennett, had pies thrown in her face, got tied to railway lines and thrown out of windows—but she was never a bathing beauty. She had the body and the face, but so did everyone else. The missing ingredient was blind luck. She lived in a rooming house with five other girls, tripping over their cardboard suitcases, pushing away dripping stockings and lace underpants just to wash her face, and living on coffee and hot dogs. Somehow Esmé had become twenty-eight years old. That scared a girl. Then she met Eddie Baker, a small-time comic for Hal Roach. He made her promises, too, and backed them up. She could stop washing banana-cream pies out of her red hair, take the Band-Aids off her knees, and move out of the rooming house. She married Eddie. For a year she didn't know where his money was coming from—he wasn't Harold Lloyd. But it was more than *she'd* ever seen. With some of it to spend on herself, she discovered she had a sense of style, a way of moving and talking that fooled people. No one would have guessed where she came from. Eddie's fast crowd thought he'd latched on to a disinherited bad girl from the East Coast's upper crust. She let them believe it. Eddie liked the way his friends looked at her, and at him —so he let them believe it too. It became their secret, their joke. It became how Esmé thought of herself. She nurtured the stories, never admitting but never denying.

James knew she was divorced, but he didn't know *who* she was divorced from. And he didn't know how many she'd never married in the first place. Esmé had Leo Olemi's word that he wouldn't tell him. Why should he? He was in on the scam. And she sure as hell wasn't about to. As long as Eddie Baker stayed snugly in his little cell across the bay in San Quentin, he wasn't going to tell either. With his head newly shaved, Eddie was booked for a long stay: life, she hoped. The only reason he hadn't gotten the chair was because he hadn't pulled the damn trigger. Besides, the gun *he* toted along for the job was from the props department at Universal Studios. His last little scheme for the "big one" had gone blooey down in LA. Two cops got in the way; one of them died. Eddie's partner had brought along the real thing; his gun worked. It was the least funny thing Eddie ever did. When Esmé found out where his money came from, she could have told him it was a dumb idea—robbing a bank usually turns out to be a dumb idea—but Esmé was fragile and tender and sweet. So Eddie didn't listen. Oh, well, there were a lot more Eddies where he came from. But Esmé didn't want any more Eddie Bakers, or traveling salesmen who turn out to have wives in Omaha, Nebraska, or two-reel comedies where the joke was on her; she was over thirty now—time to shoot for the moon.

And who better than James Alexander Hamilton, San Francisco's good-looking district attorney, to catch it for her? Esmé knew she'd never tie him legally—marriage to her would sour his career, and divorce from the rich Lizzie Stafford curdle it. That was OK. She liked it the way it was. No cooking for Esmé, no cleaning, no darning socks, no sitting around doing her nails while second-rate men with third-rate brains played all-night crap games—just quiet out-of-the way bars, evenings at her place, bed. James had the same idea about her that Eddie's friends had had. Life was fine.

Thank God for Leo Olemi. He'd brought her with him to San Francisco just after Eddie went down. He'd been in LA scouting for talent—Eddie had been one of his try-outs, but Eddie blew it. After a few years hanging around with small-time grifters, just one step up from out-and-out losers, Esmé knew class when she saw it. When a girl hasn't any talent, she uses what talent she has. Leo was one smart cookie, connected with real operators back east, and he'd spotted her worth right away. James was his idea—fishing for him needed a woman's touch. Leo sought her out, bought her the right clothes, trusting her to choose them—and she chose well; she had a nose for the right look—he skipped the rest. Esmé was a New York girl; from somewhere she'd inherited class—she got the idea.

Neither Leo nor Esmé had thought she'd fall for the mean selfish bastard. But she had. Enough to make her dizzy, but not enough to make her stupid. She'd also discovered something very interesting. James wasn't a whole lot different from the Eddies and the Leos of the world. He had the same ambitions, even the same methods. The only real difference lay in the size of his ambitions, the scale of his methods. Eddie was a two-bit crook, Leo was a smart "businessman"—James was the big time. It altered Esmé's idea of the world, and of herself. Now she knew she was in line for a few breaks. The game was the same. She just wanted to win.

Leo had rented her a little frame house on Telegraph Hill. Tents full of wriggling Chilenos no longer straggled up and down the rocks and sudden small plateaus of Telegraph; now small brightly painted houses clung giddy to its sides. Telegraph was smaller than Nob Hill. Nob slid up sedately, crested grandly, then fell away stylishly toward the west. Telegraph leapt up, bristling. From the bottom, looking up, there were no ordered streets, just a jumble of distinct blocky shapes piled on top of one another. Esmé's house was halfway up; Esmé, standing on her redwood deck, was looking down. Her house, balanced on a boulder over the Embarcadero, was painted butter yellow, garlanded with bitter purple bougainvillea. Railed wooden steps, stained white with seasalt, zigzagged down to Sansome Street, where James waited for her in his car, a Hispano-Suiza brougham. The long snazzy foreign car was parked idling under a streetlamp, gleaming in the blue-white light. Esmé, snap-brim beaver hat slanted down over one brown eye, tripped down the dozens of steps, her red fox cubby over a tobacco-brown suit keeping out the evening cold.

It took Esmé exactly one minute to find out that James was in a bad mood. Normally he drove the big brougham fast enough to get wherever he wanted to go; tonight she was afraid the destination was hell. They whipped through the busy early-evening streets, skidded around corners, tires squealing, in the apparent direction of Golden Gate Park and the Pacific Ocean.

"Where are we going, James?" Esmé waited fifteen minutes to ask that question. She didn't smoke around James, so all she had to do with her time was not smoke, not bite her nails, not scream. Each was harder than the last. Esmé's simple question was all it took. What was bothering James poured out of him. Esmé was very wise; she listened.

The control that James had over his most precious weapon, his voice, was pushed to its limit. He was talking about his wife. The usual calm flippancy he used when he told Esmé about Lizzie was now a hot nervous anger. Esmé was intrigued. Mrs. Hamilton was no threat to her because *she* was no threat to Mrs. Hamilton. Lizzie was a spoiled little rich girl, and as far as Esmé could tell, she was going to stay that way. Esmé knew the rules. But my goodness, what *had* Lizzie done?

The story James told Esmé wasn't anything like the way he'd put his marital problems to Addy Chase. He was acting with Addy at the Pacific Union Club. With Esmé the truth came out. "The silly bitch is making me look bad. Do you have any idea how careful a politician has to be about his personal life? And to top it all off, she knows about you!"

"Oh, hell." Esmé didn't like that. Wives could be a nuisance. When the little woman really started putting on the pressure, very few men came down on the other woman's side. To put it more succinctly, they took a powder.

James wasn't listening to Esmé. By now, he'd got into his stride. "I had to listen to what she thought of it after the party. But that doesn't matter, I made it clear I had no intention of changing my ways for her. What matters is what she did last night."

Esmé relaxed. *That* was exactly what mattered to her. Anything else James had to say came a poor second.

"First she disappears for twenty-four hours, running around with that smug newspaper bastard Dowie, and tonight while I was trying to think of an excuse for why I was going out, she comes out of her room in some red dress I've never seen before, looks at me like I did something to *her,* and leaves. Like that. Not a word. Leaves." James's all-American jawline was so tense Esmé could almost hear his bones crack. "But, guess what the bitch did last night! Go on, guess!"

"I can't imagine," said Esmé. This was disturbing stuff. Tit for tat from the wife was something men couldn't handle. It surprised and scared them. They actually thought it wasn't fair. Boneheads! Maybe Lizzie wasn't so stupid. Esmé didn't like that idea at all.

"She poured a jug of water, all of it, into my bed—in the middle of last night, with *me* still sleeping in it! When I woke up, I thought I'd pissed myself—until I found she'd been spying on me. Reading one of the letters I'd written to you, a juicy one. What does the little green-eyed bitch think she's doing, looking through my papers?"

Esmé made a mistake—she laughed. Until she caught the look in James's eye. Whatever he thought, he didn't think it was funny. The look on his face was so odd, like a little boy drowning, that Esmé slid over on the seat and gently touched his frozen cheek.

"I'm sorry, James, I shouldn't have laughed. It

wasn't funny." Esmé meant it. Something about Hamilton, San Francisco's hope for national attention, another woman's husband, and what a woman—San Francisco's daffy society madcap—had got to her. For all his manipulating disguised as charm, his rapaciousness pretending to be mere ambition, the way he held himself aloof—she didn't kid herself—even from her, there was that dopey little boy inside somewhere. Like there was in all men. Like all women, Esmé was a sucker for it. "Let me make it up to you." James almost drove the Hispano-Suiza into the Pacific while Esmé proved her worth.

The brougham slid up outside a moderate-sized hotel in Half Moon Bay, all red Spanish tiles and whitewash, little wrought-iron grilles around the mission-style windows, a couple of dusty palm trees and too many potted geraniums. Half Moon Bay was a nice long drive south from San Francisco down the peninsula. It was one of California's small towns, grown plump on pumpkins and bootlegging. It was nine in the evening, and the midsummer sun, like one of the Bay's fruitier orange melons, was finally snuggling down into the sizzling ocean. James cut the motor.

"Here comes business," he said. The voice was back to normal. Smooth and slippery. Esmé followed suit. "I'm meeting someone here who could get me into a whole lot of trouble if I don't handle him right. So watch and listen but keep your mouth shut. Bringing you with me means I trust you, you understand?"

Esmé nodded. She understood. Bringing her along didn't mean he trusted her. Men like James didn't trust anyone, which was the smart way to play it. It meant that James hadn't wanted to come on this particular errand alone. Taking her was, no doubt, his safest bet. Going places with Eddie Baker used to scare her; they were apt to end up badly, and for what? Going places with Leo Olemi scared her too, but for completely different reasons. With him, Esmé might wind up learning something it wasn't safe for a girl to know. With James, it was amusing. She loved to watch him throw pitches—fast balls. The guy was a whiz in power plays. She amended that. Except when it came to women. He didn't know a thing about women.

Fifteen minutes later Esmé and James were sitting in a hotel room, moderate swank for a moderate hotel. The furniture was cane, the walls had murals of early Spanish mission life: lots of priests and happy Indians and burros loaded down with Bibles. Each was holding a drink, but the man pacing the room had two: one on the go, one waiting.

Edward Laurence Doheny, Jr., was the son of a Los Angeles tycoon, Edward Laurence Doheny, Sr. Senior was one of the richest men in America, controlling California's oil production. He'd come to southern California a dirt-poor roughneck Irishman, a ragged prospector—just like his good friend Albert Fall, Harding's erstwhile Secretary of the Interior—discovered crude bubbling out of the ground, decided he was an aristocrat, and turned into a lavish spender to prove it. Senior bought a little kingdom for himself right in the middle of LA. His son was the same age as James Hamilton. With nothing like the moxie of his father, Junior did his father's bidding. After meeting the golden James Hamilton in Paris during the war, he also did James's bidding. The most noticeable thing about Edward Doheny was his mouth. The lower lip was as full as a young Negro's, but the upper was long, thin, and pinched. That made his nose look short. And piggish. Edward showed too much gum when he smiled, but since he was in no mood to do much smiling, it didn't matter. Besides that, he was essentially normal. Nice suit, nice haircut. He was a bit fleshy, but his clothes fitted. In his own environment Esmé thought he probably held his own, but not in a small hotel in Half Moon Bay. Here he was as nervous as a drop of water on hot fat. James's bringing her didn't help. Junior kept looking at her like she'd bite him if he wasn't careful.

"There's a rumor, Hamilton, a rumor, mind, that old Harding is having a nervous breakdown."

It took Esmé less than a heartbeat to realize that James was into something big. Harding! The President of the United States! Eddie Baker wasn't even worth two bits, he was a raw peanut.

"When Father leased the rights on the Elk Hills fields, Albert Fall assured us that nobody back in Washington would be any the wiser. Some friend Albert's turning out to be! They're getting wise, dammit, and they're getting wise fast. A bunch of them have set up a special committee to investigate. I told you already that two of Harding's boys killed themselves, one from the Justice Department, for Christ's sake, and Albert has already resigned from the government. That's how close the investigation's getting. Hell, I'm just a businessman. Dad's oil company is one of the biggest and the most respected in the whole United States. If this shit gets out, where the hell will I be? My God, if the fucking President can't cut it, what about the rest of us? We negotiated those leases in good faith, as a patriotic duty. The country needed money and we provided it. Fucking hell, it was *me* who gave Fall the money for them, in cash—one hundred thousand dollars. I cut you in in good faith, James. Fall told me that the government had the right to lease and that, as Secretary of the Interior, *he* had the right to do the negotiating. Now it turns out that the land was federal reserve land, navy land, supposed to be kept in trust for the goddam nation. The fucking people! When some senator thinks he's got the ear of the 'people,' guys get their fucking balls cut off. Do you know what Harding's boys have done with the money they got for those leases on federal oil land? *My* goddam money? Put it in their own pockets, that's what they've done with it! The Washington press has already got a name for the mess those assholes have dumped us in—Teapot Dome."

Sipping his drink, James had let him run. Now that Doheny had finally stopped whining, James spoke. "Excuse me, Junior, but in the privacy of this room are you trying to snow me? Good faith? You knew what the land had been allocated for, and the oil under it—national emergencies. They set it up right after the war. If someone in the oil business doesn't know that, something's wrong somewhere. And if you didn't know where your money was going, I'm Whistler's mother. Is this the story you're going to try and peddle? Bought for patriotism? If so, it stinks. I don't want you trying that on anyone else, not if you and I are sticking together on this. I'm sorry, but if we're to help each other here, you'll have to cut the crap."

Doheny's fat bottom lip stuck out farther. "No need for that attitude, James. And don't call me Junior."

"What attitude is that, Ed Junior? We're in the shit —I amend, your father and you are in the shit. The leases are in your company's name with your little signature at the bottom of the sales ticket. *You* handed the money over to Fall. As a new friend of mine would say"—James winked at Esmé, by new friend she knew he meant Olemi —"you were the bagman. Isn't that true?"

"Yes, but . . ." Doheny squirmed. Esmé enjoyed watching him. Her respect for James was blooming like a peach.

"Yes, but what? You're going to tell me that you'll tell anybody investigating *you* that *I* am involved? Is that what you'd do, Edward?"

"Well, I . . . no, of course not. But what am I going to do? This is turning into a fucking national scandal. Heads are going to roll. It could mean prison for me. Maybe for you! What do you think Fall or Harding is going to do? Christ, where's the bottle?"

James allowed himself a small smile. "I won't be going to jail, not for this. A good friend of mine is a good friend of President Harding. Mr. Harding is due in San Francisco around the end of July—let me see, that's how long?"

"Less than three weeks," said Esmé.

"Well, then, what are we all worried about?"

"What do you mean, what are we all worried about?" Doheny squeaked. "You know damn well what we're all worried about!"

Patience was in James's every gesture. He stretched his long legs out onto the coffee table, poured another drink for Esmé, one for himself, and held out the bottle to Doheny. Edward's glass shook as James filled it for him. "Don't you have any seltzer?"

"I could ring room service."

"Don't bother. We've gotten along without it so far." James let a minute go by, savoring his whiskey. He waited until the pig-nosed man was close to tears. "Maybe when the President gets here, something could be done."

Doheny turned pale. "Something done? What do you mean, something done?"

"Oh, I don't know, something."

James looked at Esmé. Esmé looked at James. "Well, all we've really got to be afraid of is the old fool talking, isn't it?"

"Yes and no." Now Doheny was sweating. He struggled with his neat businessman's tie, pulled it away from his wet neck.

"Well, that's all I'm worried about. My name isn't on anything—my shares are in your name. If you talked, I could laugh it off. If Harding talked, or Fall, it might not be so easy. So we make sure Warren doesn't—talk, that is. Simple?"

Doheny waved his hands like Pontius Pilate. The ice in his glass slopped out, landing on the hotel rug. "My God, Hamilton, whatever that something is, I don't want to know about it. You keep me out of it."

James stared at Edward Doheny, Jr., an up-from-under glance. "But you want it done, don't you?"

"Jesus Christ, we're talking about the President of the United States here!"

"We're talking, good friend, about a very nervous egg that's about to get scrambled."

The ride back to San Francisco was electric. Esmé sat on her side of the car buzzing, her eyes dazzled by the city's luminous glow as the brougham slid into downtown San Francisco. Fitzing acres of colored light giving the come-on from picture palaces, theater marquees, billboards: Arrow collars, Sunkist oranges, Ever-Ready shaving brushes. A million American lightbulbs and French neon tubes outshining the California stars.

What a vat of French perfume she'd landed in when she said yes to Leo! To smooth his way into taking over the city's bootlegging business, Leo wanted her to do a classy vamp on some lawyer up in Frisco. She found herself wooing a winner. From an orphanage on the tough side of New York to the mistress of the future President! Esmé hugged herself. Of course, she was supposed to tell Leo whatever she could learn about James. Should she tell him about this? Maybe. Maybe not.

James spent the drive telling her what *they* were going to do to make sure Harding kept his mouth shut. It was risky; hell, more than that, it could put her where Eddie was.

Her part of the deal would be easier than doing walk-ons for Ziegfeld. It was going to be the best role she'd ever played in her life. But she wasn't worried. Esmé Baker had nerve. And with this lark, she had James Hamilton.

*Chapter 10*

Smelling of American money and foreign perfume, Lizzie was sitting at the bar of the Blue Canary. Her dress was by Chéruit, a clinging red-and-gold lamé gown cut so low in front and back that it forced her to sit up straight. Even so, the swell of her small high breasts was barely covered—the *haute couture* bodice merely two wide strips of glimmering red-gold from her bare shoulders to her solar plexus. She'd pulled her black hair back into a small chignon fastened with a red rose and a ruby clip, both the real thing, and the heels of her red satin slippers were hooked onto the bar stool for balance. Lizzie was trying to look as if she belonged there. She'd succeeded so well she'd been asked her price three times. But after an hour of her snappy turndowns, she was getting left alone. The black jazz band was playing something else she'd never heard before: slow and snaky, with a lot of hissing high-hat and muted cornet. Lizzie wanted and didn't want Dido to sing. So far, no Dido. People were laughing and drinking, washing up against the long curved bar like a high tide, and there wasn't an Oriental in the place. Lizzie's nerve was going.

"If you're waitin' for Dowie, looks like you been stood up."

"Pardon?"

Appetite Ike, the barman, was squinting at her from his side of the bar. "I said, it looks like—"

Lizzie tried out a little laugh. There was some humor in it. "No, I haven't been stood up. I'm not waiting for anyone."

Ike thought about that, chewing something. "You coulda fooled me. Dames don't come here too much by their lonesome. You wanna talk?"

"Talk?" Lizzie looked at the little old man. What was left of Ike's gray hair stood up in random tufts like mattress ticking, the stretched, shining skin underneath was freckled with age, and coarse white hairs sprouted from his ears and nostrils. Plus his red bow tie was crooked. But behind the squint and the huge pores and the broken veins mapping his bulbous nose were the most curious eyes, lemur-bright and young. "About what?"

"How would I know, girlie? You're the customer. I been listenin' to Rose's customers for twenty-one years. Mostly men. The men, they wanna talk about wimmin or money. Wimmin usually like to talk about theirselves. That's jake with me. I likes wimmin. Ain't so predictable as men. So shoot. I got time."

Women like to talk about themselves? That amused Lizzie. In her case, at least, it was true. The old man was staring at her, chewing and waiting. Lizzie could talk about herself for hours. On the subject of Lizzie Stafford Hamilton, she could probably give a seminar. But somehow, somewhere, her interest had slipped down a notch or two. Lizzie found herself wanting to listen, to ask the old man questions. Lord, she had lots of questions. For instance, about Li. Who was he? Where had he come from? What was he to Rose St. Lorraine? Why was he so tall? Weren't Chinese people little, like children or dwarfs? But she couldn't just plunge into something like that. Ike might get cagey, ask her why she wanted to know. And he might tell Kit later; she didn't want that damn Dowie sitting in judgment on her. The look he'd given her the night before when she first set eyes on Li wasn't something Lizzie wanted to see again. It was hard enough to walk on. So she would have to wheedle and coax this funny old specimen, bring Appetite to the subject of Li gradually. She hadn't a clue how to do that.

Lizzie had no subtlety. She was direct, blunt and honest, though honesty was a chancy hit-or-miss kind of thing. Honest was what she felt at the moment. An hour later she could feel quite the opposite. Sometimes that was good and sometimes that was bad. It was certainly confusing—for Lizzie *and* for anyone trying to understand her. The old man was right; Lizzie wanted to talk. He was also wrong; she didn't want to talk about herself, at least not until she got a few facts sorted out. So she dived in the only way she knew how, at the deep end.

"Why aren't Addy Chase and Rose married?"

Ike wheezed, his eyebrows bristling. "That's Rose's business. If I told you, Rose'd stick lit matches under my toenails, all of 'em. Have one of them sticky things you drink on me, an' ask me another. I ain't answerin' that one."

"All right. Doesn't Rose ever come down on the floor?"

"You kiddin'? Rose makes her grand entrance after midnight. That's when this joint comes alive. If it wasn't for Rose St. Lorraine, this dump'd be nuthin' but a clip joint. How d'ya think we gets away with chargin' twenty-five smackers for a bottle of champagne? An' why? So she gets called the Texas Guinan of Frisco? It makes Rose spit. 'Cause she ain't another nuthin'. Insults the customers, calls 'em suckers, gets on an' belts 'em a song when she feels like it. Rose's one of a kind."

Lizzie had just then thought of a question she could ask Ike that wasn't about Li but, remembering what Dido had hissed at her the night before, might bring the old fellow around to where she wanted to go.

"I drink expensive champagne now, thanks. Tell me about Dido."

"It's your nickel, but girlie, you ask some big ones. Stuff that could get you an' me in dutch." Ike popped open a bottle of the Canary's best, poured some out, and slid the glass across the bar, leaning over after it. "But seein' it's you, an' seein' as how if you're gonna hang around here it's somethin' you oughta know, an' also seein' as how I don't give a good goddam, I'll tell you a little story."

Lizzie leaned forward as well. She had to do it carefully; the Chéruit gown wouldn't go with her. Her sleek black head, with its ruby and rose, and Ike's wayward tufts were almost touching. Old men smell old, a dry blow-away smell like deserted houses. Ike smelled like sourdough, tobacco spit, and cocktail onions.

"It's like this." Ike paused for effect. "That Dido showed up at Rose's first joint, Silver Street, in early 1906, year of the fire, lookin' for a job, an' Rose didn't have but one type of job for a looker like that nigra gal. She weren't more'n fifteen, sixteen, an' I'm damned if any of us knew where she learned her stuff or where she came from in the first place, but she didn't need no teachin' an' she didn't do no explainin'. Spent seven years for Rose like that, had pro'bly five men, mebbe more, die right in her room. Didn't stop any of the rest of 'em, though. They just kep' on askin' for Dido."

"Men died!"

"Yep. Gave 'em heart attacks. An' cold! You never met someone cold as that girl, 'less you bumped into the abommible snowman. We all just kep' outa her way, all 'cept Kit an' Li. But they was just kids, younger'n her. Didn't know no better."

Appetite checked the floor for signs of Rose, then spat something brown somewhere behind the bar. "For some reason, Dido took to Kit like fleas to a dog, though he was somethin' like five years younger'n her—an' white to boot. Girl, that's the only human she ever let near! I means, of course, near her heart, but I won't take bets she had one, then er now. An' Kit took to *her,* got to hangin' around Silver Street all times of the day er night, doodlin' at the piano, the both of 'em makin' up songs. Kit had him a daddy back then, but he *didn't* have a daddy, you get me? An' no ma at all. She died on him somewhere along the way. Any time the kid went on home, the bastard just beat the livin' shit outa him—a mean, shiftless, no-count drunk, that was Kit's daddy. None of us minded a bit when the kid made us his home. Anyways, Kit took that crap from his old man, but he didn't take doodly-squat from nobody else. I can't tell you, girlie, how many scrapes he got hisself into as he growed up. That boy had the charm of a minstrel, but he had him the guts of a momma grizzly. He was small an' he was wiry, but he was plenty tough, a street scrapper. Even after Boo Hoo Brown broke his nose an' both his arms. When Kit dragged hisself back to Rose, she paid for the damages, an' Dido nursed him like he was her baby. Must have been fourteen then. Boo Hoo outweighed him by fifty pounds, an' he was older by four years."

This was all news to Lizzie. When she was fourteen, she was going to *thés dansants* in her very own barouche, drawn by her very own chestnut gelding, Jingles. "What happened to Boo Hoo Brown?"

"He learned hisself some respect for Kit Dowie, but he didn't learn nuthin' else. Boo Hoo's doin' twenty-to-life in Folsom for beatin' a guy in a grocery store to death. Poor fella just didn't wanna get robbed, is all." Ike reached idly down and scratched the seat of his pants. "But as for that poor Chinese kid, Li—"

Li! Lizzie had a home run first time up at bat, and she hadn't even had to try her hand at subtlety.

"Jesus! Dido put that boy through pure hell from the moment Rose brought 'im home after the quake; bitch barely waited until we got his kid sister buried."

"You buried Li's sister?"

"Shee-it, yes! You shoulda seed what Rose did. Everythin' proper, Chinese-style, gongs an' liddle bells an' white everywheres. Had a big colored picture of liddle Su Yin, that was his sister's name, hangin' off a pole like a banner. Burnt up so much red paper for offerin's, or whatever they was, thought we'd burn the damn town down again. Oh, boy, it sure was somethin'! We couldn't find the rest of his family, not even the buildin' they died in, fire got all of it, so the funeral for Su Yin had to make do for 'em all. But you know how some folks hates niggers? Well, Dido hated Li like that, 'cause he was Chinese. At least, that's what I figure. Why else was she after him any chance she got? Anyone else she frosted, like they wasn't there, an' that went for her customers too."

Ike slapped the top of his head. "Gotta itch," he explained.

"The Chinese kid had a tough life growin' up here whenever Dido had the time to go for him. Never did it in front of me er Rose, but the rest of the time it was hell. Only person who could stop er was Kit. An' he did, too! Christ, that made Dido's ice crack! We used to laugh about it. Now"—Ike wagged the one finger he still had on his hand—"here's the point of this story, in case you was wonderin'—"

Lizzie interrupted. "I didn't know you could talk so much, Appetite. You were so quiet last night."

"Can't get a word in edgewise around Rose. Woman could talk the feathers off a parrot. So, I was sayin'. The Chinese kid was growin' like a bean plant, an' he'd read hisself ev'ry book in Rose's parlor an' ev'ry book in Addy Chase's too, an' then he started on the public liberry. When he wasn't readin', he was off somewheres in that Chinatown of his. We didn't ask him what he was doin' there, Rose said it weren't none of our business—but he'd become like a mascot to the place. Li Kwan Won was kind of a faraway kid. He didn't talk much, even after he learned English, an' he kep' outa people's way, specially Dido's. Some of the girls thought he was chicken; me, I thought he was smart. Anyways, one slow Sunday, them girls didn't have much to do, an' Li was curled up on the sofa in the back parlor readin' another book, when Dido came sashayin' down the stairs lookin' like a African devil doll carved outa ebony—hard, you know, with corners." Ike wiped his mouth and looked around. His scratchy old voice lowered. "I was tryin' to fix somethin' gone wrong with some pipe outside the window, an' she didn't see me out there. Still don't know I know, nor Li neither."

Lizzie's green eyes glittered. Her breathing was pinched. "What happened?"

"Not much, no, not much—but it was enough to keep that black bitch off him till now. Almost ten years' worth of enough. You musta noticed how big she is, taller'n lots of men, an' strong; Christ, girlie, never mistake that. Li was almost growed an' he wasn't short, but nuthin' like ole Dido. Kit an' her—like Mutt an' Jeff, right? So, Li's just sittin' there, keepin' hisself to hisself, an' she struts on over to him, then just flips Li's book outa his hands. It comes flyin' 'cross the room an' smacks into the wall, *splat!* Then she puts her hands on her hips, grinnin' down at him. Me, I woulda scooted outa there fast. But not Li. He sits there. Not smilin', just lookin' patient. So she says, 'Smells in this room. I wonder why is that?' But he still sits there. So she kicks his leg, hard too. The Chinese kid gets up slow an' starts for his book. 'Where you goin', pooch?' she calls after him. But he don't answer, just picks up his book an' starts back for the sofa. But Dido steps in front of him, blockin' his way. An' shee-it, from where even I was, she looked big! 'Didn't you hear me, slant-eyes?' she says. 'Chink dogs ain't allowed in the house.' She was talkin' real slow, like she thought he had to read her lips. By then, I thought the kid was whupped 'cause he turned an' went for the door. But Dido just couldn't leave it alone, not when she thought she was winnin'. She goes right after him, pushin' so he stumbles, an' just as he's got his hand on the doorknob, turnin' it, she pulls him away from the door an' hits him. Not an open-handed slap like wimmin do, no, by golly, a punch with a fist—"

Lizzie remembered Dido's pounding on Kit's door.

"—an' she catches him a good one right on the button. Li goes down, an' while he's down, she kicks him an' then she kicks him some more. Don't suppose you ever been kicked with them pointy-toed wimmin's shoes?"

Her green eyes round with interest, Lizzie shook her head, no.

Ike leaned in closer. It made Lizzie's interested round eyes cross. "You know who you remind me of?" he said. "You remind me of one of them kids in the movies, 'Our Gang.' Always gettin' in trouble, them kids, but real cute." Then he leaned back, and Lizzie could focus on him again. "That kickin' must have hurt like bejesus, an' Li took it. By this time, I'm thinkin' on how I better gets in there an' do some stompin', woman er no woman, even if that shiny licorice stick ups an' cripples me. You think I'm old now? I was old *then*—but then somethin' happened I ain't never seen before an' only seed a few times since. Last thing I knew, Li was on the floor, an' next thing I knew he was on his feet; how he got up that fast, I don't know. But the first thing outa his mouth is some blood-curdlin' Chinese stuff, an' then the fastest handwork I ever hope to see. Not that I saw it—all I saw was Dido flyin', an' I mean flyin', like some black crow, and Li after her, but slow, like on a vaudeville wire. Gave me the spooks. Dido came down ten feet from me, landin' flat on her back, *ooof!* It took all that cold air right outa her. Li was standin' over *her* now, not even breathin' hard. What he said was, 'I am Rose's son. This is my home, Dido. You work here. You will not touch me again.' Then he walks out. I ain't never seen that girl look humble, an' she didn't look humble then. But she sure as duck shit looked like she'd learned what *careful* meant."

A thirsty couple down the bar caught Ike's eye. The Blue Canary's five lesser bartenders were working flat out. "The long an' short of it is, 'less you got some smart Chinese moves, I'd steer clear of Dido." Ike limped off toward his customers. "Why don't you go on upstairs an' do some gamblin'?" he called back over his shoulder. "A gal who ain't waitin' ought to be doin' *somethin'*!"

Gambling? Lizzie had never gambled before, except for some foolish bets at Tanforan racetrack, but then she'd never gone to the movies alone before either. So why not? Besides, maybe the mysterious Li with the smart Chinese moves was upstairs.

The crowd around the Blue Canary's gaming tables felt different. Smelled different. Downstairs it was the sharp odor of anticipation; upstairs it was a sour fever. The faces here were strained, and the eyes carried a certain slant of light Lizzie had seen only when Mary Maud was scheming over another of her committees. But here they weren't forming committees; they were throwing money away. Rose must be loaded.

There were fewer people in this room—a high vault of dark oak paneling, conical light in smoky yellow pools over the tables, huge oil paintings of old San Francisco on the walls, an echo of cool jazz drifting up from the floor below—but the people seemed bigger, swollen with some kind of hot, unthinking need.

Lizzie wandered over to a roulette table, her Chéruit rustling between her long silken legs, her slippers noiseless on the dark carpet. Two men in evening dress turned their heads briefly from the game, gave her an appreciative once-over, and made room.

"Place your bets, ladies and gentlemen—"

The croupier was talking in a rapid clip, but it was gibberish to Lizzie. So she did what neither the man on her left nor her right did—she played the black. Black came up.

"The lady wins."

The croupier had a square face, casual eyes, and a long stick that reminded Lizzie of a hoe. He used it to push a pile of chips toward her. This was fun—and easy. The lady wins, does she? Lizzie played the black again. Then she watched the wheel spin.

Twenty minutes later Lizzie had caught the swollen fever. Her green eyes had the same slant of hard light and her chignon was losing its tight black curve against her slender neck; Li was forgotten; Ike's warning about Dido; James and Esmé. Her whole world was a little ball clicking in a spinning silver wheel, the colored chips stacked on her side of the table, the hum of strangers urging her on to higher stakes. Lizzie didn't notice when Dido showed up, a black smile on her cold beautiful face. Lizzie pushed everything she'd won onto number nine. Her heart caught like a stinging bee in a closed fist, as she heard the gasps of dismay around her. The odds on a single number were thirty-five to one, but Lizzie didn't know that. What was the matter with them? It was her money.

"The lady plays nine," she heard the croupier call. "All bets in now, ladies and gentlemen." His voice was flat. Lizzie looked up. His eyes no longer looked so casual; they looked worried. He didn't spin the wheel.

"Is there anything wrong?" she asked in the tense silence.

The croupier turned his square sweating face into the crowd, question marks in his eyes. Puzzled, Lizzie followed the question to its answer. The Chinese was standing across the table from her. The skin of her face tightened; her nerves sang with quick poison. Where had he come from? When? The croupier was asking the Chinese—he was asking *him* if he could allow Lizzie's bet. Li?

The chips, the wheel, her fever spun away. Lizzie was shaken by Li's beauty—by *his* beauty? She felt a thin whip of white lightning zap from her to him, smoking the air. It took something from Lizzie, but it gave nothing back. The electricity stayed there. With him. And died. But she had his attention, his damned attention. He was looking at her at last.

Li nodded to the croupier, yes. The man spun the wheel and Lizzie forced herself to look at it, became hypnotized, watched until it ran down, slower and slower, the little ball's connected *burr* disconnecting, separating into distinct clicks—to stop on number nine. Lizzie's head flashed up in triumph. Look at that! Look at that, you cold yellow son of a bitch. But he wasn't there. Li was gone. He'd done it to her again. The light in Lizzie's eyes wasn't slanted now. It was broken and bent and dark. Fuck him! She didn't say that, a lady doesn't, but she thought it.

"Bring me a drink, the whole bottle. And stuff your champagne."

Among the strangers, Dido laughed. That was when Lizzie saw her.

Li had gone to Rose's rooms.

At the age of twenty-seven Li Kwan Won wasn't a lost little Chinese boy any more; he wasn't even Chinese. He wasn't white either. Li was Li. An island. He dressed white. When he needed them to be, his words were white; his accent, culled from the classier customers that Rose's Blue Canary had lured over the years, was soft and soothing and careful of meaning. Li knew the power of words, his father's legacy. Like James Hamilton, Li used his voice, but for a different purpose. James was a fisher of men; when he spoke he cast a net, ensnaring others to further himself. When Li spoke, he was an artist using a palette of sound. His mind was oriental. When he spoke English it was shaded with a light ironic touch. Dropping into his own tongue, he used brighter colors, speaking with a western directness that lit up the ancient dark places. Li belonged wholly to no language, claimed no race or country. It was not his choice.

When he was ten, Li had been thrown into a white world that didn't want him. By his late twenties he had made a world among them that *he* didn't want—but was all he could have, a place for himself that he held together with all the strength of his angry soul. A twilight world of half-remembered Chinese dreams, old visions lit by a western sun. The dreams the white ghosts dreamed were harsh acquisitive dreams, jealous, violent, and righteous. When Li was a boy he had been bewildered by the rush of raw light; by the time he became a man he understood these worlds well. To the *baak gwai lo* he was Chinese. Though his English was flawless, his clothes correct, his manner direct, he was still Chinese. A stranger among a ruthless, pushing people—a race that loathed strangeness. To his own, to the Han people, though his Chinese was fluent, and in Chinatown, wearing the garb of a young male, blending by its drab colors and simple lines into the whole, his manner subtle, observant of tradition, he was not Chinese. There, he was a stranger too and his people called him *jook sing*—American-born, crazy, a half ghost. A stranger in Chinatown, where his people cowered, forced by white hatred to live together in poverty and fear and hopelessness. Where there were few young Chinese women for a young man, *any* young Chinese man, to court. Outside Chinatown, there were no women at all. America had made it illegal for Orientals to marry whites. It might mean death to try. San Francisco's Chinatown was a ghetto of bachelors.

And neither of these worlds trusted Li, because both saw the other in his face.

Once separate from his own, Li had two choices. The first was to sink under, hide, become small. The second was to rise, to grow large, too big to be hurt. Either way he would remain a stranger. When he lost his father and his mother, his brother Chang, Su Yin—especially Su Yin—there was nothing left to lose.

Li chose to rise. Like San Francisco.

He would never be a tailor as his father had wished; he would not be a scholar like his brother—for that he needed instruction in the Chinese doctrines, the tenets of Confucianism, in Buddhism, in magic. And what did the static Chinese teachings, learned by rote, or the Mandarins, have to do with America? Li would have to become educated in western thinking, western culture. So he read. If he had no teacher, no one to guide him, he would teach himself.

One of the first things the ten-year-old Li learned was what the white man thought of the Chinese. From Bret Harte's "Heathen Chinee," to Kipling, to Sax Rohmer's *Fu Manchu,* Li read it all. The dime novels of Horatio Alger taught him that any American child possessed of an earnest heart could rise from nothing by the sweat of his honest brow to become the President of the United States. Harte and Rohmer and Jack London made it clear what Alger hadn't bothered to point out in his rags-to-riches stories. Why should he bother? It was self-evident. *Any* child, as long as that child was white. Alger called the Chinese a "rather superior sort of monkey." London described them as a "wicked race, evil, cunning, and cruel." In his stories he pitted them against Anglo-Saxons. The whites always won.

The Chinese boy, lost in America, had sat stunned in Rose's rooms, books and magazines scattered on the carpet near his feet. He stared into Rose's mirror. A superior sort of monkey? Was that what was in his face? Li had looked at his hands, stretching the fingers. Weren't they human? He wished with all his shamed child's heart that he *was* white.

Until he sought out the Chinese books and the old people who could teach him. From them he learned why the Chinese called white men *baak gwai lo:* white devils, ghosts. He read about the origins of the opium trade, how Britain had forced the Indian drug upon the Chinese people to prise open an untapped market of millions, of the

French and German and British push into his father's land, slaughtering the people as they resisted modern weapons with ancient ones, the French and British sacking and burning the Summer Palace in Peking, destroying a thousand years of Chinese culture. About Crocker's "coolies," poor labor lured by the promise of wages, now trapped in a foreign land, slaves who built America's railroads when white men refused, saying the work wasn't fit for dogs. And when the tracks were laid and the easy gold was gone, the Chinese were driven from the mines they had worked, stoned from small settlements in the western states. Han people, their few women and children, were murdered in white raids. From these Li learned anger.

Four years after he came to live with the loud woman, Rose, Li went back to Chinatown. If he would be a stranger in both worlds, he would also rise in both. Take from both. Patience and breadth of mind from the Oriental; from the Caucasian, energy, ambition, the sense that a man can make the world his by vision and effort. Li had only himself—and Rose.

In 1917, America sent him to fight in Europe's war. She didn't want his mind—after all, it was a monkey's mind—or his heart. If it contained honor, if it sought peace, what could America do with that? But she needed, as she always had, his strong back; she needed the numbers, the bodies to leave on the soil of Europe. Calling cards. Tokens of her strength. Markers. There were so many left behind. Fallen among the white were red, black, yellow. Li survived. He came home to Rose's. Now, after anger, came contempt. He finally knew who America thought he was—a body for his country, a coolie for the money-makers, a scapegoat for the unsuccessful master race, the "yellow peril" for the mythmakers, a changeling for the Chinese. But on the blood-soaked soil of a foreign battlefield he discovered who he really was— Li Kwan Won: not white, not Chinese, a human being, alone—and what he wanted: value.

The only value the whites understood was the value of money. He would start there. With Rose as a white screen, a go-between, Li set himself to make money.

There was only one way for a Chinese to do that. He became a criminal, and he started with America's gift to the criminal—Prohibition and bootlegging.

There is strength in numbers, but there is power in a man who knows himself.

Framed in loops of frothy white lace curtains, Li was standing at Rose's window looking down at Mason Street. Spike in her sleeve, Rose paced the white carpet behind him, her hands moving, her soft face hard with anger. Sergeant Huggins paced with her, tongue lolling.

"The dirty dogs. What's the world coming to? How could they do it, sticking it to their own people!"

Li smiled. "When has it been any different, Rose? When has the color of a man's skin changed his soul? Greed—it belongs to us all. The Chinese merchants pick on their own poor because, aside from themselves, that is all there is in Chinatown."

Rose snorted. "Poor pickings, then."

"Poor, but available."

"But there's you, goddammit. They're your people less than five blocks away from where we're standing, getting shook down and robbed. So, what are you going to *do* about it?"

"What do you expect me to do? The Six Companies have ruled Chinatown with their goons for years, and the city officials let them run it. That way they don't have to worry about the Chinese; as long as Chinatown preys upon itself, they leave the whites alone."

Rose glared at him. "So stop them. Use *your* goons."

Slowly, Li turned away from the window and sat on an elegant divan, one of Rose's mementoes from Silver Street. "The Triad has no goons." He took a cigarette from a crystal box on Rose's low table. "As for the merchants of the Six Companies, I have already begun to deal with them, in my own way."

Rose shrieked, punching a pillow near his head. Spike howled. "Damn you, Li. Getting me all worked up for nothing. I was just about ready to grab Appetite and a gun and charge over to Chinatown myself. Why do you do that to me?"

"To see your fine red anger."

"You want to see anger? I'll show you my fine red fist."

Li drew deeply on his cigarette, let the smoke out, and said, "Ah, Rose, I spoke too soon. I should have let you and Ike loose on Chinatown. It would have been a sight. Still, we have worse problems than the roughing up of poor laundrymen. Our friend Murray Blinn is trying to move in on our business. I'm told he claims we have hijacked one of his shipments. No doubt he was hijacked, perhaps even by Chinese, but my people had nothing to do with it. I'm checking into his accusations now. In any case, three of our speaks have been strongarmed by Blinn's men in supposed retaliation."

"Blinn!" said Rose. "Saddle Mary's little snot can't do anything to us, can he?"

"I think, Rose, he already has. Murray is showing a strange confidence that is unlike him. That confidence, and certainly the intelligence behind it, must belong to someone else."

"Who?"

"I have my ideas. Soon we shall know for certain."

"Well, we'd—what the blue hell is that?" Rose strode to her door and jerked it open. "What's going on out here? Can't a lady have some privacy in her own home? Get away from—holy smoke, it's Lizzie! What's the matter with you, girl?"

Lizzie swept past Rose and Sergeant Huggins in a swirl of red-and-gold lamé, her chignon unbunned, her rose lost, the ruby clip clutched in one hand and a bottle of bourbon in the other. Right behind her came two of Li's men, pulling vainly at her arms. They both looked ashamed and outgunned. When she got to the dead center of Rose's white room, Lizzie stopped and raised an unsteady but dramatic finger, tipped by a bright red nail. *"He's* what's the matter!" She was pointing at Li. "Whaz wrong with *him?* Whaz he think I am, a bug?"

"Cripes," said Rose, "she's drunk."

"I am not drunk. I am outraged." Now Lizzie was shouting. "Why does that man keep snubbing me? I've never been snubbed, not in my whole life, an' never by a Chinaman!" Lizzie ended on a high squeak and then passed out. Her silken legs scissored under her. She hit Rose's soft carpet with an undignified thud.

Rose walked over to the warm body, snatching up the bourbon bottle before it glugged out all over her white rug. "That was some show. I could have used her in the old days. What was she talking about?"

Li followed. Lizzie's shoes had fallen off. He picked up one of the small red slippers and held it. "The lady is confusing me with someone else, someone in a movie perhaps."

"Who do you mean? Valentino?"

Li shrugged and dropped the shoe. He motioned to one of the embarrassed men, his second-in-command, O Ti. O Ti was Lan-ch'i, Blue Flag—his fighter official. "This is Mrs. James Hamilton, wife of our respected district attorney. Make sure you get her home. She has won a great deal of money from us. Get that home with her as well. And make sure no one sees you. This city wouldn't like it."

Rose was staring at Li. "You better tell your friend Rose. What's between you two?"

Li stood quietly, watching the two men carry the unconscious Lizzie out of Rose's room. Ah Chung, the second man, number 49—an ordinary fighter—took most of her weight; O Ti kept the immodest Chéruit under control. Lizzie still gripped her ruby clip. O Ti had the red slippers, one in each tunic pocket.

There was nothing in Li's brown eyes for Rose to read. "You hear me, dammit? What's going on here?"

Li looked straight through her. "Nothing," he said. "Not if I can help it. Mrs. Hamilton and I are like water and wine. Together, each would weaken the other."

# Chapter 11

In 1887 William Randolph Hearst's illiterate father *gave* him the *San Francisco Examiner*. Within a month of hiring new, firing old, redesigning the masthead from a statement to a shout, and throwing out the news, the *Examiner* became the gee-whiz paper. As one of forever-rich Willie's early editors said, "Any issue that did not cause the reader to rise out of his chair and cry 'Great God!' was a failure."

Willie's men called him "the Chief." The Chief's reporters went up in balloons; they went down into opium dens and insane asylums; if they had to, they bobbed on the sea in boats, eavesdropping on the fish. The Chief's reporters wrote up bogus sob-sister stuff that made San Francisco cry real salty tears. Hearst's rivals were disgusted. But by 1923, there were two or three gee-whiz papers in every big town in America, many of them the Chief's—because Hearst's type of newspaper made money and because Hearst's type of journalism had driven older "newsy" papers to the wall. The message was clear—compete or die. Most competed. By then, they weren't newspapers at all, they were printed entertainment. If the city editor walked in and found a quiet newsroom, he'd roar, "Get excited, everybody!", and copy would fly, typewriters rattle, and everyone found someone to phone. The *Examiner* wanted noise, fireworks, world wars, dirty deals, suicides and scandals, drums beating, cannons booming. The Chief's reporters made the news when there was none to report. To make matters confusing, Hearst also championed the underdog and fought the far-flung wealth of the Southern Pacific Railroad.

It was Hearst who, in his circulation war with Pulitzer's *World,* had tipped the balance of power from dithery waning England to cocksure waxing America. By inventing the Spanish-American War and helping Teddy Roosevelt to invent himself, with the happy connivance of the party bosses of New York State, Willie had directed history—loosing the might of America on the world as the new Empire Builder, a fresh straddler of continents.

Joseph Pulitzer, who fought Hearst's siege of New York and lost, Pulitzer, the man who had created Hearst's type of newspaper in the first place, said, "Every reporter is a hope." Kit Dowie amended that to "Some reporters *have* hope." When Dowie was a kid, reporters were stars, like his hero Richard Harding Davis or Hearst's early man in Washington, California's astonishing Ambrose Bierce: they solved murders, charged with Teddy up San Juan Hill, elected presidents, or brought the mighty down. With their typewriters, and access to a readership numbering in the millions, newspapermen made history. It was a quatrain by Ambrose Bierce that toppled Hearst, not from his mountain of riches or the helm of his newspaper ship, but from his ever holding a political office in the United States of America. Ambrose penned, and Willie rashly printed, a little ditty to the effect that it would be a good idea if someone shot President McKinley and put an end to America's misery. Right after that, someone took his advice. McKinley was assassinated by an anarchist's badly but effectively aimed bullet. Poor Willie. And he so wanted to be President. He began to build a monument to himself in California called San Simeon instead.

From the age of eight, cloth cap pulled down over his ears, in knickers and thick knee socks, Kit hawked newspapers on the windy corner of Powell and Market for two bucks a week, staring up at the mighty newspaper buildings across the street, the future in his eyes. In 1903 they were the towering *Call,* the bustling *Chronicle,* and the *Examiner*—to a boy, Market Street seemed a mile wide. Kit had stormed that glorious world with the enthusiasm and intensity of a wide-eyed hungry kid, talent blazing.

At twenty-one, Kit Dowie became one of the highest paid members of the *Examiner* staff; he got the plum assignments, hurtling around the world for stories. Kit was on the front page, his byline prominent, a desk in the corner of the city room, turning down offers from Chicago papers and New York papers because—well, because San Francisco was *his* town. Anyway, that's how he explained it to himself. But by 1923 Dowie was getting disgusted too. He didn't feel like a star any more. He didn't even feel like a newspaper reporter. He felt like a mosquito sucking the blood of America, dodging irritated swats, settling when he could, getting off fast when bloated, leaving the itch to scratch itself. Willie Hearst (by this time long gone, off setting New York on its ear) and his gee-whiz make-news attitude wasn't turning Dowie's head, it was turning his stomach. Kit's hope held; the game was still the best game in town, in the country —he had Herbert Bayard Swope's New York *World* to keep that turbulent belief alive and William Allen White's *Emporia Gazette.* Both were irreverent, aggressive, liberal: newspapermen's newspapers. But the *World* was in New York. The best reporters wrote for it. When the *World* asked him, *if* the *World* asked him, *then* he'd pack. Or so he said, if anybody asked him.

What else could be keeping him in San Francisco, that dazzlingly beautiful town he had described as "incorruptible"? Chicago was the only completely corrupt city in America, he'd written. San Francisco would never catch up. When a criminal got off the bus in Frisco he was so busy gawking at the scenery he forgot to pick pockets. And New York was so godalmighty big. San Francisco was Kit's town, the kind of place that could get KO'd by an earthquake and then pick itself up by the seat of its pants. Kit was proud of it. But the *Examiner* had become a paper for gum chewers and ah-shucksers. Bozos who read the comic strips, puzzling over words more than three letters long. And tubercular Hammett kept poking his tongue out at Kit in some corner of Kit's busy brain. "Go east," he'd say, coughing, "go east." Not a day went by that Dido didn't have something to say on the same subject. King Oliver's band was going back to Chicago to record. They wanted Dido as vocalist. Dido wanted Kit along. But Dido made no bones about it. If he wasn't coming with her, she was going alone. "Gonna shake the dust off my heels," she said. "Whadda you gonna do, pal, get buried in it?"

In the *Examiner*'s grubby city room every piece of furniture looked like it'd been in a cat fight. Kit had his feet up on his desk, his chair pushed so far over he was staring at the broken fan on the stained ceiling, counting the fly blows. There was no one around to yell, "Get excited," but everybody was anyway. The noise was deafening. Kit was so used to it, it sounded like a gentle hum. It was Kit's kind of noise, anyway. Without it, he couldn't write. Though he wasn't writing at the moment. He was using a pencil to scratch his head under his hat—carefully; the egg on his head hurt. And thinking about the Buddy Le Blond–Violet Louise rape case. Today had been the opening day of the trial. The whole thing was already beginning to smell like a forgotten fish. Hamilton, who was supposed to be prosecuting Le Blond, seemed to be prosecuting Violet Louise. He was using Stringer Bellew as his henchman, but Kit wasn't fooled. It was Hamilton's baby. Dido had told him the DA's office was crowding Violet, trying to get her to drop the charges. Violet Louise had gone into hiding. The poor kid was sick and getting sicker. And the rich bastard who'd raped her, and almost took her head off while doing it, looked like he'd get off scot-free. If that wasn't disgusting enough, the word from somewhere above, maybe as far above as the Chief himself, was "sit on it." Why? Had Hamilton got to him with his silver tongue? It couldn't be money. If there was anyone in the world who didn't need dough, it was Willie Hearst. Maybe it was the Le Blond boy's dad. Whoever or whatever it was, it was making Kit mad.

"Guess who's coming to town?" someone whispered, close enough to his ear for Kit to poke his sore scalp with the sharp end of the pencil. The front legs of his chair came down on the floor with a thud.

"Hell! Who?"

"Harding, that's who."

"Christ, George, what do I care about that, and what are you doing in Frisco?"

"Just visiting. What do you care about that? You care because I heard the old man is sticking you with the story."

"Wha'!"

"Ah, the lurid light dawns," drawled the soft voice. George Herriman was a short wide man in his early forties, a strip cartoonist whose Krazy Kat was the pride and joy of Hearst's funny papers. He was covered up to his cowboy hat in colored ink. "You get to trail the big fella around on his mission of understanding, trying to make sense of his English. Normalcy! You ever hear a dumber mess made of a word? I could puke."

Kit was alarmed. "*You* could puke! You don't have to do the story. You get to draw mice heaving bricks in Coconino County."

"Yeah, life ain't fair, is it? See you around, lil' fella. Give the Prez a big wet French kiss for me."

"Kiss my ass!"

Herriman swaggered gaily off, leaving Kit to chalk up another rotten event in what had been a rotten day. Harding! What kind of a story could he write about the President that would get anywhere near the truth? He'd get his hand slapped and his story buried. From what he'd heard, there was big trouble brewing back in Washington. Bits and pieces of what was rapidly turning into a complicated mess buzzed around the *Examiner* hourly. But only the eastern papers were giving out hints as yet.

So Kit was going to get to tag along with the well-known womanizer and hail-fellow-well-met poker player as he bamboozled a few more voting citizens. America loved Harding. He looked great. But trying to understand one of his interminable speeches was like trying to untie the Gordian knot in boxing gloves. When Harding spoke, words flew like spittle, but none landed.

"You're taking me to lunch! Come on, wake up, I need to talk to someone and you're it," said a husky voice with a familiar lilt to it.

Kit looked up to find Lizzie standing over him. She was in another one of her outfits, some kind of low-waisted full-skirted suit in a fuzzy blue material. The matching hat looked like it belonged on a Broadway sailor—say hell, he wasn't the fashion editor—but at least the flapper was out the window. A small favor but a favor nonetheless.

"Lunch? It's after four o'clock. Beat it, I'm thinking."

"Pooey."

Lizzie dragged Kit into the eatery called McGinty's Bar and Grill that every newspaperman and cartoonist in the city used, two doors away from the *Examiner* building on Market. It was all zinc-white with nickel-silver buttercake griddles. The girl behind the cash register was picking her teeth with a fishbone, one white-socked ankle crossed over the other, her shoe resting on its toe. Kit and Lizzie had to share a table with one of the guys who wrote up local sports for the de Young brothers' *Chronicle;* he spent most of his time at Seal Stadium losing money on the Seals, Frisco's home team. That didn't stop Lizzie. As soon as they sat down with their hot pastrami on rye, she was off.

For the first five minutes Kit wasn't listening. The cross fire of sure bets on boxing matches, feverish odds on *anything* against the great jockey Earl Sande, up on the greater horse Zev, who'd just won the Kentucky Derby; the *Chronicle* writer said Zev ought to be pulling a milk wagon, if he'd had to go up against Exterminator he'd have eaten dust, and if it had been Man o' War, they'd have taken Zev home in a butcher's cart. Tips on the rising stock market, table hopping, and a lot of guff from other reporters about the upcoming Harding visit kept Dowie busy. Tad Dorgan, the *Examiner*'s sports cartoonist, was bitching about the Yankees winning the pennant again. "It's a third straight. Damned if it isn't getting boring. The Babe's homers are regular as a watch." The *Chronicle* guy at Kit's table shouted, "So, we'll sic the Seals on the bastards!" In the hoots of cynical laughter that followed that ludicrous vision, Kit finally heard Lizzie's voice. It was the name Li that got him. In an instant, he was as alert as a German pointer; the hair on the back of his neck bristled, and his present from the tattooed man ached.

"Hold it, are you referring to Li Kwan Won?"

Lizzie agreed, her mouth full of pastrami. "Uh-huh, that's him. Silly name, isn't it?"

Kit controlled himself. He fought a compelling urge to tip his hot coffee over Lizzie's sailor hat and yell "Fire!" Instead, he replayed whatever it was she was blithering about before he heard Li's name. Something about James and a hot letter the DA had written to Esmé —for a moment Kit wished he could read *that*—and then a visit to the Blue Canary alone, and gambling, and Lizzie throwing a fit up in Rose's room over some bit of business with Li. Then blanko for little Lizzie. Wasn't she getting used to it?

Kit ground his teeth. Here he was again, listening to Lizzie Hamilton's brainless problems with other men. His hands itched to reach across the table, take her lovely neck between his fingers, and squeeze. Maybe it *was* time to go east. New York City couldn't have dames as dizzy as this, and even if it did, a wised-up Kit Dowie would step aside. It was too late to dodge Lizzie. She was there, under his skin like a barbed dart. Run, fella. Instead, he sat there, put his sandwich down, and looked at Lizzie. He was getting hurt. After six years of knowing her, laughing her off, treating her like a kid sister, Kit was beginning to feel pain. Alarms were going off all over his body. Why did he put up with this crazy heartless child?

"Are you telling me that you're chasing Li?"

That made Lizzie pause, her coffee cup halfway to her mouth. She put it down again. "I told you yesterday, or was it the day before yesterday? So much seems to have happened to me. Anyway, I told you I was going to do something that would really make James angry. So I thought, if he could have Esmé and you could have Dido, what about me and another man, someone so socially and politically awful that James would—"

Tad Dorgan stuck his head between them. "I hear there's something fishy about the Violet Louise rape. The word's out that the little asshole, Buddy Le Blond, is wriggling off the hook. That right, Dowie?"

Without taking his eyes off Lizzie, Kit snapped, "Not fishy, fixed."

"Yeah?"

"Yeah. Now, if you'll excuse us—"

"Oh, sure." Tad Dorgan got the point and removed his head.

Left alone again, Kit said, "Let me get this straight." His pace was staccato. "Are you trying to fuck a Chinaman?"

"I—what?" Green eyes black with shock, Lizzie stood up so suddenly her chair fell over. The table rocked; Kit grabbed for his pastrami. Lizzie stood there, coffee cup still in her hand—until she realized that although what Kit said hadn't caused a stir, *she* had.

"Sit down," said Kit.

Lizzie picked her chair up and sat.

"I ain't going to say this twice. You're headed for trouble, kid. You don't fool around with someone like Li, and that's *apart* from the question of race. You're way out of your depth and out of your class." Kit held up a hand before Lizzie could explode. "I don't mean the stupid idea of class you've been fed like mother's milk by your socialite friends—I mean *class.*" Up till now Kit's voice had had a hard edge; now it softened. "I love you in my way, heaven help me, Lizzie, and you know it, so you rough me up and I take it. But you go in the ring with that guy and I give you two minutes in the first round. And if that's not enough, you're not going to make James angry, you hopeless little fool, you're going to make him murderous."

Lizzie's proud head slowly came up under this on-slaught. She didn't get the message. What she got was a challenge. Her fierce black brows drew together. "So much the better," she said.

Swiftly, without thought, Kit reached across the ta-ble, scattering the salt and pepper shakers, and grabbed her arm. He twisted until Lizzie's eyes filled with tears. "You mutt—*who* do you think he's going to murder?"

Lizzie was insulted and she was shaken. Now she got angry. Angry enough to jerk her arm away from Kit's grasp and stand up for the second time. "Well, won't that be a joke on me!" she spat, and swept out of McGinty's Bar and Grill. On her forearm, Kit's red finger marks were already fading.

Lizzie didn't knock, she straight-armed the door of the Blue Canary and marched right in. It was late after-noon; the Canary wasn't open for business. The club looked dim and worn without the people, lifeless without the jazz. Three middle-aged women with scarves around their heads were sweeping up. A handful of chorines, dowdy without paint and feathers, were trying out a new routine on the stage. Their tap shoes echoed in the empty air. No one paid her any mind. If Li worked here, Lizzie would find him. Enough with flirting. Forget all the tricks she'd used on college boys and waiters and guys in elevators. Blunt was all she had, and blunt would have to work.

Lizzie found Li in a big back office. But he wasn't alone. Aside from baskets of fruit, flowers in bunches, and three teapots with at least a dozen matching cups, there was an entire Chinese family—momma, poppa, un-cles, cousins, four little ones, and a young woman with a newborn baby slung across her back—all standing, heads bowed, around Li's desk. There was also a young, very young, Chinese girl standing behind him.

Li looked up, saw Lizzie, and motioned for her to be seated while he finished his business. In his stunning face there was patience but no curiosity. There was also no surprise. That surprised Lizzie.

Li spoke to what Lizzie thought must be the father of the family. What he said were the first words she had ever heard come out of his mouth. The voice was soft, concerned, but the language was so strange Lizzie almost thought this whole business might be a mistake—oh, God, he didn't speak English after all!—until she remembered what Kit had said about her plan. She stayed, cleaving closer to her seat.

*"Cheng mun nay gwai sing?"* said Li.

*"Ngaw sing Jeong,"* replied the head of the family. His tone was familiar, but it was Greek to Lizzie.

*"Jeong, nay ming m'ming-baak? Ho m-ho?"*

The father bowed his head twice, rapidly. *"Ming-baak."*

*"Ho la,"* said Li. "Chi Mai?" The young Chinese girl came forward while the father backed away from Li's desk. They both stood waiting.

"Chi Mai, give this father a gift of cash."

The girl nodded, handing the old man a small envelope.

As she did, one of the two men who had grappled with Lizzie the night before appeared from somewhere. Lizzie remembered him on her way into Rose's room, but not her way out. This was O Ti, Blue Flag.

"O Ti," said Li, slipping into English, "get two others, and go with this family to their home. Have men stay with them, work with them, protect them until the Six Companies' goons get the message. If they do not, send more men. *Tsik-huk. Siu sum!"*

O Ti, preceded by Chi Mai, began to herd the family from Li's office. They all went out backward, bowing, their Chinese faces wet with happiness. *"Li seen-sang, daw tse, daw tse,"* murmured the father, the mother, the cousins, all of them. Even Lizzie got the message. Li was doing them some kind of favor and he had their hearts in return.

Lizzie and Li were alone in his office. For Lizzie, the air got suddenly thin; she had to gulp to draw breath.

Li turned to Lizzie. "Yes, Mrs. Hamilton?" There was no trace of an accent.

Lizzie had planned everything. Driving her cabriolet on the way up from Market Street, what she intended to say now had sounded reasonable. It could be as simple as a business deal. All she wanted was the semblance of an affair. The look of an affair. For Li to take her out, be seen with her. For her to be seen with him—just enough for the news to get back to James. She'd thought that perhaps she would offer Li money to cover the cost of his time. But sitting in Li's office, her legs crossed, her blue hat at a cute angle, her cheeks pinched for color just before she walked in, the plan blew inside out in her mind like an umbrella in a high wind. It wouldn't sound reasonable out loud, it would sound crass, presumptuous. Lizzie was only beginning to learn what presumption meant, but she knew how it felt—uncomfortable as hell. So she squirmed. And stuttered.

"I thought—well, you see, I need someone to accompany me as I—"

"A bodyguard, Mrs. Hamilton?"

"Oh, no! Like an escort, I mean, like a—you know who I am?"

"Of course. Who does not know the wife of the famous James Hamilton? Who does not know Elizabeth Sian Stafford Hamilton, heir to the Charles Mortimer Stafford millions? You are asking me out?"

"You could say that, in a way. I'd pay, of course. I wouldn't expect you to do it for—"

"How much?"

"How much? I don't know, how much would you—"

"I ask for nothing, I merely want to know how much you would offer."

"Well, whatever."

"Excuse me, Mrs. Hamilton, but before I agree to rent myself out by the hour, I should like to know why."

God! How could she tell him why? She hadn't thought he'd ask; the money or just her beautiful honest self should have done the job. Why couldn't he just take the situation as a compliment? It wasn't going well. Time to come up with a damn good lie. "I suppose I'll have to tell you the whole thing."

"Yes?" Li's calm was deadly, his demeanor seamless. It made things worse.

"You see, some friends of mine and I have a bet—"

"Ah! The Chinese love to gamble." He smiled.

"Yes! You understand." Lizzie began to relax. The details of her lie took shape quickly in her mind. It was going to work after all.

"Indeed, I understand."

"I bet that I could—"

Li pushed back his chair and stood. "Please, do not shame yourself further. Come with me, Mrs. Hamilton. I have something to show you."

"Shame myself further?" Lizzie began, but Li was already going out the door. Lizzie had to run to keep up with him as he strode out of his office, through the Blue Canary, and out onto Mason Street. What the hell was going on now? Why didn't anything go the way she planned it?

Damn!

They were on Grant Avenue before Li slowed down and Lizzie, holding on to her hat, could catch up with him. When she did she had a stitch in her side and a run in her silk stocking. They were in Chinatown. The few blocks she'd raced after Li took her from the world that Lizzie Stafford Hamilton knew, that belonged to her, into a land that was alien, strange, uncharted.

"This is my world," said Li, "where I was born, where I once belonged, as you belong up there." Li pointed up California Street. From three blocks away— three blocks below—Lizzie saw the Stafford mansion, crazy in its wealth. Presumption was getting clearer.

Chinatown surged around her, Chinese faces, Chinese voices. The vegetables arranged on sidewalk stands, tiny shops of jars and vials and little boxes, bare restaurants where old men sat, backs bent, eyes rheumy, slurping strange soup out of steaming dishes with strange spoons, the smell, the sound, the touch—all Chinese. Four stories above, red-and-gold pagoda roofs curled out over balconies of family washing. At street level, the colors were washed out and drab, but from the tops of street stalls, dangling down from tiny balconies, pots of feverish fuchsia and tawny marigolds burned in the sun. Drying squid, brown and grotesque, hung in a butcher shop, and live fowl squawked in crates tumbled against its window. The few women went by with wide laden baskets balanced on their heads; children, small faces heartbreaking with innocent perfection, ran through on blue-trousered legs. Hunched in a doorway was an old Chinese bootblack toothlessly singing "Ole Black Joe," and just in front of Lizzie was a shop that sold tea. Caught by its scent, she peered in.

Mounds of dried crushed leaves, brown, black, copper, were displayed on little paper doilies. One was called Butterfly's Eyebrow, another Second Pearl. Lizzie laughed with delight. With Li following, she went into a herbalist's. Rows of lacquer boxes, red with brass handles, lined the dark walls; below them, elaborately carved teakwood chairs waited for the herbalist's patients. From somewhere in the back of the shop, an old man, his beard a long thin wisp of gray, came forward, bowing as he shuffled in embroidered slippers. "You want something, missy? We have a wine brewed from snakes, withered toad to cure colds, dried seahorses? You like something for your love life, got whatever you need." Li bought Lizzie the seahorses.

She was in San Francisco, the city that had been her home all her life, but she'd never been in Chinatown. This wasn't San Francisco. Was it China? Lizzie Stafford felt so far away from home.

Lizzie turned to Li. "But I think it's wonderful," she said. What she meant was, I think it's cute, all these little people doing cute little things in their cute little costumes. Li knew what she meant. She saw it in his eyes. Well, she wasn't ashamed. What was wrong with that? They *were* cute. Mary Maud had said they were dirty. Grandmother would never let little Lizzie get closer to Chinatown than the top of Nob Hill. And the top of Nob Hill was a million dollars away. She was close now. There wasn't a white face in sight. Peddlers of hard-boiled eggs, of sea snails, of wild animals, of lovely kites like hawks or owls or dragons beckoned to her. Lizzie was charmed.

"It is wonderful," agreed Li in a quiet voice. "You are meant to think it is wonderful." He took her hand. His touch made her want to snatch her hand away. Not from its strangeness. From its vitality—the heat was there again. "Now I will show you what you are not meant to see."

Li led Lizzie up a side alley. They went only a few steps off Grant before the buildings seemed to sag. Paint peeled, iron railings rusted, garbage cans tipped over, spilling their filth onto the cobblestones, rotting food piled up against the alley walls, a dead cat putrified at her feet. Four-story buildings crowded so close over her head that the alley closed down like an airless clamp. It didn't smell here, it stank. Lizzie shrank away. Dear God, this place was a public latrine. Old men pissed in here! Li pulled her forward, Lizzie stumbling in her brittle heels, to a door in a wall. The door was dashed with crimson paint. He led her down and down dark slippery dank stairs into a black hole under the street. When her eyes adjusted, Lizzie was in a steaming pit, dark and hot and vast, tunneling its way under the buildings above. Hundreds of dim shapes bent over huge vats of bubbling liquid. Men and women, naked to the waist, streaming with sweat, stirred the vats with wooden paddles. Others beat the filth out of shapeless bundles with flat sticks.

"A laundry," explained Li. "A cute Chinese laundry. For these people, there is no way out of here except death. And to the Christian mind, where do you think these heathen people will go when they are released? Would hell be any different? Come, there's more."

Lizzie hadn't seen much, but she didn't want to see more.

"No, I think I ought—"

"Ah, but this is just the beginning. I insist on being your guide. Few whites are so honored. I expect no fee."

For what seemed to Lizzie like hours she was dragged to community kitchens where hundreds were allotted a small bowl of soup each, a handful of rice, into garment sweatshops where Chinese women worked sixteen hours a day sewing by hand in feeble light, to dark places where weird things glimmered like ghosts in tall jars, to grim bare gambling dens where Chinese men feverishly won or lost what small wages they could scrape together. There was no languid elegance here, no high-toned women to be wooed by the lure of risk. Lizzie saw opium dens where slack-jawed men lay in dreamless stupor—she could count their ribs—hotels with a mere sixty rooms that housed a thousand, shacks no more than eight feet by ten where people slept on slatted bunks, stacked one above the other. Lizzie saw listless eyes and hopeless faces.

Everywhere she went with Li Kwan Won, people made way, bowing to him, approaching Li humbly with small requests or thanking him for past favors.

Toward evening, Li led an exhausted Lizzie to a Chinese joss house on Spofford Alley.

"This is a shrine," he said. "It is not a church. There one worships. Here it is like a personal visit to speak to the gods—we have many and none is forgotten. Our temples are as if the western world had built a church to Apollo, and Wotan and Erda, the great god Pan, and the pitiful Savior and worshiped them all under one roof. But the white man squanders his past. He is like Saul of Tarsus, blinded by the vision. We Chinese are reasonable men. We do not waste what has gone before, what we have learned."

Li bought a candle and punk sticks from the temple priest. "This shrine is for Tsai Tin Tai Shing, a monkey god who is revered because he learned the language of men. For reasons of my own, Tsai Tin Tai Shing suits me. Stay here."

Lizzie watched as Li approached the altar and bowed low. He lit the candle and the incense, kneeling on the mat and calling out the name of the deified monkey three times. The strong incense stung Lizzie's eyes. Then he took two semi-ovals of wood, bowed to Tsai Tin Tai Shing again, and tossed the wooden ovals into the air. One landed flat side down, the other on its curved side.

"Tsai Tin Tai Shing will listen," he said to Lizzie.

He took a bamboo cylinder full of sticks and shook it until a single stick fell to the temple floor. Li handed the stick to the Chinese priest. The priest looked at the stick, at Li, at Lizzie, and spoke rapidly in Chinese. Li shrugged.

"What did he say?" asked Lizzie.

Li smiled. "It is not good. Times are dark. Armies march. There is no joy. But, as you see, I have been too much with *baak gwai lo*—"

"*Baak gwai lo?*"

"White ghosts, devils, your people, Mrs. Hamilton, whose God is a lover of blood. Because of this, I only half believe him."

Li stepped back from the altar of the monkey god, staring sightlessly over his head. "This blind creature with the gift of speech is my god because I cannot love yours. How could I love such an idea as the white ghosts' Christ? He drives men mad—a god only a vengeful, intolerant people could create. In the name of the lamb you have subjected whole peoples, erased cultures. Where others bless the star, the well, the worm, you exalt disease and damnation. The *baak gwai lo* are a primitive people who pillage the soul, who banish ideas, who rape the earth of her treasures. You spoil the beauty of your own lives as you steal it from others. Even here in the land of Fusang, the land the Chinese monk Hui Shen discovered four and a half centuries after the death of the ghost Jesus."

As he spoke, Lizzie thought of the Stafford mines. Grandfather had once taken her to see them. They were great open wounds in the mountain, the forests that had grown around them flattened and burnt.

Even Lizzie, whose vision was untended, thought the beautiful Chinese looked haunted. Whoever Li was talking to, it wasn't her. He stood, sightless as his monkey god, looking at nothing she could see. Lizzie didn't know what he was talking about. It was worse than listening to Kit when he was in a passion.

Li walked to Lizzie and stood in front of her, forcing her to look into his eyes. They were wild and deep and very old. Lizzie fell in.

"But you worship a monkey!" she said, stunned by his anger and bitterness.

Like raising a mask, the humor returned to Li's face. "Why not? I like the *idea* of Tsai Tin Tai Shing. I am not so foolish as to *believe* it. Now you have seen my world, Mrs. Hamilton—a world where there is little joy. What could you possibly want here? What do you want from me?"

Lizzie couldn't answer. What *did* she want from him? In a Chinatown of contrasts—outward charm and hidden horror—her problems with James and Esmé, a rich girl's struggles to know herself, seemed stupid, petty. Her thought of using someone like Li to punish her husband was like sprinkling salt on the snow. Was that what Kit had meant by class? He told her she was out of her depth, and he was right—as usual. Lizzie was finally ashamed of herself. And she was tired.

Without regard for who Li was, she had popped him willy-nilly into her plot like a pulp writer, dashing about in people's lives, thinking always of her own. Lizzie had been trying to impose flat shapes on the eternal, playing follow-the-dots on the midnight sky.

Li was watching her face. He reached out to touch her hot cheek. The tips of his fingers were as tender as a moth.

"Forgive me for trespassing on your heart, Mrs. Hamilton. I have been too abrupt and cruel." Suddenly he smiled.

For Lizzie, the smile was like hearing Kit's torch song again, the one Dido sang, "China Blues." It raced through her veins like sweet forbidden dope.

"Come, you must be hungry. I will take you to dinner. I am not your prey, but perhaps a friend?"

# Chapter 12

Dressed like swells, Coffee Trujillo and Jugs Kelly, backed up by Murray's newly imported hired guns, paid Pete the doorman their fifteen bucks cover charge each. The two new men were smooth-faced, pretty, and boyish Miles Brady from Dion O'Banion's gang back in Chicago —Miles, slim and silent, had eyes the color of oysters— and an old Five Points man, burly Joe Baglietto, who had a five o'clock shadow you could strike a match on. The sixty dollars didn't hurt; Coffee intended to get it back before the night was over. Whispering Mike was left outside in the evening fog to keep an eye on Mason Street from the comfort of the big brown Buick. Mike was chosen as wheelman and lookout because you could put him anywhere, tell him to stay, and he'd stay there till he rotted, and also because he'd never get past the doorman. Dress Mike up in a crown and scepter, drape a purple robe dragging with ermine over him, and he'd still look like a homicidal dope.

It was eleven o'clock on a Wednesday night, still early for the Blue Canary. King Oliver's band was only into its second number and Oliver's second cornet player, Louis Armstrong, hadn't appeared yet. Louis liked to wait until things got hot on the dance floor. Just like Rose St. Lorraine, he was at his best after midnight. Mostly the music was easy and slow, dinner music. Dido was on stage warming up with a number from Broadway's new all-black revue, *Shuffle Along*—"He May Be Your Man but He Comes to See Me Sometimes." At this hour the Canary was a classy restaurant—eighty or ninety people eating too much so that later they could drink too much. Rose's cook was a wild black woman from New Orleans, over sixty years old and hell with a rolling pin. The cuisine was a curiously successful mix of soul food and Cordon Bleu; chitlins vied with escargot.

Appetite Ike, who never got to bed before dawn and was back up by noon, was hunched behind the main bar counting bottles. After three years of Prohibition, the Blue Canary's stock was still the best. Rose and Li managed to keep the good stuff coming: cognac from France, Scotch from Scotland, even sticky Imperial Tokay from Hungary. Hundreds of imported bottles with intriguing labels shone warm on their shelves, long shelves that were built into a wall that could revolve at the touch of a button. Ike liked to do his bottle counting when the staff was on. That way, they *knew* he was counting.

Once Murray Blinn's boys were safely inside the Blue Canary, they got confident, letting the bulges under their arms show, talking through Dido's number, knocking over a table to introduce themselves. Coffee Trujillo got to Ike's bar, checked over the staff, noted the lack of muscle—the old guy clinking the bottles together, for instance, couldn't do more harm than one of La Pallottola's puff pastries—and ordered four beers.

Ike didn't look up. "Fifteen, sixteen—Harry'll get it for you. Harry! Beers here. Seventeen."

Harry moved over smoothly, took one look at the bunch he was dealing with, and, as he passed Ike, nudged him. Ike took the hint. He kept counting—but he also pushed a hidden button tucked under the bar. It wasn't the one that turned the shelves.

Harry, in his late forties and eager to keep on aging,

rubbed his suddenly wet hands on his short black jacket. "Yes, gentlemen? Any special brand?"

Coffee smiled. The smile got as far as his thin brown mouth. "I heard somewhere the beer's free here. That so?"

Harry grinned like a sick dog and poured the first brand of beer he could keep a slippery grip on. It was one of Li's Chinatown brews, the Snap Dragon still's Yellow Jack. Ike went on quietly counting: twenty-five, twenty-six, twenty-seven.

Miles Brady had turned away from Harry and was leaning backward, elbows on the bar, one leg crossed casually over the other, fragile-looking hands clasped over his flat stomach, holding his glass. Back in Chicago, Miles had a certain deserved reputation with the ladies. San Francisco looked like it could use him. Watching Dido with his odd oyster-colored eyes, he drank the head off his beer. "Not bad stuff. We have to get the recipe, Coffee. Get a load of the coon. Right out of the jungle. Big but yummy."

Appetite Ike grinned to himself. He nursed strong hopes that the smug little gunman would get to meet the coon—soon. Then he'd know what the jungle really meant.

Jugs Kelly giggled. He couldn't keep his hands off his gun or his eyes off Dido.

"Let's get this show on the road." Bulky Joe Baglietto shouldered up against Coffee. "Where's the boss?" he said to Harry. With his jaw jutted out and heavy eyebrows that went from side to side of his thick brow without a break, Joe looked like bad news any way Harry figured him.

"You want me to get her for you?"

"Butt out, Baglietto," said Coffee. "I'll handle this." He tapped Jugs on his padded shoulder. "Take your beer and get back and cover the front door. We got all of us we need here."

"Can't see the show so good by the door," said Jugs.

"Get!" said Coffee.

Jugs got.

"Now." Coffee turned back to Harry. "We got us a

little business deal we want to talk over with your boss. Go get 'im."

"Her," Harry corrected.

"Her? OK, so it's a dame. Go get 'er." Coffee lunged across the wide shining bar and grabbed Harry by his red bow tie and most of his starched white shirtfront. Harry came back across with him, choking.

"This ain't no discussion, barman. This is a request."

Harry couldn't say anything. He was spending his time trying to breathe.

Coffee was enjoying himself. The move on the Blue Canary was the biggest thing Murray had had him do since he'd signed on with the Blinn gang. The Canary was not only the biggest but the classiest operation in Frisco. Taking it on made Trujillo as big as it was. And without Murray along, Coffee had four guns to boss around. He liked it just fine. Unlike Murray, the boys didn't read, pulp or otherwise. The way they spoke reflected the way they lived—crude, harsh, and basically stupid. Since they conversed mainly among themselves, and rare criticism was silenced with violence, they thought what they said and how they said it was smart.

"Coffee?" said Joe.

"What?" Coffee still had a grip on Harry's tie. Harry's red face was turning purple; the squeaking bartender was only getting air by pushing himself up off the bar by his elbows.

"There's something you ought to see here."

"Unless it's the owner of this dump, I don't wanna see nobody."

"Let go of the guy, Coffee. You really gotta see this. It'll crack you up."

"Yeah?" Coffee dropped Harry, who came back down on the floor hard, landing on his knees. Ike was leaning on the bar now, chewing with interest. Rose didn't like him chewing in public, but for the moment Rose could lump it. Appetite had two wads of tobacco on the go. He was enjoying this scene as much as Coffee Trujillo was. It reminded him of that part of his wild and woolly youth when he'd been a cowpoke. Punching cows wasn't a job Ike had kept long, but he'd kept it well. Mexican standoffs were a frontier staple.

Brilliant white teeth between brown lips stretched in a good-humored grin, Coffee turned slowly from Harry and Ike and the bar. When he got all the way around he found two Chinese looking at him. They didn't look scared, but then, they didn't look anything. Two yellow faces as alike as corn kernels on the cob. Both the same to Coffee. Impassive was the word he would have used to describe their expressions if he'd known what it meant. All he saw was that they weren't packing guns or swinging hatchets. Where could they keep them anyway? The yellow geeks were in their pajamas. Black silk jammies. With blue bandannas around their geeky heads. Coffee laughed.

"Two little Chinks come to say night-night, huh? That's what you wanted me to see, Joe?"

Oyster eyes rolling, Miles put his beer on the bar and stepped forward, bowing, palms pressed together like a pretty Buddha. "No tickee, no washee."

Joe thought that was funny; he doubled over laughing.

One of the two Chinese chopped Joe so fast on the back of his thick neck that he went down like a bull on the bad end of a cattle prod. The other was making odd balletic movements with his hands. Miles came up out of his bow, jumped back, and bumped hard into the bar.

Coffee thought that was so unfunny, he drew his gun. Miles was fast. He beat Coffee to the same idea. "OK," said Coffee, "we done our laughing, no more foolin' around. I don't know how you did that, slant-eyes, but you ain't doin' it again."

Some of the Canary diners had finally caught on that something was wrong: they looked up from their black-eyed peas and champagne, waiters paused with loaded trays, the cigarette and flower girls let out shrill little eeks, but the band played on. Where King Oliver came from, this was all in a night's work. Chicago was an interesting town where it paid you to keep uninterested. But Dido wasn't from the Windy City; she was from St. Louis. Her momma was an Apalachee Indian and her pa played ragtime piano for the Gilt Edge Bar in St. Louis's red-light district, Chestnut Valley. They'd been dirt poor where she came from. People didn't dodge trouble there, they made it. Dido was damned interested. She strode to the front of the stage and cupped her strong black hands around her eyes, trying to see through the footlights.

Still stunned, Joe got up, his eyes crossed in pain, his beefy hand clamped to the back of his neck. "Let me at—"

Coffee waved him down with his free hand; his .44-caliber gun was holding steady on the Chinese who'd done the fancy chopping. "I said I wanna see the broad who runs this joint. You wanna scamper off and get her or am I gonna have to shoot you runts, one at a time?"

The two members of Li's Hung family started forward, gun or no gun.

Joe reached for the bulge under his dress jacket, and customers began moving. Dido had jumped off the stage and was headed for the action. So was Jugs Kelly, but he was running. He beat her to it.

"You fellas come to see me?"

The scene stopped dead—like a freeze shot in a Griffith movie or one of Coney Island's Living Pictures.

Rose St. Lorraine was posed at the top of the wide staircase. "What can I do for you boys?" She started down, rolling her round hips. Rose was in peach tulle from the top of her small seed-pearl hat to the bottom of her satin shoes. The skintight bodice of her frock was sky-blue snakeskin. She came down the stairs like a duchess: delicate chin up, large chest out, one pink hand trailing back over the softly gleaming banister, the other ready to wave away the hurrahs. Sergeant Huggins, her white malamute husky, followed, panting. In the sudden silence, his nails clicked sharply on the polished wooden steps. Ike chewed harder. Rose's act was terrific.

Murray's boys gawked, guns drooping.

"Ike, honey, get them another drink. They must be thirsty carrying around all that weight."

A little over two hours before Coffee and his cronies paid a call on the Blue Canary, Li took Lizzie to a Chinese restaurant on Grant Avenue. Ling Chu-tzû, the Intelligent Pearl, was unusual in Chinatown. It was as ornate as a private apartment in the I Ho Yuan, the rebuilt Peking Summer Palace of the Dragon Empress, Tz'u-hsi. Exquisite *num sing* lanterns of many colors lit the gold-and-vermilion paper walls, ebony screens inlaid with mother-of-pearl separated the tiny teakwood tables, pale pink and apple green Canton vases filled with arching branches of plum blossom stood by the round moon doors. One whole wall was a mural of spiky mountain peaks wreathed in clouds, cascades of wild white water rushing through deep valleys, spraying up against twisted root and rock in frozen foam. On a small raised stage three Chinese musicians played on flutes and two-stringed fiddles. It came to Lizzie's ear as pain and discord—like wind howling down drainpipes, singing dogs, and short sneezes. The Intelligent Pearl smelled of musk and spices and exotic unknown Chinese dishes. To Lizzie, her low-hipped blue suit and blue hat suddenly seemed clumsy.

Li led her to a private booth of latticed teakwood that glowed only with the light of a single candle. The other diners, whites and Chinese, glanced with discretion at the white woman and the Chinese man. Lizzie thought they were envious. Li knew better. At their entrance, the restaurant had snapped into high gear. Three waiters devoted themselves to Li, bowing with solemn dignity.

In San Francisco, curious tourists had only just begun to drift into what they thought of as the "mysterious" Chinese district, still exotically and enticingly tainted with the myth, legend, and occasional truth of the old Barbary Coast. Though white men had slunk in and out of its alleys for seventy years, they hadn't come to see the sights. They had come to buy young Chinese flesh. The girls, once sold for an hour to a white man, were then shunned by their own. Chinese men found no status in having what the whites had used. The Chinese prostitute was not honored by the touch of the *baak gwai lo,* but shamed.

At the turn of the century, a member of the San Francisco police force, during another of the city's periodic and ineffective vice raids, made the following statement to the press. It was sour in its pomposity: "I have never seen a decent respectable Chinese woman in my life."

His superiors compounded that stupidity by announcing, "Chinese people have no respect for chastity. Most of their women are prostitutes."

A representative of the Chinese press, if there had been any Chinese press, might have said the same thing about the whites if he had paid a visit to San Francisco during her gold-rush days. Men from all over the country stampeded to the bonanza, leaving their wives and children at home. As always, ladies of easy virtue followed them. In early San Francisco, there were few respectable white women.

For the Chinese, it had been the same. The young men crowded eagerly into the bay on sailing ships from the Far East, seeking fortune from the Gold Mountain or, later, wages for work on the railroads. Like the whites, they left their families at home. But, unlike the whites, loose Chinese women did not follow them. The females that arrived in their thousands were bought by agents of Chinese highbinders—as the yellow press called the Chinatown tongs—from their wretched Cantonese families, boat people who sold the daughters they did not drown at birth to feed the sons who were nurtured to appease the ancestors. Or stolen as young girls from rich families in the northern provinces. *Then* the women came to California, not following but forced. The best, the most sophisticated and charming, came from the Tai Ping Shan district of Hong Kong: singsong girls from "flower boats," water brothels. These few girls came willingly enough. But however they came, they were all there for the money—whether from Chinese pockets or the billfolds of white ghosts. Money is money. Men are men. The Chinese were no different. In a Chinatown bereft of families, the ghetto was preyed upon by its own. There were Chinese who were pimps, hatchet men, thieves, dope runners, slavers. In other red-light districts, whatever their sisters-in-joy did with their share was their own business; in Chinatown, the Chinese girls rarely saw what they sold their bodies for. They were sexual slaves. It was no wonder the white press saw no "respectable" Chinese women. The Chinese men came for fortune, not to settle; the wives were left at home. As the years passed and the new land became home for many who would never return to China, it was too late. The whites passed laws against the coming of the wives. With the wives would come breeding, and breeding would create more yellow people.

But now, in the twenties, with the Barbary Coast a memory trailing clouds of lurid myth, the whites were coming to Chinatown to dabble in the exotic they found on their own doorstep—to buy the trinkets, exclaim over the curious, dip their toes in the once shunned and forbidden streets.

Sitting in a booth in the beautiful Intelligent Pearl, knowing nothing of any of this, Lizzie watched as the waiters brought food. Bread baked in a mold that made the loaf into a flower or a dragon or a butterfly, then steamed with salt, sugar and pepper, swollen mushrooms called a "monkey's head," shark's fin soup, Peking grilled duck, and some kind of watermelon, hollowed out, cut in half, and stood on end. When the waiter lifted the melon's "lid," fashioned from rind, it contained another smoking hot soup of lotus seeds, chicken broth, mushrooms, bamboo shoots, and shredded ham. But the first thing Lizzie went for was the *samshu,* a fiery Chinese wine. It was a choice made from habit, but also from the queasy feeling that she'd need fortification to eat some of this strange steaming fare.

The food turned out to be fine. Well, most of it. She couldn't bring herself to sample what looked like brains in a brown sauce. But the *samshu* made her giddy. When Lizzie was sober, she talked. When she was giddy, she talked even more. She heard herself telling Li about Lizzie, about Charles Mortimer and Mary Maud, about Kit Dowie. The way he listened made her tell her story straight. Lizzie wasn't sure she could lie to Li Kwan Won. There was something in his eyes. When Kit listened to her, his eyes danced with light; they were amused. Her words bounced off him; for Kit she performed. Besides, when she talked to Kit he was always turning her words back on themselves, making her feel so damned young. With Li, the light was direct. She had no place to hide from it. With Li, she felt he thought what she had to say was important. Until she got to the part about James and Esmé. Then things seemed to go very wrong.

"—and that's how I found out my husband was having an affair with another woman. I didn't know what to do. I wanted to hurt him so bad that I—well, I tried to use you."

Li had eaten very little. He was sitting back, sipping *samshu* out of a tiny porcelain cup. Lizzie hadn't counted but she was sure he must have had as much to drink as she. Why wasn't he giddy?

"Why does the affair of your husband mean so much to you?"

"Why?" Lizzie was astounded. If there was a "why" involved, it would be, Why should Li ask such a question? Wasn't it obvious? If she had confided in any of her friends, heaven forbid, they would have gasped in shock, petted her with pity, called James a cad, and rung round for a good divorce lawyer. Even Kit was on her side about Esmé.

But Li said, "If you told me he was having an affair with a goat, I might have something to talk about, but in China, adultery is only a feminine vice. As they say, 'Husbands should be as heaven to their wives; wives as slaves to their husbands.'"

The *samshu* burned in Lizzie's nose. "What?"

"What a man does outside a wife's bed is not a wife's business. What a woman does, of course, is quite the opposite."

Lizzie stared at him, chewing her monkey's head. She was horrified. When you tell the truth, at the least you expect sympathy. "So you think like James. You believe wives are less than their husbands?"

"I do not think like Mr. Hamilton at all. Would you mind if I smoked?"

Lizzie shook her head. She didn't mind if he blew bubbles, so long as he explained himself.

Li lit a long brown cigarette. It wasn't a brand Lizzie had seen before. "I am sure you must find Chinese thought callous, Mrs. Hamilton, but that is because you judge with a western heart. In China marriage is not the result of romance, it is an economic necessity. Most of us are paired at birth. Where is the romance in that? Marriage is to form strong clans and father healthy children. If a wife is unfaithful and, worse, conceives, the whole clan suffers because the bloodline is confused. If a man is unfaithful, although there is no such Chinese concept as unfaithfulness in marriage, what is that? Why should the wife feel jealous or threatened? She has her home, her children, her married status."

Lizzie put up a fight. This man was beautiful and foreign, this man had enough charm to calm a snake, but what the hell was he talking about? Marital status? Lizzie Stafford find status in marriage!

"This isn't China, Mr. Li Kwan Won. In America, a wife gets upset if her husband sleeps around. In America, marriage is rather personal—the wife feels personally betrayed."

Li's expression didn't change; it was set in stone. "Excuse me, Mrs. Hamilton. You are right. Chinese customs are not the same, and I have no right to judge your pain in what, to the Chinese mind, is a situation that ought not to arise. In China, the woman rules the home and the home rules the Chinese. So, you see, in China the woman ultimately rules. As she does everywhere. It is only the western man who does not recognize this."

"I don't want to rule from the home. It's mine anyway. I don't want to rule at all." Lizzie was puzzled. There was something about the way he was speaking that bothered her, like a schoolboy reciting lessons. "Why do you keep saying the Chinese this and the Chinese that? What do *you* think?"

Li laughed, and the laugh was impish. He leaned forward to rest his elbows on the table and to smile at Lizzie. Like stepping through a mirror, his inscrutable oriental pose shattered. "You don't want to rule? How unusual, for man or woman. As a compliment to your uniqueness, I shall tell *you* the truth. I will tell you, Mrs. Hamilton, because China has no more sway over me than it does over you. I was raised by Rose St. Lorraine, and to be raised by Rose leaves a child breathless. She gives him so much room and she fills the air with laughter. There is not much that survives in the face of laughter. Rose's child is free to look around and wonder at the nonsense of any one tradition, any rule or custom. Rose gave a Chinese boy a fresh start. With no tradition to follow, no ancient burden to carry, no family to impose goals, I was alone—but free." Li leaned back in his chair again. "As you have done so far with me, I have been toying with you. We will start again. So please tell me, if you succeed in your attempt to do as your husband does, or at least to appear to, what would you accomplish?"

Again comfortable, encouraged by the change in Li, Lizzie thought about the answer to that. Then she said, "Revenge!" The word came out with all the emphasis she'd intended.

Li looked at her for a second, then softly said, "Yes, revenge. That I can understand. But such things have a way of backfiring."

Lizzie turned her head away from him. "That's what Kit said—"

"Kit Dowie is a strong man. Perhaps you should listen to him."

"Kit Dowie makes me feel like a baby. He never listens to *me*."

"That's not what I said."

Lizzie was mildly irritated. What was Kit doing in this conversation? She got him in, she would pluck him out. "Kit isn't important. What's important is that, somehow, I don't really feel like revenge any more. The whole idea seems silly now."

"The bud opens," said Li, looking at Lizzie with a strange sideways glance. There was something rare in his eyes, something tender. "You know, Mrs. Hamilton, Chinese men sometimes have 'wives of the heart,' and these are the times when passion can destroy a 'wife of the home.' But as I have no wife, there is no danger." The booth's intricate lattice walls cast confused shadows over Li's face.

Lizzie did mental loops. What was he saying? With

the merest hint of a flirtation, Lizzie was beginning to feel like Lizzie again. She'd taken off her hat, her blue-black hair cupped her face, and she began to use the power in her green eyes with their thick sooty lashes.

"And you want one—I mean, you would like a 'wife of the heart'?"

"Where would I find one? Here, a Chinese woman to cherish is like a blue rose—a dream. I have no family to choose for me. I'd have to return to China, and Mrs. Hamilton, I've never been to China. There I would have to search the country of my ancestors, where thought has stood still for centuries, to find one. And what would she be like, this unknown maiden of the Orient? How could I talk to her? She would find me a monster, hide from me in terror. I was raised in a western world. I would look for a wife for new, very un-Chinese, reasons, western reasons." Li paused, gazing past Lizzie. "Perhaps someday I will do that, but for now I have too much to do here."

Lizzie noticed Li's hands as he spoke. His cigarette sat in an ashtray, burning. Li was playing with the candle flame, passing his palm across the fire. They were delicate hands, elegant, controlled. And strong. Like everything else about him. Thinking the time had come, Lizzie sprang for his heart.

"Am I like a blue rose?"

The change in Li's face was swift as the fog rolling in from the sea. He was angry. But with whom? As Lizzie watched, even the shadows on the walls trembled, their shapes stretching.

"You are as lovely and innocent as a snow leopard, Mrs. Hamilton, even when you rend, and you are just as dangerous—to me. You are a white woman. I am a Chinese man. We will not play sweet useless romantic games. You have nothing to win and I have everything to lose. I don't believe in the rules that the Chinese impose on themselves, or the rules that white men impose on the Chinese—but I believe that they believe. Their delusion blackens their hearts. Their black thoughts are so strong, held for so long, they have become real. Real enough to affect even the unbelievers. We must live in the black world they have created for us all. One"—Li looked directly into Lizzie's eyes—"or two, cannot change what the multitude has decreed. If I were to touch you, Lizzie Stafford, you and I should know the fire of all hells. Hell is real. Your world would make sure of that. Mine?" Li shrugged, his anger waning with his words. "Mine? I have none."

Like a slap, Lizzie was suddenly sober. She'd slipped into what she always was with men, a flirt. It was the only way she knew how to be. Li had dashed her charm, and the truth, in her face like ice water.

There was a soft tap at the booth's closed door.

"Li Kwan Won?"

Li moved quickly to open it.

Ah Chung, the 49 who had helped O Ti with Lizzie, stood outside, head down. In rapid Chinese, he whispered to Li. The words were urgent.

The man Li had been for the last hour with Lizzie was gone. At times solemn, restrained and sober, then suddenly laughing and boyish—all these faces were gone. He listened to Ah Chung with the tension of a hunting puma, his face taut with whatever it was he was hearing.

He asked the 49 something.

Ah Chung shook his head with violence. *"M-hai. Faai-dee la!"*

Li turned to Lizzie as Ah Chung, now quiet, waited. "I must leave you. There is something I must attend to. This man will take you to your car. Before I go, I must warn you. Ah Chung says there is a man following you, a private detective."

Lizzie was still sitting at the table. A private detective? My God, who would put a detective on Elizabeth Hamilton? Of course, James! So she *was* getting to him. He would hear about Li Kwan Won after all. Forgetting what she had said of revenge to Li, Lizzie smiled. She was delighted.

Li had followed her thoughts.

"Your husband, Mrs. Hamilton, is my enemy. I have no cause, as yet, to be his."

*Chapter 13*

Appetite Ike put a bottle of rye on the bar—it wasn't the best and it wasn't the worst—then lined up four shot glasses.

"I hope the poor son of a bitch you musta left outside has his own," he said, and poured out the rye. "Don't figure you boys for cocktail men, though I got a drink I make here'd set you back on your heels: whiskey, white port, rye, an' Pernod. I calls it Frisco Hot."

"Shut up," said Coffee.

Ike squinted at him and scratched his chin. Ike always had stubble. It wasn't as impressive as Joe Baglietto's—Joe's would rasp the bark off trees—but it still made a satisfying noise under the nail of the two remaining fingers on Ike's left hand.

"You don't know what you're missin'," he said, and *then* he shut up.

Murray Blinn's mob, Jugs and Miles and Joe and Coffee, were all together now. They were bunched up by the bar looking at Rose St. Lorraine. Just behind Rose towered Dido; just behind Dido the two Chinese waited in silence. Sergeant Huggins hunkered down by Rose's side, watching the guns. From the alert look in his light blue eyes, he knew what they were for. Rose had her hand on the back of his broad white head, gently.

Harry had carefully backed off down the long bar. Harry was a wise man who had judged himself long ago, concluding that if he wasn't quite an out-and-out coward, he was close enough not to bother splitting hairs.

Downstairs, everyone else in the Blue Canary, over a hundred nervous souls, had moved as far from the action at the main bar as they could get. That meant toward the stage. Gentlemen in black evening suits, stiff white napkins tucked into their high collars, were holding their plates in one hand and their forks in the other, still munching dinner, watching the show across the silver dance floor. Women with Prince of Wales feathers in their bobbed hair, wearing short bangled gowns, rolled stockings, and most of their jewelry collections around their necks, buzzed busily among themselves. As they talked, they were stripping off brooches, rings, bracelets, and necklaces, slipping them into Rose's potted ferns, losing them amid the cracked ice in champagne buckets. If they got through this, they could dine out on the story for months. It was very exciting. The Blue Canary was always so different, so very unexpected, so chic, *n'est-ce pas?*

King Oliver's band stopped playing: black musicians leaned patiently on their horns, smoking. Lil Hardin, the pretty, petite pianist at the Steinway baby grand, was running a line of cocaine on the key of C. Half-dressed chorus girls were playing it safe by staying backstage—along with a song-and-dance team from the Trocadero called the High Steppers, touring San Francisco on a long swing out of New York City. The dancers, both chorine and featured, were tripping all over themselves trying to see through the heavy stage blacks. But Louis Armstrong, Oliver's young cornet player, blew a little blues up on the stage all by himself.

The Blue Canary was waiting. And Coffee Trujillo knew it. He was *on.* "Put the guns away, boys."

Jugs was surprised enough to protest. "But Coffee, the Chinks."

Coffee used his gun to point out the silent Chinese behind Dido. "You afraid of two Chinks in their pajamas?"

"Wha'? Course I ain't."

"So we're talkin' to the lady nice. What do you want all those people to think, that we ain't got class?"

Blinn's boys put away their guns, right where they could get them back if they needed to—fast.

Rose had been keeping her peace through all this, buying time.

"The lady's listening," she finally said, patting the curls piled on her head, curl upon curl. Rose was forty-six years old, and every hair on her head had kept its value; each one was still pure gold. The little seed-pearl hat perched on the top. "But I still haven't heard much to keep me real interested."

"We came to talk a little business," said Coffee.

"*Little* ain't my style, honey. What have you got that's big?"

"You keep on talkin', lady, it'll get big."

Rose drew in a quick impressed breath, then breathed out in big blue-eyed anticipation. "Promise me, sugar, you aren't just whistling Dixie."

"*Oooh-ee,* tell 'em, sister!" That was Dido.

Coffee paused. This was getting confusing. The dame wasn't supposed to be talking back to him, sassing him, she was supposed to be shitting herself. Plus Coffee didn't like the way Miles Brady was looking at him, almost laughing. But he couldn't get a handle on this Rose. Coffee shifted ground.

"Listen, lady. I ain't horsin' around here. You get my drift?"

"What's a lady to make out of the kind of lines you feed her, mister?" said Rose. "Good thing you haven't come to ask me for a job." She put her hand on her blue snakeskin hip and turned to the bar. Sergeant Huggins stayed put, eyes fixed on Coffee.

Another King Oliver man, bassist Ed Garland,

joined Louis's cornet. He kept up a fast slap bass while Louis blew hotter.

Dido had curled her long black body in its long silver dress around a bar stool. Yawning, she hiked up the dress. It came with the mesmeric sound of silk on silk. Dido snaked out one muscled leg, stretched it, twirling the toe of her silver shoe.

"Got me a run," she said.

"Where!" Jugs leaned his stringy neck forward, trying to see as much as Dido would let him.

Coffee found himself talking to the dog. The dog didn't blink. It just sat there staring at him, pale blue eyes wide open. The dog's pink tongue lolled out between sharp white teeth. What kind of dog was it? To Coffee Trujillo, it looked like a goddam wolf.

"Ike, honey," purred Rose, "we got any of that champagne left, the kind I like?"

Ike grinned. "Yup."

"Well, get Dido and me some, and a bowl for Sergeant Huggins. And how many times do I have to tell you about that chewing tobacco! We aren't in Silver Street. Damn!"

Coffee Trujillo was getting the shakes. Things were going sour on him. He could feel Joe breathing down his neck. Even Jugs was getting jumpy. And the grin on Miles's face had gone ice cold. If he didn't shut this old blond broad up, and fast, he was going to lose them.

While he was thinking about how, without shooting her and her dog stone cold dead on the spot, things changed.

Another Chinaman was walking toward the bar. This one wasn't wearing pajamas. This one was wearing white man's clothes, smart clothes that looked good on him, and he had a gardenia in his buttonhole. He was tall and he was smiling and he was getting from one side of the Blue Canary to the other fast. For Christ's sake, where the hell had *this* Chink come from?

Li Kwan Won entered the Blue Canary alone. He owned two downtown hotels, the Ling Chu-tzû restaurant, a distillery and brewery in Chinatown, a handful of apartment houses in Pacific Heights, five high-tone speakeasies, dozens of lesser speaks, office buildings in the East Bay, and a mansion hidden in hundreds of secluded acres across the Golden Gate in an exclusive little town in Marin County called Ross. He was also Cheng Lung-t'ou, Chief Dragon Head and Incense Master of San Francisco's branch of a feared triad, the Hung League, a triad descended from the fighting monks of Shaolin.

To keep his complicated bootlegging business going, he had a fleet of trucks and speedboats, dozens of camouflaged drops and warehouses for storage, a printing plant for bottle labels and government revenue stamps, and a cutting plant to dilute the liquor. He employed white salesmen, white lawyers, white payoff men, and a white bookkeeper. His distillery workers were all Chinese. Li owned all this, but without Rose he owned nothing.

In the United States it was illegal for any Chinese to vote, to marry white, to immigrate, to testify at a white man's trial, or to own property outside Chinatown. In the United States, a Chinese man wasn't even a citizen. Everything Li had was in Rose's name, everything he had built, everything he would build. Li and Rose were more than a partnership; they were a symbiosis. Each without the other was less. Rose had staked him after the war. With the advent of Prohibition, it was easy for a man to build an empire of shadows. Because Li was Chinese, it was necessary. Dodging the law was the only way out of the Chinese ghetto. Four shady years later, Li Kwan Won was a rich man. Li had power—but not on paper.

Walking into the Blue Canary, Li saw the woman who represented in her singular person everything that Li was in the white ghosts' world. And she was in danger. He saw it that way, but that wasn't the way he thought about it. What he thought was: Rose St. Lorraine, his mother, his mentor, his only friend, was holding off four punks with guns. She had Dido, she had Ike, she had two trained 49s, and she had Sergeant Huggins, but that's all she had. While Li had been sitting around like a fool in the Intelligent Pearl, making small talk with the wife of San Francisco's district attorney.

Li had entered from Mason Street, tipping his hat to

Whispering Mike, still sitting like a dark lump in the parked Buick, with its big engine quietly idling. Mike pretended nobody was there, in the car or out. Strolling under the Blue Canary's awning, Li winked at Pete the doorman.

"No panic, Mr. Li," said Pete out of the corner of his mouth, his eye on the Buick. "The bum they left out here thinks everything's running on ball bearings. I been acting casual, so that idea kinda sticks in his mind."

Li had arrived alone through the front, but the cream of his triad, over thirty men under the command of Blue Flag, O Ti, had come around the back way. Once in, they'd fanned out through the Canary, unseen by anyone on the main floor. Since the upstairs casino didn't open for the gambling clientele until midnight, they had the upper floors to themselves. In a few decisive seconds, O Ti had ringed the upper balcony and covered all the exits. The Blinn gang was hemmed in like a Chinese sandwich.

"Good evening, gentlemen," said Li when he got to the brittle little group by the bar. From his first casual entrance, and then all the way to the bar, Li had kept his hands out of his pockets. He bowed to each politely. "What can the Blue Canary do for you?"

Coffee didn't bother to look at him. He snorted. "I don't deal with Chinks. I came to see the broad."

Li bowed to the broad, moving himself between Rose and the Blinn boys. Sipping her champagne, Rose stepped back. Sergeant Huggins didn't move. Dido balanced herself on her bar stool.

"And why is that, Mr.—"

"Coffee Trujillo's the name, not that I need to tell you anything. Right, boys?"

The boys nodded, right. Except Miles. Coffee couldn't tell if he agreed or not. He made a quick mental note to have Murray get rid of the oyster-eyed hood from Chicago when he got back to North Beach. The guy had no respect. And a guy with no respect could get ideas. Coffee had all the ideas anybody around Murray needed.

Jugs answered Li before Coffee could stop him. "So she buys Mr. Blinn's hooch from now on in. It'd make the boss real happy if she was to do that. We got a sale on."

Joe Baglietto honked with what he thought of as laughter and slapped his beefy thigh. "That's a good one, Jugsy," he said in admiration.

Jugs grinned in self-appreciation until he caught Coffee's eye. Then he shut down like a box.

Li regarded them all quietly. "But it would not make me happy."

Coffee looked Li up and down. The look on his clever Mexican face said he thought what he saw ought to be flushed down the toilet.

"So what?" he sneered. "Who're you? Some slit-eyed rat-eater. Butt out, Chinky. We're doin' business with the lady here."

Li reached for his inner pocket, smiling when Miles jumped. He took out a black enamel cigarette case. "Would anyone like a cigarette? No?" Li snapped open the case, took out another slim brown cigarette, and lit up. The white smoke blew toward Coffee. "Why is everyone so nervous?"

" 'Cause we don't like funny moves," explained Joe, his fat fingers inching toward the polite gun in his pocket.

"I find nothing funny in this situation. Please tell Mr. Blinn that Li Kwan Won is quite satisfied with the supplier he has now. Perhaps in the future?" Li shrugged his shoulders. "Who knows?"

Coffee finally snapped. He'd been ignored by a squint-eyed short guy old enough and ugly enough to have weathered the Flood, kidded by an old dame in a silly hat, laughed at by a gorgeous nigger, and stared at by a dog—he was damned if he was going to get the brush-off from a Chinaman. Enough was enough. If these people were going to play games, Coffee Trujillo would show them a good one.

Backing quickly away from Li, Coffee shouted, "OK, that's it!" and drew his gun. Miles and Joe and Jugs weren't dreaming—they found theirs as fast as Coffee found his. "Now we talk turkey. I ain't takin' no more lip. You buy from Blinn or you don't buy from nobody nohow."

To make his point, Coffee whirled and fired at Harry. The barman ducked. Coffee's 44-caliber bullet hit the big beveled mirror behind his head, shattering the glass. Shards tinkled down onto the bottles, the crouching Harry, and the bartop in pretty melody.

The people huddled around the stage gasped, pushing farther back, stepping on well-shod toes, crushing feathers and starched dickeys, spilling dinners down dismayed backs.

"Get the picture?" snarled Coffee.

The rest of the gang were jerking with excitement, their fingers hair-triggered on their own guns.

Suddenly, Li clapped his hands once, then leapt sideways, pulling Rose down and away from the bar. Dido made the same move on her own. Ike spat, disappearing behind the bar. And Sergeant Huggins launched himself at Coffee, a savage growl deep in his furry white throat.

At the same moment O Ti and his men swung over the balcony, dropping soundlessly to the silver floor. Miles, Jugs, and Joe, sidetracked by the white dog, had enough time to turn toward the black figures but not enough time to do anything about the situation. The Chinese fighters were all over them. Coffee couldn't help; his gun arm had Sergeant Huggins hanging from it by his scissoring teeth. His gun had gone skittering over the shining floor, spinning on its blue-black cylinder, and ended up pointing at Coffee. His blood smeared the dog's white jaws and the sound of his wrist bones crunching as the dog tightened its grip was lost in the sound of Coffee screaming his head off. And Whispering Mike hadn't heard a thing. Aside from Coffee's one potshot and then his frantic hollering, the whole episode was as silent as snow. Louis and Ed Garland, the bass player, stepped up the register, drowning out the rest with jazz.

Before the Blue Canary's ogling patrons had time to start getting really scared, all the guns were gone—taken off the Blinn mob as easy as harvesting windfall walnuts.

"Sergeant Huggins!" commanded Rose, picking herself up from the floor. "Down!"

The white dog with the streaming red muzzle let go

of Coffee's arm, wagged his tail, and sat down next to Rose, licking his lips. Coffee was left staring at his mangled wrist.

Ike popped his head back up over the bar. "All over?" he said.

"What you think, Pops?" snapped Dido.

"Who won?"

"Ike," said Rose, "frankly, honey, sometimes you disappoint me."

Ike looked behind him. "Get up, Harry, an' clean up the glass. We got us the Canary to run here."

"Jeez!" whined Coffee Trujillo. "Lookit what that mutt done!"

The rest of the boys said nothing. They couldn't. O Ti had ordered their arms bound behind their backs and their mouths taped shut.

"Send Mr. Olemi the doctor's bill," said Li, "and I shall send him one for the mirror. No doubt with his new Oakland still he can afford it." He nodded at the four guns piled on the bar. "Should Mr. Blinn require these again, ask him to call round. It is no hardship for us to store them for him. Meanwhile, you have taken up enough of Rose's time. My men will escort you out the back way. Someone will inform your friend that you have all gone home. It would be a pity to have him sitting in the car all night long."

Coffee was beaten. He didn't know how; the other side didn't even have any hardware. But there wasn't a thing he could do about it. All he could manage was to keep the shame off his brown face as pajamaed Chinese roughly bundled him and his boys through the Blue Canary. The customers crowded around as they went, calling out gay goodbyes. One of the chorus girls waved a hanky. The last thing Coffee heard as he was tossed out the back door into a dark alley was the sound of laughter. The whole joint was laughing at him.

"All right!" shouted Rose St. Lorraine, clapping her hands. "Papa Joe, play us a song."

At the stomp of Joe Oliver's big foot, the band swung into "Snake Rag"—a tune heavy on cornet.

Rose grinned. "That's it. Now, everybody back to

their tables! The food's getting cold and the floor show's coming on." She turned to Li, her deep blue eyes flashing. "That showed them."

Li adjusted his gardenia. "Don't rejoice too soon, Rose. This is only the beginning. We shall meet them again—and they will bring many friends, stronger friends."

"You mean like Leo Olemi? Was that what the crack meant about his getting the doctor's bill?"

"I mean him and more."

Drinking a straight rye Ike had given her, Dido climbed back on her stool. Her cropped head came up; she had a real smile on her face. "Kit, honey!" She waved an eager hand. "Where you been? An' how come a hot-shot newspaperman goes an' misses all the action?"

"What action?" Kit Dowie had just come in, hat, as usual, pushed to the back of his head. "What did I miss? Howdy, Li. What's up?"

In a rushed babble, Ike and Rose and Dido told him in words of one syllable.

"Christ," Kit whistled. "What is this, Chicago?" He was asking Li.

Li smiled without humor. "Perhaps that is just what it is."

Dido glared at Li Kwan Won. What was Kit asking Li for? Wasn't Dido there? She could answer the questions. But because Kit didn't like her kind of trouble, she kept her bad mouth shut. Not once in all the years Li had been at Rose's had Dido forgiven him for being Chinese, for Rose loving a little yellow boy more than she loved Dido, or for what she thought was their secret—that slow Sunday afternoon in Rose St. Lorraine's big back parlor when the Chinese boy had gotten the best of her. How could she? She was still black, and blacks were treated worse than dirt. Dido needed someone lower than she was to take it out on. She'd chosen Li the minute she'd laid eyes on him. It brought her only bleak comfort, but it was better than nothing. Dido would have cleared out of Rose's years back if Kit would have gone with her.

Dido grabbed Kit's hand. "C'mon, Kit. I got a hour before the show. Let's you an' me go upstairs to my place an' have us a time. These folks can take care of theirselves."

"Hold on a minute, Dido," said Kit, color rising in his cheeks. "I only have half an hour."

Dido pushed him forward. "Time *ee*-nough, Dowie!"

# Chapter 14

Two days after her kicker of a trip to Half Moon Bay with James, Esmé sat alone in the kitchen of her cute butter-yellow house, drinking strong black coffee out of a cup big enough for a full-grown frog to paddle in, using the saucer as an ashtray. It was a quarter to three in the afternoon, and it was Thursday—Leo Olemi's day. Her friend the Italian "businessman" was due in fifteen minutes. The idea made her gag.

Esmé wasn't a lady for divided loyalties. When she had a man, she stuck with him—and a fat lot of good it had done her. But Esmé's sharp brain stopped at her finely arched eyebrows; when men got to her, they got to her lower than that, much lower. And where were all her old boyfriends, anyway? Doing time, the stupid saps. Eddy was in prison; the rest—in little houses in little towns with little wives—might as well be.

"Comes of having little minds," she said aloud to a magazine illustration hanging on her pink kitchen wall. It showed two tabby kittens rolling around with a ball of string, and she hated it. But her frequent guests, James

Hamilton and Leo Olemi, thought women ought to like little furry things like kittens, so Esmé cut it out and tacked it up.

*"Chacun à son goût,"* she said in a perfect American accent, allowing herself the luxury of another cigarette. She picked a stray brown wisp of bitter tobacco out of her teeth. James Hamilton didn't smoke and he didn't like his women to smoke, not that his wife seemed to have noticed. Esmé noticed. But then, that was her job. She was trying to give up a habit she liked, and it wasn't easy. But for her big chance, an honest-to-God main event, nothing was getting in her way. Except for Leo. What the hell was she going to do about Leo?

Down south in the City of the Angels, Esmé had only worked for Mr. Olemi; now, north in Frisco, he assumed she belonged to him. It didn't seem to matter to Leo that he'd set her up to sleep with James. To him, that was expediency; it came with the position. When the job was over, he expected her to be with *him*—exclusive property. He expected that then, though he was willing to share her now. Leo was on his way over to get laid. Terrific.

Esmé exhaled through her nose, watching the dust motes spin and scatter in the pale blue smoke. She got up and stood by her bay window. Outside her little house, hanging by the cement toes of its flimsy foundation from the sheer side of Telegraph Hill, the coy sun was shining behind the hand of a cloud and the sky was a faded denim blue. From Telegraph Hill, San Francisco looked swell. To Esmé Baker, it was a big box of expensive bonbons. Boats, with sails like triangular postage stamps, scudded on the bay. Cable cars rattled up and down the bumpy hills, getting tiny people where they wanted to go slower than they could walk. It was so cute, she could eat it up. James Hamilton was out there somewhere, making deals, revving up for the White House, his silver-blond hair softly shining in the same shy sun that shone in Esmé's windows.

Combing her long fingers through her own hair, a fox-red Castle bob, Esmé yawned. James was out there somewhere, all right, but so was Leo. And she knew exactly where Olemi was. She could hear him climbing up all her wooden stairs, cursing the climb but coming anyway.

It was three in the afternoon. The little French clock on top of her icebox said so with three sweet dings. Leo was just like her clock; he kept perfect time.

Esmé was still in her cobalt-blue silk pajamas with the gold buttons. Why get dressed? In a few minutes, she'd just have to get undressed. She hadn't bothered making up her face either. Leo liked her freckles—all of them. Holy shit, what a woman had to do to make a dime!

At three, there wasn't anyone in the Blue Canary—except the entire King Oliver Creole Jazz Band. That was after they'd scared away the two High Steppers who'd been hogging all the rehearsal time. Dido got rid of them by yodeling through their slick routine. The famous New York dance team, a tall rubbery man and a short athletic woman, went off to whistles and catcalls. Steaming as they went, dragging finery, they changed course in the middle of the dance floor, heading for Rose St. Lorraine's apartments. The big-town High Steppers had a complaint. If they'd known how Rose would listen to it, they could have saved themselves the trouble.

"I seen better legs on the back end of a cow!" Dido yelled after them.

With the dancers gone, the band got down to real business—jazz. They went into a piano boogie-woogie that had Dido jiggling up and down like a Pogo stick.

"Say, man," whooped the twenty-five-year-old Armstrong on the last note, slapping his chubby thigh in delight, "that's sure some fine playin' for a white boy! Whaz that called?"

Kit Dowie looked up from the piano, his ever-present snap-brim at a cocky angle, a cigarette smoked down to nothing stuck between his teeth, squinting as the smoke traveled up his face and into his dark eyes.

"Ode to a Dead Cat," he said.

"Eeeeow! You shuckin' me, boy," said Louis.

"Must be. It doesn't have a name."

Dido stuck her cropped head over the piano. "Then you can just as well name it after me, can't you, sweet stuff? You play better'n Momma said Daddy did, an' she swore he played him some mean black keys."

Kit smiled at the fierce and feline woman. "For you, Dido, anything. But if it's for you, I'd have to play it slower, and a whole lot meaner."

Dido purred, as warm around Dowie as a hot fudge sundae.

Joe Oliver's pianist, Lil Hardin, was sitting this song out by Garland, the bass player. She poked him to whisper, "The cold lady got herself a meltin' point."

"Wisht it was me," Ed Garland said.

Louis Armstrong, in a loud checked suit, swung up his cornet, blew three high notes, two low notes, and shook the horn, emptying the spit valve on Rose's stage. "So thaz all settled, lez try it this way, yeah?"

Keeping the derby hat that he used as a mute safely on his head, Armstrong ripped into Kit's music with the lid off.

When he finished, Kit simply said, "Wow!"

"Thaz what I think. Now we get Dido to sing it with the whole band cookin'. Is that right, Papa Joe?" Louis's bright black eyes in their pudgy black face sought Oliver's, eager for approval. "What you think?"

Joe Oliver, bald and scowling, had listened from a table near the stage. Over forty, blind in one eye, the King was slurping his way through an enormous bowl of gumbo laid on by Rose's cook. There was also a pot of coffee that he wasn't sharing, and a basket of soft bread rolls. Curtly, he gave Louis the nod.

"How the words go, Dido?" asked Louis.

"Don't know." Dido, hanging over the piano, was holding Kit's sheet music. She had on her rehearsal clothes—some kind of billowy chiffon tent the color of rust in the rain. "How the hell do I know what I sup-posed to sing? Can't read the damn words, they so itty-bitty." Dido turned the page round and round until it wound up upside down.

Kit took the music out of her hands. He said, "In-tro's like this," and then sang:

> *"Sad bones in the closet,*
> *Dead cat on the creep,*
> *If I had me a pistol—*
> *I'd put me to sleep."*

"Shit, baby!" wailed Dido, her hands over her ears. "You can play but you sure can't sing!"

"But he can write him some songs," said King Oliver, hauling himself onto the stage. "Gimme that."

Kit handed the big man his sheet music. Behind Joe's back, Lil laughed. She could read music, but could he?

Dido threw herself into a chair, where she sprawled, pouting. " 'Dido's Song' needs a bluesy feel," she said, "not that uppity Armstrong horn. He's playin' for show. I can't sing but what I feel."

King Oliver's drummer, Baby Dodds, standing behind her, leaned over and pinched her high right breast, firm and juicy as a peach. "Feel that," he said. Lil Hardin laughed, winking at Louis.

Dido rose up—and socked Baby Dodds so hard his head snapped back. "Kit! What you gonna do about this nigger man?"

"Laugh," said Kit.

King Oliver was still holding Kit's music. "Son," he said, ignoring Dido, "when we finish with this here place, we all goin' back to Chicago to see a man for Okeh Records, Myknee Jones. The band an' me is cuttin' another record for the folks. Like to use a song or two of yours. 'Course I can't pay much."

Behind the King his band snickered, the Dodds brothers mouthing " 'Course not." They were all on Oliver's blind side; he missed it. Lately, Joe had taken to packing a pistol in his trumpet case—just supposin'. King Oliver's meanness was making them mad, the Dodds brothers maddest of all. Holding some of Kit's music, Joe went back to his gumbo.

While Oliver thumbed through the sheet music, Lil Hardin moved over to the piano. "I'm gonna get my Louie to quit this band," she whispered to Kit. "Get him out from under that half-blind fat man; otherwise he's gonna be a second cornet all the way. Last time we played Frisco, we did a jitney dance hall for a dime-a-dance. But this place has class—so maybe we playin' a new Harlem club in New York City, opens real soon, calls itself the Cotton Club. This feisty woman Dido say she comin' with us. We be proud to have you along too. She sing your music mostly, don' she? An' also 'cause even if you is white meat, you got you a black heart."

Coming from Lil Hardin, that was ragtime to Dido, clean and sweet and syncopated.

"I been askin' him an' askin' him. But he won't budge."

"That true?" asked Lil.

Kit shrugged. "I'm a newspaperman. But if you were to use any of the songs, I'd be proud."

Lil laughed. "*I* be proud. But you do what you do. Like me, you is a free woman."

Shoving himself back onto his feet, King Oliver cut through the whispering. "Let's get on with this here rehearsal. We got to get this number laid down like I wants it by five."

Dido had heard that crap from Dowie before. Newspaperman! Shit! It wasn't no newspaper holding Kit in Frisco, it was that ofay rich chippie with a heart as small and black as the nail on Dido's big toe. Even in her bruised unquiet mind, Dido spat the name—Lizzie Hamilton. Dido was thinking about going to see that girl. Someone had to straighten her out, and Dido was good at things like that. Listening to the band with only half an ear, she still caught her cue. Dido stepped up and sang:

> "Seems all I ever done,
> An' all I ever said,
> Leads me, Lord, to this bare room
> An' this here empty bed."

Dido couldn't sing but what she felt. She could feel that.

Li almost had Lizzie on his mind as well. Images of her jade green eyes, the husk in her voice, feathered just beyond conscious thought—like a name that has slipped the tongue. Li was disturbed by the teasing, unsought face; he found himself vaguely angry.

The bells of St. Mary's tolled the time: three o'clock.

Seventeen-year-old Chi Mai, perfect as a porcelain doll, lay in his wide bed, sleeping. Li ran his hand over her hot naked hip, then rose quietly, put on his kimono, and, like Esmé, stood smoking, staring out of the window. Behind him, Chi Mai squeaked in her sleep.

Li's large private apartment was in a four-story building above the Ling Chu-tzû on Grant Avenue. The entire building was his. It stood on the spot where his family had died. Which was why, of course, Li had bought it, gutted it, and rebuilt it. The floor above the restaurant was used for storage, the floor above that was a shrine to his ancestors—the only ancestors he ever knew, his own family.

Li's apartment was on the floor above the shrine, the top floor. It was every bit as beautiful as his restaurant three floors below or the Li family shrine. He'd imported its furnishings from China, piece by precious piece. Influenced by western taste, it was simpler than the Intelligent Pearl. In his own rooms, lines were softer, the colors subtle: soft yellows, amber, and rose. But the ceiling was black lacquer and the floor thick with a black Chinese rug. The Intelligent Pearl's confusion of detail was for show, its opulence designed to satisfy the need for the exotic in the white ghosts' search for China. But Li had no need for the ornate.

His window looked across Grant toward the west. If he had glanced up he would have seen the Fairmont Hotel above him, standing massive against the sky on top of Nob Hill, and just behind the white marble hotel, a corner of the mad Stafford mansion. Li would not look up.

He had business at five o'clock. Li Kwan Won had called the triads of Chinatown together—"let loose the horses." After years of bloody fighting among themselves, they had been for two years all under his control. As Cheng Lung-t'ou, Chief Dragon Head, he wanted a meeting at the Intelligent Pearl. Li intended to prepare well for the conflict that was surely coming.

But the green eyes just behind thought taunted him. No, it would not be! Li turned from the window, away from the hot afternoon sun of July and the singsong streets of Chinatown.

"Chi Mai?" he whispered, slipping back into his warm bed.

"Mmmm?"

*"Ngaw joong-oy Joong-gwok soong."*

Chi Mai giggled, turned toward him, and opened her young arms. *"Ngaw hai Joong-gwok saang-gwaw."* Chi Mai was a "fragrance," a member of the Hung League. Not only that, she held high office.

Lizzie was out of his mind.

Lizzie Stafford Hamilton stood in her own kitchens, stunned for the first time in her life by the amount of people employed just to feed her. A cook, a cook's help, people to clean the mess up, pantry maids, people to serve, and people to clear away. That was only when she and James were dining "at home." When they had guests, the kitchen staff could swell to dozens. And then there were the maids under the eye of the fastidious Keiko.

It had been months since she'd visited the vast gleaming citadel of Stafford gastronomy. The kitchens were modern—everything in them was smack up-to-date and crammed full of new electric gadgets. Lizzie could afford them, and James bought them. The place hummed with efficiency. Someone could have doused it down with a firehose and not disturbed a thing. It was as twenties as that. A fly wouldn't have been caught dead in it.

As soon as young Mrs. Hamilton entered, all the busywork stopped and the chatting voices faded away to nothing.

Mrs. Gravely, the cook, was up to her elbows in flour. She had on a plain brown dress, sturdy brown shoes with laces, pink support stockings, and a starched white baker's apron. The color of her eyebrows came nowhere near the color of her hair. The eyebrows were black slapdashes on her face, the wig a shade of dead ash blond. James had hired her right after he'd married Lizzie, stealing her away from the very patrician de Youngs, their Wild West past long buried. Mrs. Gravely had to be kept hidden, but she cooked like an angel.

As soon as Mrs. Gravely saw Lizzie, her thin shoulders came up in a quick hunch, as if she expected a sneaky whack with something painful. Using the Hamilton Beach Mixmaster as a shield, she curtsied, a shallow bob on thick legs, but kept her chin up in case of trouble.

"Yes, Mrs. Hamilton?" she said, a quaver in her voice. Lizzie was a stranger in Mrs. Gravely's world of beef and paté, cakes and canapés.

"Please don't stop whatever you're doing just for me," said Lizzie. It was more of a plea than a request. "I'm just visiting." Lizzie gave Mrs. Gravely the full effect of her winning dimpled smile.

The cook stared at her, kneading dough between her fingers.

To fill in the uncomfortable gap, Lizzie said the first thing that came to her mind. "What are we having for dinner tonight?"

"Dinner?" said Mrs. Gravely. "No dinner tonight, madam. These are pies." The cook swept her floury arm out, pointing at the big butcher's block in illustration. On it were six pies.

"No dinner?" asked Lizzie, wondering what the Hamilton household was going to do with six pies. Why six?

"No dinner," repeated the cook.

"Why?"

"Mr. Hamilton told me you were dining out."

"We are?" Lizzie suddenly remembered Addy Chase. She and James were going to some kind of political dinner at his house. She'd completely forgotten. "Of course, Mrs.—um, how silly of me."

Lizzie was trying to make friends. She wasn't sure why, it was just an urge she'd had as she sat in her bedroom, counting her hats and shoes and furs. The effort had made her dizzy. Higher mathematics had a way of doing that. Now, in her own home, she couldn't even remember her cook's name. Keiko did all the planning— for meals, for dinner parties, for balls. Keiko did all the planning for everything. James advised. Her husband, who hadn't been born to wealth, nonetheless took to it like the son of a sultan. He took the whole thing seriously. Except for Keiko, James had restaffed the house. The people Lizzie had grown up with, people who still thought of her as little Lizzie and of the house as the Stafford mansion, were gone. He had replaced them with solemn strangers—and Lizzie had let him. Her first mistake. James had surrounded himself in *her* house with *his* people. It was only now she realized what that meant. Lizzie was alone in James's house.

"Excuse me," said Lizzie, "but why six pies?" It took courage to ask. The cook had started out frightened of Lizzie, but a mere five minutes had turned that around.

"Why not?" said Mrs. Gravely. "We got the blueberries."

Lizzie's efforts in the kitchen were wasted. She couldn't think of a thing to say to anyone, aside from asking stupid questions about can openers and making obvious remarks about how hot it was. And they *had* all stopped for her. From the moment she came in to the moment she left, the entire kitchen staff stood there, ill at ease and waiting. It didn't take much to realize that they were waiting for her to leave. She was in the way. She was useless. And she was taking up their time. Lizzie brazened it out for five more stiff-jointed minutes, searching through her repertory of social graces for a parting shot that would get her out of the kitchens with some kind of style. Nothing was suitable. Society doesn't teach one how to chat to servants. "I'll call you next week, darling" or "See you at the races" wouldn't do.

Lizzie backed out, smiling grimly.

It was three o'clock in the afternoon. Lizzie Hamilton didn't know what to do with herself since she'd stopped drinking. Shopping held no appeal, not today anyway, and she'd been neglecting her friends. The lunches, the charities, hunts, and races, the weddings and dances were going on all around her still, but the calls inviting Lizzie to them had tapered down to virtually nothing. She knew that all she had to do to get the phone

ringing again was to pick up her own phone, give the
operator a string of numbers, wait for ten minutes, and—
but she didn't, couldn't. Who was she going to call? Aimee Crocker, busy with her second, third, or was it
fourth husband? Gertie Arlington, San Francisco's most
pernicious gossip? Her old suitor, silly Cyril Magnin? After Li, after Chinatown, what could she say to her old
friends over Waldorf salad and iced tea? They'd think she
was crazy if she told them what she'd seen. They'd believe the squalor, the poverty, the injustice of Chinatown,
of course, they knew such things existed—but it wouldn't
mean anything to them. Just as a few days ago it had
meant nothing to her.

What did it mean to her now?

What was she going to do about it?

What *could* she do about it? Buy them something?
Set up a soup kitchen? Have cook bake them some pies?
After all, didn't Lizzie Hamilton have the blueberries?

And what could she tell people like Aimee and Gertie of Li? Even without the truth, whatever that was,
they'd be scandalized. A Chinese! Good God, Lizzie! Are
you mad? they'd say. Was she?

Lizzie had no idea. She had no one to talk to about it
either. Certainly not Kit. After the scene at McGinty's
Bar and Grill, Lizzie didn't know if Kit Dowie was
speaking to her—ever. If she spoke to Addy, the sweet
man would probably smile at her, pat her on the head,
and say, "Good girl." Then he'd get to talking about
Rose. There was Rose, of course. She could talk to Rose.

Lizzie was wandering aimlessly around in her enormous house, the house that was more a museum than a
home, talking to herself. She could have done that for
hours and still not repeat a room. At a loss for anything
better, she went back to where she'd started—her own
rooms. The sound of happy unmelodic whistling pierced
what should have been silence. Lizzie followed the tune
into her solarium.

It was Keiko. She could talk to Keiko! He was oriental. He'd want to listen.

The Japanese was in Lizzie's second-story hanging
conservatory, his small face rapt as he stroked the pol-

ished leaves of his plants, untangled new growth, fed them, watered them, cherished them.

Keiko had been one of the mansion's stalwarts since he was a boy. Charles Mortimer brought him back from Japan with a shipment of samurai armor. When the boy had first arrived, if he'd had a consignment tag on his toe, without a word of English and scared to death, he couldn't have been more of a prized bit of Charles's collections than he already was. Keiko began as a gardener's assistant; a year later he moved into the house under the tutelage of the English butler. Five years later, when he'd turned twenty, Keiko was handling all the household affairs and the old butler was gone in a snit—but claiming, to save face, that he was homesick for some place called Hammersmith, in London. This was all before the turn of the century. Keiko paid lip service to Mr. and Mrs. Hamilton but, as he had for the past thirty years, *he* ran the Stafford mansion.

"Keiko, there you are!"

"Yes, missy? You want?"

"No. Well—yes, actually."

Keiko put down his pruning shears and waited. To him, she was still little Lizzie, his mistress, his property. He took care of her like he took care of his delicate shade-loving calatheas and ctenanthe, aching in their fragile green beauty. Keiko loved them all with infinite patience.

Lizzie felt as stupid with Keiko as she had in the kitchen facing Mrs. Gravely. The most she'd ever said to the smiling Japanese in her entire life, the man who ran her home so smoothly that Lizzie never even thought it needed running, had been "Where is my topaz necklace, Keiko?", or "Lovely day, isn't it, Keiko?" as he woke her with her breakfast tray, or, at the last minute, "Sixty for dinner tonight, all right?" It never surprised her that her sixty guests were fed, watered, kept warm, and sent home carrying everything they'd come with, or that each of the sixty knew Keiko's name, and he theirs.

"Are you happy, Keiko?" she said. It wasn't a great start, but it would have to do.

"Happy, missy?"

"Yes. I mean, do you like this country? Do you like San Francisco?"

Keiko beamed at her, his little face creasing into good-humored wrinkles. "It's my home. Many years."

"But would you go back to China if I didn't need you?"

Keiko's wrinkles froze. His smile sagged. "China? Why go to China?"

"God, Keiko, I mean Japan!"

There was a worried hitch in Keiko's voice. "You want me to go back to Japan? You don't need me?"

"Oh, no! Of course I need you. I just wanted to know if you were happy here."

Keiko picked his smile up, clicking his shears. "Then you know, missy. I am happy." He waved the clippers around the solarium. "Look what I got." In the San Francisco sun, plants from around the world pressed close against the warm and soaring glass. Blooms of startling color rioted in their green. "All this is mine. Must work now. Greenies need me."

It was as good as a dismissal, and Lizzie obeyed it.

On Thursday, the twelfth of July, at the age of twenty-three, Lizzie Stafford Hamilton took her first clumsy interest in other people's lives. She got nowhere.

It was three thirty. If she was dining out at Addy Chase's she might as well start getting ready. She had lots of time to take a bath—five hours' worth. A girl could get cleaner than anyone needed to be clean in five hours.

# Chapter 15

Lizzie had been soaking so long in her scented bath the skin on her fingers and toes had puckered. The sunken black Roman tub with its gold taps was long enough and deep enough to float in. If you were careless enough to fall asleep, you could easily slip under the perfumed water and drown.

But Lizzie wasn't going to fall asleep. Her mind was too active for that. It wasn't organized, but it was busy. The full-color images crowding her head—she called them thoughts—shifted and changed faster than an old-fashioned magic lantern. Li in Chinatown, Chinatown itself, James and Esmé Baker, Kit at McGinty's Bar and Grill, Charles Mortimer's huge, fat, loving face, and—larger than life—Rose St. Lorraine. Then, of course, Appetite Ike, smaller, but life itself. Where was Lizzie in all this?

Like any human child ever born, Elizabeth Sian Stafford was the center of the universe. She was beginning to realize that although this common childhood conceit might be true after all, it was *her* universe, personal and singular. Lizzie was its only occupant. It spun, like the Milky Way, in a black void, flinging out its lonely arms to catch at dust.

There were other personal universes—dozens of them, tens of dozens, thousands—and each one as true, if any were true at all, as hers. Lizzie shuddered under the warm oiled water. Why, there were millions! More! *Billions* of universes that she was not the center of, not connected to in any way. It was a daunting vision. If she gave a Stafford dollar to every human being on the surface of the earth, all the center of their own worlds, spinning breathless on a solo flight through life, she'd be broke before she got halfway round the globe. And that was assuming she went west first. A whole lot of people would be better off by a buck. It wasn't much; it wouldn't change anything. Except make Lizzie poor.

Another daunting thought. Who was Lizzie Stafford without money?

Dido had her voice, Kit could write, James lived on ambition, Rose St. Lorraine was unique, Addy had Rose, and Li's people needed him. Even Keiko could make things grow. Left in Lizzie's care, the languid green plants with their useless floppy hands would wave a sad goodbye.

Lizzie, for all her money, had nothing. Now she was really daunted. Two hours in a hot bath and she wasn't relaxed; she was as high-strung as Rose's little pie-faced dog. Lizzie's skin wasn't the only thing that was shrinking.

She reached for the big white bath towel on a rack over her wet head, pulling her steaming body out of the cloudy water. From her slippery shoulders down, she was an angry pink.

"Elizabeth!"

"What!" Lizzie twisted her head around rapidly, the water flipping off the flat matted ends of her slick black hair.

James's voice was loud; it had echoed around her mirrored bathroom like a foghorn. Where was the bastard? He sounded like Charles Mortimer had when he'd shouted at a clumsy delivery boy one winter's day, long

long ago. The boy had broken a clay figure, one of Grandfather's pre-Columbian treasures. Lizzie was eight at the time, but the tone of James's voice brought the memory back instantly. Grandfather had been *mad*. It was the only time Lizzie could recall being frightened of Charles Mortimer.

"Come here, Elizabeth. I want to speak to you." James was ordering her!

Lizzie slipped in the bath, caught herself on the towel rack, and looked up with guilt. She didn't know what she was guilty of, but the stern voice was so accusing she was sure, whatever it was, she did it.

There he was, standing in the doorway. Through the steamy white mist, James's usually handsome face looked distorted. It was the first time she'd seen him, other than sound asleep and damp from the waist down, since their dreadful second anniversary party. He was fully dressed in evening clothes, and his right hand clutched a sheaf of limp papers. He held the papers out to her. Misted mirrors reflected enough images of paper to make a book.

"Look at this!"

"Look at what? Excuse me, but you're in my way."

James was taking up the whole doorway. Wrapping the huge warm towel around her, Lizzie stepped out of her bath and squeezed by the livid district attorney with his accusing papers. Dripping wet, she padded quickly to her dressing table. Lizzie didn't want to look at papers. They must be something to do with money. Probably how much she'd lately run up in I. Magnin. What business was that of his anyway? She paid most of the damn bills, didn't she?

James followed her, avoiding her wet footprints in the thick Aubusson.

"What were you doing two nights ago in a public restaurant with a damned Chinaman?"

Ah! So that's what it was. Not money at all. Lizzie sat down at her table with its collection of wonderfully shaped bottles: ointments, creams, perfumes, lotions. Enough for the harem of the Sheik of Araby. She bent over, drying her black hair with the white towel. Through her vanity mirror, Lizzie glanced at James.

How delicious. He was trembling with precisely what she wanted him to tremble from—anger.

Lizzie turned on her padded stool, dropped the towel on the rug, and picked up a powder puff. She was naked, but James was too preoccupied with his papers to notice—or too sated elsewhere. Either way, Lizzie felt oddly relieved. She no longer cared whether her husband wanted her. That, at least, was a liberation. "Before you tell *me* where I've been, James," she said, powdering her long neck, "let me tell *you* where I've been. It could save you a few of my dollars at Pinkerton's."

That got him. James paused as Lizzie's knowledge of his private detective sank in. She could tell he was impressed that she knew, but he wasn't embarrassed by it.

"I don't give a damn where you've been." He backed away from the dressing table. The powder was getting on his fine black pants. "I merely wanted to make it clear that wherever it is you do your slumming"—he paused for dramatic emphasis—"in the future, you'll do it in private. And lay off Chinamen. That's beneath even you, Elizabeth." He looked at his watch, an anniversary present from Lizzie. "We have an hour to get to Addy Chase's. Wear something suitable."

James threw the damp papers on the dressing table and left. He didn't even slam the door.

Absently, Lizzie went on powdering her slender body. The dressing room was coated with delicate white dust and Lizzie looked like a geisha before she noticed. It didn't matter. She hadn't given her money away yet. Someone would clean it up. The important thing was that somehow James didn't matter anymore. It had struck her while he was standing on her dressing-room carpet waving his papers; she listened to him with interest but without passion. What he said and what he did caught her attention, but not her heart. Curious.

Addy Chase still lived above Van Ness Street near Lafayette Square. The architecture of his house reflected its owner. It was tasteful, sedate, a little prim, and looked, like his love for Rose, as if it would endure forever. Set back from the square behind thick hedges of twisted cypress, it reminded Lizzie of a Georgia plantation house with its white face and gracious entrance through four carved columns of white stone. The neighborhood around Lafayette had declined in social chic since the house was built, but Addy was content to stay. And as long as Addy stayed, society came to him. Addy Chase was waiting for Rose. Someday the woman would retire, and then he'd build her a home anywhere she wanted. If society stopped coming then, the hell with society.

Addy's dining room, big as it was, could have fitted into one of Lizzie's clothes closets. Painted a dark blue-green with old-gold dadoes, hung with warm rose velvet drapery, a few Art Nouveau paintings, a landscape by Gauguin, and a small Burne-Jones picked up in France before the war, it was intimate and confiding.

For Addy, Lizzie dressed suitably. She wore the clean boyish lines of Patou, an *au courant* French designer who extolled the "real" body—no padding, no stays; he wanted women healthy, streamlined. It was a simple little dress in white crepe. Seated at Addy's table with the wives of his other men guests stiffly corseted from ankle to chin, she made the older women look overdressed, frowsy and contrived. A week ago Lizzie would have been delighted with herself for that dubious accomplishment. Tonight, she merely noted it and then promptly forgot it. There were much more interesting things going on at Addy's table. For instance, his choice of guests.

Addy had put Lizzie on his right. On his left, sweating in stiff brown taffeta, sat Adele, the plump and placid wife of San Francisco's Collector of Ports, the officious Mr. Oscar Simpson. James was down at the end, opposite Addy. Halfway along on the right side sat Mr. Leo Olemi, and next to him was the mayor of San Francisco, James Rolph, Jr. "Sunny Jim," a balding loaf-shaped dandy, rivaled Addy himself in primping splendor. Genial Sunny Jim was in his third term as mayor, so popular with the people that he had no chance of missing his fourth or even fifth oath of office. Opposite Olemi sat Mr. Robert Bent and his wife, the fluttering, gushing Hattie,

in lime yellow ostrich feathers and a prune-colored dia-
manté shawl. Given a choice between the Bents, it was a
toss-up for the winner of the gauche award. Hattie Bent
was close to hyperventilation by the high-tone company
she found herself keeping, while her husband, Robert,
walked in twitching and sneezing, sat down twitching
and sneezing, and conducted his part of the conversation
accordingly.

Addy had invited the odd couple, though the
thought had made him turn pale, because the police commissioner was a political figure who supported James
Hamilton, and this was a political dinner. Addy had
thought it over and decided that the best way to help
Lizzie was to help her marriage. And the best way to do
that was to help James. What did James want? Political
power. And who could help him achieve that? Addy and
the people he knew. So, seated next to the wife of ship-
ping magnate Robert Dollar was the assistant district attorney, Mr. Harvey Bellew. Stringer was in Addy's house
because Addy thought the fellow might be a good campaign manager when the time came. From what he'd
heard about the fellow with the red eyebrows and absurd
red mustache, he was as loyal to Hamilton as Appetite
Ike was loyal to Rose. On either side of Hattie Bent were
Herbert Fleishhacker, the president of the London-Paris-
American Bank—who'd given a zoo to San Francisco
and money to Robert Dollar and, lately, to Sunny Jim as
well—and Amadeo Peter Giannini. Though A.P. didn't
own the place outright, Giannini ran the Bank of Italy by
the sheer force of his personality.

For the necessary private finance, a few of Addy's
rich, influential, and more active friends were there with
their wives. All the men were members of the Pacific
Union Club. Addy hadn't yet brought Hamilton's name
up for membership, but the game was still early.

Until Addy told them *why* they were seated at the
same table with the Bents and Bellew, and even though it
was Chase's table, they stared. Only Addy Chase could
have made them stay. And only Addy could have invited
A.P. Giannini and Herbert Fleishhacker to the same din-

ner, or served wine in the presence of the arrogant and
abstemious Robert Dollar.

The most important personage from Addy's point of
view was his old chum, Sam Jenkins. Still fat and still
pixieish, he came with his elegant wife Mariana. She was
of pure Spanish lineage, going straight back to the aristocratic Sepúlvedas; her branch of the family once had title
to the whole of northern California and lost it when the
Americans carved up the precious land for themselves,
just as the Spanish had taken it away from the Indians.
Mariana's face was so perfect it could have been chiseled
from a bar of expensive soap.

All in all, a very mixed bag of twenty-five people ate
their way through a rack of lamb, a baron of beef, assorted vegetables, and a choice of desserts.

The number was odd because Bellew and Olemi had
no wives for the socially correct Addy to invite—and it
would take a miracle to get Rose to grace his table. She
still wouldn't marry him.

At the end of the nineteenth century, the men made
rich by the glamorous Gold Rush City, Sam and Addy's
forerunners, had been in their prime. It was an aristoc-
racy of boots and whiskers, a blithe leadership of irre-
sponsible immorality. As the century turned, they turned
with it, square-dancing through the coffers of glittering
San Francisco, pilfering with a fine impudence, encouraged by a national economic climate created by the Wiz-
ard of Washington, the man from Ohio, "Mother of
Presidents," the man who financed McKinley—Mark
Hanna. Like fat and venal Hanna, they were all oblivious
to social need. When McKinley was President, their
motto *and* the country's might as well have been "The
public be damned." For some, these were marvelous
happy-go-lucky years. No taxes, no welfare, no responsi-
bility to their fellow man. Jumpin' Jehosaphat!

Sam and Addy were young, then, and their underdog ideals sparked the air they breathed. They were just
as suspicious of Hanna's organized capital as they were of
Gompers' organized labor. Men in the middle, young
men of affluence in a middle-class revolt, they broke away
from both the Republican and the Democratic parties. By

1912, they were in the thick of it, eager delegates at the birth of the Progressive Party, wanting their hero, Teddy Roosevelt—McKinley's successor, the man who represented everything they believed in—back in the White House for a third term. Since Teddy had no party by then to back him, liberal men across the country founded a brand new party for the vigorous ex-President.

When reporters asked Teddy how he felt about his nomination for President by the Progressives, Teddy boomed, "I'm as fit as a bull moose!" After that, it was the Bull Moose Party. The then Governor of California, Hiram Johnson, was nominated for Teddy's Vice-President. For Sam and Addy, California's Johnson was the icing on a splendid cake of a splendid celebration for a splendid cause.

Bull Moose men saw themselves as the creators of a party that would level America. It would bring down the rich, advance the poor, limit armaments, give women the vote, bust trusts and monopolies, stop child labor, promote the six-day week, pay out unemployment insurance —the Bull Moose Party would "use government as an agency of human welfare." Even when the party's policies were diluted, subverted, by the conservatives among them—Roosevelt's, as later Harding's, great weakness lay in his loyalty to his friends—they still hung on. But the split by the Progressives away from the Republican Party weakened both, and the Progressives lost the election of 1912 to the Democrat, Woodrow Wilson. When they did, the Bull Moose Party gamely supported the new President, Wilson, who had many of the same ideals, marshaling their growing resources, readying their party for the election of 1920.

But in January 1919 Teddy Roosevelt died.

With him went their political hearts, the hope of having anyone to vote for. Woodrow was a good man who broke his own heart over the League of Nations, but he couldn't move them as Teddy had done—with his presence, his clear decisive mind, his humor, his sheer boundless energy. Teddy couldn't keep still. He hadn't paced, he'd raced. If denied a straight line, he'd circle.

It had been almost five years since either Sam or

Addy had actively interested themselves in politics; from 1919 on, any votes cast by either man were against, not for. But Addy, though grown more cautious than Sam, found something inside himself that still believed. And it was he who'd noticed the plausible career of young Hamilton, calling Sam's attention to its possibilities.

James wasn't Teddy Roosevelt; aside from everything else, Teddy was fat, he was loud, and he was short. James was slender, soft-spoken, and tall. The only physical similarity lay in teeth, neither man's most flattering feature. No one could take Teddy's place, but there was something about James that reminded them of when they were young, a kind of fine clean blade that might cut through the body politic. They had decided, cautiously and carefully, to groom and support James Hamilton in his future bid for the White House. The actuality was a long way off, but it would pass the time with a sweet tickle of the old fervor. For Addy Chase and Sam Jenkins, it would be their last waltz in the *danse macabre* that was politics.

Addy Chase and Sam Jenkins together had devised this little semiformal dinner party to introduce James Hamilton to the choicer elements of the Pacific Club and the money of San Francisco. Of course, that was before Addy had had his little talk with Lizzie's husband. Though something had bothered Addy about that meeting, he still didn't know what it was, and so the dinner remained on. So far, he hadn't confided in Sam; he had nothing to tell him. Best to test the water before diving in, one way or the other. Which was why Bellew, Bent, and Olemi were here.

Down at his end of the long table, James was blooming under the attention. By now, everyone knew why they were there. Addy had given a speech. It was worded more graciously than Murray Blinn's little after-dinner peptalk over in North Beach a few days previously, but it was just as succinct. When Addy sat down, the wives couldn't keep their eyes off Hamilton. Aside from James's high-bred blond looks which set most female hearts a-flutter under the worst conditions, he might also be their leader one day. There was enough charisma in that idea to seduce Elizabeth, the Virgin Queen. And Lizzie would be First Lady.

Giannini, Fleishhacker, and Dollar studied their man, counting the cost—and more importantly, the possible profit. Sunny Jim toasted James. After all, he only wanted to be governor. It would take the young man years to be where Sunny Jim would be in five—six? It could only be to the mayor's credit that he had seen so early the promise of a great man's career.

Lizzie was amused and her amusement heartened her. The blind destructive anger was gone. It was funny, but once she had something else to think about besides James, thinking about James became easy, detached. And the way she was listening was different. No, not the way she listened. What was different was that she listened at all. Until this moment, finding herself in mixed company, Lizzie would have set about outclassing the women, flirting with the men. All her life these activities had been the sole point of a social evening. Now, picking at her fruit compote, she sat composed and silent. The vaporing of Hattie Bent, the shallow bovine eyes of Adele Simpson steadily fixed on James, even the languid phrases of Mariana Jenkins threading themselves with perfect timing through the politically tangled talk of the men, brought no response from Lizzie. Without knowing it, she was listening to the undertone—the meaning beyond the words. Lizzie was paying attention.

The men were talking about the impending visit of President Harding to San Francisco. They'd gotten past the tacit acceptance of their support for Hamilton in his future career. After all, this evening was only a beginning, not a campaign meeting.

Addy was saying, "I thought I'd introduce James to Warren while he's here. No better way to start than to cultivate friendships in high places. After all, politics is who you know."

Stringer Bellew, who'd been listening eagerly all evening with growing triumph, congratulating himself throughout on his happy five-year attachment to the right man, thought it was time to jump in.

"Speaking of friendships and Harding," he began, as

the attention of Addy's table turned toward him, "I've heard that back in Washington, old Harding's friends have been—"

Addy looked at Stringer, his spoon of fruit compote halfway to his mouth.

Quicker than a bullet, Leo cut James's assistant off. "What do you think James ought to aim for first?" Olemi was asking Addy. All eyes left Stringer, swinging with interest back to Chase.

Addy, not seeming to notice the snub to Bellew, began his outline on the best way into the White House: first, perhaps, the governorship of California or a seat in the Senate—James was very young; he had time—but for the moment they had William McAdoo to think of. McAdoo had California's heart. He'd served under Wilson; he was the man's son-in-law, coming to California to build a political base for himself after Wilson's term was over. Centered in Los Angeles, he enjoyed the patronage of Edward Doheny, one of the richest men in America. But McAdoo was a Georgian. James, born and bred in San Francisco, would displace him—with San Francisco's help.

"The boy needs only one high office from which to view the presidency. Eventually the governorship, or better still as senator from California. The latter would put him in the bosom of Washington. There he would make the most powerful contacts. But for now, perhaps the state attorney general?"

Lizzie hadn't turned with the rest of the table; she was still watching Leo. What she saw puzzled her. Leo was looking at James and James was looking at a red-faced Bellew. Bellew's eyebrows and mustache were lost in his furious flush. The expression on her husband's face was the same one he'd given Lizzie when he'd ordered her away from Chinatown. How interesting—James didn't want Stringer to talk about whatever he knew of the President's friends. Why was that? And what did Mr. Olemi have to do with it?

Meantime Addy, and now Sam as well, had moved to more immediate things. They were talking about the situation in San Francisco. As district attorney, James

would have to make the most of his present position to
create a strong base for the run on Sacramento.

James was already doing that, thought Lizzie. What
was Fatty Arbuckle for, if not to get James in the public
eye? And wasn't there something strange going on about
a new rape case, a case that involved a young Creole girl,
Violet Louise, and the son of a rich banker, Buddy Le
Blond? Hadn't someone at McGinty's Bar and Grill said
something to Kit about it? That's right! The man told Kit
it was fishy, and Kit said it wasn't fishy, it was fixed. That
case was Bellew's case. And Bellew was James's man. A
few small but key things were becoming clear to her. One
of them was how far James would go to satisfy his ambition. Lizzie wondered if Addy knew that, or his sweet
apple-faced friend, Sam Jenkins?

"So far," Sam was now saying, "it seems to me that
the most important mess right here in San Francisco that
James ought to concentrate on is the growth of local
bootlegging. Our city is nothing like New York or Chicago, and we damn well don't want it to be. We have to
nip it in the bud."

Lizzie watched James as he responded smoothly.
"That is precisely what I've been thinking, Sam. I've been
working with Mr. Olemi here on that very problem."

There was something in her husband's tone that
wasn't quite right. It was smoother, if possible, than ever.
More than smug, it smirked—as if James was sharing a
joke with Olemi. At whose expense? There was no telling
from Leo Olemi. His face was still, so much of it below
the unremarkable nose, the muddy eyes hooded, the little
mouth grim. Lizzie was impressed. James, for all his silvery eloquence, was nothing compared to Olemi. The
Italian had strength. If James thought he was sharing a
prank, like a schoolboy, Mr. Olemi was a schoolmaster.
He was not amused. Lizzie was new at this; she had no
idea what was going on. But she'd bet more than a ruby
hair clip that they were up to something, and that Leo
Olemi did not consider it, as her husband did, a game.
Also, only two other people at Addy's table were in on
whatever it was: Robert Bent and Stringer Bellew. They

both had the most peculiar smiles on their unattractive faces.

Bent's was the worst. And his nose kept running. Hattie handed her revolting husband one of Addy's fine linen napkins.

Though warned once, irrepressible Stringer bounced back into the conversation. "Say, our office is right in the thick of the rumrunners. We heard just yesterday that things are hotting' up, didn't we, James? Seems there's a gang of bootleggers right in Chinatown, Chinese bootleggers, can you imagine?" Stringer quickly looked for approval from James and, getting it, continued. "And they say the leader of the whole operation works out of the Blue Canary. What do you think of that!"

Lizzie's heart leapt into her throat. She knew what she thought of that, and what Addy Chase thought of it as well. At the mention of the Blue Canary, Addy's long face went white. It seemed to Lizzie that even the glass in his spectacles frosted. That creature, Bellew, was talking about Li!

The rest of the ladies and gentlemen around Addy's table leaned forward, titillated by tales of the exotic yellow peril, not to mention the racy doings of evil rumrunners. As they did, their hands tightened with the curiosity of voyeurs, but without irony, around the stems of their wineglasses. All, with the exception of Dollar.

Stringer, excited by the attention, went on. "We've got some inside dope that tells us there's going to be a gang war between these Chinese and some white bootleggers led by a fellow called Murray Blinn out of North Beach. But we've got our eye on them. The Chinese are going to get what's coming to them, no worry about that."

"And the white bootleggers?" asked the lazy voice of Sam Jenkins's wife, seductive Mariana.

"Oh, yes, them too."

Just at this moment, Lizzie caught James's eye. The son of a bitch was laughing at her! With total clarity, she remembered the piece of paper by his bedside. The word Chinatown written over and over. Was this what it meant? Of course it did. Was James going to do something to Li? Of course he was! It would be another big feather in his cap, wouldn't it? Oh, God, this was what Li meant when he said that James was his enemy. Lizzie glanced at Addy. If he hadn't come to the same conclusion, she'd be surprised. Li was Addy's son. The poor man—and he'd been thinking of backing James for President.

What would he do now? For that matter, what would Lizzie do?

Whatever Lizzie was going to do occupied her whole mind. It was wonderfully focused.

She was in bed. It was hours later, and, aside from the rain, the Stafford mansion was quiet. Outside her second-story windows the sky was dark bullet-gray and slanted—rain swiftly slid down it, puddling up in Charles Mortimer's maze. The trees had folded their branches, huddling together for comfort. Lizzie looked at her bedside clock. Three in the morning. So far, nothing had come to her. Whatever she'd learned at Addy's dinner was nothing to what Li must already know. How the hell could she help? The brief thought of shooting James dead crossed her mind, but she put that idea away. Lizzie wanted to do something with her life, but she didn't think twenty years in jail—with her money she'd beat the rope —sounded too creative.

She switched the light on. And off as fast as she could. The telephone in James's study between her bedroom and his was ringing. At three in the morning? At the seventh ring, Lizzie heard James pick up the phone. It couldn't have woken him up. He'd never have been able to answer that quick if it had. His room was on the same enormous scale as hers. She flipped back her covers and tiptoed to the connecting door. Wasn't she supposed to use a glass against the wall to eavesdrop? She didn't have one. So Lizzie just pressed her ear against the wall instead and listened.

"What did you expect?"

That was the first thing James said. Who was he talking to? Esmé? If it was Esmé, Lizzie wasn't that interested. But the next thing she heard told her whoever it was, it wasn't his redheaded mistress.

"So step on her harder; that *is* your specialty, isn't it? . . . What do you mean, *him?* . . . I see, he called your trump, did he? That's very interesting. Well, do what you have to do."

There was a long pause while James was obviously listening and Lizzie listened to him listening. She was getting cold.

"Of course you'll have protection." James sounded irritated. "Olemi's with you on this. Don't bother *me* with details. What could be easier than getting rid of a load of Chinese? Who'll care, but that woman of Chase's?"

Lizzie forgot the cold and the slanted rain. He was talking about Rose St. Lorraine. Her charming husband James, the district attorney of San Francisco, was up to his fine eyebrows in something that no future President could get away with, not if Lizzie Stafford could help it.

"Listen to me carefully, Blinn." James's voice went on. "If you ever call me here or *anywhere* again, I'll have Leo cut your balls off. Got it? . . . Good."

James hung up. When Lizzie could hear him safely back in his own room, she turned on her lamp again, climbed back into her own cozy bed, and pulled the covers up. Next to her clock was her package of dried seahorses, a small red paper packet covered on one side with queer Chinese writing. Lizzie ran her fingers over the black dots and dashes. It smelled of Chinatown, full of ancient secrets.

Leo, the nice Italian businessman, cut the balls off Blinn? And who was Blinn? The bootlegger James's office was supposed to be chasing. And who was Blinn working for? James Hamilton, San Francisco's golden child. My goodness, you learn something every day if you listen.

Lizzie wiggled under her sheets, slipping the seahorses under her pillow.

What Lizzie had learned made her horribly happy.

# Chapter 16

Kit decided the reason he was losing at poker was because it was Friday the thirteenth. Lady Luck must be superstitious.

But Lady Luck had nothing to do with Violet Louise losing *her* poker game; it wasn't chance that dealt Violet's cards, it was her fellowman. Kit had no doubt which fellowman had done the dealing—James Alexander Hamilton, dashing ambitious young district attorney. He even knew why. Everyone knew who Buddy Le Blond's father was, and everyone knew what Hamilton wanted. Simple mathematics. Stroke a banker, win a bank.

All morning Violet Louise, in a dark gray dress with a high white collar, had sat in the courtroom, crowded with the craning salacious who came because the trial was about sex—if rape with violence could be considered sex—the merely curious, and more than a few who had nothing better to do with their time. But the biggest, noisiest bunch was Buddy's claque—the entire Stanford football team, plus most of the coaches. Dormouse quiet, legs crossed sedately at the trim ankles, gloved hands resting in her lap, Violet's small steady head, with its corona of naturally curling hair, hair the color of honey on buttered toast, was held up with pride. She never once looked toward the jury or at the accused, Buddy Le Blond.

Buddy leaned back in his chair, smirking at the jury, turning his head to the crowd behind him like a ham actor seeking applause. Buddy's brown hair was slicked down to black and parted in the middle. He had a big head, a small nose and jutting jaw, and the build of a collegiate football player. Which was what he was. Buddy played halfback for Stanford down in Palo Alto. Lacking brains, he lacked good grades. So his father bought him into college, and Stanford was proud to have him. Buddy wasn't smart, but he was the best football player they'd had for years. Kit, from a press seat, thought Violet Louise was lucky the team hadn't brought along its cheerleaders.

Violet didn't look at Buddy because Violet had seen enough of Mr. and Mrs. Le Blond's little boy—his heavy red face inches above hers, streaming with sweat, the smell of his sugary breath—before Buddy had come into her mother's hat shop he had been chewing a Baby Ruth bar. For the rest of her life Violet would retch at the hint of chocolate. What Buddy had said as he raped her in the shop's back room among the colored scraps of felt and the feathers, the fine net and the big fake flowers. What he'd done with the knife. How he'd cut her with it, carved that word on her trembling stomach, notched little nicks on her arms and neck, the insides of her soft thighs, cuts like open mouths, little mouths bleeding on her mother's hats. Oh, Violet Louise had seen Buddy. She'd be seeing him for as long as she lived.

Buddy played to his crowd; Violet played to no one. She looked at the judge. After three hours of her sad unswerving gaze, Judge Mordden was beginning to wonder who was on trial here.

Violet was the daughter of a French milliner. If Buddy Le Blond's lawyer, Harold McNutt, hadn't spread the news through the willing press, no one would ever have known she was also the daughter of Maurice Sayac, merchant seaman, a *black* merchant seaman. Sayac was dead; Violet's mother, Jeanne, took back her maiden name when she left New Orleans to settle in San Francisco. Jeanne had hoped Violet would "pass," with her creamy skin and honeyed hair. The widowed mother needed to hope. For blacks, France had an open, if primarily curious, heart; America had no heart at all.

For Kit Dowie, covering the trial was like going back two years in time. He'd sat in the same press seat, in the same courtroom; it was the same kind of case, the same rotten cards, the same dealer. Expedient injustice got all the aces again. Fatty was taken for a patsy then; it was a little Creole girl's turn now.

Kit was in the Criminal Court building's pressroom along with every other reporter sent to cover the Le Blond rape trial. The pressroom was cold and bare, painted a dark army green. Like tales of men locked away on Devil's Island, the paint was scrawled with the names of newsmen past; little scratches ticked off their empty hours.

The reporters were waiting in the pressroom, fogged with cigar smoke, the one long table covered with brimming ashtrays, leftover lunch out of paper bags, coffee-stained cups, typewriters, telephones, and copies of everybody's newspapers, because early in the afternoon the trial had come to a standstill. Buddy Le Blond's lawyer, Harold McNutt, was in the judge's chambers along with the prosecution's attorney, Stringer Bellew. Kit was waiting for the result of the confrontation. No doubt, that shyster McNutt had come up with something new and startling that would hold the case over until Monday. Mordden was a decent judge, but with both sides working for Buddy, what could he do?

Kit was trying to win some money in a penny-ante poker game, a game hotly contested by six other perpetually broke newspaper folk: men from the *Chronicle* and the *Call-Bulletin,* a guy from the *Oakland Tribune,* one from the *Sacramento Bee,* and a lady from a paper down the peninsula, even a reporter sent up from Harry Chandler's *Los Angeles Times.* The dame from the small-town paper, peppery and foul-mouthed, wore a green eyeshade

as she slapped her cards down with the panache of a
riverboat gambler. Kit Dowie may have been one of the
highest paid reporters on the *Examiner* staff, but that
didn't mean money. It just meant a little more money
than the cubs were paid. In Kit's game, the lady was the
winner. Kit folded.

Watching his colleague from the *Times* go down
with a pair of kings, Kit wondered what McNutt had got
hold of now that would put Buddy back on the streets.
For openers, on Wednesday morning McNutt had di-
vulged the irrelevant but shocking news that Violet Louise was a "nigger," or as good as, waving her birth
certificate at the jury to prove it. Judge Mordden had
been fastidious enough to instruct the jury to disregard
that sad fact, but Kit noted the immediate change in the
way those twelve differing faces, all nice shades of white,
watched the little girl from New Orleans. After McNutt's
insidious insistence on pointing out who Violet Louise's
father had been, they went from mawkish to malevolent.

Buddy's lawyer was a graduate of the grand old
school of lawyering. Thumbs hooked in his braces, his
potbelly going on before him, Harold McNutt's voice
boomed through the courtroom like a preacher tolling
doom, his rich tongue rolling off biblical quotations with
the ease of an oil spill. He'd spent Thursday, the day Kit
got in an hour's band practice at the Blue Canary, trying
to make Violet Louise out a common whore on the
grounds that her mother, Jeanne, made hats for Rose St.
Lorraine's girls.

" 'And the Lord set a mark upon Cain,' " brayed
McNutt, glaring at Violet—Kit wondered what *that* hat
looked like. "And this poor boy, *if* goeth after her he
did"—McNutt put a fatherly hand on Buddy's huge
shoulder; Buddy beamed at him—"then 'he goeth after
her straightway, as an ox goeth to the slaughter.' "

Looking at Buddy's neck, thick as baked ham, Kit
thought McNutt got the part about the ox right. All Friday morning, Buddy's lawyer had called into question
Violet's "native" intelligence. Dowie loved that touch:
shades of William Jennings Bryan. Under McNutt's
happy guidance and Bellew's limp counterattack, things

were now winding down to a case of mistaken identity. The jury was being told that Violet was too stupid to remember *who'd* raped her, if anyone had raped her at all. In that case, wondered Kit, who cut her up? Her mother, making unusual hats?

No point in wondering where McNutt got his information. He was being fed directly by the district attorney's office. Kit knew that, because Dido had told him. And Dido knew because Stringer Bellew confided in one of Rose's girls, the one he visited on a regular basis, that poor fish, *café-con-leche*-colored Lupe. Lupe had shiny suspender-button eyes, and she swayed when she walked like she still had a terracotta jug balanced on her head. She'd come to the Blue Canary from a little village in central Mexico—no one but she could pronounce its name—where the women really did carry pots on their heads. Kit called Lupe a poor fish because, whether she liked him or not, Stringer liked *her,* enough to pay for her time four days out of seven. Lupe didn't like him; she hated Stringer Bellew.

"He has verree strange ideas of what peoples do in bed together, ha!"

So Lupe told Dido what Stringer told her. Dido told Kit. Easy.

And Kit couldn't write a word of what he really knew. First, because the *Examiner* wouldn't print it, and second, because it would topple James Hamilton, or, at the very least, rock him, and that would hurt Lizzie. Once Kit let rip on the Le Blond story, he could throw in so much muck after it, James would need one of Pershing's armored tanks to get out from under the barrage. Aside from the Le Blond and Arbuckle cases, there was his connection to Leo Olemi and who Leo really was. Lately the eastern press had been full of the rise of the Torrio-Capone mob in Chicago and the takeover of New York's underworld by something being called the Mafia. Then there was his charming bedfellow, with enough bad habits to give a man nightmares, Police Commissioner Robert Bent; but best of all, there was James's war record —a record that had been left behind on the shores of France. Dowie covered the war, but he'd also kept track of James. He'd been interested in the man's career even before Lizzie got herself involved with him. Hamilton had what Kit thought of as the Ancient Mariner's "glittering eye." From the first time he met him at Phoebe Hearst's Military Ball, Kit had a hunch about James Hamilton. Kit was sent to the ball by Phoebe's son, Willie, as society hack for a day; Willie had been punishing him for something he couldn't even remember now. Kit's hunch had proved right. Over in Europe, while other poor saps got turned into fertilizer for the future crops of France, James kept well back of the front lines, wheeling and dealing in army supply. James came home from the war with full pockets. Black-marketeering for both sides in Paris was the least of it. It reminded Kit of Addy Chase's long-ago benefactor, Matthew Clinton Chase, though, compared to Hamilton, the ancestral Chase was an honorable man. Nice copy for a presidential hopeful.

Kit had the *Examiner* to thank for avoiding his growing conscience. If the paper hadn't been sitting on the Le Blond case, Kit might have had to play it fair, write it as he saw it. As it was, he had no choice but to dummy up, and keeping silent meant leaving Hamilton alone. The only thing that kept his conscience in check was what Stringer had told Lupe about the short future of Buddy Le Blond. The proposed end to the ugly trial wasn't Kit's style, but it looked like all anyone was going to get that could be given the name justice.

At least it meant he didn't have to hurt Lizzie. Kit had waited two years for Lizzie to wise up and realize exactly who it was she'd married. Lately, that was what Lizzie had been doing, in her own screwball way. Once the kid divorced Hamilton, Hamilton was a sitting duck. Kit's worries about Lizzie would be over. Or so he'd thought until last Wednesday, when she got this crackpot idea about using Li Kwan Won against James. If she kept that game up, things were worse than ever.

Meantime, Kit was right. Le Blond's attorney, McNutt, had delayed the trial with some garbage about new evidence. Evidence, he claimed in a voice meant for the press, that would clear his client completely.

Newsmen, accustomed to charades, grown cynical

by the real truth behind what ended up in print, threw on coats, jammed on hats, grabbed up pencils and typewriters, and left the rest of the mess for someone else to clean up. The pressroom cleared out fast. As they went, everyone tried to borrow a buck from everyone else. Reporters were always broke—except the lady from down the peninsula in the green eyeshade. They were also offered bets on the outcome of the case. The *Call-Bulletin* gave odds of a hundred to one in favor of Le Blond. There were no takers. Besides, all interest was now fixed on what was available at San Francisco's speakeasies.

Kit's interest was more complicated. First, he'd call in his gelded copy on the trial, then take a taxi over to the Mission district for a browse through McDonald's, first-class purveyor of secondhand books. Then he'd go home; he needed a bath. The Le Blond trial made him feel dirty. Finally, if nothing was breaking back at the *Examiner* from his city editor, he'd take Dido to dinner at Blanco's. Blanco's provided private dining rooms. Kit was sick of people, but Dido wasn't people, Dido was a friend, and eating a good dinner with her and listening to her sassy tongue in a private dining room sounded like nirvana. When Dido had to get back to the Canary to sing, he'd probably wind up at O'Flooty's. If Kit was lucky, he would catch O'Flooty with nothing to do but talk. Talking was O'Flooty's game. Listening to O'Flooty was one of Kit's. Fearless's head was bursting with words and the love of words. The grand population of literature wailed around in there like English apparitions. No one had told him that literature was dead, though he should have known, haunted as he was by its ghost.

By late tonight, Kit was sure he was going to need to talk to someone, and besides talking, O'Flooty was one of those rare people who listen.

That was the way Kit wanted his evening to go. But the only part that went well was the beginning, McDonald's, San Francisco's best secondhand bookstore. He found a complete set of Zola's twenty-volume saga of the Rougon-Macquart family, bound in soft brown leather with gold lettering on the covers. The kid with pimples behind McDonald's dusty counter said they'd deliver for a regular customer like Dowie, so Kit took home only one book, *Nana*.

Reading page five, he was hiking up Jones Street, bumping into people and muttering "pardon," when turning the corner at Eddy he spotted the pearl-gray Cadillac cabriolet parked outside the Crawford Apartments with its top up. In it was Lizzie. She had to be cooking in there. The sun was still high, hot and yellow. Oh, hell, if Kit wasn't careful, there went his leisurely bath and probably the rest of the evening as well.

"Kit! I've been here for over an hour waiting for you." Lizzie started to get out of her car.

"Don't," said Kit, snapping *Nana* shut.

"Don't what?"

"Don't get out. I'm tired. I need a bath."

"Don't be silly. I've waited this long. I can wait while you bathe." Lizzie kept on coming.

Kit pushed the car door closed on her. "I don't need this now, Lizzie."

"Need this? What's this?"

"You. I don't need you."

"Are you mad at me? For what happened at McGinty's?"

"No, I'm not mad, I'm tired. I'm not in the mood to listen to your problems right now."

"Gosh."

"Gosh indeed. I'm surprised, too." Kit dug in his pocket for his key, moving away from the car toward the Crawford's front door. "I'll see you tomorrow or the next day or when—"

"Kit," said Lizzie.

The tone of her voice made Kit turn back to Lizzie. He paused. "What now?"

"Shut the fuck up."

"Excuse me?"

"I came here to talk to you, and I'm talking to you."

Kit took a good look at Lizzie Stafford. There was a new set to her strong jaw, the shining black hair was back to straight, and the green eyes weren't coy, they were clear and direct. And she wasn't wearing another silly costume. All Lizzie's lines, her dress, her face, her eyes, were simple. It looked safe enough. Besides, Kit couldn't help it, tired or not, dirty, sick of the human race, longing for the sound of a sane voice, Lizzie got to him. This time it was through his damn curiosity. He knew he'd probably regret it, but he said it anyway, "In that case, this time I'm not just listening, I'm *talking* to you."

"That's a deal," said Lizzie, and took his arm. "I hope you've got coffee."

Kit lay on his bed, hat and shoes off, smoking and talking while Lizzie walked the length of his room and back on her long legs, repeating her short journey over and over. If this conversation had taken place in the Stafford mansion she might have hiked through half the rooms by now. *Nana* had been safely deposited on top of a pile of books that had Kit's kind of order to it; it was his French pile. Lizzie couldn't keep still. What she was saying and what she was hearing wasn't for sitting down. It was for running. But where? And when? It was disturbing and, in its way, liberating. Her color was up; her green eyes flashed like one of Gump's expensive jades.

"For God's sake, Kit, why haven't you told me all this about James and the war and Mr. Olemi and Blinn before?"

"You weren't ready to listen."

"But, they're criminals. And James wasn't a hero in France? God! We gave him all those parties and parades. Damn you, you knew it all along. He's a criminal too!"

"What's so special about James? So is Li Kwan Won."

"Is he?"

"Of course. Where did you think his money came from?"

"He works for Rose."

"Does he?"

"Doesn't he?"

"They work together."

"You mean Rose is a criminal too?"

"You could look at it that way. If you were a federal agent, you'd sure as hell have to look at it that way. On the other hand, if you were a federal agent, you wouldn't call James a criminal."

"No?"

"No. You'd call him a businessman."

"A businessman!"

"And a politician. In the name of politics, like that old-time religion, many interesting things have been done. James's crimes are against ideas and values and a man's dreams. Unimportant things like that."

"God, Kit. What am I going to do? I'm married to a crook."

"So what's new? He was a crook before you married him. Lots of decent women are married to less than decent men. For love, they stick by their men."

"I'm not standing by James!"

"Decent of you."

"Kit! Don't get mean again. I'm trying to talk to you."

"Then stop this crap about being married to a crook. Everybody in Frisco but you and the voting public and sweet Addy Chase knows about the DA. Tell me why you're deserting our James."

"Because I hate him."

"Hate binds."

"You're right. I don't hate him."

"So where does that leave you? Without hate, love dies."

"I don't feel anything."

"Terrific. What are you going to do about that?"

"Leave him."

"Jesus, Lizzie! So you leave him, then what?"

"Then? I don't know."

"Well, kid, that's better than nothing."

Lizzie's decision, sudden and final, stopped her pacing. She felt like sitting down. So she sank onto Kit's piano stool. It was either that or the floor.

Kit had his hands behind his head. He was grinning at her, but this time it wasn't like the Cheshire Cat, ear to ear and full of mischief. Kit looked relaxed and happy. For the next two minutes Kit and Lizzie sat quietly in each other's company. It was the first time, and the last, that they were both happy together. Moments like that are, by nature, brief. Lizzie, of course, was the one who broke it. She wasn't mature enough to savor the rare.

"Why are Li and Rose criminals?"

"They break federal laws. At least, Li does. Rose fronts for him. That makes her answerable as well."

"What federal laws?"

Kit held up his fingers. "Like Elizabeth Barrett Browning, let me count the ways. The Volstead Act—"

"Volstead?"

"Lord, Lizzie! Bootlegging."

"But everybody does that. I do that."

"True, but not on Li's scale. Besides, you buy, you don't sell. Then there's prostitution—"

"Oh, heck, Rose's been doing that for years."

"Being an old hand at something doesn't make it legal. Then there's opium."

"Opium!"

"Nice stuff if you can get it, and Li gets it. Then there's the matter of smuggling in Chinese brides."

"Dear God, now what are you talking about?"

"Oriental immigration. This country counts it a crime for a Chinese or, for that matter, a Japanese to enter this country in any capacity. If they're rich they're allowed to pass through, dropping dollars, or whatever they call money, as they go, but if not they get the boot. Therefore, Chinese males already here, *born* here, but with no rights as citizens—it's a moot point to our government whether they actually *are* citizens—those men who need wives, and you'll admit needing a woman is a natural American desire, have to break the law to get them. Li helps them break it."

"But isn't that good of him?"

"What's good got to do with it? It's against the law."

"Cripes."

Kit had got to his thumb. "I'm running out of fingers. Then there's the matter of secret organizations. Governments within governments. America's government doesn't like competition."

"You're talking about Li's little tong."

"Little tong! Wake up, kid. Two years ago, while you were still blushing over James Hamilton, Li waged a bloody battle in the streets of Chinatown. When it was over he alone controlled *all* the Chinese tongs—just Li. Only they don't call them tongs. White men call them tongs, from some corrupted Chinese word. What the Chinese call them are triads, secret societies. In China, they were formed as protection against the invading Manchus. In America, they protect against the whites. Before Li, some triads were good guys, a lot were bad guys. Under Li, they're both. Depends on who you are and how you wind up looking at it. Aside from the Chinese merchants, Li owns Chinatown. They're lucky it's him; he's all right for a crook. The kid I grew up with, the Chinese kid who's almost my brother, could have me or you or James rubbed out by crooking a yellow finger, and nobody'd be the wiser. That's against the law too. But it's done. Are you getting the picture? Li Kwan Won is a first-class criminal, a public enemy. He's on real shaky ground. That's why I told you to lay off him. What do you want to do, get the guy killed?"

"Me? How could I get him killed?"

"You're white, you're a white woman. If he got seen a lot with you, he'd get *seen,* you understand? If he gets seen, he gets caught, and the government takes off his head. It'd take off his head for any reason, if it could get away with it."

"Why?"

"Because he's Chinese, you idiot. The Chinese aren't wanted here. They stopped being wanted when they stopped being useful. As long as they could be used as virtual slave labor in the mines, or building the entire western half of the transcontinental railroad, or tilling the whole state of California, making it nice and easy for the white man to farm, people thought they were cute. But ever since good Christian folks thought the Chinese might try to compete for white jobs, they've become scum. Funny, isn't it? That's why they don't allow any more in, especially no more Chinese women. With women, the Chinks would breed like the niggers breed.

And the government isn't the only bunch that want Li's head."

By now, Lizzie knew who Kit meant. Putting together what she'd overheard James say to Blinn on the telephone with all that Kit had just told her, she'd have to be a complete jerk not to know. But she asked anyway, just to hear Kit say it.

"Who else wants it?"

"James and Leo Olemi, especially Olemi. Li controls an enormous bootlegging operation. James is helping him get it, so Olemi will help James with what he wants. They've already sent out their first squad of soldiers to take it from him, courtesy of Mr. Murray Blinn."

Lizzie whispered. "I know."

"You what?"

"I said, I know."

"You know! How do you know, and what?"

"I know because I heard James talking over the phone last night to Blinn."

"For Christ's sake, Lizzie, keep out of it. Leo would turn on James yesterday if he thought he had to, and you could turn out to be *why* he has to. I need another cup of coffee."

Kit jumped up to make it. Lizzie followed him into his kitchen-in-a-closet. She wasn't offering to help; it didn't occur to her.

"If Li is taking such a risk doing all these things, why doesn't he do something else?"

"And what in hell would that be, Elizabeth? Washing your clothes? Serving you chop suey in a Chinese dump?"

"Of course not. He could be a doctor or a—"

"Oh, for crying out loud, Lizzie. Li can't *be* anything. This country won't let him."

"Then he could go back to China, couldn't he?"

"Oh, sure. Why not? He's never been there. He'd fit right in. He's yellow, isn't he?"

"You know I didn't mean that."

"Are you dumb or something? You don't know what you mean. China is in turmoil. If they're not starving, they're in the middle of a revolution. Right now, there must be a hundred little wars going on for the hearts and minds of the Han people. Don't you ever read the papers?" Angry, turning with the sizzling coffee pot in his hand, Kit saw Lizzie's face. Her strong chin was trembling.

"I just want to know, Kit. I—you see, I like Li, and I want to know *why* he's a criminal."

Kit saw more than *like* in her eyes, damn her soul. It wasn't *like;* her eyes were shining more than he'd ever seen them shine for anyone, and that sure as hell included Kit Dowie. At that moment, holding a pot of twice-boiled black coffee, unshaven and unbathed, Kit gave up. In the same moment that he knew he wanted Lizzie Stafford, had always wanted her, he also discovered he couldn't have her, would never have her. Like Lizzie, Kit was liberated. The searing pain made him gasp, but the same pain made him free. Kit Dowie was going to New York.

"Li is a criminal, Lizzie, because that's all he can be. James has chosen to be what he is; Li didn't have a choice. People like James fuck America; America fucks people like Li. Now go on home and leave me alone. I got a date with my colored lady, and I need a goddam bath."

At two o'clock in the morning Fearless O'Flooty, in an old sweater, was leaning on his bar listening to Kit Dowie. His sweater was unraveling at the neck.

Dido had left at midnight. She and Kit never got to Blanco's. They ate sandwiches on their way to O'Flooty's. Kit hadn't told Dido what he was telling Fearless now, but she got the message just the same. Kit was going to Chicago and New York with her. It should have made her happy, but it didn't; it made her mad. He was going, all right, but his heart wasn't in it. He wasn't going with Dido, he was running away from Lizzie. Dido went back to the Blue Canary, her black head full of white hate.

Kit was drunk. Fearless was drunk. Practically everybody in O'Flooty's was drunk. They usually were.

There are all kinds of drunks. Drunk or sober,

O'Flooty served them all. But the kind of drunk Kit was tonight made Fearless ashamed of his profession.

Fearless spent his time being scared shitless, suffering as he was from apocalyptic torments, migraines of the spirit. He chain-smoked his cigarettes right down to his orange fingertips. He had a Celtic nose with a bristling mustache underneath. The nose started out flat and reasonably straight, but somewhere along the way it had been bent abruptly to the right. The change came from a well-connected right in one of life's Donnybrooks. But he wasn't afraid of anything physical. Everything that scared O'Flooty he carried around with him on the inside. O'Flooty's fear was personal. For the rest of what life had to offer, Fearless waded in swinging.

"Lizzie," he said, edging the name out the side of his mouth, squeezing it flat. "Lizzie. Lizz-eee." He said it a few more times, trying out different accents. "Whaz in a name? Lissen, Dowie. Let go of the broad. It's no good."

Kit picked his head an inch off the bar. "I let go. I told you. All gone." He dropped it back, cracking his skull.

"Lez you an' me go beat her up. Whaddaya say to that?" O'Flooty tried to roll up his unraveling sleeves. "Hey, Dowie? Lemme ask a question."

"Wha'?" said Kit.

"You ever had her?"

"Had who?"

"Tha' emerald-eyed, raven-haired, rich—"

"Oh, her. No."

"Then, for the love of all the gods, glinty and multiple-armed up there! You're a prize sap, Dowie. You could be missin' the disaster of your life. Plus, an' I might add, you have the opportunity to create her without the horror of pointy-toothed reality—you can have the perfect woman with you forever an' forever an' forever. An unrealized dream, the bes' kind. Something to feed on for always. You see?" Fearless pulled Kit's head up by his hair.

Dark eyes swimming, Kit goggled at Fearless. "What are you talking about?"

"We don' have to go beat her up, ole friend, ole

chum. She doesn't need messin' up to free you, boyo—you *are* free! Because without having had her, you can make up your own truth, and with your own truth, you have art!"

Kit understood completely. Just before he passed out.

*Chapter 17*

Deep under old Chinatown, it was once whispered, there lurked a subterranean world, sinister with slaves and thieves, hags in rags and filth, pestilential disease, scurrying gray rats grown big as dogs, and murder. Before the quake, whites thrilled themselves with shuddering tales of loathsome depths, layer upon fetid layer, caves of crime most foul, caverns of horror, vile warrens that would finally have burrowed to China itself—if the great fire hadn't burned away their treasured illusions.

The truth never reached the depths of the mind. But the truth was deep enough. Because the Chinese were hemmed in by hate, they could not spread out; the law-abiding took what little was given and contented themselves *above*, on Chinatown's small span of San Francisco hillside. The ambitious, the seekers after power and wealth, having nowhere else to go, went down.

Beneath Chinatown, an octopus of connecting basements and hidden passageways snaked secret tentacles. Below the busy streets lay a labyrinthine netherworld, murky haven for tong assassins, opium addicts, and lepers. Once slave girls were hidden in airless pits until they could be sold, dead bodies thrown into the darker deeper places to float, putrifying, in a slimy ooze of sewage. There were underground pawnshops and shops that sold the art of death: hatchets, pistols, stilettos fashioned into fans. Here also were the opium dens. Reached by way of trapdoors from gambling clubs, down into dank passages lit by feeble gas jets, the dens were nothing more than small bleak rooms lined with damp wooden slats for the hopeless dreamers to dream on.

The flat unmoving smoke that lay over Robert Bent's head was featureless—to anyone, that is, but Bent. To him, the deep blue smoke, smelling of burnt peanuts, with a sweet sickly undertone, was a wonderland of visions, bent dreams that writhed with meaning. He was lying curled up on his side, his feet on a bamboo pillow, trying to understand *what* meaning, as the wiry Chinese, Wong Gow, with a face full of age and merry devilment, prepared another pipe. Wong Gow was bald. Like knuckles, little points and protuberances of bone stuck out on his shiny skull.

By the flickering light of a cut-glass opium lamp fed with nut oil, the old man took up a "smoking pistol," a pipe with a polished stem of carved bamboo mounted with silver, and warmed its earthenware bowl over the flame of the narrow-topped lamp. In the bottom of the bowl there was a tiny hole. Dipping a slender wire poker into a small buffalo-horn box containing bitter Turkish opium, Wong Gow took out only the amount that stuck to its point, then held the poker over the flame. The heat of the fire made the tiny piece of black opium swell to twenty times its original size, until it no longer looked like black molasses but melted India rubber. Then he gently rubbed the pill of opium against the inner surface of the pipe's bowl. When the steam inside the heat-expanded pill was gone, the old man patiently held the poker over the flame again, roasting the opium in its heat, then rolling it in the bowl of the smoking pistol, over and over, until the opium was finally reduced to a soft solid.

Wong Gow then inserted the point of the poker into the hole in the pipe's bowl, twirling it until the opium stayed in the pipe. The poker came out clean and easy. The old man smiled at his skill. He roused Bent and gently put the stem of the bamboo pipe into the man's thin, quivering mouth, keeping the bowl over the flame. Eyes squeezed shut, Bent inhaled intensely, while the opium frizzled and sputtered like a guttering tallow candle. The old man kept the pipe between Bent's eager sucking lips until thick smoke poured out of the police commissioner's pinched nose, and Bent sank heavily back on his hard wooden divan, oblivious.

Wong Gow wiped the bowl of the pipe with a damp sponge and waited. Both he and the pipe were ready for Bent's next dream.

Robert Bent was under Pine Street off Grant Avenue. The opium den the police commissioner used was on the outskirts of Chinatown, where a white man could occasionally get a smoke. *Baak gwai lo* weren't allowed in the opium dens. But the police commissioner was an exception. Bent thought it was because the Chinese were afraid of him. The truth was less flattering. Li let the nervous policeman in because there he could keep close track of the man's erratic and uncertain maneuverings. And because he talked in his sleep.

Robert Bent, curled up like a baby, thumb in his mouth, blank eyes half open, began to babble.

Smiling, Wong Gow bent his tufted ear to Robert's mouth. He listened intently, nodding his knobby bald head on its stringy neck like a ripe sunflower on a thin stalk.

After two minutes of lucrative listening, Wong Gow pulled twice on a tassel that was connected to a rope that ran from behind Bent's divan, up the wall, and through the floor above.

Five minutes later, fragrant Chi Mai, with a rustle of silk, slipped through a panel in the wall.

*"Hai mee-ye see? Hai m-hai ho gan-yiu-ge?"*

Wong Gow put his finger to his lips. "Shhh."

Slender and alert, Chi Mai stood beside Wong Gow —and Bent babbled on.

* * *

"But you've got to tell me where Li is," protested Lizzie.

"Honey," said Rose, feeding Spike strawberries, "because of Addy, I think the world of you, but I'm damned if I'm putting Li on the spot just because you ask me to. I'll tell you straight, he isn't for playing with."

Lizzie—dressed for finding Li—in a long slit skirt matched by a slender cowl-necked tunic, both in black velvet with silver worked down the tunic's long sleeves, no jewelry, and her blue-black hair shining in severe Egyptian geometry—stood in front of Rose St. Lorraine, trying to tell the truth. She had no idea what Li had told Rose about her, if he'd told Rose anything at all. Lizzie also had no idea what Li thought of her, if he thought anything at all. All she knew was that she must find him. After talking to Kit Dowie—Lizzie had grown used to the offhand way Kit talked to her, but lately he was getting downright rude!—she had two damn good reasons. First, she had to apologize for herself. She'd already done the explaining over dinner at the Intelligent Pearl, but she didn't really know how awful she'd been in her arrogant presumptions. Now, thanks to Kit, she did. Second, she had to tell him what she knew of James. Then she intended to leave Li alone. Period. Forever. Cross her heart. Honest.

And there Rose sat on her chaise longue, her fingers stained with strawberry juice, frowning. Guarding her oriental gosling like a mother goose. Geese can be dangerous. Lying on the floor at the foot of Rose's huge bed, Sergeant Huggins whimpered in his dreaming sleep. All four doggy feet thought they were gaining on a fleeing alley cat; Rose's white rug rucked up under them.

So Lizzie told Rose everything. About Esmé and James, all she'd told Kit, what she'd meant to do with Li, adding a bit about Kit's moods. It took her two embarrassing hours. Rose managed to listen without saying a word; Ike wouldn't have believed it. When Lizzie was finished, it was midnight and Rose was getting ready for the Blue Canary. It was Saturday night. On Saturdays, Rose gave her customers their money's worth and more. She was struggling into a confection of cream velvet and yolk-yellow tulle, the kind of thing that Lizzie had only ever seen in drawings of the Gay Nineties.

"Help me with this damn dress, sugar." It was the first thing Rose had said for over an hour. The dress over her head, Rose was stuck somewhere between her armpits and chin under a mountain of crackling froth. Lizzie started from the top and dug down to Rose's golden head, found the right yellow ribbon, and pulled. The dress tumbled the rest of the way down Rose's hourglass body in its complicated corsets and stayed there.

"Thanks." Rose stood primping in front of her Wild West mirror. Ike had won the thing with a pair of threes from a guy who owned a bar in Yuba City, way up in gold country. It was over six feet tall, wider than that, and framed with naked gold women in the most curious poses. "How do I look, honey?"

To Lizzie, Rose looked like a lemon meringue pie. But adorable.

"You look eatable," said Lizzie.

"Good. Because tonight I intend to sing the suckers downstairs a song that's going to make them cream their best Saturday pants. Wake up, Huggins. We've got a show to put on."

The big white dog picked his head off the rug, cocked his ears in Rose's direction, and yawned, his pink tongue curling back in his enormous fanged mouth. Lizzie thought of what Kit had said about the beast and some bad guy named Coffee. Nice doggie. She sent that placating thought to Sergeant Huggins. Sergeant Huggins blinked his pale blue eyes at her. She hoped he was smiling.

"Rose?" Lizzie called, as Rose was trying to get out her door into the hallway, crushing her yellow tulle. "You *did* listen to me. You *are* going to tell me where Li is?"

Rose gathered up the front of the dress and pushed on through the door. When she was clear, she turned and smiled, her dark blue eyes thoughtful. "Heard every word, honey. Fascinating."

"And?"

"And I'll tell you, on the condition that if you're seeing him, you promise you won't end up hurting him."

"Rose, I don't want to hurt him, I want to help him."

"Wanting ain't doing. But sometimes a woman has to trust her instincts. So, honey, you'll find him on Pine, corner of Grant Avenue. Blue door, peephole, no markings. The place isn't usually for whites, though if you tell them Rose sent you, they'll let you in. Now, girl, don't bother wishing me luck, I got all the luck I need. Just pray for the people downstairs. Tonight, I feel hot as pastrami."

Rose, preceded by Sergeant Huggins, put one hand on her hip and swayed down the hall. Lizzie watched her go. At the top of the grand staircase leading down to the Blue Canary's gaming rooms, she called back.

"Lizzie?"

"Yes?"

"You ever wonder why Kit gets himself in such moods?"

"Because he's got a mean streak; you said so."

"Ever think you might have something to do with that meanness of his?"

"Me? No. Why, what do *I* do?"

"Honey, being dumb isn't *always* being cute."

Rose St. Lorraine began her regal Saturday-night walk down the staircase.

Lizzie lost her Pinkerton by driving her gray cabriolet down Market Street to the Ferry Building, parking it right out in front, then nipping inside, buying a ticket for the last boat trip of the night, waiting until her man got on the ferry with her, then nipping off before he could do the same. She waved goodbye from the dock as the snoop from Pinkerton's set sail for downtown Alameda, far to the north of San Francisco. Even if he dove off the side and swam, she'd lost him for the night.

The blue door wasn't as easy. Rose hadn't said *which* corner of Pine and Grant. Lizzie tried each. On the fourth try, feeling silly and conspicuous, she knocked three times on a blue door.

The peephole snapped open.

"Yes?" The voice inside was soft, disembodied.

"Rose sent me."

The peephole snapped shut. Lizzie stood there. She was just about to knock again—with spirit—when the blue door opened.

"Welcome."

Just inside, a Chinese girl in lavender silk bowed, moving aside to let Lizzie pass. The girl came to Lizzie's shoulders. She was tiny but perfect, from her powdered oval face with its small flat nose, the hair, even darker than Lizzie's, gathered in a heavy bun tinkling with miniature wind chimes, to the embroidered slippers on her tiny feet.

"You come." The girl led Lizzie to an exquisite bar of teakwood. "Here you ask, you get." She glimmered off, disappearing through a red-lacquered moon door.

Lizzie ordered a champagne cocktail from the bartender. He was a black man, almost as small and just as dainty as the girl in lavender silk.

Sipping her champagne, her nerves singing, Lizzie looked the room with the blue door over. It wasn't as beautiful as the Intelligent Pearl. But to her western eye it was just as Chinese. It was dark and intimate; the only light came from three little painted paper lanterns. The room smelled like the inside of one of Keiko's boxes, strong cedarwood, but underneath the cedar there was a hint of something sweet, a sticky, cloying smell. Lizzie heard the sound of tiles clicking in a back room, the hum of hushed voices. There were some whites here, shadowed in teakwood alcoves, but they were far outnumbered by Chinese. From what she now knew of the California Chinese, these must be merchants. All were well dressed in western clothes, their black hair worn short and slicked back like silent movie actors. Moving among them were small Chinese singsong girls, each as perfect as the girl who had opened the blue door.

There was no stage, but there was another jazz band. The musicians were white, the singer black. It wasn't Dido. It was a huge woman in a green turban and a short spangled green dress. The dress was so tight the seams were spreading with the strain.

When Lizzie entered, the woman in green wasn't singing, she was leaning over the piano listening to a soft melody the pianist was fooling around with, her glossy black face dreamy and still.

Before she sang, she was ludicrous, a mountain of flesh quivering in a hideous dress. But when the music started, she changed. And when she sang she shouted, pushing her great breasts out, grinding her hips under the short green dress. Her big round belly wobbled, and her heavy black face twisted down in a thunderous holler. She held on to her turban with one huge arm and windmilled the other. The room with the blue door was stunned into silence. What was Chinese shattered into New Orleans black.

Lizzie didn't know what the difference between this woman and Dido was, but it was the difference between satin and burlap. They were both real, but the fat woman in green was tough. Dido insinuated, whispered in your ear; this woman shouted you down, blew you off your feet. Lizzie was getting to like the blues.

When the song stopped, the room became Chinese again. But there was no Li.

"Have you any more rooms besides this one?" Lizzie asked the dainty black bartender.

"Who wants to know?" The man looked her over, the white of his eye rolling.

All Lizzie could think to say to that was to repeat, "Rose sent me."

The bartender broke into a sweet-toothed smile. "You say Rose? In that case, chile, take your pick. We got mah-jongg, we got *pai gow,* hell, we got Chinese checkers. You wander on back, you find some game you be wantin' to play. An' since Rose sent you, you take another cocktail along. No charge."

"Why, thank you."

She chose the first of three round moon doors, following the click and tinkle of tiles. Here Chinese were playing mah-jongg. It was nothing like the way white gamblers lost their shirts or like the desperate gaming dens she'd seen with Li. There was the same flush, the same excited onlookers, but the smell was different. It wasn't a fever, but a flow. Gambling is in the Chinese blood, as natural as eating and drinking. They were enjoying themselves. It wasn't sexual, it was a game.

No Li.

Nor was he in the second room, with its *pai gow*— Chinese dominoes—players, or the third, where people were betting on cricket races or doing strange things with bones and tiny black-and-white pebbles.

Lizzie had no choices left except one. This was a door marked PRIVATE. It was western, nice and rectangular, made out of dark oak. She opened it before anyone should think to stop her, and went through. The door led into a short hallway. And to two more doors, both private. Lizzie trembled, suddenly afraid of meeting the man she'd come in all innocence to apologize to, to warn. She turned the knob of the first door. It was an office. No one was there. She backed out. The second door then. Her last chance. If Li wasn't behind it, she was going home. Lizzie Stafford Hamilton's trek was finished. She would take it as an omen. No apologizing, no warning. Leave Li alone. Holding her glass of champagne, Lizzie opened the door.

"Oh, my God!"

Li was lying in tumbled silk sheets the color of hot rose. The room was deep in shadow, lit only by a candle by the bed, but beside Li, Lizzie could see a small dark head on a white pillow, black eyes big in shock, staring at her.

"I'm so sorry, I was—oh, shit." With one swift motion, Lizzie drank the rest of her champagne, set the glass on a table by the door, and began to back out.

"Stay."

At Li's command, Lizzie froze.

She watched as Li rose from the silken sheets, naked. His tall northern-Chinese body was as beautiful as his face, his soft voice, his hands, his eyes. Lizzie blushed and looked away.

"This is Chi Mai, Mrs. Hamilton." Li put on a Chinese robe of plain yellow silk.

"*Hamilton taai-taai, tso sun. Gay ho ma?*" said Chi Mai in a contented voice, like the purring of a pedigreed cat.

"Chi Mai says she is pleased to meet you."

Lizzie tried to smile. "Thank you. I mean, her." Her throat hurt as she spoke.

Li looked at Lizzie's empty glass. "You drink like a man."

"I need to. You're full of surprises."

Why did she say that? It seemed that everything she did, all she said, was never what she intended. Finding Li in bed with a lovely Chinese girl was not the way she assumed things would go. But lately, nothing was simple and nothing went as expected. Once, being rich and young and cute meant Lizzie could count on her days and nights as immutable, each one glorious in its sameness—like a string of cultured pearls. Was that only a few weeks ago? But now? She was on her hands and knees picking up beads. A simple meeting, a simple apology, a simple goodbye: that was all it was supposed to be. If Lizzie had been thinking, it might have occurred to her that looking for an attractive unmarried man after one o'clock in the morning could pack not only a surprise but a wallop—for Lizzie.

"I surprise you? Did you think I wasn't a man? That I was merely a Chinese?" Li turned to the young oriental girl, who had risen in the bed and was now sitting up, staring at Lizzie. She was as naked as Li had been moments before. Her breasts were bare, unashamed—small and pert.

"Chi Mai, *lau seong.*"

"*Choei-been.*"

Chi Mai quickly gathered her clothes. Without bothering to put them on, she left the room by a door hidden back in the shadows.

"And now, Mrs. Hamilton. You visit again. Your choice of hour and place is always amusing. What can I do for you this time? Surely it is too late for another tour of Chinatown?" Li seemed calm, but his eyes had a charming menace.

Lizzie was afraid. She backed away. "I came to tell you—I'm sorry."

"Sorry? What have you done now?"

"Nothing. That is, nothing more than I've already done. I wanted to apologize for last Wednesday. For my stupid pride and my thoughtlessness."

"You must not ask forgiveness for what is natural to you."

"You mean, I am naturally thoughtless?"

"It is a gift."

"But—I'm trying not to be."

"That is all the apology I need."

There was nothing more to say. It was finished; Li had accepted her apology. Now, as she watched him tie his thin yellow robe, she understood—he expected her to leave. And there was her promise to Rose. Lizzie was lost in pain.

By the soft light of the candle's flame, his taut skin gleamed gold, the aching line of his neck, the fine arch of his alien brow—strange untouchable beauty, hers for only this one timeless moment. When she turned, he would be gone forever, spinning thousands of years away from her, back to a strange people, lost in strange thoughts spoken in a strange tongue—oh, God, Lizzie!

She was dying in this room, secret with envious shadows and the intimate scent of Chi Mai, a musk that lingered like sighs on Li's rosy sheets. Lizzie's heart beat slowly in her white throat; her white skin shivered under black velvet. A part of Lizzie Stafford was fading away like a whisper, forgotten in the wind. She had not come to tell this mysterious man she was sorry. Nor to warn him about James. She came to Li because—she had to. There was nowhere else to go.

"I'm lying," she said.

"I know."

Some struggling something in her mind put up one last fight. "I came to tell you that James is going to hurt you, you and your people, he's the one behind Olemi and Murray Blinn—"

Stepping quickly away from the bed with the rose sheets, Li put his hand on the back of Lizzie's pale neck.

She gasped. His touch was no longer tender; it was a harsh grip, possessive. He was hurting her.

"You should not be telling me this. You should not have come here. You and I must not be on the same side."

"I wanted to warn you—"

His hand was burning her skin.

"You are still lying, Mrs. Hamilton."

Roughly, Li pulled Lizzie toward him. He dug his fingers deep into the soft black geometry of her hair, pulling her head back until the green eyes were forced to look up into his beautiful Chinese face. His alien eyes burned with a copper light.

"Goddam you, white ghost," he murmured.

Her heart slipped sideways.

"Then help me. Tell me to go away. Tell me to get the hell out of here."

"I can't. This is a game we shall both lose." Li's hand twisted in her hair. "The devil will take it all." He bent her backward, kissing her long white neck. "But we will play."

Lizzie, with a sob, set her sights on Satan.

*Chapter 18*

Fearless O'Flooty kicked Dowie's foot. "Wake up. It's six o'clock."

Kit Dowie rolled over and fell off O'Flooty's couch. "Who gets up at six in the morning?" he mumbled, picking himself up from the floor.

"It's six in the P.M., boyo."

"What? Holy shit!" Kit looked for his trousers, until he discovered he was already wearing them. He was also wearing his shoes, tie, and jacket. All he really needed to find was his hat and a toothbrush. "What the hell day is it?"

"A fine fat Friday, July the twentieth, 1923. How would you like your eggs? Fried, fried, or fried?"

"Fried."

"Nice choice."

Coming out of the fug of another day's drinking, Kit remembered everything, almost. He was in O'Flooty's dinky Vallejo Street apartment, and O'Flooty's apartment was in an old shingled house on Russian Hill. Nob, Telegraph, and Russian hills rose on the northwest side of the sea-locked city like bubbles on the ninth wave. In the 490 square blocks of San Francisco real estate that fed the great fire of 1906, the frame houses around O'Flooty's were the only ones of their kind spared—not by the exhaustive effort of a mobilized city or by the grace of a fickle God, but by determined householders flatly refusing the military order to abandon their homes and run for it. With mops and towels drenched in soapy water bucketed from bathtubs, and with the help of a tough old lady with an endless supply of siphon bottles, they held back the flames for two days. In the end, between Green and Broadway, Taylor and Leavenworth streets, there was still a bit of old San Francisco—like the stone in the heart of a plum.

Kit had been on Vallejo a whole week, he had a hangover that felt terminal, and O'Flooty's looked like any other bachelor abode he'd ever been in—disgusting.

It was stacked to the ceiling with old magazines, newspapers, and political tracts, decorated with O'Flooty's dirty clothes, used dishes, stinking ashtrays, and unmatched cutlery. Only one of the four windows opened, the one in a kind of cupola built onto the side of the house. O'Flooty's pet pigeon, Just in Case Pie, hobbled in and out of the window on its deformed feet. Just in Case Pie slept on the *inside* of the sill. You could tell from the two inches of pigeon shit. The place felt just like home to Kit.

"Did I go to work today?"

"You did, and every day, though not much good it did the paper. Got here an hour ago, slept since. Told me to wake you at six. Eat this."

Cigarette burned to nothing stuck in his mouth, Fearless thrust a cracked plate into Kit's hand.

"Shit, I remember! It's President Harding night," said Kit, balancing the plate on his lap. "Some advance crony from his Ohio gang is in town, instructing the press on how to kiss the President's ass." Two eggs eyed him from under bacon eyebrows. Kit ate the whole face. "The press is supposed to toddle along with sharpened pencils so everybody knows what questions Harding wants us to ask. *I* want to be there so I know what questions he *doesn't* want us to ask. Then I can ask the sap."

"You told me already, Dowie."

"I did? When?"

"Today, at five o'clock. Now," said O'Flooty, taking the empty plate away from Kit and tossing it near the sink. "I said to myself, almost a week ago this very hour. I said, Fearless, give the lad seven days, and by the end of them, by God, he'll be as good as ever he was. No woman can keep this boy down for long. You aren't trying to prove me wrong, are you?"

Kit shook his head until his hangover rattled.

"That's the ticket. Have a mug of coffee and stop all this mooning around. Here, you're wearing out your welcome. Besides, I'm tired of that black beauty, the fearsome Dido, coming around. She scares me to death. Me, a pugilist with prizes to prove it, and a poet!"

Kit took the coffee. It was as black and as bitter as Dido. "Have I told you what happened in the Le Blond trial?"

"You did, more than once."

"The son of a bitch was acquitted!"

"The man's going to tell me again." Fearless sighed and turned his back on Kit. He went and fed Just in Case Pie a piece of bacon fat.

Kit talked to himself. "Buddy Le Blond comes up with a surprise witness who swears he was with him the whole time whatever was happening to Violet happened, *if* anything happened. And it's Violet Louise who gets run out of town. Shit! Now he's hitting every speak in Frisco celebrating, him and his fucking football team. Except for the Blue Canary. Rose won't let him in."

"It goes to prove, football is a vile sport."

"And I don't notice James Hamilton's little promise to Stringer Bellew coming to pass, either."

"What promise is that?" Fearless came back from his pigeon feeding. "You didn't tell me about a promise."

"To make Bellew feel better about getting the guilty bastard off, Hamilton promised him that Buddy wouldn't be walking the streets of San Francisco for long."

"And how do you know that?"

"A little Mexican finch told me."

"Did it now? I await the final episode with interest."

"You aren't the only sucker, but no one's betting on it. I'm sick of the whole thing, O'Flooty. I'm sick of the *Examiner,* and I'm sick of Frisco."

"Crap, boyo. You're not sick, you've just got growing pains."

"Says you." Kit rubbed his blue chin. "I need a shave and I'm damned if I can even remember what the hell story I was on today. Can I use your razor?"

"And why not? When you used it for the sixth time, I gave it to you."

Kit wobbled up from O'Flooty's busted couch on rubbery legs. "Where's the bathroom?"

"Holy smoke, Dowie! Where it's been all week." Shaking his shaggy head, Fearless took Kit by the shoulders and marched him to a door. "In there. Remind me to check my hooch. The stuff I get from Li Kwan Won must be poisoning half of Frisco."

Less than a minute later, Kit popped back out of the bathroom, shaving cream smeared over his dark tired face. "Fearless, have I seen Lizzie this week?"

"No, not you or anyone else. Not even her husband, not that he seems to be caring. The man's been out and about with a redhead. Careful places for sure, but nowhere's careful enough."

"Where is she?"

"How the hell should I know, you idiot? And *you* shouldn't want to know. The lady can take care of herself —and if she can't, it's time she learned. Keep shaving."

Above the Blue Canary, one high hill to the south of O'Flooty's, Rose St. Lorraine was in bed with Addy Chase. Spike and Sergeant Huggins were there as well. Spike was curled up in a hairy little brown ball on Rose's satin-and-lace pillow, and Sergeant Huggins sprawled full length between them, white paws in the air. If they'd both had litters at the same time, if they *could* have puppies, there'd still be room in Rose's barge.

"Sugar?"

Addy was falling asleep with a smile on his long face. "Hmm?"

"You know where Lizzie is?"

"No. Should I?"

"I was just wondering."

"Scratch my back, sweetheart. No, not there, *there*. Ummm."

A full minute went by. Something about the way the silence sounded made Addy open his gentle brown eyes.

"You worried about something, Rose?"

"That girl made me a promise. I've been wondering whether she kept it."

"Don't worry about Lizzie, honey. She's all right."

"She isn't the one I'm worried about."

Esmé stood in the great hallway of the Stafford mansion and gasped. Keiko took her coat with immense dignity.

"Jesus H. Christ!" she said, twirling around in awe. "It's bigger than the *Titanic!*"

In full and proud possession, James almost grinned. He remembered his teeth just in time. "Wait till you see the rest."

Esmé hung back. "The rest? What about your wife? You said we'd just pop in for a minute. If she catches me in her home—"

"Mrs. Hamilton left days ago. I don't expect her back for some time."

"Left?"

"Gone. Disappeared. Vanished. The peace is sublime."

Esmé had been around. Men's wives don't just vanish. Plus, they sure as mud don't walk away from millions, their own or anyone else's. And if they do, husbands are supposed to at least pretend to be concerned. A frisson of distinctly unpleasant suspicion traveled from her red head to her suddenly tense toes.

"Gone where?"

"Do I know? Do I care? Come see the master bedroom."

Esmé gave the grave Japanese butler a weak smile

and followed James up a center staircase of ridiculous gilt mermaids and seashell lamps so wide that Henry the Eighth and all his wives could have walked down with their arms linked. The butler didn't smile back. He gave Esmé the freeze and, holding her coat like a pet skunk, turned on his heel.

"Ma! Where's my dog?"

Saddle Mary, every gray grizzled curl on her head held stiffly in place by hair pins, her blood-red lipstick seeping into the lines around her thin lips, bit into a Zu-zu gingersnap. She was lying on the sagging couch reading a new issue of *Photoplay* and getting cookie crumbs between the pages.

"Jugs took him to the park to piddle half an hour ago, Murray. Keep your shirt on." Mary flapped the magazine. "Lookit Mae Marsh! Ain't she the bee's knees?"

"I don't want nothing happening to Tommy."

"Ain't nothing happenin' to that mutt. What could happen? He's so dumb an' so fat, he couldn't even get run over, an' if he did he wouldn't feel it."

Murray Blinn and Coffee Trujillo had just come back to Murray's North Beach teashop and speak after a meeting with Leo Olemi.

It was over a week since Coffee Trujillo had fallen on his public face at the Blue Canary. The feisty Mexican hadn't gotten over it. He would never get over it until he'd paid that Chink back. Every night since it happened, he'd lain in his bed thinking up new and interesting ways of snuffing the yellow bastard. Coffee astonished himself by his imaginativeness.

"So it comes down to this: we go back into the dump blasting," said Murray. "Leo wants the Blue Canary's business, *I* want it—so we get it, even if we hafta use an army. Leo's recruiting them now." He was poking around in Mary's horror of a kitchen for something to eat. Every time he did that, he was left wondering why he bothered. "We tried being friendly, and where did it get us?" He picked up something that could be food—but *whose* food? "You know what, Coffee? Seems like to me, manners is a dying art. Ma, ain't we even got any fruit?"

"We got a banana."

"It's black, Ma!"

"So?"

"Christ, I gotta hire that woman a maid," Murray whispered to Coffee. "Ma just ain't got what it takes for housekeeping."

Coffee looked at Murray's mother. The sight made him sick. If only Murray would let him try out the things he thought of before he fell asleep—on *her.*

"Sure," he said. "Mothers oughta be taken care of."

Murray smiled at Coffee for that. It almost made up for the Mexican's bungling at the Blue Canary. Almost but not quite. Next time they paid a little visit to that blond dame and her Chinese friends—and after talking it over with Leo today, next time was sooner than they thought—Murray was going along. *And* he was taking Tommy. Rose St. Lorraine had a dog—well, goddammit, Murray Blinn had a dog too.

James was right when he told Esmé that Elizabeth Sian Stafford Hamilton had disappeared—vanished into another world. In the narrow concepts of time and space, she was no more than half an earthly mile from most of those whose lives she had touched in her twenty-three years. But in other, more rarified dimensions of spirit and mind, she was as removed as if she had voyaged to China itself.

Lizzie was in Chinatown; she was in love. Both were conditions of the soul, and both were intoxicating. But just beyond the bright lights—the heightened senses that Li awakened in her: sweet raptures of touch, brief and tender encounters of spirit—lurked shadows of premonition, like demons in the tunnel of love. Small shivers of delicious dread, an unutterable sadness: this could not last, was not meant to last.

In Li Kwan Won, Lizzie had not found cynicism, much less bitterness, but a clarity and breadth of mind that left him too aware: left him, finally, detached. When she touched him, she felt the warm living body, heard the soft words, but sensed a barrier: something curiously above and beyond her she could not reach. Though they had plunged in together—heedless of drowning, reckless of the threatening deep spread out beneath—Lizzie was swimming out alone.

She filled in the chill empty space with herself. She gave what she never knew she *had* to give. It was *her* passion, and it seemed inexhaustible.

Li Kwan Won and Lizzie Stafford were in Li's Grant Avenue apartment above the Ling Chu-tzû.

Lizzie hadn't been home to the Stafford mansion, hadn't been anywhere, since she found Li on Pine Street. She'd left Li's apartment only once, to buy something to wear. Besides the black silvered velvet, her entire wardrobe now consisted of silk Chinese cheongsams—skin-tight and slashed high on the thigh—embroidered slippers, and little quilted jackets. She'd sampled half the menu from the Intelligent Pearl, learned to make tea in pearl-blue Sung cups, to make love, and to smoke opium. Li gave her Patna, the finest: its morphia content milder than Turkish opium, there was no bitter aftertaste. He called it "traveling clouds"; to smoke it was to "bite clouds."

"Alcohol is a nightmare; opium is a dream." Li exhaled deep blue smoke. He passed the pipe to Lizzie. "Perhaps this will release you from the bootleggers."

"All of them—except you." Lizzie took a tentative draw on the pipe, wriggling her nose.

For a week, Li had come and gone, faithful to his mysterious business. When he was out, Lizzie was lost. She wandered the rooms above the Ling Chu-tzû, running her fingers over fine pieces of lacquer, looking at paintings in tinted inks, milk-blue vases holding sweet peas that an old Chinese, Li's servant Wong Gow, changed every day, Li's books—like Kit, he had so many, but his were neatly on shelves. Again, like Kit's, Lizzie hadn't read them, but unlike Kit's she had a reason: many were in French, German, or Chinese. The things in Li's home were arranged with the chance delicacy of scattered leaves. They appealed to the mind, not the emotions.

The only time Lizzie came alive was when Li was with her, holding her. They did nothing but make love and talk. Lizzie's long white limbs lay tangled in Li's. Li was golden, not like James Hamilton's unexplored blond body—unexplored, that is, by Lizzie. James was covered with coarse blond hair, but Li was as smooth as cornsilk. For the first few days, Lizzie did all the talking. Li listened, looking at her with his slanted sable eyes. After a day, slanted eyes were the only eyes in the world. But now, as dusk, like a vampire with manners, drew a gentle black cape over Chinatown, Lizzie, protected in Li's strong warm arms, listened to *him*.

"If my sister, Su Yin, had lived, she would have been as you, Lizzie—except for your jade eyes. A young woman of strength and passion. I would have cherished her."

The traveling clouds had taken possession of Lizzie's mind. Li's voice gave her not words but a wash of watercolors, like a painted movie, a movie with sound.

"I will tell you a story, Lizzie. Maybe then you will understand better who I am. And maybe then you can run away, back to where you belong."

Run away? She would never run away from Li. Not from whatever he may have done, not from what he might do. In her long pull for the sea, she was too far out from shore to swim back.

Lizzie, her mind clouded in smoke, curled mists of sweet opium intricate as blue lace, wasn't in Chinatown listening to her lover telling a story, she was with him in a Chinatown of eleven years ago, a ghostly sixth member of Li's triad, the Night of Two Moons, keeping pace with them as they traveled through Li's memory.

"We were five figures in black, one of them myself—sixteen years old and as eager and thoughtless as a young bloodhound—running in perfect silence through the dark streets of Chinatown. As we passed the cribs of the singsong girls, their shrill cries followed our swift flight with plaintive monotony. This was my triad, these fighting men, *boo how doy,* and we stalked like predators of the night through shadowed alleys, led by our master, Wan Yun-lung. Beside him raced the dim shape of a man we called Ma Mien, Horse-face, and another, Niu T'ou, Ox-head. Just behind these two was O Ti, a man of songs—a poet and a scholar—but on this night he ran like a leopard. Running at his heels, I kept pace with O Ti; it was my place to be last. I was new to them, had only just 'entered the circle.' I was fresh and untried.

"We carried no weapons. Wan Yun-lung had been sent by the politician Sun Yat-sen to America to rouse the western Chinese. Sun's rebellion in China had toppled the two-hundred-year stranglehold of the northern Manchus. But it was a victory that could turn hollow at any moment. The people were divided by the greed of warlords. By sending Yun-lung to us, Sun hoped to raise men and money for his cause.

"And so, in San Francisco's Chinatown, he gathered around him those of us he felt were the most promising. I was bursting with pride to have been chosen for the Hung League: me, Li Kwan Won, without family, without wealth, raised by a white woman, Rose of the loud voice. To inspire us, Wan Yun-lung needed nothing more than himself and his training in the military arts. He told us, 'There is a saying, "The officials draw their power from law; the people, from the secret societies." ' He taught us, yellow men born on the Gold Mountain, the secrets of the triads. He gave us the gift of the Buddhist monks of Shaolin, an ancient monastery in the province of Fukien, a refined discipline that avoided violence. He cut off our queues. He lifted our vision above Chinatown, called to us to look homeward, toward the land of our people, to China. I looked back with the rest, and what I saw was hope.

"That night we were not running to attack but to defend. Somewhere ahead of us was our prey, men of a rival triad that did not concern itself with ancient things, with ideals of honor, but with slaves and drugs, extortion and murder. They were hunting a young man from the Night of Two Moons, Little Cricket, for he had committed a grave error against their bandit family. He had fallen in love with a young Chinese woman, a whore, and stolen her from her crib. Little Cricket fled with the girl, the bandits pursued him, and we pursued the bandits. Wheels within wheels.

"Little Cricket and his woman had disguised themselves: the lover as a shrimp fisherman, the girl as an old man. Because of the girl's feet, bound and misshapen, she could not run. She hobbled. The man who loved her enough to risk his life hoped that the guise of an old man with a stick would hide her lily feet. But his hopes were nothing. To reach the safety of a ship bound for the Orient, he had to take her across the wide Embarcadero— out into the open, where they were seen by the avenging bandits. We, the Night of Two Moons, could do nothing to help them; they were still too far away.

"The young man, in a last desperate effort to escape, put the girl over his shoulder and ran. It was useless. The bandits were upon them. Dropping the girl, Little Cricket turned to fight. I knew he would die. He knew it too. But he stood his ground, shielding the girl behind him. With one quick slice of a hatchet blade, a bandit cut the lover's head from his shoulders. It bounced off the wet cobblestones, then rolled slowly into the gutter, coming to rest face up. The girl, expecting the same, bowed her own head.

"We and our master slipped across the street and faced the bandits.

" 'Why have you done this to Little Cricket?' asked Wan Yun-lung. 'Would not the loss of the girl be enough punishment for him?'

"Hatchet Yee, who had done the killing, stepped proudly forward. 'Your man had the right to buy but not the right to steal. The girl belongs to my triad. We are returning her.'

" 'So you are not cutting off her head as well?'

" 'Why should we damage our own goods? The girl is worth three thousand dollars.'

" 'And what is she worth to herself?'

" 'Worth to herself? She is nothing to herself.'

" 'Wan!' I, who was standing back as they talked, moved out of the shadows. 'Look!'

"The members of both triads turned. I pointed toward the docks. From between the quiet warehouses, a gang of white devils, hoodlums, had appeared, no doubt attracted by our conflict. They were armed with brass knuckles, hickory sticks, and knives.

"Hatchet Yee picked up the passive girl, threw her over his shoulder as her dead lover had done, and, with his bandits, ran away. It was a wise thing to do.

"But the Night of Two Moons remained. We could not run. We had not yet done honor to Little Cricket. He was one of us. We had to take his body back and send his bones to China. So we stood waiting, facing with silence the oncoming devil ghosts. They strode toward us, jeering. There were five of us, three times as many hoodlums. Before the quake, their kind would have burned Chinese homes, branded lone Chinese with red-hot pokers, slit ears and tongues. They would have hung Chinese pigtails on their belts with pride, displayed them like the scalps of Indians. Now they contented themselves with murder.

"The hoodlums taunted and abused us. One of them kicked the head that was still in the gutter. Little Cricket spun on his hair, gazing at the black and spinning sky. The *baak gwai lo* thought we were defenseless. We carried no hatchets, no guns.

"Like a Chinese ballet, we used the precious skills we had been taught by Wan Yun-lung. To have fought these white devils, to have won, and then to leave them alive would have been to face the outrage of later vigilantes—more white devils bent on defending white honor. To have fought these devils and lost would have meant to die. The Night of Two Moons had no choice. We had to win, and when we won, we must win finally. None of the fifteen hoodlums could be left alive to raise a cry, to lie and bluster and bring death to Chinatown.

"The hoodlums, to their short-lived and intense surprise, didn't stand a chance. Though they outnumbered us by three to one, though we Chinese were not on our home ground and were not armed, it was over almost before it began. The hoodlums had chosen their own deaths. We were merely the means. There was no dishonor to us.

"But one of them had been hanging back from his fellows, watching from the shadow of a warehouse door.

He saw his friends go down to the Night of Two Moons, and just as all was quiet he fled. It was I who saw him. I who chased him. I who caught him. The ghost, his pocked face hideous with fear, crouched at my feet, begging for his miserable life. I could not give it to him. His life meant the death of my people. I had no choice. I allowed him to stand, to unsheath his knife, to change his destiny. He could not, just as I could not. His death was quick and merciful—but, though swift, it was death none the less. And I was the Death Master.

"I had never killed before. It was not as I had thought it would be, not as I had read of it. It was so easy to kill a man. I felt no remorse or pride. There was no accomplishment here. It had to be done, and it was done. It was the snuffing out of a candle, the closing of a music box—the flame and the music were gone.

"But I had become separated from Wan Yun-lung and the Night of Two Moons when I chased the devil. I did not return to Chinatown. I went to the Blue Canary and there I saw Dido. After my first kill, I saw the *haak gwai* who hated me so, because she herself was hated so. But by then I was a man. I had killed, I had been Death. There was nothing she could say to me, no meanness she was capable of that could touch me. There was no kindling in the ash."

As Li talked, Lizzie lay quietly on her side, along the length of his body, looking at him. When he was finished, lying still, his eyes closed, his breathing shallow and steady, she said nothing. Li's silence and the waning opium released her from the past. She was here now, beside him, her soul in her deep green eyes, wanting to hold on to this man, to pull him with her out into the sea.

"I will have your baby," she murmured. "I will give you back your Su Yin."

Li opened his eyes. The muscles of his body stiffened against her softness. Lizzie glimpsed in his face a kind of fury and contempt that he had kept masked by exquisite irony and serene humor.

"That will never be!"

The beautiful voice was hissing at her.

"We have this. It is enough!"

*Chapter 19*

It was July the twenty-third, had been for four and a half hours. Dawn on what would be a hot Monday in the summer of freewheeling San Francisco's seventy-seventh year. In less than an hour Chinatown's seductive streets would be filled with the cacophony of overburdened trucks and handcarts, yellow men hurrying to work in the laundries and sweatshops, what wives there were pinching the first fresh vegetables of the day, little children—no long lazy summer for the sweet spawn of the Orient—laboring to open the family stores. Now, all was dark silence, mirroring the stillness underfoot. Even the Chinese underworld had to sleep sometime.

Halfway along a littered alley off Chinatown's Sacramento Street, a gray rat suckled her young in a discarded tea crate padded in warm, comfortable rubbish. Blind and hairless, pink and fat, mewing like miniature kittens, the hot squirming bodies sought their mother's nipples. The big rat had come home to her crate after a satisfying night of scavenging, her gray fur sleek with pork fat. Black eyes closed, sensitive whiskers twitching on her pointed snout, she lifted an obliging back leg for the ninth baby, snuffling blind along her hairy flank.

A chain scattered in deafening pings over the crate.

With a squeak of alarm, the rat jerked its coarse gray body away from her young, scampering to her feet. Her two long orange incisors snapped at the threatening air. Eight helpless bodies, clamped to her teats by powerful suction, went with her. The ninth was left curling its translucent body in confusion, the stomach and heart dark pumping shapes against thin pink skin.

"Pipe down!" hissed Coffee Trujillo, lighting a match.

Coffee, Jugs Kelly, and Whispering Mike were huddled around the loading doors of a big blank building that backed onto the narrow alley. The front of the building opened onto Grant Avenue. Except for their own faces, lit eerie from below, none of them could see a thing. It was still too dark.

"Dropped 'em," explained Whispering Mike, living up to his name. He held up a pair of new steel clippers. The light from Coffee's match made them beautiful. "Slipped on the garbage, an' the chain fell off. This place stinks. Ain't nobody awake, anyhow."

"They will be, you keep that up, you dope." Coffee poked Jugs, a shadowy form standing beside him. "The boys all here?"

"Sure, Coffee. Everybody in place, just like you told 'em." Jugs was weighed down by two .45-caliber Thompson submachine guns, one his, one Miles Brady's.

"Everybody" was Coffee's four men, plus two more soldiers recruited only that Friday from Leo Olemi. That made seven, counting Coffee. The Mexican felt grand. His army was getting bigger. At the Sacramento end of the block-long alley, burly Joe Baglietto was lookout. He carried his own tommy gun tucked under his arm; its barrel poked an inch into the street. The other end of the alley exited into California Street. The brown Buick purred at the curb on California, its long hood pointed downhill. One of Leo's men sat in the driver's seat, waiting, both hands ready on the wheel. The second Olemi loaner made up a bookend with Joe; he guarded the alley's California end.

The most agile, Miles Brady, was climbing a drainpipe. The pipe, groaning with rust, had a tenuous grip on the back of the big brick building. He'd climbed up far enough to read an old sign painted on the blackened bricks: JIMMY LAU'S HAND-ROLLED CIGARS. The building wasn't a cigar factory any more, hadn't been since the quake. Jimmy Lau's was gutted by the fire on the first day; all that had been left was the shell of the brick building itself and the smell of burnt tobacco. Now, it was a mah-jongg factory making hundreds of intricate mah-jongg sets each day to feed a growing market of mah-jongg fanatics. All over America the click of Chinese tiles echoed in the best back parlors. America may not have liked the Chinese, but for the moment she loved their games. So in Jimmy Lau's old building Li Kwan Won made mah-jongg sets. At least that's what the new sign said above the loading-bay door. And it was true. It simply neglected to say that more than mah-jongg was made inside—Li also made hooch. The sign should have read LI KWAN WON'S MAH-JONGG MANUFACTORY AND SNAP DRAGON STILL. But of course it didn't. This was Prohibition. Next door was the back entrance of a high-class Chinese restaurant, the Intelligent Pearl. Momma rat's cozy tea chest, emptied of its fragrant China tea, was a restaurant castoff.

"Clever little bastard," said Coffee. He couldn't see the mah-jongg factory sign, but he knew it was there. The place had been sniffed out on Saturday, as he and Murray Blinn were drawing up the plans for this adventure.

"Huh?" Whispering Mike worked his clippers on the larger chain.

"The big Chink inside here, pretendin' he's making Chink games for silly old white dames to play."

In the yellow light of Coffee's waning match, Mike's stupid face tried to look like Mike knew what Coffee was talking about. Mike gave it up and busied himself with the chain. Whispering Mike had feelings; he was tired of being razzed. It took him years to figure it out, but it had finally dawned on him: if he didn't understand what someone was saying, the best thing to do was to shut up. If he shut up, nobody took a verbal poke at him.

The second chain snapped with a steel crack that made Coffee wince. He lit another match and waited a full half minute before speaking. "All right," he whispered, "wait until Miles gets this joint open from the inside, give him two minutes to scout around for what's where an' who's what; you got that, Mike? Two minutes—"

"Gimme a break, Coffee. I know what a fuckin' minute is."

"—an' then we go in. After that, no matter what happens, I want this job done right, goddammit. No leavin' nothin'. If it moves, shoot it; they're all a bunch of Chinks anyway. An' no talkin' to nobody that thinks we oughta maybe sit down an' discuss things. I ain't got no manners left. Right, Jugs?"

"You got it, boss."

Coffee loved the word "boss." It warmed his trigger finger. Things were now moving like he wanted them to move. No more pussyfooting around with the niceties. When you wanted something, you didn't ask, you took. What's the point of asking, anyway? If someone asked Coffee for what was his, he sure as shit wasn't going to hand it over. They'd have to break his arm to get it. That's how things were done. You broke arms. Because if you didn't, you'd be the one wearing the fucking cast. Coffee ought to know. His wrist was tender with unhealed dog bites. No one was biting Coffee again. None of that shit. Any more asking, and Murray Blinn could find himself another lieutenant. And if Coffee Trujillo went, he'd take what was Murray's, including Jugs Kelly. The painted pansy didn't deserve him. A man needed someone like Jugs around. Someone to call him boss. Coffee's match went out, leaving him holding a bent black stick.

"Hey, boss, Miles is in." Jugs lit another match. In the flare, his pinched face looked like a three-year-old's attempt at carving a jack-o'-lantern.

"OK, signal Joe an' the other guy, what's-his-name —we're goin' in."

Jugs waved his match, then dropped it onto the

stones of the alley. No need to step on it; it went out with a sizzle in the slime under their feet.

"This place gives me the creeps, Coffee. Chinks is filthy."

"What say you an' me an' Mike go clean 'em up, then?"

With a heave of his broad shoulder, Mike pushed open the loading doors. Inside, the "mah-jongg factory" was as bright as full morning. All the electric lights were on. Coffee and his boys, now caught up with Miles Brady, who took his tommy gun back from Jugs, paused to soak the Chinese operation in.

"Some still, eh, fellas?" said Miles, smears of rust on his old trucking jacket and brown pants. "The place takes up practically the whole block. Looks like they must make thousands of gallons of high proof here every goddam day." Miles's oyster eyes gleamed. "There's three whole floors of it, plus a place where they make the games. They're bottling, labeling, packing it all right here."

Coffee Trujillo felt like he was standing at the altar of the only kind of god that made any sense. Everything he'd ever wanted was spread out before him like Mammon's buffet. Coffee inhaled the sweet-sour smell of bootlegger's heaven.

A dozen or so booze-filled vats as big as Hollywood swimming pools curved wooden rims over their heads; thirty-six-gallon barrels, hundreds of them, were stacked one on top of the other in towering pyramids; copper and glass tubing twisted like vermicelli from vat to vat. Running around the upper walls was a catwalk, and three sets of stairs led from the huge first floor up into private darkness. To their left was a fleet of covered trucks, parked hood to tailgate, chrome and paint glowing under the overhead electric bulbs. To their right were packing crates labeled with the operations products: Snap Dragon Spirits—gin, whiskey, rum, bourbon. The whole gamut from bottle to blotto. Coffee's mouth watered.

"Anybody here, Miles?"

Miles nodded his smooth head. "Yeah, this floor there's a couple of Chinks toward the Grant Avenue side putting labels on things, a white guy wearing an eyeshade in an office upstairs, counting pieces of paper. Didn't see nobody else up there. Came through a skylight quiet as a mouse. They don't expect nothing. We're jake."

"OK. Jugs, go round up the Chinks. Miles, get the guy in the office. Bring 'em down here an' do it quick. I wanna get this over as fast as it takes me to piss."

"You want me to salute?" Miles gave Coffee a big smile, his perfect teeth dazzling.

"Can the crap, Brady. Just do it."

Miles snapped a salute anyway, spun on his leather heels, and followed Jugs.

"Remind me, Mike, as soon as this is all over, to plug that Chicago punk."

Whispering Mike had trouble with subtleties. That kept him in the dark about 90 percent of his life. But Coffee's point about Miles was as clear as a game of marbles. "Yeah, Coffee. No trouble."

Coffee decided that poaching Whispering Mike from Murray was also in the cards.

Miles was a pain in the ass, but you had to give it to him. He was fast. Shoving the white bookkeeper along with the live end of his tommy gun, he was back moments before Jugs. The bookkeeper had eyes like a goldfish behind his thick eyeglasses. Hands held high over his head, his eyes were swimming with fear.

"What's all this?" he demanded. Even scared, he had time to be outraged.

"Whaddaya think it is? It's your birthday. We brought a surprise. So shut up an' enjoy."

Jugs, herding three quiet Chinese, joined the little group. "Not a cheep outa the little guys."

Coffee had Mike put the four of them into the cab of the first truck in the line. Mike locked the doors behind them.

"You boys stay in there an' be nice," said Coffee. "That way mebbe you come outa this with your skins still on. OK, Jugs, let's do business. An' don't stand on the floor. Before you know it, this place is going to look like a tidal wave hit it."

It took Coffee's idiot army five minutes to machine-gun every barrel, bottle, and crate in the building. Snap Dragon gin, whiskey, brandy, and rum gushed out onto the cement floor until the Blinn boys could have done the backstroke in San Francisco's biggest, most lethal cocktail. Miles Brady, halfway up a staircase and heady with the fumes, was laughing. With all the noise they were making, his laughter wasn't a problem. But what he did next was. He spun on the stairs, spraying bullets in a fine arc, and one huge vat split open with a liquid shriek, Yellow Jack beer frothing from its splintered sides with the force of a busted dam, surging for the line of trucks.

"Hey, Coffee! Watch this!"

Miles pumped rapid-fire into a truck three back from the front. With a low booming *whumph!* the engine exploded, sparking out gaudy streamers of flame. They jumped like furious orange monkeys from Miles's truck to the tailgate of the truck in front of it. In a second both trucks were engulfed in a ball of red boiling flame and up to their heavy bumpers in swilling Yellow Jack; heat miraged the walls behind them five feet away. The truck in front, the truck with the Chinese and the bookkeeper, sucked fire up its exhaust.

Miles Brady watched all this, handsome face glowing in the hot glare, oyster eyes reflecting pink, still laughing. "Lookit the Chinks!"

The men locked in the cab of the burning truck were trying to get out, their faces like an Edvard Munch painting pinned behind glass, mouths perfect O's of imploring horror.

"Shit!" screamed Coffee. "Let's get the fuck outa here!"

Farther south than the area once known as South of the Slot lay the western terminus of America's mighty railroads, the railroads that had been built at immense cost to the Chinese coolie and immense profit to the robber barons of California. South of the Slot was named for the simple reason that the tough working-class neighborhood was below the trolley-car slot that ran the length of Market. Although it was razed in 1906—right back to early Indian sand—the southernmost spread of the holocaust had been contained at Townsend Street, leaving the sprawling freight yards of the Southern Pacific Railroad untouched. The freight docks saw ships sailing out, sitting low in the sea with the lucrative enterprise of San Francisco, and sailing in—north from the Panama Canal, launched from the eastern seaboard and Mother Europe, and west from the wide Pacific with the tumultuous trade of the Orient. The trade had hardly paused in its frantic loading and unloading. An earthquake couldn't stop business; a fire merely provided a coffee break.

Near the docks of the Pacific Mail on the top curve of China Basin—the shale of the basin lapped by the gasoline oil of the saltsea bay—stood a wooden warehouse, relic of the 1880s. If you stood directly in front of the old warehouse with the bay behind it, its white paint peeled off twenty years before, you could get seasick. The building leaned at an interesting, possibly dangerous angle. But whatever danger there was in the angle was a long time coming. The warehouse withstood the quake leaning, Leo Olemi bought it leaning, and under his ownership it would stay leaning. Leo chose the area because no attention was paid to it. For a man who kept a low profile, it was like lying flat on the ground. Leo had his offices on the top floor, using the flimsy back wall to butt his desk against to keep it from sliding through the open window. Speaking of angles, the window was a pip. It framed Mission Rock out in China Basin, a rock that looked like a cubist plum on Jack Horner's thumb, with no known angle at all.

Leo Olemi, heavy hands folded, heavy face without expression, sat listening to Murray Blinn. Everything Murray said had to be shouted above the squeal of straining metal, the clang of connections, and the hiss of steam coming from the rail yards. A neglected cigarette, burning on its curved paper spine, stank in an ashtray on Leo's desk. Spread out beside it was Tuesday's edition of the *San Francisco Examiner*. Leo had it open to page six. Down at the bottom was a small filler about a break-in at a Chinese mah-jongg factory; there was no byline. That was about it: no mention of a fire, nothing about anybody dying. Leo didn't know it, and wouldn't have cared if he had, but it was Kit Dowie's piece. He might have liked to know that Kit had considered the story front-page. Gangland murders weren't usually buried on page six. Christ, gangland murders weren't usually copy, not in San Francisco! When Kit brought the piece in, his city editor, smelling a big story, agreed, until the old man found out the "big story" was about the Chinese. "Chinese don't buy papers, Dowie, you know that, and what's more to the point, Chinese stuff don't *sell* papers. So it gets buried." The city editor went through Kit's three-column write-up with a blunt blue pencil. "The fire got put out and it was just a few Chinese went to heaven, or wherever they go." Kit was used to this kind of crap from his editor. There was no surprise. Rose owed him ten bucks. She bet on a newspaper having principles. But then, Rose, even with her hard-boiled outlook, had some very soft ideas. But he tried one last shot. "What about the dead bookkeeper, the dead *white* bookkeeper?" The city editor shrugged. "He worked for the Chinese, didn't he? Now get the hell out of here and go find us something interesting, something that *matters.*"

Murray Blinn, dressed to kill in orange plaid, thin yellow hair stiff with smelly paste, his eyebrows freshly plucked, was standing in front of Leo, keeping a good grip on the desk to enable himself to remain reasonably upright.

"So after what the boys did, Leo—"

"Mr. Olemi."

"—yeah, right, after that, Li Kwan Won ain't got a still no more. It'll take him two weeks to get that operation going again, if it ain't burned down by now."

"It didn't burn down. I sent one of my boys to check."

"Well, that's OK, ain't it? You didn't tell us to burn it down, just to scare 'em. We did the job. An' as I was sayin', it'll take him weeks to get back on the road. An' what the hell if he does? That was just our calling card. Wait till he tries to move his stuff out of Chinatown. Then he'll find out he's bottled in his own hooch. Li Kwan Won may be a big man in Chinatown, but out here in

America he's nothin' but dog shit." Murray giggled at his own joke. " 'Bottled,' get it?" he shouted.

Leo listened to Murray with distaste. He had wanted the job done. The job was done. He was pleased. But having to suffer Murray Blinn telling him about it was almost unbearable. He lit another cigarette; it took its place next to all the others. The stink masked the stink of Murray Blinn.

"Fine, Murray. Now I suggest you get on back to make sure he stays bottled."

Murray worked his way up the floor. At the top, he turned. "The East Bay distillery ready yet, Mr. Olemi?"

Leo waved him out with a languid hand. "Soon, Murray, soon. Concentrate on the Chinese."

As soon as Murray slammed the crooked door that led down to Berry Street, James Hamilton came through the one that led to a back room. He'd been pacing in it since Blinn's arrival fifteen minutes earlier. James had no intention of doing anything with people like Blinn face-to-face ever again. A future president had to be very careful. Now he was angry. Since his anniversary two weeks back he'd learned a few things about Leo Olemi, but not enough to let his anger show. He kept his voice down, but high enough to beat the trains.

"I don't need a war with Chinatown, Leo. I merely need a dead Chinaman. Without him, Rose St. Lorraine won't know whether she's coming or going. Addy Chase as good as told me outright that Li Kwan Won is the brains behind whatever she does. We get rid of the brains, and all that's left is one scared old lady. I need that property she's holding. The city airport deal is coming up for a vote in less than a month."

Leo Olemi raised his muddy eyes like a cobra raising its hood. "Let Blinn handle it in his own way, James. The way he does things is his trademark: messy. Look what happened at the Chink still. I ask him to go in with a few men and bust the place up. What do I get? Three dead Chinks and a dead bookkeeper. The press can't sit still on that kind of thing forever. He'll have the good citizens of this town down on his ass soon enough. Anything that happens to one Chinaman, anything that happens to *any*

Chinaman, will point directly to him. The way he's going, you get what you want and I get what I want. Without the Chinese business, I control the bootlegging from here to Sacramento. Without the Chink, you get Rose's plot of sand. Though why you need money, having the wife you have, is beyond me." Leo stubbed out the smoldering cigarette. Without Murray stinking the place up, he didn't need it. Olemi studied James Hamilton. He could explain things to the ambitious young dope a hundred times a day if he had to. After all, Hamilton had every chance of becoming a lot more important than he already was. The dinner at that stuffed shirt's, Addy Chase, proved it. A possible president in the pocket was better than gold. Nobody in America was going to vote for Leo Olemi. Power secondhand was better anyway. You weren't in the firing line, and you didn't have to shake hands with a nation of morons. Politicians changed like the seasons; Leo Olemi would last forever.

The way Leo put the obvious calmed James down. Leo was right. Leo also had another quality that James decided to add to his own repertoire: patience. If patience was something you acquired with age, James didn't have time to wait for it. He'd start now. He straightened his hat, his tie, his white carnation boutonniere.

"It's simple, Leo. My wife's money is ultimately *her* money. I need *my* money. And you're right. Let Blinn handle it any damn way he pleases. I've got something bigger than a few hundred acres of sand on my mind. President Warren G. Harding is on a boat somewhere between here and Alaska. I've got a party to plan."

Hamilton's Hispano-Suiza was parked out of sight behind the building; it was nosed up against the wooden fence that separated Leo's wobbly warehouse from the rail yard. The noise out here was no worse than it had been in Leo's office. Driving away from Olemi's leaning office, James's slick mind was working as fast as the railroads behind him. Once Leo, through Blinn, got rid of Li, James was going to have to get rid of Leo. Contacts like Olemi weren't a good thing to have for a young politician. What if Addy Chase or Sam Jenkins got wind of what the Italian really did for a living? And who had sent him west? One whiff of the New York connection and they'd drop James like a hot cake knife, Lizzie Stafford or no Lizzie Stafford. Playing one side against another was James's game. When Blinn went down, the district attorney was going to bring Leo Olemi down with him.

The big car was headed back to the better side of the tracks. There was only one thing now that was bothering the fair head of James Alexander Hamilton. Pinkerton's had caught up with Lizzie. The bitch was holed up in Chinatown. Now James had more than a plot of sand against Li Kwan Won.

# Chapter 20

Murray Blinn's smug estimate of the recovery of Li Kwan Won's mah-jongg factory and Snap Dragon still was off by more than a week and a half. It only took the Chinese three desperate days of round-the-clock labor to rebuild the great wooden vats, bubbling again with young Yellow Jack and the finer brew Topaz Silk, to absorb the loss of three trucks, and to repair or replace bottles, crates, and labeling machines. If the Snap Dragon had been owned by Murray, the plucked and pomaded son of Saddle Mary would have been off in his timing by months. With the dubious help of Coffee Trujillo and the boys, the Snap Dragon might have managed a gala opening for Christmas.

The white ghost has a short and convenient memory. Popular history forgot the Chinese: their strenuous, and at the time welcome, part in the birth of California was erased as savagely as the gold had been erased from her wild mountains. By 1923 the yellow man, now unaccountably squatting in the precious center of a vibrant white city, appeared to be without skill, without intelligence, without industry. To those wishing to exploit him, the clannish secretive Chinese had just brains enough to wash the clothes of his betters, clean the grand houses, and hawk fruits and vegetables in the streets. Even the more compassionate of the *baak gwai lo* thought of him as a docile child willing to work cheap, just as they thought of the black man as a possible missing link and the red man as a hopeless savage. Simple minds, simple tasks. To those who saw him as a sly threat to white labor, who used his unwelcome presence to explain joblessness to the Anglo-Saxon, the Chinese harbored vice like decay harbors maggots. The odd Oriental was viewed with arrogance or patronage—but, either way, always with ignorance.

Inside Chinatown—in a small country of his own making—the Chinese worked with a will. Three Chinese dead and one white bookkeeper were nothing compared to the amount of Chinese labor Li could command. In cold business terms, their loss went unnoticed. In terms of humanity, their loss was an occasion for the mourning of a whole people. On Tuesday, the afternoon of James Hamilton's visit to Leo Olemi in his quaint leaning warehouse by the clash and clang of the railroads, Chinatown held a funeral for four. There were no wives, no children to grieve. Li, for precisely this reason, used no married men in his bootlegging business. But that did not mean there were no families to pay their proper respect. In China, all villagers are family. In America, lacking the villages where a man could look back generations and find a direct ancestor tilling the same soil, members of entire Chinese districts became family. The funeral procession was followed by thousands.

No one came to mourn the white bookkeeper. There wasn't time. The man was from Great Falls, Montana, almost a thousand miles away from San Francisco. He had grown up in the shadow of the Rocky Mountains. The unfortunate bookkeeper went back to distant Great Falls by train, first class and feet first, on Wednesday morning to be buried close by the source of the Missouri River. The bodies of the three Chinese were prepared for shipment to Canton. Unless his bones came finally to rest under the still revered earth of ancient China, no man could join his ancestors.

Monday's dawn raid on the Snap Dragon works, Murray Blinn's little calling card, held no surprise for Li. It was inevitable, in one way or another, the moment Coffee Trujillo had his gun taken away from him and was forcibly turned out of the Blue Canary. Calmly, Li had waited for Blinn's second move. Now that it had come and in a way that was prepared for, he put into operation his considered response. As Murray so nicely put it, outside Chinatown Li was dog shit. But inside Chinatown, in the narrow alleys and streets overhung with tiny balconies of burning cineraria, Li Kwan Won might as well be emperor. By law, the white ghost patrolled his streets in the form of armed police, but never alone and never to any effect. The Han people policed themselves, and since the coming of Li Kwan Won they did it well. No Chinese sought out the official *baak gwai lo* for justice, he went to Li. Where once he might have gone to the Six Companies for help in bringing his wife to California, selling his soul in exchange, to borrow money, or to settle familial disputes, he now sought Li.

It was not democratic, but democracy was something the Chinese were never allowed to experience—not in China and not in the Mother of Democracy, America. Of course, America had never actually been a democracy either. She was ruled by the few for the few, though the "people," whoever they were and whatever that meant, were given a passing thought now and again—mainly to assure their votes. It was in the interest of those same few to govern a happy workforce, so they did what they could, whenever it caused the ruling classes no great harm. After all, this was what the Founding Fathers had had in mind when they drew up their elegantly phrased Declaration, no matter what was thereafter taught the nation's children, those faceless votes of the future. Chinatown was truly fortunate in the rapid rise of Li Kwan Won. He may have been a dictator, but he was a benevolent *Chinese* dictator.

Kit Dowie, lying hatless on a park bench, had come to these conclusions about Li and Chinatown by talking to O'Flooty. The ideas on democracy were, so far as he knew, all his own. But if his boyhood friend was a benevolent dictator, he was the only one in history that Kit could think of. Dowie had run with Villa and Zapata down in Mexico—somehow living through the experience—in a revolution that went on and on and on. As Ambrose Bierce had said, "To be a gringo in Mexico—ah, that is euthanasia." And Bierce was right; he'd vanished in Mexico before the Great War. Christ, even though it was supposed to have been officially over for six years, the Mexican revolution was still going on. He'd seen the peasants lay down their lives for their charismatic, strutting leaders. But aside from speeches—representing the American press, Kit heard impassioned speeches from the endless white dust of Chihuahua to Zapata's captured Morelos—Dowie had seen little of real benevolence in either the handsome mustachioed Emiliano Zapata or the hot-blooded Pancho Villa. What he'd seen and written about was bloodthirsty expediency and the rapt sacrifice of the individual. Of course, both Mexicans having since been assassinated, they had no real and lasting power to prove themselves one way or the other. And then there was the gloomy awakening of the Great Bear. Kit had never been to Lenin's new Russia, but he'd heard about it. It didn't sound too benevolent either. But you never knew—miracles were supposed to happen now and again on God's great earth, dizzy with all that spinning.

Kit's bench was in Portsmouth Square, Chinatown's only open space. He was sunning himself fifteen feet away from the spot where, in 1846, the first American flag was raised in San Francisco and, in 1851, the first man in San Francisco's short history was publicly hanged. Not only had he the honor of being the first man to hang in Frisco, but he was hanged by the first of San Francisco's chillingly effective vigilante committees. One John Jenkins was strung up by his protesting neck for stealing an entire safe from a nearby store, dumping the heavy iron box in the bottom of a small boat, and then rowing like hell for the open sea.

Fearless O'Flooty was sitting on a bench opposite

Kit's, his long legs, ending in huge boots, stretched out across the dirt footpath, his head thrown back to give his face the full force of California's noonday sun. The summer fog had graciously skipped a day. The long thin shadow of one of the square's symmetrical poplar trees lay across his stomach, neatly cutting Fearless in half.

"Pass me a doughnut, Dowie."

Kit never noticed it before, but now he was thinking of Zapata, O'Flooty looked just like the swaggering Mexican with his black walrus mustache and swarthy skin, until he opened his eyes—they were the startling blue of lapis lazuli. He was also a foot taller.

"You ate them all."

"I didn't."

"You did."

"Well, by God, I'm starving now."

"We're in Chinatown. Eat something Chinese."

"I hate Chinese food. I want a doughnut."

"Then you'll have to run the Blinn blockade."

"Bejesus, that's right."

"Forget your stomach, O'Flooty. And leave me alone. I came to this damn bench for some peace and quiet. I'm writing."

"And what for, boyo? Out in the open the goddess Truth suffers from chilblains. Nobody's going to print it."

"I'm a writer. When I find a great story, I write about it. I'll find someone to print it."

"You'll find someone when those bootlegging bastards blow Chinatown and every Chinese in it right out of San Francisco. And then only to shout 'Hurrah!' "

Heading for Clay Street on the south side of Portsmouth Square, a scurrying clutch of very old Chinese hurried by them, buried in curious bundles.

"There goes Li Kwan Won's army now," said Fearless, rubbing his tiny paunch as he watched them with his beautiful blue eyes.

Kit looked up, resting his note pad on his chest. "That means lunch is over. I'm getting back to Li's still. We might be missing some action. You coming?"

Leaping to his feet, O'Flooty forgot about doughnuts. "What do you think, Dowie? The trick is to dazzle the bastards. On such a grand day as this, it's me for protecting my investment."

"Sure you are, Fearless."

Grinning, Kit grabbed his hat from under the bench and followed O'Flooty's long-legged gallop across the worn yellow grass of Portsmouth Square. Protect his investment? The only investment Fearless O'Flooty had in the Snap Dragon was his waterfront speak's stock of booze. He could get that anywhere. Fearless O'Flooty was in Chinatown because he was a born advocate of the underdog. And he didn't give a damn whether they were right or wrong, or whether he liked them or not. He fiercely championed the cantankerous Tom Mooney, though hating Mooney the man. As Fearless said, who can stand the bastard? But Tom Mooney was rotting in San Quentin, along with another labor agitator, Warren Billings, for supposedly planting a bomb at San Francisco's Preparedness Day Parade in 1916. Ten people were killed, and the United Railroads swung the blame onto Tom. Everyone thought he was the only local radical rash and stupid enough to try it. With no evidence, the URR and San Francisco's political machine called up a prostitute, a spiritualist, a dope addict, and a pathological liar to perjure themselves. It worked. Tom Mooney and Warren Billings were behind bars. And Fearless O'Flooty went into a rage that earned him more black eyes than all his other causes combined. And now Chinatown. In America, there couldn't be many dogs lower than the Chinese. He was also there because wherever there was a fight, O'Flooty was right in the thick of it. Witness his bent nose.

Chinatown was under siege. Murray Blinn had blocked off every street leading in or out with an army of hired guns, most from out of town. Smart boys from Chicago and Cleveland, New York and St. Louis, with Olemi footing the bill for their services, patrolled the perimeter of dark confusing alleys and steep streets cluttering the fine flanks of Nob Hill—from Broadway to Bush, from Stockton to Kearny. Whatever the cops on the beat thought of a sudden swell of snappily dressed street layabouts, collars up and hands stuffed in their bulging pockets, they didn't say. They didn't have to; Robert Bent and his cops were well paid to leave them alone and keep their mouths shut. Li's trucks couldn't get out. But his people could. Every man, woman, and child carried Snap Dragon bottles away from Chinatown—hidden in laundry carts, under mounds of Chinese greens, or on their bent backs. The barrels of Yellow Jack and Topaz Silk went through the underground warrens, one leading directly to the Blue Canary a safe block outside Chinatown, another to the Chinese speak on Pine and Grand Avenue. Whatever Murray could do, Li could easily counter. Virtually everyone in Chinatown owed Li for something he'd done for them. Most of the grateful recipients had no hope that they'd ever be able to repay him. Working to get Snap Dragon booze past the Blinn mob was a godsend. The siege was a source of joy. If Murray Blinn could have known his caper was turning into a community festival, he might have been discouraged.

Lizzie was on the ground floor of the Snap Dragon. No more Parisian couturier clothes, no brittle heels, no square-cut emeralds, no marcels or high-buffed nails. From even a short distance away, Lizzie could have been mistaken for a Chinese boy. With her black hair tied back in a loose bun, blue tunic and pants, and soft black slippers, all she needed was a straw coolie hat. But up close, the resemblance ended forever. No Chinese had green eyes. And no boy had a face like that. It was Lizzie Stafford Hamilton, all right. What her fierce brow and strong jawline had always portended had come true. Her wide unpowdered cheekbones glistened with sweat as she sorted what crate went where, by what method, and with whom. Families of Chinese crowded around her, taking their no-nonsense assignments. In Cantonese, they called her Miss Blue Trousers, shortened by the children, and then by everyone, to just Laam, Little Blue. But whatever they called her, they did what she said.

Kit hadn't seen Lizzie since he'd gently but firmly thrown her out of the Crawford Apartments almost two weeks before. Pencil behind his ear, cigarette stuck in the corner of his mouth, he entered the Snap Dragon on the run. Just inside the doors of the loading bay, he stopped dead, and O'Flooty ran right into the back of him.

Disturbed by O'Flooty's echoing *Oof!,* Lizzie snapped a green look at them both. "Kit! Come here, I need help." She had scarcely paused in her distributions, taking only enough time to tuck a stray wisp of hair back behind her ear. "Good, you've brought a friend. Help me pick this up. God, I wish I had taken Chinese at school."

"They don't teach Chinese at Miss Murison's School for Young Ladies," said Fearless, shoving Kit out of the way, his Mexican mustache on his Irish face bristling at Lizzie. Kit was speechless.

Lizzie didn't bother to look up. "Well, they should have. Look at all these people I can't talk to."

Kit stared at her. Was he having a nightmare? Was she kidding? Holy hell, little green-eyed Lizzie Stafford was worrying him all over again. His week of drinking and talking O'Flooty deaf had brought him to his senses; happily, he thought it was a remote kind of worry. She'd gone to Li. He should have known she would, he *had* known it, but until now he couldn't admit it to himself. Kit Dowie had been covering the siege of Chinatown ever since the Blinn mob cooked the bookkeeper and three of Li's men. But he hadn't seen Lizzie. Talk of Little Blue had passed him by; he spoke no more Cantonese than she did. Such stupidity was surely self-defense? But he couldn't deny her now, not with little Lizzie barking orders like the *Examiner's* city editor when a big story was breaking. Kit suddenly had a vision of Lizzie, stripped down to her lacy white camisole, burning at the stake. Kit was sure she didn't know what was really happening here, or how dangerous it was. How could she? But she was involved. Kit had known Li Kwan Won since he was eleven years old and he still hadn't figured him out, him or his people. Lizzie had only a two-week crash course. It wasn't enough for a people centuries old. But now, with something to care about, something to *do,* she looked like she could lead a crusade into hell. Kit was afraid that Lizzie Stafford was going to turn into Joan of Arc if someone didn't get her out of Chinatown. And the only person who could do that was Li Kwan Won.

"Where's Li?"

Lizzie jerked her busy head up. "In his office. You're not leaving me again?"

"Take Fearless O'Flooty here, with my compliments. He's got a strong Irish neck." Under his breath, Fearless growled at Kit. "I need a word with the boss."

But Lizzie wasn't listening. She was trying to make herself understood by an old woman in black, bent under the weight of the Snap Dragon's unbonded Scotch.

"No, *Laam sui-je,*" the old woman croaked. There wasn't a tooth in her mouth.

"Yes, yes. Oh, for goodness' sake, Mr. O'Flooty. Try to make this woman understand: six bottles, not ten. She can't carry that many."

"I understand. I can earry. I carry more all my life."

Climbing one of the three staircases up to the Snap Dragon's encircling catwalk, Kit suddenly stopped dead. What the hell was he doing? In the first shock of seeing Lizzie, and such a changed Lizzie, his only fixed idea had been to get her out of Chinatown. Why? The gesture of an old friend? The natural protective response of the male toward the female, *any* female? Hell, no. Kit couldn't fool himself, he wasn't any good at it. The truth made him clench his fists. He wanted to stuff her back into her high-class silks and satins; he wanted her propped back up on top of Nob Hill. The horrible truth was that he'd cheer if she got another marcel, began to chatter over tea at the Fairmont, or bitch about James and Esmé Baker. Lizzie as she had been was no longer a danger to him—he was sure he'd gotten over *that* Lizzie. As long as she stayed that way. But *this* Lizzie? The new model stunned him, set him back on his newspaper heels. How was he going to handle her now? Kit wasn't trying to protect Lizzie, he was trying to protect himself. She was going back. Li would agree. Women had no place in a war. Because Kit Dowie couldn't take the pain of seeing her in the middle of it, growing up without him.

Li was in the bookkeeper's office, seated calmly at the dead man's desk. From a distance, Lizzie could pass for Chinese; from the same distance, Li might be mistaken for white. It wasn't just the western clothes. It was the firm set to his shoulders, the amused tilt of his head. In America, as in China, the Chinese bowed a lot. Unless in parody, Li never bowed at all.

Even in the middle of an all-out siege the office was like the eye of a tornado: papers neatly in stacks, orders, invoices, the coming and going of Li's men—quiet, dignified, and very efficient. Like a glossy Buddha, O Ti stood tall at Li's side. As Lan-ch'i, Blue Flag, it was O Ti who planned and directed the military movements of the Night of Two Moons. It was Blue Flag's fiercely held opinion that now the Blinn boys had caused death, more deaths would be nothing to them. Li Kwan Won's, in particular, would be everything. Unasked, O Ti, arms folded over his barrel chest, jaw thrust out, was Li's constant bodyguard. Li, though inclined to trust fate, gave him his head.

Before Li noticed him, Kit had a moment to absorb the feeling in the Snap Dragon office. He was sure Li was enjoying all this. There was no sense of hurry, no fear. Li directed the complicated operations with grace, maintaining delivery under the threat of a gang war to dozens of speakeasies, hotels, and restaurants as if it were business as usual. Even the mah-jongg games were getting made. You had to admire the guy. America missed her chance on a terrific general a few years back in France.

All Kit carried was a notebook and spare pencils. The notebook was thick with details of his three days in Chinatown. Except for Lizzie in the middle of everything like Annie Oakley dressed as a coolie—or was it Calamity Jane?—this whole thing was exhilarating. Though Fearless was right, damn him: the *Examiner* wasn't covering the story, nor was any other newspaper in town. Hearst was in California for a change, but not too close. He was down south in Big Sur collecting more stuff in his undaunted attempt to buy the world. He had more unopened boxes and crates cluttering up his unfinished castle, San Simeon, than Charles Mortimer Stafford had hauled into the Stafford mansion in over forty years of trying. But then, Hearst did everything, not necessarily better, but—more. Just like Charles Mortimer, Hearst had no taste. Most of what either one of them bought from people eager to sell, people who could spot a sucker coming when they saw one, was elaborate junk. Hearst was also pressing his great weight, in more ways than one, on some poor sweet actress with an endearing stammer. Because of Marion Davies, Hearst was now not just the most flamboyant publisher in America, he was on his way, if he could, to cornering the movie market. And his only star was smothered little Marion. Thousands more than Kit Dowie were getting sick of seeing her admittedly cute kisser planted in Hearst's roto pages every Sunday. With all this going on, the Chief still found time to take an interest in his first paper, the *San Francisco Examiner,* and to squash stories that didn't appeal to him or to his far-flung interests. Kit wasn't surprised. He knew Hearst would sit on the Chinese story. The Chief wouldn't print until, as O'Flooty said, it got *out* of Chinatown, became news for the folks, and sold papers. Well, the hell with that. Kit would pay his own money to have it printed if he had to; he'd write a book; he'd do something. This wasn't a bootleggers' war, it was much more than that. It was Chinatown's stand against America—and America didn't give a good goddam. Three city blocks away from where he stood, Mr. and Mrs. San Francisco went about their daily business, unaware and unconcerned about what was happening in Chinatown. He wondered if Lizzie knew *that?*

Seeing Kit Dowie framed in the doorway, Li smiled. "Kit. You have returned to take more notes?"

For a split second Kit was caught off-balance. He'd spent his life standing back. While others loved or fought, schemed for office, for riches or for honor, Kit merely hung around, just as he was doing now, and watched them do it. Then he went home to write it all down. So? What was wrong with that? Kit regained his balance with the supple backbone of an alley cat twisting in the middle of a two-story drop.

He shoved his hat to the back of his head, flipped a spindly chair around backward, and sat in it that way, chair tilted up, his elbows propped on Li's desk. "That's the artist for you, old friend. Some create with money, some with blood; I'm a sucker for words."

Li laughed, a nice easy sound. "And am I, in your opinion, an artist?"

"Sure, you're a magician." Kit kept a light touch, but he bore down heavier when he said, "Maybe you ought to make a few passes over Lizzie. Turn her back into a princess. The kid's gonna trip over something. She's game, but dammit, she's raw."

The two men smiled at each other across the desk. Kit thought he knew what Li was feeling, but he was damn sure that Li knew what Dowie was feeling. His old friend had compassion enough not to mention it.

"Lizzie is impetuous, Kit. She trips over herself with an awkward radiance."

"You said it."

"And you think she ought to go home, that she is playing a game?"

"Don't you?"

"I've thought so since she arrived. That is, I've thought she should go home. As for a game, what is not a game? To play one here or there makes no difference."

"Maybe. You have a point. But some games play with rough rules."

"Ah, yes." Li's brown eyes shone with a curious fatal light. Kit wondered what he was looking at, but whatever it was he saw, Li would never tell him. Li had played his whole life close to the chest. That he allowed Kit Dowie to come as near as he did was a compliment, and Kit took it that way. Li said, "Some games are much more interesting than others. This one is the preamble to the most dangerous of all."

"A preamble?"

"Of course. This is a game of charades. I am meant to guess who Blinn really is, but of course I do not need to guess. I know."

"You mean Lizzie's husband."

"I mean Mr. Leo Olemi. James Hamilton is the more corrupt, but there is a weakness inside that can be reached. Olemi, in his way, is an honest man. He does not pretend to be better than he is, and that makes him strong. Leo Olemi is the man who counts. His game will be much more exciting than the little one we play today, the one that pretends to be about the business of bootlegging. Of course, it is only Murray Blinn who is foolish enough to believe that that is what we are doing. Mr. Olemi uses him to play for power, and when he has achieved that power by removing the irritant of myself, he will remove Blinn. You see why Leo's game is so much more dangerous?"

"So you aren't fooled?"

"Did you think I was?"

"I thought if you didn't know all this by now, I wasn't going to tell you."

"The objective reporter?"

"Sure. I'm supposed to tell the story, not make it."

"It is curious then that you continue to work for Mr. Hearst."

"That hurt, Li. But you're right. I intend to quit by the end of next week. I'm going east with Dido to see if New York is ready for me yet." Kit got up from his chair. O Ti moved forward a step. Kit took a good look at his round pockmarked face and sat down again. "For Pete's sake, what's the matter with him?"

*"O Ti! Dowie seen-sang hai ngaw lo paang-yau."*

Kit pointed at O Ti. "A bodyguard? You think someone's gonna go for you?"

"It is not what I think that matters. O Ti appoints himself."

"Oh." Kit stayed in his chair. "But, dammit, I want one last Frisco story. Christ, why won't they let me write it?"

Absorbed in his own frustrated passion, Kit missed Li's little smile to O Ti. It was not to the triad's benefit to have this story told. Secrets, "theatricals"—their name for ritual—shadow play, all these were at the heart of the Hung League, of any triad. Even among themselves nothing was what it seemed. All was hidden in cant and elaborate ceremony. It was not just *baak gwai lo* antipathy that kept Kit Dowie silenced. There were others besides Willie Hearst who had influence in San Francisco.

"And what a story, Li! I've got so much on Hamilton now it makes my teeth hurt. This little game, as you call it, may be one thing to that bumbling baboon, Blinn, and another to Olemi, but to James Hamilton there's even more at stake than money and Leo controlling California for the boys back east. And I can't print a word of it."

Partly to distract and partly as a gift, Li gave Dowie something to chew on. "You mean Harding."

Kit sat up in his chair. "I do? President Harding? What about Harding?"

"He comes to San Francisco soon."

"Christ, I know that, I'm stuck with the damn story. I was talking about James helping Leo by bottling up the police, in return for Leo's putting the pressure on you. I got fed the story from his secretary, a Mrs. Heney. She spies on him because she's the only dame in town who doesn't think Hamilton is Sir Launcelot. Why are all the clever ones so ugly? She told me James wants you out of the way to get at Rose. Something about selling to the city some land she owns down in San Mateo County—once it's his, of course. What about the President? What's James got to do with Harding?"

"James is preparing a surprise for him. Something that might surprise us all."

"Did Lizzie tell you this?"

"Lizzie does not know."

"Then how do you know?"

"Our police commissioner, Mr. Robert Bent, often comes to taste the simple vices of Chinatown. He talks in his sleep."

"You mean to Chinese whores?"

"I mean opium. Girls are of no use to Mr. Bent."

"Holy smoke!" Kit flipped open his notebook and scribbled madly. "The President is due the twenty-ninth of July. That's only three days. Jesus Christ!"

"I wouldn't worry about your story. You are a writer, and a writer has many pages in his book. Words last through time—action fades like a smile."

"Yeah, but I haven't got time for fading smiles. What's the bastard up to? *Why* is even more interesting. What's he got against the President? And what's he gonna do about it, whatever it is? I'll bet that Baker broad knows all about it."

"Why and what is something I will discover. When I know more, you shall know more."

Kit fell silent. His pencil made doodles on his note pad instead of words. He'd reported on dirty deeds and shady deals since he was sixteen, but none of them touched him. He didn't know the people involved. Hell, they weren't people, they were stories. This time everyone around him, people that mattered to Kit, were involved in a mess he had only glimpsed the edges of. The center was fuzzy, still nascent, still unwritten. Kit Dowie couldn't stand back from *this* story and just watch. He had to do something. But on whose side? Who were the good guys and who the bad? It should be obvious—James and Leo were the ones in the black hats. But, as he'd said to Lizzie, if they were criminals, Rose was also a criminal. She was the best madam in San Francisco. Li was a criminal as well, a bootlegger. A bootlegger? Jesus, he was a murderer! After the war, Li had told Kit about the killing of the young white bandit. Though he never mentioned the Night of Two Moons, Kit wasn't slow. Li was involved in some kind of secret society. And Li's society broke laws. For a newsman to turn a blind eye was to break more laws. But if the laws were unjust? Why was it a crime for a woman to use her own body any way she pleased? Why was it a crime to sell alcohol to a country of millions who wanted to buy the stuff? It was just like Rose said: You make a stupid law, and you get a bunch of lawbreaking citizens. Once they break one law, they find it easy to break another. Nothing was black and white, and the color gray brought on cynicism, like a headache of the spirit. Kit drew a good likeness of Li on his note pad.

"The problem isn't lawlessness," he said, "it's ambiguity. Nobody can tell what's good and what's bad any more."

Li turned Kit's notebook around, added little horns to the portrait, then slid it back. "What is good and what is bad? Do you know? Have you ever known?"

"Chinese puzzles, for Christ's sake. We *need* to know. I need to know. Otherwise, what the hell am I doing?"

"The puzzle is simple. Choose what *you* think is good. Choose, and honor your choice."

"Li, you drive me crazy." Quickly, Kit held up his hand. "Don't say it."

"What was I going to say?"

"You were going to tell me that if I went nuts, then I chose to go nuts."

"An interesting idea."

"This whole mess is interesting. Now Lizzie can't even go home. Chinatown is at war, her damn husband is up to his neck in plots—he's lost face by her being here. Who the hell knows how he'll pay her back for that? Why don't you take her to the Blue Canary? Rose and Addy would watch her. She has to be safe there."

"Because she wants to be here."

"Tell her to go away."

"I have. I have given her every opportunity, but, as you can see, she stays."

"Then take away her choice."

"You love her that much?"

"Don't you?"

"I love her enough to let her keep her freedom."

"Her freedom might get her killed."

"Freedom is all we have—the lack of it *will* kill her."

"Then *I'll* take away her goddam choice."

"That choice is yours."

"Fuck you, Li."

*Chapter 21*

Kit didn't waste any time. He did exactly what he told Li he would do—he got Lizzie out of Chinatown.

"Listen, kid. I don't give a damn if you never speak to me again. This is no place for Lizzie Hamilton."

"You mean no place for a woman?"

"I mean no place for *you.*"

It took Kit Dowie, Fearless O'Flooty, and an old friend of theirs, a scrappy Irish cabdriver named Jim, three hours of gentle persuasion—followed by Fearless's losing his patience and clipping her on the jaw—to do it. But ultimately, Lizzie went, yelling her head off. And weeping with frustration that there was no point in punching anyone in the mouth. By anyone, she meant Kit. It took strength to make it stick, the kind of strength men had—or women truck drivers.

To her despair, Li hadn't been any help at all. He'd stood there with that inscrutable oriental smile on his now-beloved face, and the inscrutable O Ti at his elbow like a Chinese twin, still taking messages from and giving orders to his busy triad—which meant, for over three days now, all of Chinatown. He was saying by his silence that it was all for the best. The best? For whom? Lizzie was spitting with rage.

Li was as calm as a deep-sea clam. "To tell you the truth, Laam, I haven't the faintest idea who will benefit most. I hope that it will be you."

That's what he'd said! She couldn't believe it. "You mean you haven't got an old Chinese saying to cover this situation, Li? I'm surprised."

Li had laughed; then he'd taken her dark furious head between his hands and kissed her on the forehead, while she glared at him, speechless in her frenzy. Her hands itched to garotte him, to feel the smooth handle of an ax. A crossbow, prussic acid, anything would do.

"You will be close by. Kit's friends are taking you to stay with Rose. I will come when I can."

That's when she'd started yelling and when O'Flooty had knocked her out cold with a seasoned prizefighter's accurate touch. After that, she didn't remember a thing until she woke up wearing a long pink nightie in a bedroom above the Blue Canary, with Rose St. Lorraine standing at the foot of her bed. Rose was wrapped in a kimono printed with every kind of flower that the designer could think of. Rose looked like spring in San Francisco's botanical gardens. Spike, as usual, was up her sleeve, and Sergeant Huggins, ever the gentleman, panted at her side.

"Hello, sweetie," said Rose. "Say hello to Lizzie, doggies." Spike yipped; Sergeant Huggins yawned and wagged his white plume of a tail. "I got you out of those sweet Chinese clothes and the canvas sack Fearless and his cabbie friend brought you in."

"Sack?"

"You came through with a shipment of Yellow Jack. They didn't want to get you all dirty down in those dark tunnels."

Flipping back the covers, Lizzie tried to leap out of bed. "I'm going back! Ow!" Her head spun and her jaw ached.

"No you aren't, honey." Rose snapped her fingers. "Sergeant Huggins! Guard!"

Sergeant Huggins stopped yawning, stopped his tail-wagging, and bared his spectacular fangs. Defeated by force for the second time, Lizzie fell back onto the pillow.

Rose covered her up again. "I brought you some coffee and a bun, honey. You missed breakfast."

"Breakfast? What time is it?"

"Must be a little after three."

"And I just missed breakfast?"

"You should know the Blue Canary doesn't get up until noon."

Lizzie was catching on. "You mean this isn't Thursday anymore?"

"No, baby. It's Friday. Somebody must have slipped you something to make you sleep. You've been out for close to a full day. Hold on; I'll get Ike to bring you up an ice pack. You got a beauty of a bruise blooming on your chin. Meantime, you've got this room all to yourself. Dandy, isn't it? All pink. Maggie, my Polish girl, she's gone to visit her folks."

Taking the beady-eyed smashed-face Spike with her, Rose headed stately for the door.

Lizzie decided to cry, clotting her thick black lashes and pinking the whites of her green eyes. She twisted the Polish whore's sheet between her fingers. "You mean that's it? Why are you, of all people, doing this to me? No one would have dared kick you out of the Klondike."

Rose stopped halfway over the threshold. How was she going to tell this girl she didn't have the sense of a donkey? No one could throw Rose out of the Klondike because Rose controlled the Klondike. Lizzie Stafford couldn't even control herself. It was fine with Rose to endanger yourself as you grew up, but to take others with you—that was quite another thing. Rose's loyalties lay with Li. "That's truer than you know. But I've been asked to keep you out of Chinatown. And that's what I mean to do. Honey, you promised me you weren't going to make trouble for Li."

"I haven't made trouble. I was helping, and I was good at it. Ask him."

"Oh, hell, I believe you were good at it. If there's one thing you've got, it's spunk. And you've got brains, now that you decided to use them a little. So for heaven's sake, Lizzie, use them some more. Haven't you got it yet? You're going to get my boy killed if you hang around Chinatown."

"But I love him, Rose."

"That just makes it worse. Be a good girl and let him do the visiting. That way, you both have a chance."

"I don't want him to visit, I want to live with him."

Rose got mad. She almost loved Lizzie, but she wasn't sure she liked her. "Are you crazy? White girls don't live with black boys, or red boys, or yellow boys. If they found life on Mars, white girls wouldn't live with those boys, either. And if they did, hell! Nothing usually happens to the girls, but the boys get strung up by their balls—that is, if they still got balls. Li is as fatalistic as the stars, but I'll be damned if I'm letting him sit down in front of a rushing freight. And you, Lizzie Stafford, are a whole train. The idiot loves you, just like poor Kit loves you. And Rose? Dammit, honey, I love everybody, even you. That's because you remind me of me. I did a lot of dumb things when I was younger too, but you might be setting a record."

Lizzie was listening, but selectively. "Li loves me? He told you?"

"You kidding? Of course not. He doesn't need to."

"In that case, I know why Grandfather left me all his money. I know what to do with it now."

Rose was tapping her foot. "Oh, Lord, Lizzie. What are you talking about?"

"I'll use it to protect Li."

Rose gave up and followed her own advice. Which was: Don't bother to give it, no one listens. "Eat your bun. Ike'll be up in a minute." With a rush of riotous kimono, Rose and Spike were gone.

So there was Lizzie, trapped in a pink room above the Blue Canary, with a big white dog with big white fangs looking at her. Lizzie reached out a slow cautious hand and scratched Sergeant Huggins under his soft chin. Sergeant Huggins gave her a happy toothsome grin. Very very carefully, Lizzie sneaked a foot from under the covers on the side of the bed away from the dog.

"Good dog," she was saying. "What a lovely dog you are."

She had both bare feet out now, and was sliding away from Sergeant Huggins, slithering under her covers. Her feet found the pink carpet, then her knees. Her head was still under the blanket when she heard Sergeant Huggins growl. It sounded serious.

"Damn!" Lizzie scrambled back up and popped her head out. Sergeant Huggins had all his teeth out again.

"I'd forget it if I was you," said Appetite Ike, bobbing in on his unequal legs with a bucket of cracked ice and a clean towel. "That dog only listens to Rose. An' me. Back off, Huggins. Gimme some room."

Ike sat himself down on Lizzie's bed. Under his weight, the bed barely sagged. There wasn't much of him left.

"Ike, I have to get out of here."

"Where to?" Ike gave her a horrible squint. It was meant to be friendly. Then he clamped a towel full of cold ice onto the point of her firm chin and held it there.

With Ike and his ice attached to her determined face, Lizzie found it difficult to talk, but that didn't stop her. "Home, my home—up on the hill."

"You mean you ain't plannin' on runnin' back to Chinatown?"

"What's the use? No one wants me there. Not Kit or Li or Rose, or you either, I suppose."

"I'm like Li, girlie. I want you to be wherever it is you wanna be. But if all the other folks think different, whaddaya gonna do? As they say, you can't fight City Hall. Meantime, what're you feelin' so sorry for yourself for?"

"Am I feeling sorry for myself, Ike?"

"Hell's bells, whaddaya think? You did what you could, an' I 'spect you done enough. Let the boys handle it now. You had yourself an adventure, an' you ain't lost nuthin'."

Through wet sticky lashes, Lizzie looked at the old man who was holding an ice pack to her chin. He was ugly, he was bent, he was little, and he smelled like the wet end of a cigar, but she hadn't liked anyone so much for as long as she could remember. Except for Rose St. Lorraine. Though she suspected Rose's liking for her had dampened a little. There wasn't much she could do about that, except give up Li—so there wasn't anything she could do. But no matter how much she liked Ike, it didn't change the fact that the old man was wrong. She *had* lost something, only she didn't know what that something was. It was time to go home, back to the house Grandfather had given her, that she'd spent her whole life in. Why should she have to hide in the Blue Canary? It was her house, leaping on its hill above San Francisco in all its arrogant flamboyance, not James's. They might be able to keep her out of Chinatown, but she'd be damned if she couldn't go home.

"Let me hold the ice pack, Ike, and do me a favor. Call this dog off. I'm going home. Tell Rose that's where I've gone, and thank her for the bed."

"I wouldn't worry about Rose, girlie. You wanna get out of here, an' you ain't intent on botherin' nobody down the hill, she won't mind where you go so long as you're safe."

Appetite Ike came to this conclusion with all the assurance of someone who didn't know what Kit knew, and Li as well: James Alexander Hamilton was worse than Chinatown.

"Sergeant Huggins, let's you an' me leave the lady alone."

Dressed in a ribboned and bowed frilly something she'd found in Polish Maggie's closet, Lizzie walked home. Home was only three short blocks straight up Mason Street in the full slanting light of the afternoon sun. When she got to the top, she could have turned to the right and marched three blocks straight down to old St. Mary's, and she'd be in Chinatown again. But Lizzie hadn't been lying to Ike; she wasn't going back to Chinatown. At the corner of Mason and California, where the glorious Fairmont Hotel glimmered a flat Greek white against the yellow sky, she turned left. Lizzie needed to talk to somebody.

Stopping in front of the Stafford mansion, catching

her breath, she knew who that somebody she needed to talk to was going to be. Charles Mortimer was the person she most wanted to see in all the world—but, damn him, Grandfather wasn't in the world any more. Seeing him would be seeing his ghost. Lizzie had the sudden eerie feeling that wherever Charles Mortimer Stafford was now, he'd kept track of everything she did. So her choice fell to the person nearest—Grandfather's best friend, Addy Chase. There was a chance it might be like talking to Charles Mortimer. Standing on California Street in her borrowed frills, looking up at the waving towers of Charles Mortimer's mad mansion, the house that architecturally made no sense—the house she'd brought her young groom to when she was still little Lizzie, blind and stupid—now made no sense emotionally.

Without Grandfather, Lizzie talked to his house. I'm growing up, Charles Mortimer. What would you say if you saw *how,* if you knew who I loved and who loved me? What would you say to that, you fat wonderful old man? You were so rich you could buy whatever you wanted. You were luckier than me; you wanted what a person *could* buy.

Like a climber after struggling up Tamalpais, Charles Mortimer's personal mountain, Lizzie sat down breathless on the top step of the mansion's marbled entrance. The air up here was thinner, harder to breathe. She wasn't thinking or holding another disjointed conversation with herself, she was feeling, searching her clamoring nerve ends for a clue, a key to unlocking the box that had snapped its lid down over her heart. Her vision had faded, leaving a wash of bleakness that bleached out the colors she'd seen only a day before as vibrant leaping brush strokes. Gone as soon as Kit had walked up to her in the Snap Dragon. That was right after he'd had a word with "the boss." One look at the little line between his dark eyebrows, the trick he had of pulling the skin at the corner of his mouth, and she knew that what was coming was bad. Kit was in his serious mood.

Dwarfed by the pillars and columns of the Stafford mansion's unwelcoming front door—even the dark glossy-leaved oleander bushes growing in massive gargoyled stone tubs were bigger than she was—Lizzie realized that it wasn't the loss of Li that had leached away the colors. She hadn't lost Li. It was the loss of something in herself, a sense of purpose and direction that went kaplooie when they threw her out of Chinatown. Without purpose there is no meaning.

The sudden discovery of what she had really lost burst out of Lizzie before she could check herself. The pain in her voice broke the protected silence of Nob Hill: swaddled in riches, it was a high rare place, unused to pain.

"I felt *useful* in Chinatown! Useful! God damn Kit Dowie to eternal hell!"

An elderly couple, arm in arm on an afternoon stroll, turned their hatted heads away.

The Stafford mansion's great front door opened with a thick *whoosh* of rich air. Lizzie, risen from the step in the grip of her passionate revelation, turned to take on all comers. Heaven help James Hamilton.

"You all right, missy?"

It was Keiko. He was so happy to see her, he grabbed her hand and kissed it. Lizzie was so happy that Keiko was happy, she kissed him back. On the top of his head.

"Where's Mr. Hamilton, Keiko?"

"Him not home. At work."

"Good."

"You bet, missy, very good."


Three cautious feet into the hushed splendor of the Crocker family's St. Francis Hotel on Union Square— why did Addy insist on meeting her here of all public places?—*the* Mrs. Gertrude Arlington, who'd been splendidly dominating the fashionable Mural Room, attacked Lizzie.

"My dear Elizabeth! Where have you been hiding yourself? There have been all sorts of rumors flying around—of quite the most delicious kind. I love your frock!"

Mrs. Arlington was San Francisco's answer to the younger of New York's two Mrs. Astors. She was terribly gay, terribly rich, terribly bold, and, though now growing long in the tooth, was quite up-to-date in a short skirt and a gold turban. Mrs. Arlington shocked society in the most deliberate way, smoking cigarettes in public, writing for the newspapers, and publishing books, such as *Red Cattle,* which had jolted the staid. Her charge was set on high, but never high enough to stun. Grand Mrs. Arlington, never out of the social press, suspecting that Elizabeth Stafford Hamilton, whom she considered her successor, had been stepping over the line chalked deep on the social sidewalk, took Lizzie's elbow and forced her into a corner behind an enormous jardiniere.

"Hurry up, Elizabeth, before Ned spots you. We'll never get to talk if he sticks his oar in."

"Ned Greenway! Is he here?" Lizzie's faded heart sank. Not old Neddie. This was a game she'd played all her life, and now, only a few months after quitting the side, she was back on the field running the wrong way.

"Darling, where isn't he? He's here with Mrs. Atherton. You don't want to see her, or Aimee Crocker." The Gertrudes despised each other. They were in the same line of business, but Atherton, G., wrote better books.

"Please, Gertie," pleaded Lizzie, "I have Addy waiting. I'm already late. Perhaps another—"

"Time?" Gertrude Arlington, not to be put off, pressed. "When? Lunch? Here? Tomorrow?"

"No, not here."

"Too public? What's that on your chin? What *have* you been up to?"

"I'll tell you all about it tomorrow. You come to my house for breakfast."

"My dear, I never go anywhere for breakfast. Unless, of course, I still happen to be there when the sun rises." Wagging her absurd turban, Gertie winked at Lizzie.

Lizzie was shocked. Gertie was older than Rose St. Lorraine.

"Well, then, when—?"

Gertie pounced. "I shall arrive, alone, tomorrow at

one o'clock prompt. Tell Keiko I am partial to anything that isn't in aspic."

Gertie let go of Lizzie's arm, twirled on the ball of her foot, and caught Ned Greenway, who was waddling eagerly toward them. "Ned! Come with me. Our Elizabeth will see you next week. She'll call you, won't you, Elizabeth?"

Dumbly, Lizzie nodded.

Old Ned, heart set on his Lizzie, bleated, "But I—"

"Neddie!"

"Yes, Gertrude."

Mrs. Arlington led the defeated little man away into the babble of starched shirtfronts and glittering headbands that cluttered the Mural Room. The Mural Room was *the* place to be seen, on Monday afternoons and any night before eleven; after eleven, society sought the speakeasies.

Lizzie was left free to find Addy, practically hidden beneath the fronds of a giant palm in a little dining area off the very public Mural Room. In the Mural Room everything was lit with the blaze of gigantic crystal chandeliers and the teeth behind smiles; where Addy sat under his palm tree in its Chinese pot, things were a little better. There was only one chandelier, a modest effort that left the diners in peace. All in gray, from his neat spats to his silken mustache, Addy rose from the stiff velvet banquette. Before he was fully erect, he was taller than Lizzie. The sight of his mild morose face blinking behind eyeglasses and overreaching palm fronds, a face as dear to her as Charles Mortimer's, lightened her heart. Lizzie kissed him on both thin cheeks.

"Oh, Addy," she began, "I have so much I—"

"Lizzie!" Frowning, Addy cut her off. "Rose has been worried about you."

Lizzie's little speech died on her lips. She'd come to explain herself, to elicit sympathy. Addy's beginning with sympathy for Rose made Lizzie immediately cross. It was Rose who'd set Sergeant Huggins to guard her. Was no one on Lizzie's side? Not even Addy Chase? Things had not begun well.

"You mean worried about Li," she said, intending to

sting and succeeding, as she slid onto the banquette beside him. The velvet rucked up the chiffon of her dress, a complicated affair that looked like a hundred gossamer scarves tied in clever knots, leaving bits of delectable flesh exposed to the grateful eye. The color of the banquette was wrong, a blood red against the green of the scarves. But the pale green chiffon made her eyes go the green of a young leaf in the rain. Her chin, masked under a layer of heavy makeup, was the color of a ripe plum.

Sitting back down, Addy sniffed through his long nose. "If you must be unkind." His long bony fingers tapped the silver cigarette case on the table. "What would you like for dinner?"

"I'm not very hungry."

"I am, my dear. Therefore, I shall choose. Waiter!" Addy ordered chicken Kiev for three.

Lizzie was alarmed. "Three!"

"I have taken the liberty of inviting a friend."

"But Addy, I wanted to talk to *you*, alone."

"I know. He will be here for the main course."

"He? Who?" Lizzie's nerves had had enough. Was Addy betraying her too? Did he mean James Hamilton? Lizzie had left the house by a side entrance just as James was coming in by the front. Keiko had kept his promise to warn her. Keiko had also told her of Esmé Baker's visits. The Japanese was scandalized. Any loyalty that he had felt toward James had evaporated like boiled sake.

With long thin fingers, Addy ripped into a soft bread roll. "Samuel Jenkins is joining us. He's going on to a meeting at the Pacific Union Club, where I later intend to join him. We're beginning to put into motion the machinery which will make your husband our next candidate for state attorney general. I had already made arrangements to dine with Sam when you phoned." Addy spread out the wide palms of his hand. "So, you see, my dear—"

"I hate it when you call me 'my dear.' It means you think I'm a fool."

"Does it?" Through the spectacles perched on the end of his sensitive nose, Addy studied Lizzie Stafford Hamilton. She endured the hard gaze for as long as she could, then blushed. Addy was equal to her ill temper. "I suppose you're right, Lizzie. I do think you're a fool. All of San Francisco is talking about you. Well, all of it that matters to us. The people we know."

Lizzie got crosser. "They've been talking about you and Rose for years. It hasn't done either of you any harm."

"But that is different. Rose does not belong to society and cannot be hurt by it. She lives in a world of her own creation. I am a man, and a man can pretty well do what he likes so long as he doesn't flaunt it. It also helps to contribute to charities and attend social events. Otherwise, a man of means and breeding can get away with anything, whereas—"

"A woman can't." Lizzie sounded resigned, not bitter. Even cross, she had common sense.

"Just so," said Addy with equal resignation. "The way of the world, Lizzie. And we're not going to sit here wasting time discussing it. A woman finds herself either in one world or the other. There is no crossing over. Rose taught me that. From what I gather, you have crossed over, farther than any other woman I know. That bruise is very unladylike. Never lead with your chin, child. Still, besides myself and Rose, few are aware of precisely how far you've gone. You can still cross back."

"You mean away from Li Kwan Won?"

"That is exactly what I mean."

"You don't think he's good enough for me? Or good enough for society?"

Addy sighed, chewing on a bread roll. "On the contrary. Until recently, I would have said the opposite for you as well as society, but the concept of who is good enough for whom is entirely beside the point. There is no place for him in our world, nor for us in his. It shames me to admit that this is not a judgment on Li, but on us."

"Addy," protested Lizzie, "you and Rose raised Li. He *is* in your world."

"He is in my heart, not my world. Should he wish it, even I could not gain him entrance there. Are you so blinded by *your* heart that you cannot remember that he is Chinese? And, being Chinese, what that means in San Francisco, in all the western world? You were raised in a cosseted hothouse of privilege and snobbery by virtue of Charles Mortimer's money. An elite closed world. Without careful and unremitting maintenance, our delicate society would wilt and wither away. In Europe, admittance is a matter of birth; in America it is, more often than not, money. Therefore, American effort is the frantic making, and then the maker's equally frantic protection, of money. But neither world admits the Chinese." Addy paused as he sought the waiter's eye through palm fronds. The man glimmered into full view. "Mrs. Hamilton and I would like wine. A very dry white. I trust your judgment, Stephen."

"Certainly, Mr. Chase."

"I imagine that is so in China as well. I mean the protection of the class that holds the purse strings." Addy continued without missing a connection. "Or in any foreign culture. It is human nature, after all. The English fool themselves into believing they are admitted everywhere by virtue of superior morality and strength of character, when in actuality they are held in derision and suffered so long as their military strength, and nothing else, is superior. We Americans, on the other hand, believe we hold the upper hand because of our one true twin-headed religion—money and democracy."

The waiter reappeared with a bottle disguised as a water pitcher, which Addy briefly glanced at, approved with a nod, and drank a whole glass of as soon as it was poured.

"If you think all this, Addy, why are you a part of it?" Lizzie ignored her wine; she felt too noble to drink it.

"Oh, my dear Lizzie, I was born a part of it. I cannot deny my heritage, even though there are times when I should very much like to. Perhaps that is my weakness. Like so many who tend society's hothouse and the privileges of wealth, I too love democracy. But I do my best to have sufficient money to keep it as far away from me as possible."

Lizzie held her breath; an idea of pure beauty constricted her throat. Addy, of course, was right. That *was* his weakness. It would take a unique and implacable strength to deny her birth, her training, her world. So far, what she had done had been mere gesture, nothing more than paddling near a regainable shore. Lizzie Stafford could swim, but could she dive? The possibility went through her like a rock through a pane of glass. She looked at the sweet gentle man sitting next to her. She was hurting Addy Chase. Why? Because he was telling her the truth, *his* truth. Lizzie felt suddenly ashamed. It was a feeling she was beginning to know well. "I'm sorry, Addy. I ask you to talk to me and I behave like a desperate brat. But I love Li. I love him with all my heart. And I know he loves me, I do." Lizzie's green eyes filled with tears. "God, Addy, what do I care if I lose society, your precious hothouse? I still have money, as you say, to protect me."

Addy smiled a sweet sad smile. "I know you love Li, Lizzie. You love him as I love Rose. And Rose is a whore—"

"Addy!"

"Nothing less than the truth. My beautiful whore. But for me, the difficulties with Rose have been nothing compared to what you face with Li. A man is forgiven his weakness, because the state of man is to be weak. A woman is never forgiven, because a woman's lot is strength. Being strong, what she does she is solely responsible for."

"I don't need forgiveness."

One tear spilled down Lizzie's hot cheek. It caught in the corner of her mouth. The taste of sudden salt surprised her.

"Ah, but you will. And when you need it most, it will be denied you. By throwing away your own world, you burden Li. By burdening Li, you endanger him. And then again, by throwing away your world, Lizzie, you endanger and isolate yourself. Your heart has taken you into a foreign country. I'm afraid, my dear, you've gone on a journey that can end in nothing but tragedy. What will protect Li from your heart? Money cannot shield him from the hatred of our world." Uncomfortable in the presence of Lizzie's tears, Addy veered off. "And what do you think all this is going to do to the man you married? And to his future?"

With the introduction of James, Lizzie regained her spirit. Her anger softened the pain of Addy's words. The thought of endangering Li, so often repeated by so many, was a thought she would not, could not, examine. But the thought of endangering James! "I don't give a fig about James's future, now that I know about his past and, even worse, his present."

"Indeed. You fascinate me."

"I'll do better than that. I'll horrify you."

"Oh, good." Addy was as relieved at the change of subject as Lizzie. He'd been advocating a course he himself had followed halfheartedly, expecting Lizzie to do much more than that. Hypocrisy tired Addy; expediency caused him despair, yet he had lived with both all his life. "If this is going to be politically revelatory, please wait for—ah, Sam! Just the man." Addy rose for a second time. If Lizzie felt short around Addy Chase, Samuel Jenkins felt like a dwarf. But he'd been feeling like that for so long, it hardly mattered. Sam arrived with the chicken Kiev.

"Mrs. Hamilton. How delightful." The fat man squeezed his stomach between the table and the banquette, settling down with a plump sigh. "I am here!"

Addy shook his beautiful groomed head. "Indeed you are, Sam. But perhaps things will not be as delightful as all that. Lizzie has something to tell us about our candidate."

Fat had kept Sam young. It filled out his cheeks, banishing wrinkles; it made him wheeze and squeak and kept his color high. "How exciting!" To Lizzie, he'd stepped out of *The Pickwick Papers,* one of the few books she *had* read.

Munching buttery chicken, drinking two more pitchers of good white German wine, Addy, but more especially Sam, managed to keep quiet, except for the odd question and muted expletive, for over an hour. When Lizzie had finished telling them everything she knew about James, Addy gently tapped his lips with the crisp white napkin, drank off a full glass of wine, and beamed at Sam.

"Ah, well, Sam," he said. "Lizzie has given us a truly precious gift—a clear case of something to fight."

The fat man beamed back at him. "We haven't come up against anything so fine since Boss Ruef."

Lizzie listened in growing amazement. "Then you aren't horrified by what I've told you?"

"Horrified?" Sam patted Lizzie's hand. "Us? We've seen too much to even be surprised."

Addy was pushing away from the table. "It brings my blood back to the boil. My God, to know the enemy! It makes me young. It also explains that night with James at the Pacific Union. I knew something was wrong. Excuse me, dear, but Sam and I have a very special meeting to attend. We'll see you home. I have my car waiting, and the club is so near your own house." Excited, Addy turned to Sam. "Dear God, old man, what do you think Hamilton has in mind for poor Warren?"

"Your guess is as good as mine." Sam laughed. "As if the President didn't have enough to worry him."

Marveling at their reactions, but, more than that, pleased by them, Lizzie gave the full force of her dimpled smile to Sam Jenkins. What she'd had to tell of James had gone well. Much better than the painful conversation about Li. The fat little man melted under Lizzie's light; he smiled back as he helped her up from the banquette.

"Dear Lizzie." Sam sighed.

"Samuel," warned Addy. "Remember the Alamo."

Reminded of the temper of his volatile Spanish wife, Sam's smile dropped at Lizzie's feet. Graciously, she stepped over it and took his arm.

On the way back up the hill in Addy's car, Lizzie knew Addy was absolutely right. She must make a choice and, having chosen, never go back. For the precious sense of worth she'd tasted, she could put anything at risk. The possibility that anything included Li was something not to be considered.

"Goodbye, Gertie Arlington," Lizzie whispered.

Interrupting his fevered conversation with Sam, Addy turned toward her, "Excuse me, Lizzie?"

"I was just saying goodbye, Addy."

"Goodbye?" Addy peered through the windshield.

"Oh, yes, we're here." Addy opened the car door for her. "Good night, Lizzie. If you can forgive the distasteful truth, please consider what I said this evening."

Lizzie already had—and made her choice.

On a ship nearing Seattle, President Warren Gamaliel Harding was thirty-six hours away from San Francisco, holding his gut. Only Warren knew he was cracking up, but everyone knew he was sick. Doubling over with pain, the President sighed. When trouble came to a man, it wore cleats.

# Chapter 22

It was a few minutes before noon when Keiko tiptoed into Lizzie's darkened room with her breakfast tray. On the black lacquer tray was a silver tea set, a pansy-patterned cup and saucer, two slices of cinnamon toast, a crystal bud vase, and one once-dewy red rose. Lizzie was sound asleep, tangled up in her linen sheets, her head under a pillow, one small white hand trailing on a Savonnerie rug. There was a month-old *Vogue,* a new *Harper's Bazar,* and a copy of Helen Hunt Jackson's *Ramona* on the rug close beside her fingertips. Lizzie had managed to get to page thirteen in Mrs. Jackson's story of the doomed love of a half-breed girl for a full-blooded Indian, before using a gold spoon as a bookmark. A large onyx ashtray on her bedside table was stuffed with butts and a crumpled pack of Benson and Hedges; another pack, half smoked, lay beside it.

"Missy?" Keiko set the tray on a small antique table at the foot of the heavily draped bed and crept up on Lizzie. "You 'wake now?" He removed the pillow in its cream linen pillowcase from Lizzie's head. If nothing else, his lady was alive; Lizzie snatched it back.

"What?"

"You eat breakfast now. This third one I bring. Flower getting tired."

"No." Lizzie's "no" was muffled. She'd put the pillow back over her head.

"Yes," said Keiko. "Air bad. No good."

Enough was enough. Lizzie had left instructions for Keiko to wake her, and wake her he would. He pulled the tasseled cord that opened her heavy silver-gray curtains. San Francisco's tempestuous sun tumbled with triumph into the room. He raised the tall windows, one after the other. They came with gratifying ease. Charles Mortimer built erratically, but he built well. Then Keiko windmilled his arms, escorting the stale smoky air out of the room and welcoming a stiff sea breeze in. Satisfied with his efforts, he marched back and fought the pillow off "missy."

"Go away, Keiko!" Lizzie now lay blinking painfully in the cruel light and shivering in a wind straight from Santa's workshop.

"No. Not go. Mrs. Arlington comes at one o'clock. If Missy not up, she yells at me."

"Oh, God, Gertie!"

"Oh, God, yes, missy."

"Well, shut the windows at least."

"When air clean, I shut."

"The air's scrubbed! Shut the windows."

"You get up?"

"I'm up already. Jesus, Keiko!"

Keiko waited until Lizzie had both bare legs out of bed, nodded happily, and shut the windows.

When Charles Mortimer died, Keiko grieved for months and then put little Lizzie at the center of his life. Charles Mortimer's granddaughter would take Charles Mortimer's place. She was still little Lizzie, his "missy," even after she'd married James Hamilton. Mr. Hamilton's recent behavior had both shocked and angered Keiko, but missy's sudden unexplained two-week absence disturbed him deeply; the Japanese had pined for her. Through the gossip of an army of servants attending the fine Nob Hill houses, Keiko could get no word of where she'd gone. No one seemed to know. Wherever it was, the cabriolet had gone with her. Had Mr. Hamilton bumped missy off for her money or for that redheaded woman? Keiko spent his time taking notes on James Hamilton, all in Japanese, collecting bits of paper from Hamilton's room, hovering near the study door when James made or received phone calls. He'd learned a great many things about the district attorney but nothing about Mrs. Hamilton. Three times Keiko picked up the kitchen phone, watched by a curious Mrs. Gravely, and listened to the operator's "Number, please?" but each time hung up before saying a word. If missy wasn't killed, Keiko's call to the police could make missy lose face with the city. And then, as suddenly as she'd gone, missy was back. He found her sitting on the doorstep like an orphan child, wearing the most awful dress. Her return gave him back his peace and his symmetry; Keiko was delighted. Missy was the Stafford mansion's heart. But habits once formed die hard. Keiko still spied on Mr. Hamilton.

Hands folded, Keiko turned back from Lizzie's windows, tall windows so far above the San Francisco skyline that they saw only the deep noon blue of the Californian sky. "You eat toast, drink tea—I go get red carpet for Mrs. Arlington."

"Red carpet? Have we got a red carpet?"

"I kid."

"I dress. Get lost." Lizzie looked for her slippers with her feet and found them under the bed. "Keiko, it's Saturday. Is Mr. Hamilton at home?"

"No, gone since nine o'clock." Keiko winked at Lizzie. "Not here much anymore. Not to worry."

"James doesn't worry me, Keiko."

"You lucky."

Keiko skipped off.

As the door shut behind him, it occurred to Lizzie that for the second time in her twenty-three years she and Keiko had just had a real conversation. The first was only the day before, when he found her sitting on her own front steps. They were suddenly easy with each other.

The Japanese, always there, always perfect, often unseen but always vital, always kept his place. But something had changed him. Lizzie thought it must be Esmé's visits. The change pleased her more than she could say. Aside from anything else, it was another slap in the face for James.

When Sam and Addy dropped her home after their dinner at the St. Francis, she'd immediately phoned Rose St. Lorraine. She wanted Rose to tell Li where she was and where she was staying. Li hadn't been to Rose's yet. Lizzie had left a message for him. The message was simple. Tell Li I'm safe, tell him I love him. "Sure, honey," Rose had said, all that kindness back in her low musical voice. "He's safe too." Then Lizzie had told the anxiously waiting Keiko—he was terrified she would disappear again—that Gertrude Arlington was invading the Stafford mansion for a private lunch, and then promptly forgot about Gertie. She was too busy for the next six hours, her mind grappling with agitated schemes, her heart fretting over the absence of Li, her body missing his, smoking cigarette after cigarette, trying to read, while what was left of her wanted to get to sleep. Old St. Mary's tolled five in the morning before she'd dropped off, exhausted.

Sunlight simmered on the silver tea-paper ceiling and the silvered drapery over her bed like light through a porthole, while Lizzie hopped around on one foot getting dressed.

Gertie Arlington! God, what would she tell her? A sudden trip to Europe? Of course not. No one could get to Europe and back in two weeks, unless they had an airplane. Lizzie owned almost everything, but she didn't own an airplane—not yet, anyway—and as far as she knew, there wasn't an air service that flew the Atlantic. An illness awful enough to demand quarantine? That wouldn't wash either. She didn't look like she'd been at death's door. Two weeks on Chinese food and Lizzie looked as healthy as a milkmaid. Somebody dying in the family? But Gertie knew everyone in Lizzie's family, and those few who weren't already dead were just fine. All these faulty explanations, and more, flipped through her mind. It wasn't the time to tell Mrs. Gertrude Arlington anything truthful. It was never the time. Gertie would tell Neddie, and, after that, who wouldn't know? Let society's number-two literary goddess find out for herself —when Lizzie Stafford Hamilton was gone. Lizzie settled on a tale close enough to the truth to make it easy to remember: a clandestine love affair. She made up her lover's coloring, background, and attractions as she ate her cinnamon toast, drank her tea, and dressed. Today she would wear something very proper. Another Patou with sporting lines, a soft gray silk dress coming to well below the knees. Simple gray shoes with white toes and an ankle strap. The ensemble was going fine until Lizzie looked into her mirror. The left side of her chin looked like one of Luther Burbank's Santa Rosa plums. A dab of mascara on her thick black lashes, a touch of rouge on her high cheekbones, masses of foundation on her chin, Chanel No. 5, and her most expensive and unusual diamond clip earrings to deflect Gertie's attention—and Lizzie looked less than twenty-three. Closer to sixteen. But the mind behind the clear brow, straight black bangs, and bruised chin felt older—much older.

Lizzie got downstairs before twelve thirty. Much of the mansion's first floor had been arranged with an eye to pleasing the grand Mrs. Arlington. Keiko was so happy to be receiving the "best" visitors again, even if Mrs. Arlington walked right over him, that he'd filled the reception rooms with the wildflowers of late July. But it was the small private dining room in a bay overlooking the back gardens that he'd given his all to.

The Stafford mansion had an Italian room, a Spanish room, a French room, a Swedish room, a Russian room, a Chinese room, a room stuffed with Japanese samurai armor, an English room, a tapestry room, a music room, a round room where all the furnishings were curved to fit the walls, and enough spare bedrooms to take on the Fairmont Hotel's overflow. Lizzie hated the Swedish room. It was dominated by massive portraits of massive Nordic royalty hanging high and heavy on high walls. Everything was constructed of cold stone painted iceberg blue. It looked frozen. Through two twelfth-century, thankfully unpainted stone pillars Charles Mortimer had had transported from a fortified French chateau, one suddenly found oneself in the *salon des muses.* Here all was trompe-l'oeil. Nine Grecian ladies in painted drapery, heavy of thigh and button-mushroom breasted, stood in six-foot painted niches artfully posing. From here it was a zig through the Spanish room, somber with twisted dark wood carvings and Charles Mortimer's family motto, self-penned and tongue-in-cheek—"All for One"—scrolled around a self-created family crest, a zag past the forty thousand books in the English library, books bound in leather, dark blue, dark red, dark green, dusted and oiled, and *voilà*—the *petit* room for intimate dining. The table sat twelve. Today it was set for two: crystal and silver, fine china, pale green linen and lace, California wildflowers in rare vases.

This room looked over Charles Mortimer's cunning maze. It would have dropped straight into a moat, but a friend with some knowledge of engineering told Charles that if he went ahead and dug one the house would probably fall over. So, no moat. The private dining room was Venetian. It was all in green, greens upon greens. Aquamarine and beryl green, bottle and pistachio, the green of grass, the deep green heart of a wave, and that secret green winking in the bottom of an old well when the sun is high—green from the damask wall coverings to the fittings on the Venetian glass sconces. Lizzie's eyes were all these greens as she stood in the only room in the Stafford mansion that she actually loved.

Keiko had laid out a cold lunch on the long refectory table. Wines were cooling in silver buckets, Gertie's favorite brand of cigarettes waited in a carved wooden box. Nothing was in aspic.

It was 12.25 P.M. and Lizzie had over a half hour of nothing to do. Fending off Mrs. Arlington's noisy curiosity disguised as friendship wasn't something to do, it was something to endure. The only thing she wanted to do was phone Li, the only place she wanted to be was with him—in Chinatown. But Addy Chase had made sense; she'd promised herself she would do neither. When she saw Li Kwan Won again, it wouldn't be tucked away in a pink working bedroom above the Blue Canary. It would be somewhere safe for them both. There would be no sneaking or hiding. She had it all figured out. This time, Lizzie would do something right. But for now, the seconds were ticking by like Chinese water torture—drop after drop—each drop, each second, experienced as a man experiences a life sentence in solitary confinement. Lizzie shook herself. She had thirty-five minutes. In thirty-five minutes one could do anything, if one did anything at all. Thank God, she hadn't got out of bed at Keiko's first offering of breakfast.

Lizzie went for a walk. In her house there were places it took time to walk to. She would go and admire some of Charles Mortimer's odder collections. Lizzie hadn't seen the Egyptian room in ages. When she was a child, before the earthquake, she'd hid in the gaudily painted sarcophagi. Until her maid, Irma, ruined that game by learning to look in the mummy cases first. To get to the Egyptian room, one had to walk through the long gallery. Lit from the east, the gallery was like the Hall of Mirrors at Versailles with a window embrasure of faux marble every ten feet. Then across the main reception room, heels clicking on the Caen stone flagging. This was where Lizzie was when the chimes sounded. Of everyone in the house, she was closest to the front door. She was so close it would be silly to wait for Keiko or one of the maids to answer. Lizzie swung to her right and went through a circular hallway. Two stories above her irritated head bubbled a dome of amber glass. Depend on Gertie's eager appetite for gossip to make her early—and rude.

Lizzie swung open the heavy oak door.

"Oh, God!"

The big beautiful black Dido strode past her. Without saying a word, Dido smiled at Lizzie. Dido's smile was dreadful; there was nothing civil about it. She wore red; silken red tassels at the end of her short red skirt swished past her red-stockinged legs, a red slouch hat tipped down over her black eyes, and she had a red fox stole thrown over her shoulders. The fox fur was long enough to wrap around her neck twice and still touch the floor at both ends.

"A joint like this an' you gotta open your own door, sweet stuff?"

Dido's strides had taken her past Lizzie. She was farther into the house than Lizzie was. Without waiting for an answer, Dido kept on walking.

Lizzie slammed the door shut and trotted after her.

"Where are you going, Dido?"

"Hell if I know. I ain't never been here before. Where's there someplace to sit down an' get a cuppa coffee? Wouldn't mind somethin' to eat either. What's a body supposed to do? Drop bread crumbs to get around? Shee-it, girl. This place is *big!*" Still walking, Lizzie still anxiously following, Dido put back her head and yodeled. "Wow! You got some echo. Oh, lookie—food!"

Somehow, Dido had worked her way unerringly back to the little green dining room. She was forking cheese, cold meats, and a huge blob of caviar onto a plate. "Wine, too. How nice. You knew I was comin'?"

Lizzie had had time to gather her wits following Dido's great long strides. Lizzie had long legs, but Dido had stilts. What the hell did Dido want? What was she doing here? And how dare she come, anyway? Lizzie know she was coming? Dido was the last person on earth Lizzie would have invited to the Stafford mansion. Li had told her a little, very little, of Dido's past, but Appetite Ike's story was enough for Lizzie. That, and the few times she'd come face to face with Kit's good "friend."

Dido poured two glasses of wine, handed one to Lizzie. Without thinking, Lizzie took it.

"Dido, as Rose says, 'Cut the crap.' What do you want?"

"Well, honey, since you put it that way, I'll tell you." Dido perched herself on the edge of the refectory table, her plate in her lap, her endless legs crossed in their sheer red stockings. The table was strong enough to take her weight without shaking a dish. The fierce grin was replaced by something Dido probably thought was appealing. "I'm gonna surprise you. I come to ask you for a favor."

"*You* ask *me* for a favor?"

"You're right. It ain't a favor." Dido scooped a spoonful of black caviar into her red mouth. "Dido don't ask nobody for favors. She learned long ago that nobody gives nothin' away. But tradin', now—folks like to trade. An' there ain't nobody else *to* trade with but you. Ain't nobody else got what I need."

"I don't know what you're talking about."

"You help me, I try to help you."

"Why should I help you?"

"Dammit, girl, I ain't actually askin' you to help *me*. I'm askin' you to help Kit."

"Help Kit? What does Kit need help for?"

"Girl, you dumb? My man is crazy 'bout you."

"Kit Dowie? Crazy about me?" Lizzie choked on her wine. Wasn't that what Rose had said just after she'd set Sergeant Huggins on Lizzie? Was everyone mad? Kit thought of her as a kid; most of the time Lizzie irritated the hell out of him. And he'd been the one to bundle her out of Chinatown. If he loved her so much, why get rid of her? "I'm sure he's not, that he doesn't—"

Dido looked at Lizzie like she was something soft Dido had just stepped on. "You for real? You blind as well as dumb? Runnin' round after that Chink, keepin' Kit right up to the minute on your progress. I told him you didn't have no heart."

Lizzie felt like a body with a brand-new bullet hole in it. She had to consciously accept the fact before collapsing. Kit love her? My God, it could be true. Dido must know. Dido loved him. Oh, hell, Kit Dowie; what a mess. Lizzie didn't love Kit, she loved Li. Kit was her friend, her big brother, the person she went to when she was in trouble—the person who kept her level when the world tilted. Lizzie poured herself another glass of wine, and another for Dido as well. Dido was quiet now, picking at her caviar. Her slanted red hat covered her eyes. But Lizzie, sitting below her at the table glittering with silver, could look up into her strong black face. Kit was Lizzie's friend, had always been her friend. And Dido was Kit's. Dido's fierce heart made her as true a friend to Kit as Kit was to Lizzie. She'd come in all her heady pride to ask a woman she hated to help the man she loved. Could Lizzie do the same? For God's sake, can't you be someone's friend, Lizzie Stafford?

"If that's true, Dido, what can I do, what do you *want* me to do?" Lizzie's voice was low and soft, hardly there at all.

Catching the change of tone, Dido's changed with it. "Leave him alone. I ain't askin' for you to leave him alone so's I can have him. I'm askin' you to leave him alone 'cause you makin' him sick, you tyin' him down. This ain't easy for me, you gotta know that. But my man gets hisself over you for a day, a week, an' you come bouncin' along with your chat an' your troubles an' he's sick all over again. Lord, I ain't never seen drinkin' like I saw Kit doin' at O'Flooty's place 'bout the time you went off with Li. I want you to go tell him you just ain't there for him, you ain't never gonna be there for him—cut him loose, girl. Let him get outa this town. He keeps sayin' he's gonna go, but he don't. He keeps findin' some reason to hang around. Now, he's got hisself involved in that Chinaman's fight. He says he's writin' it down, but it ain't that. It ain't Kit's fight. He's gonna get hisself hurt."

Lizzie stood up and, shoving a Sèvres china chafing dish aside, perched herself next to Dido. The two of them sat there on the table, washed in watered green light, drinking wine out of crystal and nibbling cheese. The seconds ticked away.

"Kit's drinking?" Lizzie finally asked. "Was it bad?"

Dido twirled her red toe. "Bad enough."

Lizzie had recovered some of her old spirit, but only enough to put a crease between her green eyes. "Kit threw me out of Chinatown. Look at my chin. Fearless O'Flooty did that."

"I was noticin'. But *that* man! Hot damn! Every time Kit gets near that crazy Irishman, he gets hisself another lump."

Lizzie remembered the lumps Kit got from the tattooed man at O'Flooty's blind pig and flushed. "How the hell do you expect me to throw *him* out of Chinatown?"

"You don't have to throw him out, honey. He'll

walk away quiet. He'll go if you make him strong, an'
you can do that by breakin' his heart."

"You want me to hurt Kit?"

"Ain't you been hurtin' him all along?"

Lizzie accepted that. Lowering her eyes, she nodded.

"Listen, you do that, an' as I told you, Dido can give
you somethin' about your Li. You won't like what I tell
you, but it's a gift all the same. I can tell you what you
been dealin' with. Stuff a rich white girl like you can't
never understand 'cause you ain't never had to live it."
Dido looked around. The wealth in only one room of the
Stafford mansion was enough to dim her eyes. "I ain't
never seen nothin' like this place in my whole life, an' I
thought the first time I saw Silver Street it was somethin'.
'Course I was only just turned thirteen."

"Thirteen, Dido? Ike told me you were sixteen when
you came to Rose's."

"That old coot been talkin' about me? Then he's
been guessin', 'cause aside from Kit I ain't told nobody
nuthin'. What's my business is my business. But I'm
tellin' you as my part of the deal. You know somethin'
'bout me an' then you know somethin' 'bout Li."

Dido lit two cigarettes she'd dug out of the carved
wooden box on top of the table. She handed one to Lizzie. "What we gonna use for an ashtray?"

"Your plate."

"You don' mind?"

"I must own a thousand damn plates."

Dido laughed. Lizzie had never heard her laugh. It
was lovely; the laugh rang through the Stafford mansion
with a child's purity. "This ain't so bad as I thought, rich
girl. An' though you bad, you ain't *so* bad." Dido inhaled
the smoke of her cigarette, looked at its gold tip, and
came to some kind of decision. "I ain't thought about
when I was young for years, but now I'm doin' it, it's like
it's fresh as shit. An' I mean shit, 'cause where I'm from
an' how I grew up don' smell no other way. Honey,
gimme some more of that wine."

Lizzie gave them both some more wine.

Dido tipped it back. "I don' know what you was
doin' when you was a chile, but I been a whore since I

was ten. Lived in a boxcar by the St. Louis railroad tracks. Me an' my ma dined outa garbage cans in alleys, an' I wore the same dress till it fell offa my skinny black body. Shoes? Who had shoes? Me an' her was sued outdoors as many times as we got in."

"Sued?"

"Evicted. That's when I learned to sing. I sang to keep warm. Standin' in the Union Station watchin' the glory trains pull out was all the playin' I ever did. Wasn't no one gonna pay to teach me singin' so *I* paid, an' I did it by sellin' my ass. First john I ever had was a sadistic dwarf."

"God, Dido."

"Wasn't so bad, once I learned to close my heart. My pa never come nearer to me than between my momma's legs. An' my ma was tellin' me she wished I was dead since I can remember knowin' how to listen. But I made me enough money to leave Momma in her rage an' her rags an' get outa that boxcar. Lord, I hated that woman! Only pet I ever had, my momma ate. He was a chicken, don' you laugh at me—"

"I'm not laughing."

"Well, you laugh an' Dido'll slap your face. I loved that goddam chicken. When the only thing you love gets et, you stop lovin'. An' that's what I did, I stopped lovin' an' I stopped feelin'—till I met Kit Dowie. Ain't nobody gonna eat Dowie; I saw that in him when he was eleven years old. An' I saw it in Li Kwan Won. He's like me, honey. You understand? The lovin' got burned out of him. Tell you the truth, girl, I feel sorry for you. You don't want the man you can have, an' you can't have the man you want."

"But Li loves me!"

"Oh, honey. Sure he do. Maybe even as much as Kit do. But not with all of hisself. It ain't all there. That's the gift I'm tryin' to give you—don't get your heart broke by a man with but half a heart."

"Lizzie Stafford!" Gertrude Arlington's voice rang through the imminent air like a great bell.

Lizzie's head jerked around. "Oh, heck! I forgot Gertie." Dido was already staring.

Gertrude Arlington, wearing another curious gold turban, stood open-mouthed behind a white-faced Keiko in the door of the little green dining room.

"Lizzie! What is this—this *woman* doing in your house? Isn't she a—"

"Nigger? Whore?" offered Dido.

Both Keiko and Gertie gasped.

But Gertie had spunk. "If either will do, young woman, why not?"

Dido put down her wineglass and stood up. No one, with the exception of Addy Chase, was taller than Dido. And Mrs. Arlington was a whole lot shorter than that. When Dido stood, Gertie shrank. The astonishing black Amazon in red walked up to society's turbaned dragon.

"Lady, where I come from, a whore is a whore, a thief is a thief, a nigger is a nigger, an' a bitch is a bitch. Where you come from, a whore can be a debutante, a thief can be the President of the United States, a nigger is a dead man, an' a bitch can be a rude broad in a stupid hat." Turning from the apoplectic Gertie back to the stunned Lizzie, Dido said, "We gotta deal, girl?"

Lizzie slowly nodded.

Dido flipped her long red fox back over her shoulder, sweeping china and silver from Keiko's beautiful table, and walked out. With tears in his eyes, wringing his distressed hands, Keiko followed.

Wide-eyed, Lizzie watched her go. It was the greatest exit she'd ever seen.

Gertie Arlington turned a furious beaked face to Lizzie for an explanation—and an apology.

"I've heard you're getting to be quite the Jezebel, Elizabeth Hamilton, but I never—"

"Excuse me, Gertrude." Lizzie hopped off the table. "I'll have to cancel lunch. I've just promised to do something for a friend."

Lizzie had had enough of lying.

# Chapter 23

His knobby bald head catching the light from a bare high-watt bulb, Wong Gow cleared a space on the table-cloth with one sweep of his sinewy arm. Li deftly whipped away his cup of *samshu* as the old man pushed at the plates, tipping tiny teacups and scattering small round serving boxes. "Now I tell all fortunes," he said, shoving up the black sleeves of his cotton gown like a magician proclaiming, See, no tricks.

Fearless O'Flooty, huddled into himself on the far side of the round table, belched. "It is a thing of wisdom to tell the world who you are first, and not to let the bastards figure it out for themselves. This is due to the possibility that they might be right." He was pickled on *samshu;* a wet butt stuck in the corner of his mouth jerked up and down as he talked.

Kit Dowie, seated next to Fearless, hadn't finished his meal; he followed his moving plate, stabbing at it with a pair of awkward chopsticks.

Fearless fixed Wong Gow with a rolling eye. "Get in

a few blows before they get their teeth into you, by God. I want the little devils to see me as I create myself."

"Shut up, O'Flooty," said Kit through a mouthful of *deem sum,* a kind of Chinese dumpling. "Wong Gow is telling fortunes."

"Lies," said Fearless. He stuck two stubby fingers in his mouth, pulled back his mustachioed upper lip, and exposed toothless gums. His two front teeth were missing. "If you will look closely, you can see for yourself the proper evidence I have here of sticking your teeth into lies—and meeting dentists run amuck with pincers. It would be a fine thing to feel *their* teeth under brass knuckles."

Fearless got Kit's full attention. "Where's your teeth?"

"Left 'em somewhere, bejesus."

"Well, shut up anyway."

In a modest little Chinese restaurant called Hoong Foong, Red Wind, off Stockton Street—if nothing else, it had tablecloths on its twelve tables and the best *deem sum* in Chinatown—Li Kwan Won, Kit Dowie, the implacable O Ti, Wong Gow, and a silent Chi Mai had just finished a late supper. O'Flooty drank his. It was Saturday night, the twenty-eighth of July.

The white ghosts' siege was petering out, running out of gas if not bullets. There'd been no one to shoot at. Li's trucks had stayed safely in the Snap Dragon; his speedboats, under canvas, bobbed at their mooring lines. But each speak, each hotel, each restaurant had received their deliveries on time, all bottles and barrels accounted for. For Blinn's gunmen to have caught and inspected every laundry cart, every shrimp boat, every old woman with a bundle on her back, they would have needed the services of the U.S. Customs. Under Li's calm command, Chinatown had gone about his business with barely a hitch; by the time of Lizzie's enforced leaving, Murray Blinn was already wasting his time and Olemi's money.

Sleeping in Li's apartment above the Intelligent Pearl since Thursday night, Kit had been in and out of Chinatown all weekend, running between the *Examiner* building on Market Street and the Snap Dragon on Grant.

President Harding was seriously ill. The news had flashed down by telegraph from the private express train carrying the presidential party south. They'd all transferred from the good ship *Henderson* and reboarded Harding's private train, a train now somewhere in Oregon on a nonstop run to San Francisco. Though no one else aboard the *Henderson* fell ill, Warren G. Harding had been stricken with food poisoning—evidently from contaminated crabmeat, crabmeat they had all eaten. Kit couldn't find out how bad Harding was; how serious was serious? Since talking to Li, Kit's interest in the President was consuming. From the moment the man set presidential boot on San Francisco's sand and rock, buried under seventy-odd years of glamorous cement, Kit Dowie intended to dog his footsteps. Whatever James Hamilton had in mind for Warren, Kit meant to be there. The telegraphic messages coming into the *Examiner* offices at the rate of four an hour were garbled and contradictory. Just how sick was the President, and why was he the only one?

The President of the United States? Warren Gamaliel Harding? For the American voters of 1920, the choices had been thin on the ground. As one old-time senator put it, "There ain't any first-raters this year." With nothing to choose from, America chose nothing. It had happened before, it would happen again. Warren G. Harding came out of nowhere. Theodore Roosevelt was in his grave; Woodrow Wilson, once a "frozen flame of righteous intelligence," was mortally tired, fatally ill, and politically dead with his noble (but way before its time) fixation on a League of Nations. America was sick of helping other countries. Look what she'd got out of it last time: war. Everyone else—peripatetic William Jennings Bryan, New York's Al Smith, Wisconsin's La Follette— was too regional, too polarized, or too cranky to capture a whole country. But Warren Harding, now—he wasn't anything or anybody. Owner and editor of a small-town newspaper in Ohio, the *Marion Star,* Harding did not crusade, which suited America just fine. After the waste and horror of the World War, America wanted walls, not crusades. That year the League of Nations was the issue, the *only* issue. Standing for nothing in himself, the people made Harding stand for whatever they liked. H. L. Mencken summed it up: "Tired to death of intellectual charlatanry, the voter turned despairingly to honest imbecility." That and his looks got Harding the job. In return, America got her greatest political scandal since the awesome Crédit Mobilier under Grant's administration some fifty years before.

Tall and straight and broad of shoulder, Harding possessed a grand mane of hair and a truly noble brow—behind which lurked very little, and though that very little was sweet-tempered and amiable, sweet-tempered and amiable does not a president make. In Warren's case, amiable unmade. His glad-handing, poker-playing good-old-boy retinue, brought with him intact from Marion, Ohio, as he ascended the throne of America, created a web of such intricate double-dealing, such bare and outrageous theft and chicanery, that America had never seen the like. For a while, Harding didn't see it at all. Like a sweet celluloid emperor, he stood before the adoring public "bloviating," as he put it—a good word for Warren; it meant talking without saying a damn thing—as his cronies from Ohio robbed the country blind. Though a few of his presidential appointments were serendipitous—Charles Evans Hughes as Secretary of State, Herbert Hoover as Secretary of Commerce, and Andrew Mellon as Secretary of the Treasury—the rest were a total disaster, most notably Albert B. Fall as Secretary of the Interior and Harry Daugherty as Attorney General. Albert virtually sold the country to private interests and pocketed the proceeds. And Harry, up against stiff competition, was the biggest crook to ever hit Washington; considering how many crooks Washington had attracted since the capital rose from its swamp, that's saying a lot. Harry Daugherty was like a cheap patent-medicine man; he thought Washington was a great big carny and the people it governed a load of suckers ripe for picking. Selling presidential pardons, stealing trial evidence for a price, holding whoop-'em-up orgies, both Albert and

Harry generally had a good and lucrative time for three years.

When the truth began to leak out, the press called the whole murky mess Teapot Dome. Teapot Dome was an oddly shaped butte in the state of Wyoming. This butte, and all the oil under it, was one of the things Fall sold, though he called it "leasing"; another was the Elk Hills oil fields in California. The latter went to the Dohenys and, through Ed Doheny, Jr., to James Hamilton.

When Warren and the rest of Washington finally caught on, the slow-witted President was torn between his colorfully venal friends and his oath of office; between his naturally good and simple heart, his honest intention to do whatever was right—not that Warren ever quite figured out what that was—and his loyalty to the good old boys. But before he could make up his mind, it was too late. Washington had had enough. Everything and everyone was under investigation, not least of all, the President himself. It wasn't that Warren didn't know what the hell was going on in his administration—after all, it was the way he and his friends had done business for years back in Marion, Ohio. In Washington, his friends were only doing their normal business on a grander scale, business not for the country but for themselves. And what was America all about if it wasn't business? It was more his innocence, rather than his connivance, which had caught up with Harding. All at once he discovered that, yes, he knew Fall and Daugherty and his glut of office-holding Ohio friends were running the country by those same old corrupt small-town rules, but, my God, you don't mean to tell me that it's illegal! It was making important people mad, people who had the power to call for Warren's head.

As Woodrow Wilson had done a few years before him, the President figured his last chance to avoid the wrath of Washington was to stump the country, go to the people. But he went a very nervous man, tired and confused and heartsick. All hell was breaking loose back in Washington, and the tidal wave that was coming was, like everything else, way over Warren's head.

Meantime, Harding had sailed the high seas—after barnstorming the country by train, meeting and greeting people from state to state, shaking their hands from the back of his railroad car, the Superb. The people, equally unsophisticated, were still unaware of the brewing mess. They were thrilled to see the President. Outside Washington and the big cities, Teapot Dome meant nothing—yet. Now, back on his train, Harding was on his way to San Francisco, due south from the wilds of Alaska, sick with fear and shame and poisoned crabmeat.

Meanwhile, in the humble Hoong Foong restaurant, Wong Gow rubbed his gnarled hands; he'd cleared the table and placed parchment black with wriggly calligraphy in front of him—ready for an after-dinner séance of sorts. "I tell the fortune of Li Kwan Won first, using Tzu Wei Tou Shu, Purple Star Calculation. I do Pa Tzu, Eight Characters."

Seated with his back to the bare wall—O Ti insisted on staying between him and the door—Li demurred, but Wong Gow spoke over his vague protests.

"I tell simple Chinese horoscope. You listen." The old man made lines on the white tablecloth with a chopstick. "You are *hou,* a fire monkey, born in Year of Monkey, 1896. United States is *hou* also, also a Fire Monkey. 1776. You are same. Young, quicksilver, cunning. There is great energy in both. Also always truth, even though it causes pain. But you are Ping Shen Hou—Monkey Climbing Up Mountain. There is also possible carelessness." Toothlessly, the old man laughed. "Is it a wonder you find everything you need in this young country?"

Li laughed with him, sipping his rescued *samshu.* "Everything I need, Wong Gow?"

"Oh, yes, maybe you don't see this, or how strong you are, Cheng Lung-t'ou. If you were *baak gwai lo,* you would see better how easy things are for you. And now, how dangerous. As proverb say, 'When a dragon is stranded in shallow waters, all the shrimps laugh.'"

Li clapped the old man on the back. "Wong Gow is the perfect Chinese. Deny him his proverb, and his tongue would go dry in his mouth."

"You want proverb? I give you proverb. 'Discipline begins with fear of death.' How you like that?"

"I have no fear of death."

"Then you have no discipline."

"Why should I fear death, Wong Gow? 'A man who can ride a tiger never dismounts.' "

"What you mean?"

" 'Death is bigger than a mountain, smaller than a hair.' Death is both too big to see and too small. Why waste time searching for it? It will come when it is ready. Meantime, I ride my tiger because I can."

Wong Gow snorted. " 'When one end of the Milky Way sags it is time to wear padded clothing.' I seek only to give you a padded tiger." He used one of his thick-ridged fingernails, yellow with age and curled like a rose thorn, to describe Li's chart—twelve boxes around a larger center box. "These are palaces, Tzu Wei, pole star, here, see? Ming palace. Very good. Whatever you ask, you get."

O Ti interrupted. "I get whatever I ask if I fight hard enough for it."

Wong Gow's shining bald head nodded vigorously. "Same thing. Some people fight hard, get nothing but cracked skull. That no proverb, that my own idea."

It was almost midnight. Aside from Li's table, there were few in the Hoong Foong. And aside from Fearless and Kit, they were all Chinese and all known to O Ti and Li Kwan Won. Three men, eating before beginning their night's delivery of Snap Dragon beer, sat by the door talking quietly together. Two others, three tables away, had finished their meal. They played a quick and intense game of *pai gow*. The rhythmic clicking of the big dominoes, the murmur from the trio by the door, and Wong Gow's fortune-telling had put Fearless to sleep. He was stretched back in his chair, his weight forcing its front legs off the floor, his mouth, framed in its Mexican mustache, open, not yet snoring. O'Flooty had found his two front teeth. They'd been in his jacket pocket all along; now they were back in his mouth. Kit Dowie, listening with half an ear to Wong Gow, was smoking and watching Chi Mai.

More attentive to Wong Gow than Li, Chi Mai had her chin in her cupped hands and her elbows on the tablecloth, leaning forward to catch the old man's words. She was wearing the kind of thing that Kit had last seen Lizzie wear, a simple blue tunic buttoned from under her left shoulder with ornamental frogs, blue trousers, white socks, and embroidered black slippers. Her hair was loose, drawn from a center part and hooked back over her small ears. Lizzie's hair was almost as black, but none could be as black as Chi Mai's—not even Dido's. It absorbed the electric light. And the almond-shaped eyes, large and slanting up, were black as well. Chi Mai was superb. The proportions of head to body, nose to chin, the line of the serious pink mouth, made painful beauty of geometry. Kit caught himself—painful beauty? Why does beauty give pain? Because all beauty dies? Or because it lies? It cannot be held, cannot be possessed. Beauty was the only thing he knew that could fill where it left empty. There was no humor in the girl, or in her beauty, as there was in Lizzie. But there was strength and the terrible purpose of a warrior.

Kit was entranced by her. Chi Mai hadn't changed since he'd met her ten years before. She'd been seven years old, born three months after the quake and fire, the daughter of a crib girl; no one knew the father. The little face was as serious then as it was now, adamantine of chin and eye. And all that purpose, all that firm unwavering belief and fearsome loyalty, was directed at Li Kwan Won.

"And someone born in the year 1900?" Li was asking Wong Gow. "What would this person be like?"

Kit saw Chi Mai stiffen. If he hadn't been watching so closely he wouldn't have noticed a thing.

Wong Gow rubbed his bald head. "The year 1900? That is *shu*, the rat. A metal rat." He drew a few quick characters on Li's parchment. "I need time to figure out. Would be an idealist, emotional, sensual, eh? But there is a great love of drama. Must be curbed for peace." The old man looked into Li's face with a sly understanding. "'It is fortunate to meet a friend, most unfortunate to meet a pretty woman.'"

Kit also understood. Lizzie Stafford was born in the year 1900. Both he and Wong Gow knew Li didn't mean Chi Mai. Chi Mai was *ma,* not only a horse but a fire horse. If Chi Mai had been conceived in China she would have been aborted, even if she were an only child. Chinese dread the children of the Fire Horse. And if the child is female, so much the worse—she would bring disaster in her wake, to family and husband. Wong Gow went on. "Such a rat person would suit a monkey. If the person was female, she would make a good wife for a fire monkey."

Kit studied the young Chi Mai's perfect oval face as she listened to Wong Gow tell Li of Lizzie Stafford. He knew what it was he saw. This was certainly love. He recognized it by her simple sacrifice of self. Chi Mai made no demonstration, did not berate Li for Lizzie, or complain to him of *her* need. Chi Mai loved Li Kwan Won. If her loved one loved another, if he wanted someone else, then another was what Chi Mai wanted for him. Chi Mai accepted what was, as she accepted birth and death, the Fire Horse and the tenacity of grass. Dynasties would weaken, ice caps melt, even stone would wear away, but grass, like love, left its seed. Chi Mai put her faith in growing things—that which survived and, in surviving, was renewed.

Wong Gow tapped out a paradiddle on the table with his curved fingernails. "But back to monkey, all is not good. This year is Year of Boar. For the monkey, you must be more careful than ever. There is difficulty in business, insults from your enemies. It is not a year in which to trust anyone, not even your best friend."

Li smiled. "I do not need fortune-telling to tell me this, old man."

Wong Gow waved a chopstick. "You take an old man serious, you know what's good for you. 'A wise man in a fool's service is like a pearl dropped in lacquer.' There is also danger for—"

A woman, Jeong-lo, older than Wong Gow was old, balder than he was bald, had appeared by their table, bowing and smiling anxiously at Li. Her teeth were very small, very close together, and very rotten. Jeong-lo's family, one of the many Li had helped against the powerful Six Companies, owned this little restaurant of the Red Wind.

"*Li seen-sang, chaan-yuen?*"

Li nodded his head. "*Ngaw sik-duk ho baau, sik-jaw, m'goy. Nee-dee soong sup fun ho sik.*"

Jeong-lo beckoned toward the back of the restaurant. From behind a bright gingham curtain a young boy came eagerly forward. Moving with agility around the stretched and sleeping body of O'Flooty, the old woman and her grandson began to clear away the dishes. From his side of the table, O Ti helped by stacking the little round boxes that earlier contained the *deem sum.* The party of three men by the door had already left. The two who had been playing *pai gow* were pushing back their chairs, also getting ready to leave, picking their teeth and laughing.

Li rose, cutting off Wong Gow, who very clearly had more to say. "Perhaps, like our wise friend Fearless, we should all get some sleep?"

Kit yawned. "Good idea. Things are slowing down in Chinatown. I haven't been home since Thursday, the place probably needs dusting."

"You have finished your story on Chinatown's little war?"

"Finished it? So far, all I've done is take notes—that and roll a lot of barrels through tunnels. I won't have time to write it until I see President Harding safely off the premises."

As Li moved slowly away from the table with Kit, and O Ti was five feet to their left with his armful of little *deem sum* boxes; as Wong Gow stood over the sleeping Fearless O'Flooty, shaking the Irishman's shoulder, and Jeong-lo and her grandson together flipped the cleared tablecloth from the table, Chi Mai, still seated, her back to the room, was quivering like a newborn fawn.

Something was wrong. The two Chinese men were still laughing. How long had they been laughing? What was so funny? The sound of their laughter, beginning to echo now in her uneasy head, was strange—not moving away but coming closer. What could be so funny? What could make them laugh so? And why was the laughter nearer, rather than farther away? Surely they were leaving, going toward the door to the street. Why? Chi Mai swung her head around suddenly and caught a glint of light on a thin scream of steel.

"Li!"

Li swiftly turned and, in turning, braced himself. He had neither time nor room enough for anything else. Throwing herself from her chair with awesome speed and grace, Chi Mai flew between the moving blade and Li, her body edge on to the two "sons of lepers," thigh muscles coiled for a powerful kick.

Chi Mai's chair went spinning, catching the back legs of O'Flooty's. O'Flooty went over backward, waking just before he was knocked out cold on the hard floor. Throwing the boxes into the air, O Ti came around the table before any of them landed, grabbed the two men by the hair, and knocked their heads together with a hideous crack. And the body of Kit's girl warrior sank quietly to the floor beside the oblivious Fearless.

"Chi Mai!" Li pushed away the keening grandmother, kneeling beside her.

Kit was sick with fear. Leaning over Li's shoulder, he could see no blood. "How is she? Is she—?"

"She will live. The wound is glancing."

"Jesus, thank God. Chi Mai saved your life."

Li looked up at Kit. "I will make sure that her gesture will be worth more than that. O Ti! These two, put the bodies in the deepest tunnel. I am taking Chi Mai to Rose. Mr. Blinn grows angry. I am surprised at his patience. Now *I* shall surprise *him*."

# Chapter 24

The steaming black train carrying the presidential party, her fuming brass stack snorting out short bursts of hissing smoke and her whistle calling like a sweet one-note calliope, wailed into the station off the Embarcadero in a warm summer rain. It was Sunday, July 29, and it was eight o'clock in the morning. Too unhappily aware of the President's illness for bunting and brass bands, sophisticated San Francisco greeted the President and Mrs. Harding with wistful welcoming faces under wet umbrellas; composed fathers held their yellow-slickered children above the quiet dripping crowd; wives with snug cloche hats and light summer colds wiped their noses on little lace hankies.

Without his famous smile, Mayor Sunny Jim's face looked like a pale lima bean above his stiff collar. San Francisco's bald mayor, with his white toothbrush of a mustache, stood under a huge black umbrella held by a very small aide and gave a short and, for once, a sober speech. The length of his greeting was more to save his silk top hat, the jauntiness of his blue four-in-hand tie, and his custom-made boots than in consideration for the President's recent health, or lack of it. Sunny Jim would give a speech anywhere—cow-milking contests, frog-jumping competitions, bathing beauty pageants, snow-queen parades—but the arrival of so grand a personage as the President of the United States made his boutonniere quiver. When he'd finished speaking to the waiting people, accepted the applause from a public that actually liked their laughing mayor, Sunny Jim dashed past the cordoned-off ticket office, up the slick red carpet, his round bottom waggling, to greet the President, followed by the aide with the umbrella, the president of Stanford University, a gaggle of imposing medical men, a squadron of police, and a horde of eager newspapermen.

At any other time Kit Dowie would have resented the early hour, would have held back, his cynicism sharpened to a fine point by years of political high-jinks. But not this time. Now he was right on Sunny Jim's expensive heels, elbowing out surprised comrades, worming his way as close as possible to the action. Kit wasn't going to miss a thing, and one of the things he hadn't missed already was the absence of San Francisco's young and usually visible district attorney from the mayor's side. But whenever and wherever and however James Alexander Hamilton put in an appearance, Kit Dowie would be there. Meantime the police commissioner, pasty-faced Robert Bent, was in some kind of hastily constructed receiving line, along with his senior police officers, sneezing as he held back a crowd that wasn't pressing. Boisterous San Francisco was behaving itself.

Accompanied by his wife, Warren G. Harding stepped firmly from the hissing train onto the slippery expectant carpet with a straight back, a red geranium in his buttonhole, good, if swarthy, color, clear eyes—and an unclear conscience. But few were aware of what occupied the President's mind. That anything occupied it at all was a miracle of imposition. His wife was right behind him. Mrs. Florence Harding was a shock; before Kit could lose his first startled impression, he quickly scribbled in his own unique shorthand, *President—bellowing prime beef. But no longer the oiled and curled Assyrian*

*bull that William Allen White has described. First Lady—*
*plucked vulture, shrill and starved.*

At the sight of their President, perhaps a little pale around the great eyes and mouth but nonetheless hearty, the black lake of umbrellas below him lifted, shaking with genuine cheers. Sunny Jim took one of Mrs. Harding's frumpish flapping arms through his, her well-groomed husband took the other, and together the trio swept through the crowd. Mrs. Harding looked like a midwestern housewife dazzled by a vacuum-cleaner salesman, Sunny Jim like a Broadway actor at the end of a long and successful career, and Warren looked like a king. Over the concerted protests of doctors, Warren refused a wheelchair. As the presidential foot touched the puddled cobblestones of the Embarcadero, the Hardings and the mayor of San Francisco were swallowed not by the common people but by newspapermen. Kit Dowie, first among them, stuck to the President's side like static electricity. He watched as Warren broke into a great homey smile, bit off a hunk of chewing tobacco, took in as many of the press as he could without losing his timing, and said, "Shoot."

They were all drowned in babble, exploding flash cameras, huge new radio microphones, and waving paper. The questions were easy to field. Harding was an old hand at the expected.

"How are you feeling, Mr. President?"

"Much much improved, just a touch of the old stomach, you know. Getting better by the minute."

"What do you think was wrong with you?"

"Damned if I know. Doctors can't say either. Must be some bug that just likes presidents, since I was the only one so honored."

"How's the trip been?"

"Wonderful. As I always say, America is a nation of friendly people."

"Mr. President, over here, please! Just why are you making this trip?"

"That's simple, son." Warren hugged scrawny poultry-faced Mrs. Warren. The woman simpered as the cameras turned her way. "Flossie and I wanted to get on out and remind the people of this great country that it is *their* country, that they have the right to a say, that the government isn't some distant impersonal thing, no, by God, the government is human just like them."

"Say, Mr. President!"

Warren swung his head in a friendly arc to find the new voice.

"We've been hearing some disturbing news from Washington recently. Perhaps you could substantiate . . ."

Kit was proud to note the question came from a Frisco newsman, even if for the rival *Chronicle.* Harding started moving. His aides began to push the press away. "I'm tired, boys, haven't quite shaken that old bug yet. Just you let me get a good night's rest, and I'll answer every one of your questions tomorrow. That's all for now, thank you for coming. Mrs. Harding thanks you too, don't you, dear?"

Mrs. Harding screeched something that was lost in the bawl of an excited radio commentator; the man from KDN was shouting into his bulky mike. Blinded by flash guns and deafened by the powder explosions, the President ducked his head.

Kit wasn't really listening. He'd even tucked away his pencil and notebook. To write up his story of the President's arrival, all he had to do was make it up. Nothing was getting said, nothing asked. The knives weren't out for Harding yet. His fellow press even bought that old "tired" ploy—or, out of politeness, pretended to. When the press is polite, the story is dull. By tomorrow, Harding's staff would have supplied him with the right answers, answers that would sound good and mean nothing. Meanwhile, all Kit needed was time and place, some local color—the rain, the umbrellas, the kids in the yellow slickers, Sunny Jim's butt wobbling on the mayoral dash up the red carpet—for a little harmless humor, a few platitudes, a bit of bombast, the usual stale jokes, his own sharp style, and the story was written. For the moment, his city editor expected nothing more. Besides, most of the front page would consist of a banner headline and photographs anyway. What people were really inter-

ested in was Harding's health—and the fact that the
President of the United States was in San Francisco at all.
And what Kit was interested in was this man's connection to James Hamilton. In his position close by Warren's
side, Kit had time to study the President. What struck
him first was the smell. Under the sodden reek of the
man's wet raincoat, the pungent hair oil, the slight stink
of ill health, was an acrid hint of something else. Kit had
a good view of the President's heavy pink face, the graying hair curling over his collar, the seemingly open face
turning to first one, then another of his questioners, smiling, pretending to be amused, or concerned, or even—
most difficult of all to pull off—informed. The smile was
right, the tilt of the huge maned head, the crinkle around
the gentle trusting eyes. But the whole was wrong.

Kit had once been to the holding pens of one of
Chicago's great slaughterhouses. He'd stood on a long
covered porch stuck on the outside of the largest abattoir
and looked out over a hundred pens. What could be more
innocent of thought or deed than a cow, more uncomprehending of subtle concepts like "the past" or "the future"? Until he'd heard of Harding, Kit's answer was:
nothing at all. Yet supposedly knowing nothing, thinking
nothing, feeling nothing, the poor doomed animals stank
of fear in those crowded pens, their lathered trembling
flanks pressed together, their big soft brown eyes showing
white, the delicate nostrils flared red. Mr. Harding, prize
bull and beloved of the people, smelled like that: a bovine
sacrifice. Interesting.

The great man, the great man's less than great wife,
his scurrying entourage of Cabinet men—Wallace and
Hoover among them—plus wives, secretaries, Secret Service men, Mayor Sunny Jim, smiling once again, and assorted city dignitaries, piled themselves into a long row of
waiting cars with little flags on them and pulled slowly
across the wide wet Embarcadero, through the cheering
crowd, away from the station and the docks. Warren
hung out his window and waved. The crowd loved it. The
whole soaking presidential kit and kaboodle were off up
Market Street to the rebuilt Palace Hotel, where the entire top floor was reserved for the Harding party.

Kit followed, jumping onto the running board of a loaded press car, only to find himself fifteen minutes later, drenched to the skin, stuck in the very grand Palace Hotel lobby along with all the other reporters. Dozens of Bent's police were guarding the stairs and exits. The arrival of a President, of course, was accorded more and classier coverage than the Buddy Le Blond trial. Not just the major cities were represented; reporters came from every town in California that was big enough to have a newspaper, every ethnic publication from Chinese to Mexican, and there were no second-stringers. Kit bagged a position by the main elevator doors, wedged between a potted palm three times taller than he was and a big brass spittoon. Unless Warren chose to exit by a fire escape, Kit couldn't miss him. And that's where he stayed until a presidential aide, with a fine stammer and a white-knuckled grip on a clipboard, told them all they were wasting their time; everyone might as well scram. Looking around at the noisy lobby, Kit thought the aide could have been taking pity on the press but was more likely responding to a request by the harassed hotel management. Waiting newspaper folk never sit still: the lobby was bedlam. There were extras to get out, a voracious population to satisfy; America was dependent on the press for news. The President would not be down, shouted the aide, until the morning—if at all. Doctor's orders. After getting a good whiff of Warren, Kit believed him. The President needed at least twelve hours to have some convincing answers drilled into him. Maybe small-town America let Warren chug through on his private train without asking probing questions, but San Francisco was bound to have a few more daring souls—like the guy from the *Chronicle,* for instance, and Kit Dowie. Plus, there was no James. If there wasn't any district attorney to watch, if the press couldn't get to Harding, if the guy was going to hole up for the rest of his stay in his hotel suite with that frump of a wife, there wouldn't be much happening between now and tomorrow morning. Kit gave it up and left.

It was ten in the morning. Kit stood on the steps of the Palace Hotel and looked out over Market Street through the steady gray rain. Twenty-eight years in this town, twelve of them as a reporter. Just down the street was the spot where he'd hawked papers as an eager kid, where he'd stood and watched the Call building burn down. Kit shrugged at it all, hunched up his shoulders in his wet jacket and strolled the short block to his own paper, filed his story, and then, because he couldn't think of anything else to do, went on up to Union Square.

San Francisco's most elegant city square had dressed up for the President. There were enough wet American flags flapping on flagpoles, or draped over department store balconies, or fluttering from private windows to give Betsy Ross the fits.

Shoving his hands deep into his wet pockets, Kit crossed Geary Street, splashing straight through puddles into Union Square. No one was there, no one stopping; even the pigeons were hiding under the benches to keep out of the rain. A few souls, hidden under umbrellas, hurried through the streets that squared the city green full of rain-slick traffic, everyone head down against the stiff summer downpour. But Kit kept walking until he found the bench he wanted on the Stockton Street side of the square. It was no different from any of the others, all curled red iron backs and smooth wooden seats; his was just as solitary and just as wet, but from it he could sit, get wetter, and look over at the St. Francis Hotel and the Victory Monument. If he wanted, he could also look up and to his left to see the Fairmont and, of course, the Stafford mansion.

Rain in a California summer. It was sweet, clean, sudden to start, and reluctant to stop. Behind Kit the useless floppy hands of a lone English chestnut tree shivered, wringing with the wet. After the 1918 Armistice, Kit had spent a summer in England. Where the chestnut tree came from it was always raining, and if it wasn't raining, it was thinking about raining, and if it wasn't thinking about it, it was trying to forget. On the other side of the bricked path, beds of massed summer flowers, colors running in the rain, tipsy with too much drink, leaned over and drooped their petals in the mud.

Kit sat there alone, soft warm water collecting in the

brim of his hat, down the sides of his shoes, dripping from the end of his nose. Digging in his coat pocket, he took out a pack of cigarettes and a book of matches. Blue Canary matches. Getting a match lit took half a book; after that, lighting up was easy. Smoking was impossible. In less than a minute his cigarette hung from his fingers limp and dead. Kit gave that up too.

Where was James Hamilton? You'd think a guy with that much ambition would be right up there beside Sunny Jim getting his picture taken with Harding. And that wasn't taking into consideration what Li had said about James's curious intention toward the President. What was going on? And where? Kit's eyes strayed from the top floor of the St. Francis to look even farther up, to the very top of Nob Hill. Was the DA home? Modestly sitting out the President's arrival? Why? Waiting for something only he knew about? Friday morning after his talk with Li, Kit had sought out and found Esmé Baker on Telegraph Hill; she'd slammed her door in his face. Kit had to hand it to Hamilton. He didn't stint on his women—Esmé was a stunner. Red hair, brown eyes, and some skin! James Hamilton's women, Lizzie—abruptly, Kit stood up. All the water that had been gathering in the brim of his hat went into his lap. So what? He couldn't get any more miserable or wet.

Turning his back on Nob Hill, Kit started the short walk back down Stockton Street—and then he was going home. He needed the sleep. Sometimes even reporters had enough sense to get out of the rain. Kit didn't want to catch tuberculosis and wind up coughing his life away like Dash Hammett.

Meantime, the kid was all right. Last night Kit had checked on Lizzie. After that nasty little close call in the Chinese restaurant with Chi Mai, Li, the old man, and Fearless, Kit had gone straight to the Blue Canary. Rose and Ike said Lizzie had gone home the same day she'd arrived, Thursday. Both innocent of the character of James Hamilton, both proud that Lizzie had kept her word and not returned to Chinatown, they were pleased with the girl. Rose had got one phone call from Lizzie. She'd come to her senses.

Kit listened without taking off his coat. Ignoring Dido, who had tried to tell him something, Kit had dashed back out of the Canary and run all the way to the top of Nob Hill. Once there, he leaned on the buzzer until Keiko came.

"Mrs. Hamilton here, Keiko?"

"Oh, yes, Mr. Dowie."

"Hamilton too?"

Keiko had frowned, rubbing his eyes, while the corners of his lips turned down. "Yes, him too."

"And she's all right?"

"Oh, yes, no problem. Missy home now. You want come in? Everyone asleep, but I get."

Kit had backed off. "No, I don't want you to do that. Just an idea I had. Forget it. Sorry I woke you. And Keiko—"

"Yes, Mr. Dowie?"

"Don't tell her I called."

"What you say, I do."

Typical of the dame. Sweet-talking her way out of disappearing for two weeks. God, she could talk herself out of anything. Well, Kit Dowie wasn't listening any more. By then it was three in the morning. No point in going to bed. Kit had spent Saturday night at the *Examiner*.

Now, to make his day complete, the unseasonal rain stopped the moment Kit shut the front door of the Crawford Apartments. Still, it was a day alone—maybe it would be a good Sunday after all. His city editor loved his story on Harding's arrival, especially the part about the mayor, and Kit had nothing to do for the rest of the morning. The Chinatown siege was over, nobody cared. The President hadn't dropped dead of crabmeat poisoning, and whatever was going on in Washington—the thing that was haunting Warren—wasn't big news yet. There was no juicy murder to cover, no major fires, no earthquakes. A man needed an earthquake now and then. It put things in perspective. Kit Dowie would work on a song. After that maybe a nap, then he'd call Dido, take her out to dinner—he owed her one for his abrupt behavior Saturday night at the Canary. Then he'd go back with her to Rose's and try out his music on King Oliver and Louis some more. At least *that* could still make him happy. When he was playing, he wasn't thinking about Lizzie.

Kit turned on the gas fire, took off everything he'd been wearing, left the whole mess soaking in a pile on his rug, put on a dry pair of socks and some roomy shorts, wound up his gramophone, and put Mamie Smith's recording of "Crazy Blues" on the turntable. Then he sat himself at his typewriter. He'd write a letter to Ben Hecht in Chicago. Another newspaperman was the perfect person to tell his troubles to. Kit had typed out, "Hey, Hecht, I'm going to take your advice and come east" before the phone out in the hall rang.

"Shit!"

By the time Kit could get to it, one of his friendlier neighbors, the young whore from number 29, smelling of hot cologne, her sandy hair frizzled and her pug nose freckled, had answered. It didn't matter. The call wasn't for him anyway. Kit's appearing in the hall dressed in black knee socks held up by garters and a pair of striped shorts didn't matter either. It made the pug-nosed lady, one very nice leg up on the hall stool, laugh. Her high brassy Brooklyn laughter warmed Kit faster than the gas flames. It brought him home to himself.

Kit spent hours at the piano. Writing to Hecht would end up like whining. Getting the cramp out of his fingers with Rubinstein's "Melody in F," he launched into ragtime. Stride breaks and a witty bass line brought concentration. The song he came up with was great. Screw Lizzie. Kit had his music and his words. He called the new song "Houdini Heart."

When Dido sang it, she'd understand.

It was about that Stafford kid again.

# Chapter 25

Shocking-pink-and-red dressing gown crumpled, yellow hair up in jerky pasted spikes, eyebrows perfect commas of surprise, Murray Blinn cuddled a drooling Tommy. Both he and the bulldog were sitting on Saddle Mary's favorite couch, the one she read her movie magazines on. Murray always sat himself on it very carefully. If he didn't, he'd get smothered in a cloud of dust. He had copies of Wednesday's *Examiner, Chronicle, Call-Bulletin,* even the *Oakland Tribune,* spread out on the coffee table in front of him. He also had copies of Monday and Tuesday's newspapers. Murray had read each one of them three times—from the front page clear through to the sports. He was surrounded by bay-area newspapers. Half the pages had worked loose, fluttering to the filthy carpet below. Once beige, the carpet was now several shuddering shades of brown, but most of the muck was under a second carpet of newsprint.

"Not a thing *again,* Ma, not a goddam thing! There's stuff about the President arriving and being sick or something, there's piles of stuff on Capone and what he's up to back in Chicago, but not a thing, not a fucking thing, about me and what I've been doing right here in Chinatown! It makes me sick! And on top of that, Li Kwan Won had another good night's sleep. The Chink guys I hired to pop him have disappeared right off the face of the fucking earth—Coffee says it's like a hole opened up and swallowed 'em. Jesus! Can't anybody do anything right?"

Ominous spits and crackles were coming from behind the closed kitchen door. Suspiciously, Murray sniffed. Something was burning. Why did the old broad have to go and make him breakfast today of all days? He wasn't in the mood to pretend to eat it, and Tommy wasn't looking too perky either. Why couldn't she let him send on down to the La Pallottola for something that wouldn't poison anybody? Was it his birthday? Nah. Today was the first of August. His birthday wasn't until mid-September. Hers, for Pete's sake? Jesus, was it hers? If it *was* his mother's birthday, he hadn't bought her a thing. Murray's heart skipped a beat until he remembered Saddle Mary was born in January.

Kicking at the newspapers piecemealing her floor, Saddle Mary made her entrance. There was nothing in her hands except a mirror and a scuffed makeup case. No plate came with her, heaped with unnamable crap, no billowing black smoke rolled behind her, nothing was on fire. Murray sank back onto the harsh horsehair in relief.

"You hear me, Ma?"

"Hear what, honey? You referrin' to all that swearin' you been doin'? You know I don't like words like that in my own home."

"We ain't made the papers again."

"That so?"

"An' it's for sure now we didn't get the Chink. Whadda we hafta do to get our names mentioned, blow up City Hall?"

"Blowin' up things already been done. You tried the Chink papers? Bet you're in there."

"Are you kidding, Ma? Even if we was, who can read those scribbles?"

Saddle Mary yawned, seating herself at what passed

for a dining-room table, propped the mirror against a
bottle of sour milk, then tumbled out the contents of her
case onto the scarred tabletop. " 'Course I'm kiddin'."
Mary selected a jar of something, wrenched it open,
sniffed it, then dug three fingers in and produced a great
gob of white goo. She slapped the goo on her chin.
"Whaddaya wanna be in the papers for, anyways?"

"Capone's in the paper every damn day. Everything
he does makes the front page, even here. Can you imagine him sitting around scratchin' his ass in Chicago having to read every newspaper in town trying to find his
own name? It must be 'cause I'm dealing with Chinks.
Nobody wants to read about the little yellow bastards,
not unless we wipe 'em all out. What was you doing in
the kitchen, Ma?"

"Curlin' my hair. Can'cha tell?"

Murray looked at his mother. Her gray hair looked
like electric corkscrews. Her eyes and mouth were three
black holes in a soft landscape of white plaster. Some
day, when he was as rich as Capone and had as classy a
place as Raffles, he was not only going to get her a maid,
*two* maids, but her own hairdresser. She'd burned her
damn hair again.

"Looks great, Ma."

"Don't it though." Mary patted her singed curls.
"Meanwhile, it seems to me, Murray, you oughta play a
bigger game, you wanna make the papers. An' I wish
you'd get that slobberin' mutt offa my furniture."

Murray clutched Tommy closer. Still waiting for
breakfast, Tommy licked his face. "What bigger game
you mean?"

"Well," Mary drawled, collecting her thin wrap
around her thick waist and squirming in her spindly
chair, "you ain't gettin' nowhere in Chinktown, an' you
can't get to Li Kwan Won even with hired Chinks, so it
seems to me you oughta get outa Chinktown—an' bring
them Chinks to *you.*"

"How?"

"How!" Mary snorted, turning in her chair to stare
at him. She'd wiped half the mess off her face. Underneath, her skin had gone a deep pink. "I wasn't aware I

raised me a dope. Think about it. You wanna be like Capone, you act like Capone, it ain't hard. It don't take a lotta brains, what it takes is a lotta moxie. Whaddaya *think* will draw the head Chink out? By fillin' the Blue Canary fulla lead, that's what!"

Murray sat up, licking his lips. Olemi had given him his head on this operation, and he hadn't said anything about leaving the Blue Canary, or Rose, alone. The idea glimmered before him with all the beauty of a million bucks in the bank. It was the kind of thing Al would pull off. "Mother," he said, "you're a pip!"

A vicious glint came into Saddle Mary's piggy eyes. "An' what's more, while you're at it, you can make sure Rose St. Lorraine ain't neglected when you go handin' out presents. It's been ten years, but I ain't never forgot her stealin' Chi Mai offa me. Her an' her uppity yellow friend."

Murray groaned. Here she goes again. Poor old bat. Aside from her adventures in the frozen north with his vanished old man, it was her favorite story.

"I paid good money for that girl—she was gonna be big, big business, my Chi Mai was. An' then I get one, maybe two tricks outa her, an' that busybody bitch comes to take her back to Chinatown. So I laughs in her face. An' Rose says, OK, so she'll pay for my Chi Mai. Pay for her! I had at least five years of big bucks comin' to me with that child. Hell, she was somethin' to see, an' only seven."

This time, remembering made Mary's pink-and-white face go red. When her face got purple, Saddle Mary threw things, and her aim was terrible. Murray was getting worried.

"Who cares, Ma? Calm down, that was ten years ago."

"Who cares? I care, you little runt!"

Murray flinched.

"An you're gonna pay 'em both back for me. It wasn't so much what happened after that—all them Chinks, led by that little crud Li Kwan Won, bustin' into the house, breakin' up the furniture." Mary spat in disgust. "It was what the lippy broad said to me—*me*, Mur-

ray—made me mad. That's what you're gonna get her
for."

Hurt by his own mother's calling him a runt, Murray's nose was running; Tommy licked that too. He'd
heard this all before—hell, heard it? Wasn't he eighteen
years old then and hiding behind his mother the whole
time? Murray had his own personal reasons for hating
Chinks. He gave Mary her usual cue. "What did you say,
Ma?" With his mother, Murray was a study in patience,
the perfect son.

"She stood there smilin', and then she said, to me,
your goddam mother, Murray—she said I wasn't good
enough for a dog to piss on." Saddle Mary leaned down,
jerked off her dirty pompomed slipper, and heaved it at
the wall. The apartment in North Beach had another
crack in its peeling plaster. "You're gonna go in person,
Murray—*in person,* you hear?—an' you're gonna piss on
*her!*"

While Murray Blinn, fingers stained with printer's
ink, was furiously turning the flimsy pages of every newspaper printed in and around San Francisco, Lizzie Stafford Hamilton was sitting on one of two cases of
monogrammed Vuitton luggage, shivering with rage.
Aside from all her servants, aside from Keiko and his
sensitive plants, aside from one hundred or so rooms of
haphazardly accumulated museum pieces, Lizzie was
alone in the Stafford mansion. Or she might as well be.
Keiko was somewhere downstairs. The closest telephone
was in the room that James used as a study, locked between Lizzie's bedroom and his. James had pulled hers,
the one with the private number, right out of the wall.
The bells that connected her to Keiko, wherever he was,
or to Mrs. Gravely down in her kitchens, even the bell
that went to the gardener's house, were all disconnected.
James had locked Lizzie in her own rooms, along with
her packed suitcases. Then he'd done something to the
electric bells. After that, she supposed the bastard had
whistled off to the garage, climbed into the Hispano-
Suiza chosen by her for his thirtieth birthday and paid for
by Stafford money, and finally driven off to work. On a

Wednesday morning it was about time he decided to be Mr. District Attorney again. Her resolve, weakened over four awful days of waiting him out, was back with a spitting vengeance.

In the Vuittons was everything Lizzie had intended to take with her: very few clothes but hundreds of photographs, so many they'd been pulled out of their frames to lessen the weight, letters, though none from James, sentimental keepsakes—silly things she would miss, like diaries, bits of shell or ribbon or china, things Charles Mortimer had given her, or Addy, even Kit. Her dried seahorses Li bought her that first day in Chinatown. Then there were things she needed that weren't at all silly: title deeds, checkbooks, stock certificates and bonds in their ribbons and bows, wills, keys to safe-deposit boxes, keys to wall safes, plus every bit of jewelry she could stuff in. Jewels were valuable. One never knew when one would need ready cash. Where Lizzie thought she was going, emeralds might be the only currency short of gold ingots. Lizzie packed her cases on Saturday, right after her promise to Dido and even before Gertrude Arlington had swept out of the Stafford mansion in a terrific huff. It was the fastest packing she'd ever done. With no idea when James was coming home, no idea where he'd gone in the first place, Lizzie was determined to clear out without seeing him again. All she'd managed was her packing. James came back at three o'clock on Saturday afternoon. She hadn't been fast enough.

He'd walked in, seen her coming toward him through the long gallery, spun on his heel, and climbed the main staircase. She was sure he hadn't seen what she had in her hand, some bauble she coveted from the Egyptian room. And he hadn't said a word. James had ignored her. Which was just fine with Lizzie. No longer drinking, without the fury that bootleg alcohol gave her, scenes were something she wanted to avoid. She'd simply keep out of his way and wait until he left again. Thank God, the packed Vuittons were out of sight up in her bedroom. For months now, James seldom went into her rooms, so —with just a little more luck—he wouldn't see them. Sometimes a big house was a treasure.

Dutifully, Lizzie went down to dinner Saturday night. She could play a few more games for the sake of peace. It wasn't easy to do, demanding not courage but patience and a straight face—Lizzie's short suits. But dinner turned out to require neither. That night, James had his meal alone in his study. She was relieved. Keiko hadn't seen the suitcases either. As far as he was concerned, it was just another evening at home for the Hamiltons.

James spent Saturday evening in his study making phone calls. Lizzie didn't bother to eavesdrop. She was no longer interested in a thing he said or did. From the moment she could get herself and her Vuittons out of the damn door, James would be a thing of the past. He already was, he just didn't know it. Lizzie nerved herself to wait. She could leave on Sunday.

But on Sunday, the day President Harding arrived, James Hamilton went nowhere. Lizzie spent the entire day buzzing with anxiety. No one phoned her; she phoned no one. What was happening in Chinatown? There was nothing in the papers except a short tongue-in-cheek report on the President's arrival by Kit. Kit himself was in one of the front-page photographs, squeezed in by Harding's elbow. Lizzie studied his grainy newspaper face. In spite of what Dido had said, Kit looked as cocky as ever. What was happening at the Blue Canary? Couldn't at least Addy call her? But then, how could he? James was on the phone constantly. But there was her private line. Perhaps Addy had tried when she wasn't in her rooms.

Waiting for James to get the hell out of the house, visit his doxie Esmé Baker, or take a drive in the car— when Lizzie divorced him she'd let him have the car but very little else—she even found herself waiting for him to talk to her. The imminent silence was becoming more than a little tiresome: it was nerve-racking. But he did absolutely nothing, except ignore Lizzie some more. His ignoring her was like blowing one of those dog whistles. It was for her ears alone. Lizzie felt like a poodle; her head rang with tension all day. Somehow, even though they weren't speaking, James managed to be wherever she was, or close enough for her to be constantly aware of his irksome presence. She passed the time working on a jigsaw puzzle. It was the only thing that kept her from screaming. It was obvious by Sunday evening that she was going to have to wait until he went to work before she could get out of the house. And Keiko had said he wasn't home much any more! Jesus!

Leaving when he was out was the only way she could think of going, unless she wanted to confront him. She could, of course, just leave. Endure whatever scene there was bound to be, pick up her suitcases, and go. Lizzie had played with that idea for a few moments and rejected it. There was no point. People only fought when there was something to fight for. Lizzie didn't want a damn thing from James. And she didn't want to listen to what *he* wanted. The tactic of silence, aside from setting her teeth on edge, did nothing at all to Lizzie. The fighting was over.

Lizzie had just about decided to make a run for it when James was asleep—until she remembered the last time she'd arrived on Li's doorstep without warning. But surely this time? No, she couldn't do that to herself. Li had never said he loved her; there had been no moment when she knew with certainty that he was hers. Up in her bedroom late Sunday night, Lizzie began to doubt. What if she was about to make a complete fool of herself? Running away to a man who didn't want her. What Dido had said haunted Lizzie: Li could only love with half a heart. Oh, God, what if everyone was right? Their voices began to clamor in her dark head: Addy, Rose, Kit, Dido, all saying *no*. Were they right and Lizzie Stafford wrong?

She did not make a midnight dash for Li. Lizzie was learning.

Monday morning came and went without event. James didn't go to work, not Monday or the day after. What the hell was he up to? Was this his way of punishing her for her disappearance, for Li? If it was, it wasn't working. It wasn't his silence that was finally getting to her, but his increasingly detested presence. The waiting was growing worse than her distaste of the scene they'd go through if she just walked out in front of him. Her jigsaw puzzle got bigger.

James condescended to come down to dinner on both Monday and Tuesday. With thundering silence, they'd eaten in her beloved green dining room. Keiko broke forty years of tradition—*he* talked to *them* as he served, almost chatted as he cleared away. The poor thing was nervous. James's only response was a few grunts and a curt thanks when Keiko poured the wine. Lizzie hated James more for that, for making poor Keiko uncomfortable, than for almost anything else he'd ever done.

Lizzie also worried about Kit, remembering what Dido had told her. She'd promised the woman she'd speak to him and she meant it, even if it was as humiliating as hell. After all, Dido might be wrong. After two days of Lizzie's seeming to do absolutely nothing, Dido probably thought Lizzie wasn't going to keep her word. Lizzie tried to phone Kit nine times—but no one answered at the Crawford Apartments, not even Number 29. Kit and Dido were problems that would have to wait until she could get the hell out of the house.

By Tuesday night, Lizzie could no longer sleep. James had to go back to the office sometime, didn't he? He'd spent Monday and Tuesday on the phone. Why was he working at home? Surely it couldn't be to keep an eye on Lizzie. He couldn't know what she had in mind. Hadn't even socked her for disappearing for two weeks. The way things were going, Lizzie wondered if he'd noticed.

Pacing her room, smoking, Lizzie changed her mind three times. She would go. She wouldn't. She would—she ended up opening the suitcases again, checking and double-checking that she was taking everything, that all the important papers were there. Poking through a pile of Charles Mortimer's old photographs, she came across one of Keiko. God, at the time it had been taken he couldn't be more than fourteen at the most. A skinny little Japanese kid dwarfed by the paternal mass of a smiling Charles Mortimer beside him, Keiko's hand bur-

ied in Stafford's. They were standing on a pier somewhere, it must be in San Francisco; there was nothing
Japanese about it except the little oriental boy squinting
in the cold sun. The picture was probably taken the day
Keiko had arrived in the United States—a daguerrotype,
brown with the passing of forty years. Keiko! What about
Keiko? Her leaving the first time had hurt and worried
him. What would this leaving do to him? It might hurt
him a lot more. But that was simple, Lizzie. When everything had calmed down, when James had gone his own
way, Lizzie would come back and collect Keiko. She sat
down at her desk and wrote him a letter. It took her two
hours. Writing his name on the envelope, she added,
*Open when I'm gone.* She couldn't take the risk of his
reading it before she got out of the house. Who knew how
he'd react?

Finishing just before dawn, Lizzie sneaked up to the
Stafford mansion's top floor where Keiko's private suite
was stuck away, under the complicated eaves. She slipped
the letter in its thick cream envelope under his door and
went back for the third morning in a row to wait for
James to leave for work.

Lizzie was still waiting three hours later, running to
her windows from time to time to check on whether the
car was ready. Coming back from the sixth or seventh
peek, Lizzie started. Her door, without a warning knock,
simply clicked open. And there was James: standing in
her doorway, dressed to go out, a smirk on his tanned
and too-handsome face. At least he wasn't laughing. She
would have smacked him.

"Suitcases, my dear?" James shut the door quietly
behind him. "Where are you going?"

Oh, hell, the suitcases! Of course. Why bluff? What
was the point? The only reason she'd waited four boring
dreadful days instead of walking straight out on Saturday
afternoon, James in the way or no James, was to avoid
just this kind of confrontation. Well, that was shot to hell.
She couldn't avoid it now. Maybe, like Kit's hustling her
out of Chinatown, it was best. Lizzie stared at James's
unsmiling mouth, holding her ground. James never

smiled. Why hadn't she noticed that before? And the beautiful mouth was weak, even a little prissy around the corners. He was thirty years old and looked twenty-five, but his eyes were fifty. There was no youth or humor in them. She hadn't noticed that either. Framed in her tall windows, hands deep in his jacket pockets, he stared through Lizzie. Lit from behind, the color of his hair, the ice-blue eyes, were glorious in the clear morning light. James Hamilton shone so brightly one could miss the dim man beneath. A tall man who never smiled but knew how to smirk, a ruthless man, brittle and proud. He was holding himself as he always did, with the kind of control that could become rigid. But she used to think her husband was graceful, dignified. And the way he dressed: too carefully, too showy. And worst of all, he was a snob. A seeker of approval. He wanted not only the approval of society but that of the whole damn country. My God, why was she seeing all this now? Who cared if what James truly was was so obvious? Who cared now if she should have been able to see it all along? That she'd lived with him for two years, been courted by him for four more, and been stupid and blind for all of them? His reasons for choosing her, for waiting until Charles Mortimer died before he asked her to marry him, were suddenly as clear and heady as wine. But what mattered, what she took heart in, was that she wasn't blind now. As for being stupid—Lizzie was working on it.

"I asked you, Elizabeth, where do you think you're going?"

"None of your business."

"Isn't it?"

"I don't think so, James."

"Little Lizzie doesn't think so. Isn't that sweet." James moved toward her. Lizzie clenched her fist. If Dido could deck a man, perhaps Lizzie could at least—

"Don't touch me, James."

"Oh, my dear Elizabeth, I have no intention of touching you. Tell me, though, are you planning something short, or—"

"I intend to be gone for a long, long time."

"Do you now?"

"Yes."

"And if I say no?"

"Who cares?"

"I take it that means *you* don't."

"Right on the button."

James went around Lizzie, who turned with him, keeping him in front of her, and opened her closet doors. The doors were fluted panels of silver set into the grisaille walls. When the panels were open the automatic light in the walk-in closet switched on, and the spoils of years of busy shopping spread before them. Sables and silver fox, chinchilla and sealskin, slippers, ball gowns, hats and capes, gloves neatly stacked, suits and sweaters, scarves and silk stockings—enough to clothe a small town, a very rich small town.

"You won't need clothes?"

"I'll buy more."

"Spoken like a true Stafford." James shut the closet. "A lovely day for traveling, isn't it?" he said, as he strolled back to her door. "You'll be relieved to hear that I intend to return to work today. No more waiting for Lizzie."

Lizzie said nothing. But she ground her fine white teeth. So he knew she'd been waiting for him to leave. No doubt the son of a bitch had stayed at home for just that reason, to watch her squirm.

James opened her outer door, pausing for a moment. Lizzie hadn't taken her eyes off him. "By the way, Elizabeth. I've just announced my intended candidacy for state attorney general. It should appear in the papers today. You do realize that my rich socialite wife is part of that ticket?"

"Are Leo Olemi and Murray Blinn part of your ticket too?"

"Let's just say they're backing me."

Lizzie hugged herself. She couldn't wait to see his face when she said what she had to say next. "Hasn't Addy Chase told you yet?"

"Told me what?"

"That he and Sam Jenkins have no intention of supporting you."

"And why is that?"

"Oh, just a little something they heard."

James looked at Lizzie. If Lizzie expected temper or dismay, she was disappointed. What he did was smile. From that distance and with the sun over his shoulder, the smile was splendid. "Hearing things," he said in his best voice, "and proving things are not the same. Whatever you have persuaded Addy Chase to believe of me, I am still seeing him tonight, and he is introducing me to someone very special—President Harding. You have heard of him? It is going to be a very important evening for me. Whatever you have told your old friend can be untold. I too can be very persuasive, much more persuasive than a young wife who's been cheating on her husband. Meantime, enjoy your rooms, Elizabeth. You'll be seeing a lot of them for the next few days."

Lizzie's phone rang. Both she and James turned to stare at it. But before Lizzie could make a move to answer, James strode to the phone, yanked it from the wall, tucked it under his arm, took the key from her door, stepped through, and locked it from the outside.

Lizzie sat down on the sturdier of her two leather cases.

Swell.

How long had James been planning this?

And *now* what the hell was she going to do? Whatever it was, her dithering was over. It was one thing to choose, another to be forced. By locking her in her rooms, James had tipped her hand. Lizzie was going.

Except for the ever-attendant figure of Chi Mai, Li Kwan Won was alone in his office at the Blue Canary. Chi Mai, her side bandaged, small head bent over the "little jacket"—the secret books of the Triad—kept quiet. O Ti, at long last deciding Li was safe enough to be allowed out of his sight, was off gambling on the upper floors.

Li took a small leather-bound book from his desk

drawer. In the little book was a poem Wong Gow had written, and that Li had translated into English.

> *Perfect beetle*
> *Circling dung.*
> *In perfection egg begun.*

> *Perfect bee—*
> *Perfect flower,*
> *Ritual of perfect hour.*

> *Perfect web—*
> *Perfect fly.*
> *What a perfect way to die.*

> *Spider, fly, beetle, bee—*
> *Cornered in Geometry.*

The old man himself, Wong Gow, had just left the room. But before that, he'd spoken for fifteen minutes without stopping, determined to tell Li what he'd divined from the oriental stars.

"But you understand, *Li seen-sang,* I only warn. All this can change. Fortune change, you listen. 'Ignore an old man's advice and one day be a beggar.' One lucky star this year, two unlucky—but you fool 'em. I help."

Li listened, quietly smoking. Change his fortune? He had known the face of his fortune since the moment Little Sister had died in his arms. The Fire Horse brought death to Li's family; to Li it gave a life of separateness. Detached, calm—there was a kind of peace that came with isolation, a cold joy that belonged to a life lived in the mind. The once-boy had leapt on the horse's burning back, knowing that to ride was to feel the flames—but the furious gallop, however brief, would light the dark night of his life with cold crazy sparks. Li had nothing to fear from fate. He would neither seek it nor avoid it. Only once had he attempted to turn away the fierce force of the stars—but Lizzie Stafford Hamilton was as much his fate as the Fire Horse had been Su Yin's. What could a man do but stride forward to meet such a calamity? This he had chosen for himself. Lizzie was free to choose as well. He would not help. If fate, in the form of a wild dark child from Nob Hill, came to him again, he would welcome her. But Li would not go to her. That much he would do for Wong Gow.

Li had set his "surprise" for Murray Blinn in motion. O Ti was about his "cold work." Sometime in the middle of this night Blinn would know the high cost of the hurt to Chi Mai. To the soothing sound of Chi Mai's rapid quill and clicking abacus, Li read Wong Gow's poem again. Over the years he'd read it many times. Tonight the meaning was cold and clear.

# Chapter 26

Just behind Addy Chase, James Alexander Hamilton stepped, head high and jaunty, from Herbert's Bachelor Restaurant. Herbert's catered to men only—usually very important men, though who decided a man's exact degree of influence was a toss-up between the taste of the watchful management, the known truth, and a hopeful patron's personal ego bolstered by wealth or enough moxie to give the appearance of it. Addy and James passed on all counts, though between them the last was James's sole province.

Hamilton was winging it on good cocaine just snorted privately in one of Herbert's manly toilet cubicles. Once outside in the salty San Francisco air, James thought the moon looked like a potato chip in an India-ink sky. But the stars were a thousand spinning coins, tossed up and all coming down heads.

James felt terrific, a high roller on a winning streak. Whatever nonsense Lizzie had told Addy—though during their evening together neither James nor Addy had referred to her telling Chase anything at all—surely must have been dispelled by the past two hours over Mendocino oysters, vintage wine, and rare roast beef. If anyone could, James managed to gloat. Tonight of all nights, Hamilton's tongue was not only silver but platinum. He had the old man bedazzled, bedeviled, and back in his pocket. No one was going to stop him from entering, and then winning, a race for the state attorney general. After that, people like Addy Chase were unimportant. As for Lizzie. Christ! What did she think he was, stupid?

James's mind was way ahead of his body. While the latter continued to execute elegant graceful necessities, like paying the check, tipping the waiter, and following Addy Chase out into the starry night to hail a taxi, his mind was in a crude looping spin. The way James was thinking was not the way he spoke. In his thought, unlike his speech, he allowed himself few adjectives. It was becoming a kind of free-wheeling vers libre with a lot of crudity for spice.

Coming back on Saturday afternoon and finding his wife darting around the mansion with a bit of Egyptian junk hidden in her hand didn't so much surprise as anger him: what did she think he was going to do, kiss and make up? The little cheat had been in Chinatown with a Chink! It made him sick. He'd gone directly to her rooms, seen the suitcases—it didn't take Einstein to know what she had in mind. Hamilton wasn't having a public breakup of their marriage. He still needed the green-eyed little dope, would need her for some time to come: her social position, her contacts, her money. Charles Mortimer's spoiled Lizzie Sian Stafford wasn't going anywhere without James.

His senses stretched and humming, registering everything but retaining nothing, James climbed into a taxi behind the dapper figure of Addy Chase. His silence was electric as his mind dipped and swayed with racing thought. God, it'd been a hoot waiting Lizzie out for four days, watching her fret and fuss. And what an education, learning what Lizzie did with herself when she was stuck at home! Without spending money, or fooling around having lunches with Kit Dowie or one of her equally pointless friends, or holing up with a fucking Chink—

James gave himself a secret smile; he could have put that bit about the Chink better, same words, all they needed was a little rearranging. But James stopped his mind from dwelling on Chinatown or, worse, what his wife would be like in bed with a Chinaman—revolting! Besides, with the thought of Chinatown came thoughts of Blinn. Murray wasn't living up to expectations. That imported gun caper had gone as limp as a cheap hotdog. And James had no idea what Blinn was doing now. But Lizzie, the brainless moron, had whiled away two days doing a 2,000-piece jigsaw puzzle of a Swiss Alp, while James spent four days pretending he didn't know a thing about those suitcases or what she'd been up to while she was gone.

But all good games had to come to an end. It was Wednesday; Harding was feeling better. For a while, it looked like the President was never going to leave his hotel suite or return Addy's calls—in which case all Hamilton's plotting was for nothing. When two days had passed, he began to hope Warren would drop dead. That would shut him up for sure, and James would have had nothing to do with it. But Addy phoned. Harding wanted to see his old friend. From that moment on, James knew everything was going to go his way. He had things to do, and they didn't include playing cat-and-mouse games with his wife. As early as Sunday he knew he was going to have to lock Lizzie in her rooms. It would be easy holding her. The servants, with the exception of Keiko, were hand-picked by himself. They'd do as he told them. As for Keiko, the little Jap had been informed that missy was sick and to leave her strictly alone. James had been very firm about that. After his business with the President was concluded, he'd think of something more permanent for taking care of Lizzie.

Which reminded him—Esmé! If this evening was going to work, he needed Esmé. Jesus, the damn redhead had better be where she was supposed to be. Of course she was; he could count on Esmé Baker, the girl had a heart like a lion. He had nothing to fear from Esmé. As for Lizzie—what the hell was he just thinking about? Oh, yes, a damn good way of keeping Lizzie out of trouble.

There must be something she still feared. It didn't seem
to be the loss of her name, maybe not even the loss of her
money. The loss of her mind? But that was already gone
if the idiot didn't care about money or position. So blackmail wasn't the answer. Maybe he could drug her with
some of that Chinese opium his Pinkerton man told him
she'd become fond of—and then keep her out of sight. A
bit melodramatic, but hell, if he wanted to deal in melo-
drama he might as well go all the way and stage some
kind of handy accident. A fatal accident? James followed
his own catherine-wheeling mind into places that made
him a little nervous, but his consciousness went anyway
—ducking and feinting, propelled headlong by cocaine. A
widower could still make it in politics—think of the sympathy vote! He wouldn't have to do anything himself; he
could get someone Olemi knew, a professional hit man;
maybe he could even find one to do it without Olemi
knowing. Yes, maybe he could! Meantime he and Addy
were getting out of the taxi, now pulled up in front of the
Palace Hotel. It was ten o'clock; the President expected
them. The potato-chip moon over the Ferry Building at
the foot of Market was fine and fat and laughing.

Addy Chase followed James into the hotel's grand
lobby.

A few of Bent's sleepy police were on duty. Without
asking questions they waved Addy and the district attorney on into the elevator. On the ride up—at that hour
they had the elevator to themselves—Addy maintained
the silence he'd begun as they left Herbert's. A silence he
needed, sweet peace he'd earned after his meal with
Hamilton. From the moment Chase had stood up to greet
the young man in the restaurant, James had talked without pause, the words coming faster than water over
Yosemite's Bridal Veil Falls. Addy had never seen or
heard anything as pure and uncluttered as James's total
self-absorption. The older man got the peculiar feeling he
was eavesdropping. It was a brilliant monologue. Too
brilliant. If Addy hadn't been warned by Lizzie, didn't
know what he now knew, he'd have gone under in the
first ten minutes, would have found himself cheering at
the highlights. Tonight, James was like an enameled

scarab on a gold pin, a highly colored, brittle bug. Addy was exhausted; was the boy that excited at the prospect of meeting the President?

Even though he believed every word Lizzie had told him, Addy was still taking James to meet the President of the United States. Why not? The word was filtering through about the scandal back in Washington—what good could Warren do James now, or, to put it another way, what harm could James do Warren? And if he did mean harm, as Lizzie suggested, the presence of a third party—namely, Addy Chase—ought to prevent that.

As far as Addy was concerned the meeting was pointless, but both he and Sam Jenkins had decided to let James down easy. Their principal backers, Fleishhacker and Giannini, hadn't been privy to everything Addy and Sam knew but weren't slow to catch on that something unfortunate was up, that enthusiasm for San Francisco's golden youth had waned. After Sam and Addy had met them at the Pacific Union Club on Friday night, everyone was now sitting—and waiting. By the time they got tired of that, time would have passed, James would get the message—and Addy could forget he'd ever attempted a last flutter on this or any other political hope. Best to remember the innocent days when he and Sam believed a vote could change things. Whatever Teddy Roosevelt was really like, neither Addy nor Sam had ever gotten close enough to dim their dreams. For Addy, politics gave its last gasp with this brief dalliance with Hamilton. In a way, he was relieved. The only thing that vexed him now, something he'd sat with Sam long into last Friday night discussing, was: should they, or should they not, actively take part in bringing Hamilton down? Neither one of them could make up his mind. The most positive thing Sam did was not to come along to introduce James to Warren, said his conscience wouldn't allow it. Addy disagreed. Pulling out at the last minute could rebound on Lizzie.

So now here he was, getting out of an elevator with James Hamilton, whose silence was turning out to be as loud as his verbal torrent in Herbert's, and whose almost unnaturally blue eyes were beginning to make him nervous. Before it had really begun, Addy was waiting for the evening to end. Still, resigned to getting through it, Addy knocked on a hotel door.

"Addy Chase! You old son of a gun!" Warren Harding, a full whisky and soda in one hand, a cigar between his fine white teeth, jerked Addy into the top-floor suite, winking one wild bloodshot eye. Addy, taller than the President but much thinner, came easily.

"Doctor told me to go to bed, but he didn't say *which* bed. Ha ha! I got Duchess Flossie the suite next to mine, put her and all those damn flowers and most of the baskets of fruit and nuts everybody's been sending us in there with her an hour ago. Hell, you Californians grow some odd things—avocados! I've never eaten anything tasted so foul in my life, and I don't intend to start now. Doctors are making me live on caffeine and digitalis. Anyone ever tell you you look like Abe Lincoln, Chase? *I* did? Well, goddammit, I would, wouldn't I?" Warren pushed the long-limbed Addy into a chair. "Sit down. Rest your feet. Been waiting to talk to you all day. All my little elfin aides are tucked into their wee little beds, the doctors have given up poking and prodding me and gone the hell home, and we have the place and the night to ourselves." He advanced on James, beefy hand extended. "You must be this hotshot DA I've heard so much about, and not only from my good friend Addy Chase here. You're thinking of running for higher office, boy? I'll let you in on a little secret: it's not all it's cracked up to be. Missed you at the train station Sunday morning. You weren't there, were you? No, I didn't think so. Never mind—some of us have jobs to do, right? Have a drink, have a cigar, a piece of fruit—you play poker, son?"

The President of the United States was pathetically happy to see them. He couldn't stop talking, pacing, pouring drinks from the overwhelming bar stock supplied by the proud Palace management, sweeping newspapers, front pages full of his public face, off chairs and sofas. The Harding smile was wide and fixed but the pink-rimmed eyes were somehow hurt; they had a puzzled, damaged look—as if he was haunted from the inside. Even James noticed.

"Can't stay in bed, feel fine, absolutely well. Keep telling them that whatever the hell was wrong with me is gone now. Food poisoning, that's all—nothing serious. But they're all on me like ticks on a mutt."

Addy, from his enforced chair by the fireplace, accepted a huge tumbler of whisky with a whiff of soda, saw James receive the same—and was amused by the President's ability to silence the fabled tongue of San Francisco's district attorney by sheer volume.

With his guests seated and watered, Warren relaxed, standing with his back to the fire. "I heard California was the sunny state, boys. When I got here it poured on me. Since then all the sun I get is through hotel curtains."

"This is San Francisco, sir." James was stunned by a man who could talk longer and louder than he could, but he was recovering quickly. All the man's soft spots were showing. He was already thinking of asking the President where the bathroom was; the cocaine was wearing thin, but maybe he didn't really need it. Warren was proving no adversary at all. "Weather changes from one day to the next."

"Like politics, eh, Addy?" Warren stopped grinning. "Suppose you've both heard what's blowing up back in Washington?"

"A little," admitted Addy, sampling the President's whisky. A bolt of pure flame felt like it shot right out the top of his head. Someone in the Palace was making some pretty raw hooch. Blinking his eyes to clear the fumes, Addy thought Warren hadn't changed at all. The old bull was wounded, but he was still as innocent and foolish as ever, which made his faults innocent and foolish, like the indecencies of a small child.

Warren rocked back on his heels. "Well, Addy, don't you believe it, not about me anyway."

Addy looked at the nervous man, leonine and grand, leader of the greatest country on earth. Addy couldn't hold Warren's eyes for a second, brown and mild and forgiving as his own were. "I don't believe it, Warren. Not about you," he said gently. What he meant was: his old friend the President was obviously a fool, he was weak-willed and weak-minded, but he wasn't a crook. The mere fact of his third year in the White House shook Addy more than anything the President's appointees were up to; it said something about the people who voted for him, rather than the President himself. But by saying so little, Addy meant more than he said.

Warren took it for less. The booming voice had lowered, become almost a plea. "It's my friends, Addy, my goddam friends, they're the ones making me sick. By God, Harry—Harry Daugherty himself—came all the way west to be with me when he heard I was ill, bless him. And damn him too! He's sleeping down the hall right this minute, the best and the worst friend a man could have. They wanted government jobs, I gave 'em government jobs. I had a right to choose my friends for them, didn't I? A man wants to work with people he knows. Hell, when I got elected, no one was more surprised than me, and I didn't know a damn soul in Washington. I'm just an old Ohio boy. And after that, I owed so many favors—all politicians owe favors. That's the way it is. And what's wrong with that? Happens in business all the time. How was I to know what my friends would get up to once I wasn't looking? Being President isn't easy, Addy. Everyone giving you advice, all of it different: do this; no, do that—God's teeth, one little mistake and you got the whole world on your ass. My friends didn't ask me before they went and did anything; I'm only just finding out about it all now, just like everyone else is. But sure as shit, it'll be my neck on the block. I'll tell you something my father once said to me, Addy; he said, 'Warren, it's a good thing you wasn't born a gal, you'd be in the family way all the time—you can't say no.' "

And then the President of the United States laughed, a great belly laugh that made Addy remember why he liked the man in the first place. Warren G. Harding might not be a good President, a man of gas but no substance, but he was a hell of a lot of fun to drink with. "Well, I've got only myself to blame, haven't I? It's my stew, I chopped the onions—no wonder I've got to be the one doing the crying. Come on, get up! We're going to see that gal of yours, Addy—Rose St. Lorraine. A man can't visit San Francisco and not see a landmark like your amazing lady Rose! I've had enough pussyfooting around with pipsqueak aides and Secret Service men and the persnickety press, not to speak of the Teapot Dome crap. I want to go out and have one hell of a good time. We'll sneak down the back stairs; the Secret Service boys are half asleep. Who'll ever know? You game, boys?"

James had been carefully listening, resisting the urge to impress the President with his own voice. What he'd learned was a little different from Addy. One: his plan for the evening was a winner; he didn't even have to be the one to suggest the President go out. Two: as he had thought it wouldn't, his own name didn't seem to mean a thing to the talkative Harding; it brought no niggling reminder of Ed Doheny, Sr. *or* Jr., and the Elk Hills leases. The President was only worried about his own skin. And three: that a politician had better be very very careful choosing his friends. So much for Leo.

As Warren and Addy gathered their hats and coats, a confident James decided not to ask the way to the bathroom.

Popping the Blue Canary's plump maraschino cherries into her painted red mouth one at a time, Esmé Baker sat on the same bar stool Lizzie had used the night she listened to Appetite Ike tell his story about Dido and Li. Esmé, her back to Ike's bar, leaned lightly on her elbows, her stockings sheer black, red-gartered just above the dimpled knees, her legs crossed. For this night, this very special night, she looked just as James had instructed her to look: very available, but at a sky-high price. Wardrobe and makeup at Universal Studios had taught her a few tricks, but Esmé didn't need many. The only thing that seemed out of place was the size of her purse. Sitting on the floor by her bar stool, it was big and heavy enough to qualify as luggage.

Esmé had no trouble dressing for her part; what Hamilton had required she be for a night, she was anyway. Among the men she counted as acquaintances, the

vainglorious DA was about the only one who didn't
know it. Esmé differed from Rose's girls in only three
respects: her clients were long-term, they were one at a
time—seeing Leo Olemi while she was working James
was not Esmé's usual style—and they all paid in install-
ments. In her cynicism, the worldly Esmé thought the
whole arrangement wasn't much different from being a
wife. What the hell, it was better. No kids, no contracts.
If a girl didn't like the setup, she was free to move on to
something new.

Wearing a simple black dress, a short black jacket
with long slashed sleeves tucked tight at the wrists with
ebony beads and fanned high at the mandarin collar with
glossy black feathers, and a cunning little hat, Esmé
perched on her bar stool and waited. Her hat capped her
fox-red hair in black velvet. Esmé's face was shadowed
and shaded and made mysterious by a thin spidery veil.
Beneath it Esmé's carefully bored brown eyes narrowed.
Up onstage she'd just seen the pushy newspaperman
who'd come snooping around her house after dirt on
James. She smiled, remembering; all the guy got for his
efforts was a bent nose. But she didn't recognize the two
men, both slightly drunk, who argued a few feet away
from her. Fearless O'Flooty and Dashiell Hammett were
not in Esmé's world.

"You wanna talk, lady?"

Esmé turned to face the hideous little bartender
who'd asked her that, his face made more astonishing by
the snowy dicky and red bow tie. "You kidding? I'm
busy. Buzz off." Esmé took three more of the old man's
cherries, swung back on her bar stool, and, while she ate
them, waited some more.

Appetite Ike wasn't too pleased. The redheaded lady
didn't look like she'd come calling on Rose for a job, she
looked like she already had one and had no intention of
paying rent on the office space. While he mulled over
what he ought to do about that, the Blue Canary was
doing its usual brisk Wednesday-night business. The
dance floor was full of its normal well-dressed and well-
heeled clientele. Kit Dowie and Lil Hardin were playing
a hot duet on the piano, Armstrong was modestly follow-

ing King Oliver's cornet with his own, and Dido, having nothing to sing but doing it with style, was leaning on the piano tapping her heels and jiggling her ass. Because it suited her and because she loved it, Dido was wearing what she wore the first time Lizzie had ever seen her— silver: silver bugle heads on a long silver dress, silver slippers, silvered eyelids, and thin silver earrings like wings swept back over her ears.

By the time they strolled by Pete, the Blue Canary doorman, Harding and Hamilton were chums, already on a first-name basis, Addy Chase bringing up the rear. Pete was used to important people showing up at what he thought of as "his" joint. The Blue Canary drew 'em from everywhere, big and small: show business, politics, the rackets, high society, low society—it was Pete's job to check heads and to make sure, if they were important enough and wanted it, they got as much privacy as the Blue Canary could offer. They weren't always presidents, but most of them behaved like it. For instance, the smooth and snooty district attorney, who probably thought he was slumming. Warren Gamaliel Harding didn't act like a president, he acted like the bank manager of a lucrative branch office. The President clapped Pete on the back and gave him a cigar. Pete put the cigar in his pocket as a souvenir.

Though Addy had suggested they come in the back way, through his and Rose's, and of course Li's, private entrance, Warren wasn't having it.

"Tonight, Chase, I'm a private citizen. Sure, I snuck out of the hotel, but that's because I was hiding from my own staff. Here, I don't have to hide from anybody, do I?"

Addy couldn't think of anyone to hide from. It was Warren's choice anyway. If the President of the United States wanted to be seen in a speakeasy, what was Addy Chase supposed to do about it? Besides, he was sure Rose would be thrilled to have the President show his face in her place.

"I'll go on up and get Rose, then, get her down as soon as I can; it's early but I'll push—the Blue Canary isn't anything without Rose. James, you take care of Warren while I'm gone. Introduce him to Appetite."

"Great, Chase. You do that." Harding was looking past Addy; like most every other U.S. citizen, he was eagerly sniffing the heady air of illicit alcohol, cool women, hot jazz, and risk.

James, exultant at the unexpected ease, led Harding directly to the main bar, picking a spot a few feet away from Esmé and avoiding the thin man who was coughing into the face of a guy who looked like a Mexican bandido. Esmé and James ignored each other. If Esmé was here, then Rose's girls Lupe and Carol, the Canary whores James had bribed through Stringer Bellew, were here too —doing what they were paid to do: waiting. Everything was perfect.

"Appetite Ike," James announced with pride, "this is Mr. Harding. What would you like, Warren? Anything at all. You name it, Appetite can make it. And whatever you have, I'll have."

Harding held out his hand to Ike. Greeting the President with one of his horrible squints, Ike deliberately returned the handshake with the left hand, the one missing the fingers.

Undaunted, Harding took it and gripped firmly. "Couldn't be the war, you're too old for that."

"Lost 'em in the Klondike," snapped Ike, who hadn't voted for Harding. "An' I ain't too old for nothin'."

"Ah, the Klondike! I was a young man then. I had all the world before me." Harding's eyes misted. "Sometimes wish I could start again. You can make anything, old-timer?"

Ike scowled at the "old-timer," but he took it without flinching. "Yup."

"In that case, Ike, make me something of yours, something nice and strong."

Ike grinned. There went the Pernod. "Two Frisco Hots comin' right up."

Warren leaned in close to James. "You know anyone else?"

Hamilton's heart picked up speed. Wasn't he going

to have to do any persuading here? He had a funny feeling the President had a copy of the script. "Are you thinking of anyone in particular?"

"I am indeed." Warren gave him a lurid leer. "I'm thinking of the lady in black two stools along, the lady with the red hair."

Bingo! What could go wrong now? James straightened his perfect tie, shot his French cuffs, and introduced the President of the United States to his mistress. Esmé Baker. In his introduction, he left out the part about the mistress.

Ten minutes later, Esmé led Warren up the Blue Canary stairs to the private back rooms on the second floor. She carried herself with dignity and her purse with effort. If she and Warren had turned to the right, they would have entered the gaming rooms. Harding eyed 'he familiar smoke-filled rooms with hunger, heard the clicking of spinning balls, the riffling of cards, but turned left with Esmé. He'd have time for that later. It was going to be a long night.

Unnoticed by Warren, Hamilton followed at a safe distance. But Kit Dowie noticed. From the height of the stage, he saw the President enter with James and Addy, saw Addy go upstairs alone. What was going on? Kit was suddenly confused. If Hamilton was up to something, what was Chase doing in the middle of it? Then he saw James put Esmé and Harding together. That *was* something. Kit stopped playing to think it over, leaving Lil to carry the piano part alone. He caught O'Flooty's lapis-lazuli eye. Fearless winked at him and nodded his shaggy head toward the main staircase. So Fearless was wondering about Hamilton and Harding as well. Should he follow James, as James followed Esmé and Harding? Did Addy know about this? Kit's instincts told him to wait it out. And his reporter's luck put him, as ever, in the right place at the right time. With a practiced gesture, Kit shoved his crumpled hat to the back of his head, winked at O'Flooty, and came back in on the low notes.

Now safely upstairs but startled, Harding stopped just inside the door to the room Esmé had chosen. "Two more?"

"On the house, Mr. Harding." With skill, Esmé kept him moving. "What could be better than a blond, a brunette, and a redhead?"

Warren couldn't think of a thing.

Catching his unspoken answer, Esmé smiled. "Just a little added surprise. Girls, this is Warren. Warren, this is Lupe and Carol."

Lupe, the coffee-and-cream-colored Mexican, eyes like shiny black beans, and Carol, a honeyed blonde with skin like a nectarine and great swimming blue eyes, were curled like sugar spoons in the lacy double bed. At Harding's entrance, they yawned and stretched and beckoned.

Lupe crooked a little finger. "Come here, honeys."

The President stood for one minute, looked first at Lupe, then at Carol, then back to Esmé, and said, "What the hell! Last one in is a chicken." He ripped off his coat and snapped his suspenders over his broad shoulders, struggling with the buttons on his pants.

Just before he made a dive for the giggling, jiggling bed, Esmé picked her purse off the floor and went through a side door. It led to the room next to Lupe's; it was Carol's and it would be empty—just as James had arranged. As Esmé slid through, she called over her shoulder, "I'll be back in a minute, everybody, but don't hold things up just for me."

James, already in Carol's room, pulled Esmé through. "Is everything all right?"

"It's perfect. It couldn't be better." Esmé pulled up her thin black veil and gave James an enthusiastic kiss, hot with admiration. "My God, honey, that's the President of the United States in there, just like you said!"

James Alexander Hamilton, tall and straight, elegant and blond, light-blue eyes icy, was in command of himself; he removed her arms from around his neck. "How much time?"

"Give him ten minutes; he's just getting started. Carol and Lupe know what to do." Esmé knelt down and opened her enormous purse. Inside was a professional camera, a flash, and enough film for Griffith's *Birth of a Nation*.

"Here, James. You get this together. I'm so excited, I'm shaking."

James took the camera, loaded it with film, and readied the flash.

Head over heels in love with power, Esmé walked slowly to Carol's bed, leaned over the edge, and flipped her black dress up over her round white bottom. She wasn't wearing a chemise. Under her beaded dress and slash-sleeved feather-collared jacket, she wasn't wearing anything.

"James . . . ?"

James looked up, sucked in his breath, and frowned. "For Christ's sake, Esmé, not now."

"Yes, baby," she breathed, "now."

Lizzie was still locked in her rooms. As soon as James had left she'd pulled the place apart trying to find a spare key, a nail file, a hammer, a stout shoe, anything to open the door. Two hours of that, and then fifteen minutes of screaming for help at the top of her voice, achieved exactly nothing except a messy room and a sore throat. Where the hell was Keiko? Why couldn't anyone hear her? The answer was simple. The Stafford mansion was a fortress and every room in it a padded cell, or as good as. The solarium had hinged glass panes set into its soaring glass roof, but the roof was two stories above her head. Even using Keiko's ladder, where would she go from there? The windows that opened, in her bedroom and her sitting room, opened onto a fifty- or sixty-foot drop, even before she took into consideration the angle of the street she'd land on if she jumped. Oh, for the long golden locks of Rapunzel! Yelling out the window into the clean rain of a short shower got her a few curious looks from a few busy pedestrians, an answering ring on a bicycle bell from a newsboy in a rain slicker as he sped away down California Street, wet hair, and a bad case of vertigo. A little after four in the afternoon, Lizzie, exhausted, threw herself across her unmade bed and fell asleep. One thing she did not do was cry.

Lizzie was awakened by a timid tap at her door. Her room was dark with the kind of dark that meant night.

The rain had long since stopped, and it was quiet enough to be way after midnight. Lizzie might have missed the knock if she weren't also starving. Scrambling, confused by sleep, she got to the door before whoever it was could try again—or, dreadful thought, leave.

"Keiko! Is that you?"

"Yes, missy. Mr. Hamilton say you want leaving alone, say you sick. But I worry. Mr. Hamilton not a good man. I go to bed, get letter. Sorry, but I open. Now I worry more. Also, what about plants?"

"Mr. Hamilton is a shit. Get this door open!"

"You not sick?"

"Do I sound sick?"

"You sound mad."

"That's not the half of it. Open the door. The bastard's locked me in."

"Locked in?"

"Keiko!"

"Yes, missy?"

"Open the goddam door!"

"I have to break."

"Fine. Break it."


James, lying spent across Esmé's slim freckled back —she was holding the both of them up, her knees locked and her hands flat on Carol's monkeyskin bedspread— looked at his watch.

"It's time! It's got to be. Come on!"

Esmé used one of Carol's hankies to wipe herself dry, tucked it under the mattress, hitched her dress down, but kept her veil up, and followed James. On the way, she picked up the camera. The sounds that came through the connecting door made them smile at each other.

"Now!" stage-whispered James, and he swung the door open, rapidly standing back to keep out of Esmé's way. At the same moment, Lupe, flipping off the sheets, uncovered the double bed.

Esmé's flash caught Warren G. Harding, the presidential tool empurpled and swollen, in a tantalizing tangle of tinted flesh. It was positive and clear, and it made a pattern to ponder on. All the President's aides and all the President's kin wouldn't have any trouble at all, spotting the President's skin.

As the President himself looked around, blinded by the flash, caught in the flesh, his eyes were wide open and innocent—like the eyes of a stag in oncoming headlights just before impact. Raising one white palm, whether to plead or to forgive James never knew, the rest of Harding began to turn purple. And Carol started to scream.

All James said was, "Good grief," as the President died.

# Chapter 27

Slinging the heavy camera over her shoulder, Esmé Baker moved quickly to the bed, clamped her hand over Carol's hysterically shrilling mouth, and held it there, while Lupe, wriggling her disgusted nose, gingerly picked up the President's right arm by one of its limp forefingers and then dropped it. The arm flopped back onto the wrinkled sheets like a dead fish, fingers curled up—as useless in death as in life.

"We got trobble, Meester Hamilton?" asked Lupe. There was no response from James. "Meester Hamilton?"

"James!" snapped Esmé, struggling with a surprisingly strong Carol. "Wake up! What should we do now?"

For answer, the district attorney, in a room above a famous speakeasy owned by what he thought of as his worst enemy, a room occupied by two naked whores, one having hysterics, and that one in a headlock by his own mistress in black with a camera around her neck, his unfaithful wife locked in her rooms three blocks above him, and the newly dead body of the President of the

United States flung pale and naked across a double bed right in front of his eyes, picked the closest chair and sat on it. At least Harding had the decency to die on his stomach.

Hamilton's mind, earlier a silver screen flickering with a thousand images, was now a total blank, without sound, without movement. The stunning blue eyes were almost as dull as the President's. Faced with something he couldn't talk his way out of, the totally unexpected and the completely unthinkable, James did the best he could—he stopped thinking.

Esmé let go of Carol, who promptly began to cry, and strode desperately across the room to stand in front of Hamilton. She snapped her fingers under his nose. "James! Goddammit, take charge. We've got to do something. James!" Not even a nerve twitched in James's handsome jaw. Esmé slapped him across the face—hard. She'd seen people do that in the movies. It was supposed to rouse a person from shock, wasn't it? James must be in temporary shock. What the hell else could be wrong with him?

Hamilton's golden head snapped sideways and then slowly came back to the same position. "What?"

Thank God! He was talking again. "What?" Esmé asked, dumbfounded. He was talking again, but was that all he had to say? "Jesus Christ! What the hell is the matter with you?"

"Matter with me?" he repeated.

Esmé was now faced with the same thing James had just experienced, something unexpected and unthinkable. James Hamilton, her source of power and unlimited ambition, was gone, a washout. Temporary shock or not, Esmé was left, when she needed the guy most, when he needed himself most, with a shell. A beautiful shell, she now suspected with dismay, that just might be, probably was, the whole man. In an emergency, granted it was a humdinger of an emergency, James was proving himself nothing. And it was his problem. He'd dreamed it up; the whole thing was for him. If this had been Leo Olemi she was standing in front of, she wouldn't be standing there at all; Leo would have taken care of everything without pausing to draw breath. Whatever had to be done, would already be doing; even Eddie Baker was up to more than this. But it wasn't Eddie and it wasn't Leo, was it? It was the lately gorgeous district attorney of San Francisco, the basket Esmé'd thought of putting all her eggs into, and nothing was being done at all. She remembered the way James had handled that other guy in Half Moon Bay, Edward somebody or another, and had an unpleasant revelation. So fine, James was a terrific bully. But just like any other bully, he collapsed when the worm turned.

Oh, Esmé. You bought a ticket on the big ride. And like all the other damn rides you've ever ridden, it just went round and round and round. What are you going to do now?

There was only one answer to that. Sweet and fragile Esmé Baker was going to have to get them all out of this mess herself. And, though tempted like sin, she couldn't do the obvious, what anyone in their right mind would do—namely, run for it, leaving James to take the shit that was surely coming, because, aside from feeling a small amount of remaining loyalty, what good would that do? The jibbering Carol and even the cooler Lupe wouldn't keep their mouths shut. Not for this. And why should they? They'd be pointing fingers faster than kids in baseball caps around a broken window. No, they were all in for it. This was the goddam President, not one of Eddie's dumber moves. Esmé had no intention of standing around until the law came. She was getting out of this. But how? What would Leo do? Whatever it was, Esmé had to drop her helpless act. Men! At thirty-one, Esmé was beginning to wonder if she needed them.

"Lupe!"

The Mexican looked up at Esmé, happy to have somebody say something, do something. Nobody had paid her for this. The picture should have been taken, they said nobody would ever see it besides the man they were paying her to pose with, the dead man should be alive and putting on his clothes by now—everybody should be going, it was time it was all over. And the sniveling Carol could hustle her fat gringo ass back into her own room. Lupe was getting sick of her whining. "What we do, lady?"

"What can we do on our own? Go get Rose St. Lorraine. We're stuck without her. This is her place, she knows the ins and outs here—she'll want to help, she'll *have* to."

Lupe smiled. The lady with the red hair was right. That was the answer. Rose! Rose would take care of everything. Of course, she'd be mad at Lupe for taking money without sharing, but Rose was a good woman, she forgive. "You said it! I bring double quick."

Naked, Lupe scampered out of the room, leaving Carol curled up by the body of Harding—a body already growing cold. The hot little pink whore, squeezing her eyes tight, noisily sucked her thumb.

Without thinking about why, Esmé moved as far away from James as she could get. It was a natural reaction; it felt right. If James noticed, he made no response. But Esmé was getting the picture. She was on her own here.

Li Kwan Won got there before Rose St. Lorraine. It was a full two minutes before he was joined by Rose; he had time to take in Esmé and the camera, James slumped in a chair, and the scene on the bed.

In that two minutes Li got the picture as well. It wasn't as complete as Esmé's, but it was a fairly colorful picture anyway. There was no answer here to "why?"— Li knew nothing about Doheny and Hamilton's involvement in the purchase of government oil leases—but "how" was simple enough. So this sordid little mess was what James had in mind for the President? Hamilton disappointed him. Li, with only hints from a babbling Commissioner Bent, had imagined something more devious, more *creative,* from Lizzie's husband. Once again an enemy proved as hollow as a paper dragon's head, and "what begins with a dragon's head often ended with a snake's tail."

"Mrs. Baker. Mr. Hamilton." Li bowed politely, then took out his cigarette case, snapped it open, and held it out to Esmé. "Perhaps you would like one? I am told that Mr. Hamilton does not smoke."

"Thank you." Esmé took one of Li's cigarettes; she also took the light he offered. From the depths of his chair, James found energy enough to scowl at Esmé's smoking, though he ignored Li. Esmé exhaled in his direction.

None of this was lost on Li. Not the line of Hamilton's neck and shoulders, the dimness of his eyes, or the spirit in the eyes of his redheaded woman. This was James Hamilton's mistress. For her courage alone, Li could find something to admire in the district attorney.

Hamilton had posed him a very pretty problem. The sudden death of America's President Harding in the Blue Canary—Li's Blue Canary—was a very interesting, not to say rare, problem. No time now for finding out why the President was here, though the manner of his death was obvious enough. It was also funny in a macabre kind of way, but there was no time for laughter either. It was also obvious that the district attorney, for whatever reasons, had made a few fatal miscalculations. Hamilton's business of course, but, though his, it would not look good for Li or Rose's business happening where it did, or as it did. Therefore, Li concluded cleanly and quickly, it would not happen that way but some other, a way that would leave all concerned happier than they were at the moment. Except, of course, for the unfortunately dead head of state. Still, wherever he was now, the President would no doubt be grateful to have his death arranged in more fitting a fashion.

Li smiled to himself. Even James would leave with some content—because there was also no time for too much detail. Those responsible for original causes would have to wait for justice. Li had little enough time to sort things out for Rose and himself without worrying about fair play. The concept of what was just could not concern him; justice was a word that many used and few recognized. But then, as Wong Gow might say, "Perhaps being James Hamilton was justice enough."

Li had just bent his busy head to light his own cigarette when a half-dressed Rose came bustling in, followed by a breathless Addy Chase, O Ti, two more of Li's men, Chi Mai, and Lupe—now wearing one of Rose's kimonos. Rose stopped short at the door, putting her hand to her mouth to stifle a scream, but Addy kept on coming. He went directly to the President's side, took the stiffening wrist, and tried for a pulse.

"He's dead," said Addy.

Esmé let out a short dry laugh. "Who's this, the house doctor? Tell us something we don't know."

Addy colored. "What you don't know, young lady, is how much trouble you're in."

Rose, recovering her usual poise, kept unusually quiet. Whatever needed saying or doing, Li would say or do. With pride in her "son," she stayed out of the way. Li held out his hand for peace. "Oh, yes, Addy, the lady knows exactly how much trouble she's in."

The tone in his voice made Esmé look closely at Li. Whose side was he on? She couldn't tell. But she could tell that around here whatever this man said went. His was evidently the last word. He was also a Chink. Esmé was used to foreigners, though where she was raised, nothing was really foreign. Jews, blacks, Italians, Spanish, every northern race that Europe had ever thrown up, Orientals—as a kid on New York's Lower East Side, she'd played with them all. As a woman, she played with them still; the games were the same, only serious. Grown-up games were for survival. Esmé, smoking Li's cigarette, thought that under certain interesting circumstances she could like this tall stylish Chinese—she could like him a lot. Then she caught sight of the tiny and delicate Chi Mai. The girl had skin like an eggshell and eyes that saw as much as Esmé herself saw. Well, there went that idea.

Shock shortening his long face, Addy suddenly noticed James.

"Hamilton! What are you doing here? What's Warren doing here? Is this your fault, man?"

Carol started sniveling again.

"Never mind, Addy," said Li. "We can work the truth out later; now we must change it. This is not what America would like to think of her President. We shall give them a truth they can believe. It will also give us a chance, like historians and poets and politicians, to be very creative." Li turned and snapped his fingers for Blue

Flag. O Ti quickly stepped forward. Esmé was impressed. Even Leo's men never moved that fast. "I cannot leave this matter in lesser hands, Lan-ch'i. *You* must get a car ready and back it up to the delivery door—a closed car; the gray Dodge will do. And O Ti?"

The big man jerked his head forward in a quick bow. *"Ho?"*

"This does not change this night's 'washing of faces.' *Faai-dee!"*

*"Ho la!"* O Ti left the crowded room on the run.

"Chi Mai, keep that girl quiet—"

By "that girl," Esmé knew the Chinese meant Carol. Before Chi Mai could obey, Esmé sat herself next to the naked little blue-eyed whore and held her hand; she wasn't gentle. She kept her hold on Carol while her eyes stayed on Li, fascinated. When a girl makes a mistake, she makes a whopper. She had chosen James, that was Esmé's mistake, but this man, this Chinese man, was Lizzie Hamilton's mistake. Or was it? Hell, it was the kind of mistake Esmé wished she'd made. James was huddled down in his chair only a few feet away. There were signs that he was making a comeback; the blue light in his eyes had a hardening glint, the thin graceful hands gripped the arms of the chair, the cleft in the jaw was beginning to jut. As far as Esmé was concerned, he might as well have been on the moon.

Evidently, Li felt the same; he turned his back on James, hardly pausing as he laid out his plans. "The President has had a heart attack; he could have had it anywhere. Does anyone know if his people are aware he's gone?"

Addy answered. "No. Warren managed to get out without the Secret Service's noticing. I knew James intended something, but I had no idea it would go to this—"

"That's fine, Addy." Li smiled at the distressed Chase. "You are not the one to blame here. And now we shall do what the President did in reverse: get him back without anyone noticing. His hotel? Which one?" Now, and for the first time, Li addressed James directly. "Which one, Hamilton? A contribution, please."

Brought back to his senses by rage, James half rose from his chair.

"Palace, top floor." The answer came from Esmé, not James.

Glaring at her, James sat back down.

"He will go back then to the Palace, and he will die there. In his own bed. You two!"

In unison, the two 49 members said, *"Ho!"*

"Dress him, put his hat down over his face, and between you support him down the back stairs. You understand? He is just another drunk. It is not unusual. O Ti will be waiting; he will drive all of you to the Palace Hotel. And you!"

Esmé, sitting upright, felt like shouting *Ho!*—whatever that meant—but this time Li was talking to James. Hamilton's icy blue eyes were finally focused. And Esmé hated what she saw in them: petulance, spite, resentment—small things, mean things, shining with a petty light. Small? Esmé shivered. No, please God, no more small men. James had sat up again; raising his golden head, he looked straight at Li. The Chinese brushed away the loathing like a man brushes away lint.

"You, Mr. Hamilton, will have to get the body back to its rooms. However you do that is your problem—being Chinese, my men won't be allowed in the lobby, front or back. Once O Ti delivers the President to the hotel, I wash my hands of what you have done here."

Following Li's succinct orders, or getting out of the way, everyone in the room except James started moving. Rose picked up the President's clothes, helping the two 49s to dress him. Addy arranged his hat. Chi Mai moved close to Li. And Esmé let go of Carol and stood up, intending to help the two Chinese down the back stairs with their burden of dead weight. Li stopped her before she got past the end of the bed.

"I'll take the camera, Mrs. Baker. Mr. Hamilton won't need that photograph now, will he."

Slowly, like an unintended strip, Esmé slipped the camera from around her neck, her brown eyes fixed on Li's, and handed it to him.

"No," she whispered, "he won't."

Li accepted the bulky camera, removed the film, and held it to the light. Then he smiled at the redheaded woman in the cunning black hat and the black beaded dress, her fox face framed in glossy black feathers, and, like Lizzie, Esmé died a little. She pulled down her spidery veil.

Downstairs the Blue Canary, oblivious, was smarting with the slap of jazz. The King Oliver Creole Jazz Band played Kit Dowie's "China Blues." Joe Oliver, sweat beading his round black head, black cheeks swollen with effort, made the air crack with a cornet solo so long and so loud the people at the jammed tables were standing; excited white faces leaned forward into the weighted notes. Dido, taller and blacker and infinitely more beautiful, was propped on the piano just behind Joe. Dido, her silvered eyes closed, the muscles of her slim arms and flat stomach taut, waiting for the break into lyrics, was going where the music took her, a very private place that everyone in the Canary could see. Dido went where they all wanted to go, somewhere hot and rapturous, where poverty and the cold and killing white eyes could never reach her.

Ike mixed his lethal brews with both hands; Harry and four other barmen couldn't pop bottles fast enough for the demand. Fearless O'Flooty, his front teeth firmly in place, laughing like an idiot, was lunging across the bar taking his own, and Hammett, quiet but for the eternal coughing, shared the booty. Waiters and cigarette girls, busboys and flower sellers, worked the floor with the precision of Henry Ford's production line. Above them, Rose and Li's gaming tables were taking people's money away as fast as they could lay it down, and in private rooms the Blue Canary's girls were taking breath away as well as money. The place was hot.

But Kit Dowie wasn't going with it. A little into "China Blues" he'd picked up a saxophone, leaving Lil Hardin the piano, and was doodling around with it, hitting all the right notes but with the wrong feel. His conscious mind, the niggling irritating part, was focused on James Hamilton and Warren Harding.

It was getting close to an hour since the DA and the President had gone upstairs. Kit knew why the President went, his reputation with the press as a poker player and ladies' man was no secret, but why with Esmé? And why had James gone up a few minutes later? What the heck was the DA up to? Kit had one more item to add to all this mystery—it was after twelve. Where was Rose St. Lorraine? Rose never missed her midnight entrance. It was one of the Blue Canary's attractions. Rose's odd and worrying absence did it; Kit couldn't sit still a second longer. The musician in him wanted to play, but the newsman wanted to snoop, wanted Kit to get up off his ass and find out what was up. The reporter won. He'd made up his mind; he was going upstairs and answer some questions. The hell with the President's privacy. Just as Louis Armstrong stepped forward to introduce Dido, Kit put the sax down and stood up. And almost fell over.

Good God! Of all the people in San Francisco, what was Lizzie Stafford doing here?

Coming in past Pete the doorman, Lizzie was working her way through the intoxicated crowd with a couple of huge suitcases. She also appeared to be wearing more than one dress and, even though it was midsummer, the first—no, by now it was the second—of August, a full-length sable coat. Kit pulled himself together and regained his balance. Now what?

Lizzie saw Kit a second after he saw her and waved, dropping her suitcases. He started to smile back—until the crooked grin on his dark face froze. Behind Lizzie, the main doors of the Blue Canary crashed open, followed by Pete, face drained of color and a bloody bloom of red spreading across his starched white chest. Following Pete came Murray Blinn. Kit had the presence of mind to register Blinn's lime-green plaid jacket with a mustard yellow handkerchief in the top pocket, a dopey-eyed brindle bulldog waddling at Murray's feet, and a Thompson submachine gun in his hands. The details of the rest of the gun-carrying mob were lost to him, except one; there were a lot of them and they weren't just carrying tommy guns, they were intent on shooting people with them.

"Lizzie! Watch out!" Sleek heads everywhere turned toward the stage. Kit dived off the edge, pushing through the astonished crowd, and made a flying tackle for the equally astonished Lizzie, bringing her down in a welter of glass and crockery, lit candles, and dark sable fur.

King Oliver stopped dead in the key of E, his good eye telling him all he needed to know; Chicago taught strong lessons. Moving his fat with balletic ease, he reached down, snapped open his cornet case, and found his pistol, and Dido, hearing Kit yell, looked up over the footlights to see what he saw and saw enough to make her heart leap into her mouth. Dido pushed Louis behind Baby Dodds's drum kit, sweeping Lil Hardin with him. Baby Dodds was already there, lying on his top hat. The only thought Dido had time for was the worst thought she'd ever had in a lifetime of breathing mean air. Kit Dowie's first move was for Lizzie. Lizzie! Who'd never done anything for him in her whole life—not even when Dido went to her on her knees, begging. For one terrible moment, Dido fought the urge to stand up tall and welcome the howling bullets. For some reason, she didn't.

"God, life gets a grip," she whispered to no one; no one could hear her over the white devil dealing out sudden arbitrary cards over her head. Instead, she hitched up her silver skirt, jumped over the footlights off the stage, and crashed into the fray. Because the oyster-eyed lunatic was the only one laughing, Dido had singled out Miles Brady.

Appetite Ike was angry. He recognized the Mex, Coffee Trujillo, and his pals, Jugs Kelly, Joe Baglietto, and Miles Brady. Back, were they? He watched as his precious bottles exploded like a string of firecrackers, all coming in his direction, one bottle after the other, all spraying the shining bar with biting booze. Ducking, Ike made a quick grab at the end of the line, got hold of a last bottle, and, gripping it by the neck, marched out from behind his curving counter, swearing and limping and squinting.

Harry, peeking over the bar top, shouted, "Ike! Get

back here, you old fool!" then ducked back down as
Miles Brady swung his tommy gun around, aiming for
Harry's head. Fearless O'Flooty, who'd thrown himself
flat at the first burst of fire, was crouching down in front
of the bar with Hammett. He reached for Ike's gimpy leg
to trip the idiot up, but missed.

Ike swung his bottle over his head. "Mr. Brady, look
what you done to my bar!"

Miles turned his attention from Harry, saw Ike, and
laughed. Then casually, like an afterthought, he blasted
the old man in the stomach. Ike went down as he lived—
honest as hell and just as angry. And Miles, still laughing, stepped over the body. Dido, black and shining, leapt
on his back, dug her long red nails into his eyes, and
squeezed.

Upstairs, in Lupe's room, everything changed. With
change, brought by the deafening racket coming up from
below, a racket no one needed explaining, came individual response. James Hamilton, having finally begun to
move, moved fast. He simply ran out of the room, heading for the back staircase, leaving Li and Esmé and Harding to fend for themselves. Watching him go, Esmé
shrugged in disgust. He no longer surprised her. Then
she shooed along Li's men, propping Harding's body between them; they'd both stopped and were hesitating at
the carnage they heard below.

"Go! Keep moving!" she urged.

At a nod from Li, they obeyed her. Esmé went with
them.

Lupe jumped into bed beside Carol and covered
them both up, but Rose and Addy, Chi Mai, and Li
headed for the most noise.

"No!" shouted Li. "You three stay here." None of
them listened. But Li, running ahead, didn't know that
until they all got to the top of the stairs at the same time
and bunched up behind him, staring down at the pande-
monium. Li had left his plan too late. Wong Gow was
right. This enemy was not hollow.

Blinn and his boys, finished with shooting up the
first floor of the Blue Canary, were at the bottom of the

same staircase that Li was coming down. The whole place was frantic with vivid confusion, people screaming, thrashing to get out; on the stage the Dodds brothers were holding down Joe Oliver's arms to keep him from popping off crazed and random pistol shots.

Looking up, Murray's little eyes glittered. There was that bitch, Rose St. Lorraine. And holy shit! If it wasn't the Chink too, right at the top of the stairs. Like sitting ducks, like bull's eyes, like dopes, like the answer to all his troubles. Ma was right. Saddle Mary knew her stuff. This was the way to do things. Shoot 'em all, do the job right, show 'em Murray Blinn was here. Blinn felt the sweet spirit of Capone in his blood. Stepping past the slobbering Tommy, he raised his gun.

Behind him, held down by Kit, Lizzie struggled to rise. She was up on her bruised hands, pulling away, as Fearless O'Flooty, blood on his mustache and a fearful pain in his blue eyes, crawled toward Kit. Distracted by the wounded Fearless, Kit loosened his grip on her waist, and Lizzie wriggled free. She got to her feet just in time to see Rose St. Lorraine and Addy Chase, Chi Mai and Li Kwan Won—and Li? Oh, God, no!—go down in a red rain of bullets.

"Please!" Lizzie screamed, the sound of her own torment drowning out the hideous thump of a body as it hit the silver dance floor, falling twenty feet from the top of the Blue Canary's shattered stairs.

# Chapter 28

The Blue Canary was as active at eight in the morning as it had been at midnight. Down on the main floor, chorus girls, the High Steppers dance team, the King Oliver Creole Jazz Band, Fearless O'Flooty, and Dashiell Hammett, all still awake and still shocked, drank themselves electric on coffee. Fearless, a blood-caked furrow over his left eye, had a newly acquired pair of crutches and one bandaged leg. Hammett was untouched. Carpenters were ripping out the long curved bullet-shattered bar. Behind it Harry, bent with shock, was counting bottles, and cleaners mopped up the puddled blood.

Hammett was trembling with creative inspiration. "This is my next story, Fearless! Gunmen from all over the country come to San Francisco to knock over a big job! I'll put this town on the criminal map!"

Fearless hadn't stopped talking since he'd picked himself up from the floor. He swung up one of his crutches and hopped on his good leg. "It's a question of life," he was saying as Hammett wrote himself notes on a cocktail napkin. "It has a way of springing at you, hungry for blood. Writers can only offer violent shadows."

Hammett, caught in a great short story, wasn't listening.

Up in her room, a few doors down from Rose and Addy, only Dido slept. Red drapes drawn, black satin sheets over her cropped black head, drugged on laudanum—it was the only way Dido knew to stop the mad film in her mind: Kit Dowie leapt off the stage over and over, dodging silver bullets, running for Lizzie. Away from Dido.

Li Kwan Won was in his office making phone calls. Lying silent on the couch by the closed door, Lizzie Stafford, her suitcases stacked neatly beside the wall, using her sable as a blanket, was watching everything Li did. She was on her third cup of coffee and her fifth aspirin tablet. She knew Li so much better now. Upstairs Rose was in tears, her blond hair ringleted by her twisting unhappy fingers; out on the Canary's silver floor, every light in the house up full, everyone was shouting across everyone else in short harsh sentences, staccato with the discovery that words changed nothing—everyone except Hammett. But here in Li's office, there was nothing to say.

To Li, death was life. And life a quick step toward death. He was arranging funerals. What little talking aside from business he had done had been to Lizzie. And that only after she'd helped Rose St. Lorraine pull him away from the body of Chi Mai. But all he'd said was, "Surviving is worse than death."

Lizzie had never seen death before. Three years before this clammering summer, Charles Mortimer and Mary Maud had lain bloodless in their coffins, sedate and waxen. That wasn't death. It wasn't life either. It was nothing. Death was Chi Mai, broken and bent, the back of her head shattered on the silver floor and the dead face perfect. The long black hair still pulled back in a chignon, baby-fine strands loose on the hairline; Chi Mai hadn't lived to see age line her skin or time mark her brow. The pretty pink mouth, the closed eyes, lids a sweet blue were all too beautiful, too cold to touch.

Death was the blood on Lizzie's shoes, the pool of thick red that closed after her footprints, the great smear of crimson, like an obscene ink blot, that had followed Ike's body as he slid down the bar—death was the quiet that came with the last swinging of the Blue Canary's doors as the men with the tommy guns left, laughing. Life was the inrush of breath and the bedlam that erupted after that. Life was Kit Dowie picking himself off the floor, sweeping his dark eyes over what had become of the Blue Canary in less than five minutes, pausing for a second on Lizzie's escape to Li, and then turning his back —to take out his note pad.

For little Chi Mai, there were no dying words, no gentle cradling as she breathed her last. Things like this didn't happen in *Harper's* or *Vogue*. It was not a lovely still life of literate anguish and romantic loss. It was messy. It was babble and chaos. It left the living with unseen wounds and a hideous mute fear. Death was just as Li had described it that night he told Lizzie of killing the *baak gwai lo:* the flame and the music were gone. Chi Mai was gone. The old man, Appetite Ike, was gone. Pete the doorman was gone. Gone where? Was there somewhere to go? They had each left a void and Lizzie had tears for them all. But what good were tears? They soothed the living.

Now, hours later, as she lay silent on the couch, listening to Li make his calls, Lizzie could not cry. She was tired. Her makeup made smudged black thumbprints under her green eyes; her hair, uncombed, tangled around her head. Lizzie trembled from shock, the tips of her fingers were numb, the nails hurt—and the tender skin under her thumb-printed eyes jumped with fatigue. Death had come calling, and after such dying, who was truly alive?

Was Li? A man from a forbidden race, half in love with death. His skin, the color of pale opium, the slight hint of beard on his smooth face shadowing the strong chin and full lips, the sweet little upcurve at their corners vanished, the fold on the upper lid of each eye more defined, more foreign than she remembered. Lizzie Stafford shuddered under her sable. She was seeing Li. All night while Rose cried and Addy Chase devoted himself to her pain, all night while people shouted and cursed, the red tide of shocked horror washing through the Blue Canary, all night while people attended to themselves, Li took care of them all. It was Li who calmed, who made order of the chaos, who told people what to do—frightened people needing to be told, people with vacant eyes holding on to Li as they would to a raft in a flood. He brought them all home again after a night of blood and fear and echoes of the dead. But who took care of Li?

Seeing him, perhaps for once Lizzie could touch him. He was alone; Li was as lonely and as lost as she was.

Pushing off the sable, Lizzie left the couch and crossed the room.

"Li?"

Li Kwan Won's dark head came up; he put the phone down and looked at Lizzie. The blood sang in her veins. He was there. In his eyes, Li was there for her. She could help him. Lizzie would take care of Li.

"Ike was an old man," he said, pressing his head into her belly, still sitting as Lizzie stood, his arms tight around her waist. "He had done many things—his death was honorable. But Chi Mai? She followed, used herself as a shield for me. I had time. Why didn't I stop her?"

"You couldn't stop her. She loved you."

Li pushed Lizzie away and looked up into her tired eyes. "You knew that?"

"Yes, Li, I knew that." Lizzie knelt down and put her head on his shoulder. "And you loved her too, didn't you?"

"Yes."

"She loved you and I hurt her."

"Yes."

"God, I'm so sorry."

"We are both to blame."

"We hurt her, Li, but we didn't kill her. Chi Mai knew what she was doing. You told me once, remember? Life is like a spring dream, dying like going home. I have no excuse. I loved you. I still love you."

"You are right, there is no blame. The student

teaches the doubting master." Li cupped Lizzie's strong chin in his hand, tilted it up, and kissed her. There was laughter somewhere deep in his eyes. "Life is like a dance of shadows. The body like a mask. Surely, it can only be by dying that one sees through the shadowed dance where death shines with a fierce white light." Li stood, and as he rose he gently lifted Lizzie with him. "I have sickened of this world I have created. Come with me, Lizzie. We will begin again. And first, we'll go tell Rose what I've decided to do."

Murray Blinn got out of bed at dawn. This day, waking was a keen pleasure. This day was Murray Blinn's day. Today he was sure to make the front pages of every newspaper in town. Leo Olemi would contact *him* for a change. In his narrow single bed, Murray stretched with pleasure and remembered what he'd gone to bed in —everything except the shoes: plaid lime-green jacket, blue slacks, lime-green socks, sock suspenders, shirt, tie. Cautiously, Murray felt around in the bed. Well, the tommy gun wasn't in here with him anyway.

In the room next to his, his mother was snoring like a singing saw. Slipping Moroccan slippers over his virulent socks, Murray padded to their connecting door and gently shut it. The old girl needed what she called her "beauty rest"; let her sleep. After all, she'd been up until four in the morning with Murray and the boys—all, that is, but Miles, who was in the back office of Leo's pet doctor getting his eyes seen to—reliving with them the triumph at the Blue Canary.

"You sure you got Rose? You sure?" she kept interrupting their story to ask.

And Murray kept answering, "We got her, Ma. We got 'em all. The way things were, how could we miss?"

Now it was past first light. The first thing Murray usually did when he got up was to pomade and comb his yellow hair; this morning the first thing he did was stand at his filthy window and look down on North Beach. You never knew: maybe his work at the Canary merited a special edition. Murray had to spit on the windowpane and then wipe it with the linen sleeve of his lime-green jacket to see more than a smear of dawn-gray street below. Nothing doing down on Grant Avenue. The little newsstand in front of the Italian Sports Club—boccie ball was about as sporting as the club ever got—huddled, small and still and silent, in the last of the morning fog. Murray put his hands in his pockets and rocked back and forth on his Moroccan heels: the first editions wouldn't be off the press and on the city streets for an hour or so.

Murray spent that anxious hour making a pot of coffee and drinking the whole thing black. And chain-smoking. His bulldog, Tommy, asleep under the table, guttered, soft hairy lips flapping, competing with Saddle Mary for volume.

Until—ah! Patience and an early rising were rewarded. Murray heard the sound of Carlo, the rheumatic guy with the North Beach newsstand, slamming open his wooden shutters. And the thud of heavy paper bundles as a delivery van dumped Thursday's news on the shivering sidewalk.

With carbonated veins, Murray pattered down from the top floor, his slippers slapping on the soles of his lime-green feet, and out onto his own front stoop.

"Hey, Carlo! It's Murray. Which one you got, the *Examiner?* So, great, gimme three."

Murray, clutching his precious papers, galloped back up all those stairs, giving himself a stitch. Catching his breath, rubbing his side, he threw the papers on the table. They came down right side up. Some trick of his sight made the headlines not black but red. They jumped at him. BLOODBATH IN FAMOUS NIGHTCLUB! MANY WOUNDED! FIVE DEAD! And just underneath, in smaller type but still huge, *On the Spot Report by Kit Dowie.*

Murray did a little dance of glee. He'd done it! The front page! The *whole* front page! And more on the second and third. Murray couldn't sit; using his index finger to keep his place, he read every word standing up.

Ten minutes later, the veins in his neck stretched like piano wire, he screeched "Ma!" and, snatching the papers, darted into Mary's room like a kid who'd just seen the bogeyman. He pounded on her heavy shoulder. Saddle Mary felt like a dead sponge, and the rank smell of fresh booze and stale dentures in her dark airless room hit him between the eyes. Murray gulped at the dirty air. "Wake up, Ma!"

Mary opened an early eye, fish-gray and furious. "Wha . . . ?"

"Read this!" Murray thrust the papers at her. "We got big problems. And it's your fault, you told me to do it."

"What the hell are you blithering about?" Saddle Mary squinted at the screaming newsprint a foot in front of her face, ran her dry tongue over what was left of her dry teeth, and woke up fast. She pulled herself upright and grinned.

"Front page, huh? Well, it's just like I said, ain't it?"

Murray jabbed at the flimsy paper with a forefinger stained with newsprint. "Oh, yeah, Ma, it's the front page all right. But go ahead, read the small stuff. Where's Rose St. Lorraine? And the head Chink? We got a seventeen-year-old Chink girl, an eighty-year-old bartender, one grifter of a chorus girl, one customer, and the damn door-man. And that ain't all! They're sayin' I'm crazy. They're callin' me a madman, a kid killer. Read it!"

"I'm tryin' to." Saddle Mary was still patient. Experience with Murray told her things were never that bad; he was an excitable, sensitive boy, that's all.

The sensitive boy was wiping his dripping nose with his fingers. "And the worst thing, the fucking worst thing, is that the frigging police commissioner was there. Upstairs somewhere. Christ, Ma, what was Bent doing there? You know what it means, don't you? It means that now to save his face, he's got to make up some damn story, and he'll go after my ass when he does it. Bent is supposed to protect me, that's what Leo pays him for, but now! They're screaming for fast action, and this reporter, this Dowie, is naming me, our address, most of the names of my boys, descriptions of 'em, everything—eyewitness stuff—saying I oughta get shot down like a dog." Murray looked puzzled and hurt, his pasted yellow hair clamped to his skull. "Me!"

From under her covers, Mary kicked him.

"Shut up an' get out. Let your ma get dressed, have

her some coffee, an' then we talk this over calm. Go on, scram—an' don't forget to put the coffee on."

There was a sudden hubbub down in the street. Noise was nothing in North Beach; it was a loud neighborhood. But noise accompanied by mourning sirens, screeching brakes, and the squeal of windows opening up and down the block *was* something. Like everyone else, Murray pulled up his window and stuck his head out. Clutching her tatty robe around her tired bulk, Mary followed him.

"What's up?"

"Can't tell, Ma. Hey, Carlo! What's all the rumpus for?"

The man with the newsstand, just taking delivery of another enormous stack of papers, looked up. "President of the United States, he dropped dead! Got a special edition here."

"Oh."

Murray pulled his head in and shut the window. "It's nothing. The President kicked it, is all."

"What?" Saddle Mary pushed him out of the way, yanked open the window again, and stuck her own head out. Grant Avenue was running with people. They were grabbing at Carlo's papers before he could get the heavy twine half off the bundles. "Carlo! Yoo hoo! Hold up the front page!" she hollered. The headline was large enough for Mary to read three stories up. "Thanks, sweetie, that's swell of you."

Mary's greasy gray head came back in the window, and when it did her worn face was pink with one big smile.

"Murray, think of it! President Harding died in Frisco!"

Murray Blinn stared at the woman like she'd dropped something on his foot. "So what? Who cares? It's me who's got the problems."

Mary slapped him. It was a friendly little slap, but it turned his cheek plum-red before her hand was clear. "Don't you get it, you moron? Now, the President dyin' right here in town, *that's* news. You go on down an' get yourself a paper now, read the headlines. You was a one-edition wonder, boy. You say you got problems? The President's wiped your problems off the front page for good. By the time this town gets over Harding dyin' on their doorstep, they're gonna forget about you, seventeen-year-old Chink an' all."

Dawn came twice for Murray.

"Of course! You're right! Say, Ma, that's great!"

Rose St. Lorraine couldn't breathe for all the flowers. An hour after Murray and Mary finished another pot of coffee, Rose was lying in bed above the Blue Canary. She was fine, just a few bruises from Addy's falling on her. Addy, meantime, was in bed beside her, his arm in a hardening cast; he'd taken a clean bullet through his left shoulder. Rose had been crying. She hadn't slept once since Murray's visit. It had been the most jam-packed night of her eventful life. The confusion, the police, ambulances, the press had gone on until dawn. The last body they took away was Appetite Ike's.

When the early papers hit the streets of San Francisco, the people started coming. And the phone started ringing. Calls came in from all over the state: Ninx, owing everything she knew to Rose, doing good business down in Los Angeles; old Klondike miners in luck or out, scattered over the northwest; Aimee Semple McPherson phoning direct from her new Angelus Temple, in her excitement mixing the outright profane with a brief nod to God—with her old friend Rose, Aimee didn't bother too much with her God game. Even when the news of Harding spread like blue fire over spilt gasoline, the phone kept ringing and the people kept coming. In ones and twos, in little groups, staying for a few minutes, crying with Rose over Ike. The Blue Canary was a San Francisco monument. Everyone knew and loved Rose or at least had heard of her. Sam Jenkins, Mayor Sunny Jim, the Pacific Union Club boys, Giannini and Fleishhacker, customers from throughout the years, acts in town that had played her stage. It was mayhem. And over the protests of Addy, Rose let them all come. It was better than thinking about Chi Mai. Better than crying over Ike all alone.

"Li!" Rose St. Lorraine held out her rounded arms as Li and Lizzie entered her white room. Spike swung in her yellow feathered sleeve. "Rose needs you."

Lizzie was shocked at Rose's appearance; if she could have seen herself, the shock would have been greater. Age hadn't taken Rose down an inch, but grief had. The loss of Ike put lines in her skin, took color from her golden hair, gave gravity a hold on her face. Rose was fighting, but it was an uneven contest. The dark blue eyes looked lost.

"What am I going to do without Ike, Li? That old fart was all I had."

Addy Chase looked at Rose, his brown eyes full of hurt surprise. "All you had? You have me, Rose."

Rose patted the good right arm that held her. "Oh, sure, of course, sugar. I've got you. And hell, you've got me. But without Ike, I'm not as much as I was."

"You're as much as you ever were."

"And you, Addy Chase, are a damned fool. I got a big piece chipped off me last night, and it hurts so bad, I feel like jelly inside. Nothing ever made me feel so bad before." Though she'd cried all night, Rose still had tears. Sergeant Huggins, curled in a big white hairy ball at her feet, howled along.

Though Rose wore a canary yellow negligee, Addy Chase was fully dressed. In a morning coat, striped trousers, and highly polished black button shoes, he lay beside Rose slim as a straw, his elegance intact. Even propped up by pillows in Rose's absurd Egyptian bed, his arm in a cast, he was taller than Rose, taller than the headboard, and as gallant as ever. Addy took life as it came, and he took Rose in the same way.

"I'll take whatever's left, sweetheart."

Rose buried her face in his steady shoulder. "Oh, Addy!" She cried until she laughed. "Oh, hell, I just remembered Bent! Coming out when it was all over, his pants halfway to his knees, blinking like an owl, saying, 'What's happening?' And Harding! Does Lizzie know about the President yet?"

Lizzie, who'd seated herself on Rose's white velvet

chaise longue, nodded. "Li told me this morning. What happened to James?"

"Who knows, honey? He slunk off fast when the shooting started."

"The man is a cad," said Addy, wincing with pain. Rose laughing hurt more than Rose crying.

Rose patted the bed beside her. "Come sit here with me, Li."

In silence Li sat, waiting for Rose to wind down.

Rose wasn't ready to be quiet yet. Her pain wouldn't let her. "And his little redhead seeing it plain. And still taking control, pulling his fat out of the fire. She did it, too. Harding dying in his own bed! The papers are saying he died of apoplexy. Now I wonder how that little redhead got Mrs. Harding to agree to that?"

Addy tried to scratch under his new cast. "Shouldn't think it was too hard, Rose. What else could the woman say? That her husband died in a back room at the Blue Canary with not one but two ladies of the evening for company? Think of the press on that."

"As Appetite always said, sheee-it!" Rose hooted. "Hot damn, I'd love to hear what the redhead has to say to James Hamilton this morning. What a night! What a scorcher of a night! Can't remember anything like it since the quake!"

Li, finding himself next to Sergeant Huggins, stroked the dog's huge head. Sergeant Huggins stopped howling and licked his hand.

"Listen to me, Rose," he began when Rose showed signs of slowing up, "we have things to do."

Addy, who had always felt it was his business not to know too much of Li's and Rose's, struggled to rise. "If you two are going to talk about—"

"No, Addy, stay," said Li. "I want you to listen. This night has taught me many things. I could foresee much, but I could not foresee this—not Ike and Chi Mai. I knew that our visitors would be back and that they would bring friends. But I didn't know what it would really mean. I am at fault. I should have known. Wong Gow warned me—in my conceit, I thought he meant me. Because I believed that, I waited too long. What I have caused to be done this morning, should have been done before now. My pride kept us unprepared. So now I must do more."

Rose, quietly hiccuping, blew her nose with a lace hanky. Spike complained, and she scratched his chin. "What more, honey?" She knew Li longer and better than Lizzie did. There was no point in arguing with him. Of course it wasn't Li's fault. That was Chinese thinking. But Li was Chinese.

"We are changing our business. We will reopen the Blue Canary. But no more bootlegging, no girls; the Snap Dragon will change, make mah-jongg, cigars, who knows? Who cares? We will use the money we have made to buy more land, add to what we already own. The *baak gwai lo* sell paper to each other, more and more each day, the stock market is a pyramid of paper that will blow away in the wind that is coming, leaving it as the miners and the timbermen left the mountains—dry and bare. But we will keep the real gold, the land itself. San Francisco needs to expand, and there is nowhere for her to go but south."

"But Li," said Rose, "south is only sand."

"Then they will build on sand, *our* sand. And here in Chinatown we will create another nightclub, a Chinese nightclub. I shall call it the Chinese Rose."

Addy listened to Li with a growing joy—no bootlegging, no more girls! Aside from his twenty-year obsession to marry her, it was all he wanted for Rose. "What do you think, sweetheart?"

Rose sneezed. "What do I think? What will be different, Addy? What are we going to do with all that money? So there's no girls. We still have to buy booze if we run nightclubs."

"But we don't have to make booze." Li was patient. "What will be different is what we do with the money. We will put it into Chinatown."

"You mean buy the place, honey?"

"No, I mean help it."

There was a sharp knock on Rose's door. Lizzie jumped and Sergeant Huggins lifted his head, curled his pink lips, and growled.

"Oh, God, who's that now?" moaned Rose, finally tired of her unending visitors.

Li opened the door. It wasn't another caller offering sympathy; it was O Ti. He had come not to see Rose, but Li.

O Ti hurriedly bowed in turn to each in the room, then pulled on Li's arm. *"Li seen-sang, ngaw yau dee see-gon seong toong nay gong."*

*"Lan-ch'i, hai mee-ye see? Dang yat tsun,"* Li said to O Ti, then turned back into the room. "I must go. Wait for me, Lizzie."

The green of Lizzie's eyes brightened in her pale tired face. Wait for him? It would take another earthquake to move her.

As Li left, the room was filled with the voices of Rose and Addy and Lizzie, already living in the new world that they and Li would create.

Li led O Ti down the main stairs, through the babble of the Blue Canary, not glancing at the woman who scrubbed the floor at the foot of the staircase, and shut them both in his office.

"It is done? You have them all?"

"Yes, Cheng Lung-t'ou. The Night of Two Moons found them early this morning. Their faces have been properly washed. Most were sleeping. There was no trouble. We left a calling card at each visit as you wanted. The bodies have been removed."

"And Blinn?"

"He was last. And awake. Because of that, we had to kill the old woman too. It could not be helped."

"No," said Li, "it could not be helped. What of Harding?"

Blue Flag's great round pockmarked face broke into a grin. "Ah, yes—the President. That was well done. The Hung family could use Hamilton's red-haired woman. She is like a man. Because she could not carry the President's body alone, she got help. I took her to her friend, a big man with nothing in his face—"

"That would be Leo Olemi."

"Yes, the woman called him Leo. He went with her

into the Palace Hotel. No trouble. There will be no connection with us. I drove away and left them. Then my men and I did the other, as you told us to."

"You did not see James Hamilton?"

O Ti shrugged with disdain. "That one? No. He has hidden himself. If a man has fallen down a well, there is no need to stone him. Hamilton has lost so much face with his woman and with you that he might as well be dead."

Li dropped into English. "A dead man is a dangerous man."

O Ti, not at home in English, did not understand him.

# Chapter 29

Leo Olemi's eyes shifted like the mud at the bottom of a cold river. This wasn't a social call; Leo didn't bother taking off his hat or dull brown coat. Brown hat, brown suit, brown shoes: Leo planted himself in the middle of a room in the Stafford mansion that looked to him like any minute in could walk some goofy old king of France. The layers of Persian carpets under the soles of his shoes—so thick it was like walking around on a mattress—reminded Leo of times when he was a kid and his mother caught him jumping on the bed. She didn't have much to say about it; even as a stout and silent boy, Leo didn't take lip from anyone. But first he'd gone on an astonishing voyage of envy. To get to Hamilton he'd been led from the amber cathedral of a front door, through a Pennsylvania Station of some kind of foyer, down the mansion's long gallery, and past open doors that promised enough exotic loot to satisfy a pirate. Some setup! In well-concealed wonder, Leo followed an oriental runt through Hamilton's dandy hilltop house. To him, all Orientals looked the same—when you've seen one, you've seen them all. Funny that Hamilton would hire a Chink. The quiet mind Leo kept under his hat mentally shrugged. But so what? If you could keep them in their place, Chinks made the best menials. Someday he'd hire one himself.

The Stafford gold and silver and crystal looked at him with a satisfied sneer. Leo sneered back. This was the kind of place he'd always intended for himself. After last night's fuck-up, he might not get it as soon as he'd hoped, but what the hell, so it was later; he'd still get it. The way Leo Olemi played the game, patience was everything.

He was watching James Hamilton pour himself another shot of good Scotch out of a cut-glass decanter. Leo had turned down the offer to share. It was nine o'clock on Thursday night; his town, Frisco, down at the bottom of this high-class hill, was silly with news of Harding, the cops were scattered all over the place like pepper in soup, and here was Frisco's pretty DA already as cut as his fancy decanter. Hamilton was buried in newspapers— he'd been doing a lot of reading. In a far corner, the radio was turned down low, but the muted whine of constant up-to-the-minute broadcasts made a nice backdrop to what Leo had come to say.

They were alone in the Stafford mansion, James sitting on a maroon brocade sofa with Leo standing ten feet away. Menacing as a gargoyle, Leo was doing all the talking. James, for a change silent, was too busy putting the Scotch away. Olemi saw the tremor of the slender hands, the white around the frozen blue eyes, the nervous tic of the fine skin around the mouth. Olemi had his number. The guy had lost his nerve—when the chips were down, Hamilton had a yellow streak Leo could have taken a pratfall on. Still talking, Leo lit a cigarette and began to walk, circling the sofa, forcing James to twist his ashen blond head to follow what he was saying. As he figured, James followed, all right. The guy hated every word Leo had to say, but, like a layman at an autopsy, he listened in fascinated horror.

All day Leo had had the police on his back; the article by Dowie named names. And the press. He'd talked to reporters until he was hoarse. But he'd prepared for that; his answers were simple, pat and believable. Nothing had happened that he didn't expect to happen; he'd had his cover ready for days. Figuring that Blinn would get around to pulling something like this—it was just a matter of when—Leo Olemi prepared well for what was bound to happen next. And everything went just like he figured, right down the line, except that it had all been a waste of time. Li was alive and likely to remain so. Hamilton wasn't going to get that sand from Rose St. Lorraine he coveted any too soon, and, as far as Leo could tell, Leo himself wasn't going to pick up the pieces of Li Kwan Won's operation any sooner. As for Blinn, the way he went about handling the Chinese problem was no more and no less than Leo thought it would be: satisfyingly stupid. But Leo had made one miscalculation. He'd thought it would be just like it was, but he'd also thought it would have results. Taking an army and shooting up a crowded nightclub with machine guns—and still not hitting the target! Christ! A guy had to laugh. But whichever way it went, Leo had made sure he was in a position to do the laughing. His full report, and plans for the immediate future—the East Bay distillery was showing a fat profit—were already on their way back east. He was in the clear with the big New York boys too.

So what the hell? Public suspicion was one thing—fueled by that reporter, Kit Dowie—real evidence another. Leo Olemi's connection to the Blinn gang was going to be harder to find than one particular grain of sand on Rose St. Lorraine's beach.

Meantime, Leo's boys had reported back. The story they told impressed him. Blinn's North Beach speak, the pastry shop, the whole building, had been cleaned up like it'd been hosed down. They'd found that ugly squat-nosed dog there, alone and howling. And that was it. No Murray. No Saddle Mary. It was the same when they got to Coffee Trujillo's squalid room on Turk, the place Jugs Kelly used in the Mission District, Miles Brady's hideout down on Battery, Whispering Mike's and Joe Baglietto's digs over a pawnshop on the corner of Second and Howard. Each the same, but with one exception—for the rest of Murray's mob there wasn't even a dog left behind to

howl. What there was was nothing. His boys told Leo the
hunt had been kind of eerie. Though they hadn't stuck
around to do much snooping, they'd found real easy what
they were meant to find.

What they were meant to find? What Olemi was
meant to see and, through Olemi, James Hamilton? Leo
felt in his pocket, clicking tiny tiles together. Twelve
pieces of some kind of stone. Two for each missing man,
if you didn't count Mary. Mah-jongg tiles. On each was
the imprint of one bamboo and one circle. Leo didn't
know what the symbols on the Chinese tiles meant, but
he knew what they'd been left for: to tell him that Li
Kwan Won had been there first. Leo also knew there
wasn't any point in looking further; there wasn't any
Blinn mob any more. Nice touch for a Chink. Leo smiled
to himself. Next time he wouldn't underestimate the yellow bastard. All in all, that was really his only mistake.
Hamilton wasn't a mistake, he was an experiment.

Sparing himself effort, Leo told James Hamilton all
this in words of no more than two syllables. Then he
tipped the contents of his pocket out on the low table
with the cut-glass decanter and all those newspapers. The
mah-jongg tiles rattled over the table's gleaming surface,
all twelve coming to rest on newsprint.

Leo loved James's response to the spinning stones.
The blue eyes almost popped out of his blond head.
Olemi went for the jugular. "And what about the Presi-
dent—dying on the same night? Some coincidence, eh,
James?"

James managed a quiet, breathy "Yes."

Leo, now just behind Hamilton's head, popped a
knuckle. The sharp snap made James jump. "But even
though it's just bad luck for Harding, there's a stink
brewing. Your wife's friend, that hotshot reporter Dowie,
is on it like a tick. He ain't gonna leave the story alone
like he found it, easy and simple. Funny, but it seems he's
not buying the idea of the President dying in his hotel bed
lonely as a cloud, though Harding's old woman is swearing it's true. She's telling the press her husband suffered a
relapse of that old food poisoning. There's even a rumor
going the rounds that the guy's wife killed him herself to

avoid some political scandal, and one that says he did it himself for the same reason. A scandal? You know anything about a scandal, Hamilton?"

James was in misery. "No. What could I know?"

—"True. What could you know? Stuck here in Frisco, just a humble public servant. We're a long way from Washington, ain't we? But if Dowie is right, what happened? Jesus, how many guys had it in for the poor bastard?" Leo was on his eighth circuit of the couch. "You think he died in his bed, Hamilton?"

James shook his head. "I don't know and I don't care."

"Really? Now, I wonder why that is? But can you figure it? Dowie's on a crusade—and he's got our old friend Bent behind him. Seems Bent is trying to save his ass after the sorry spectacle he made of himself the night before. His own cops found him in the Blue Canary hiding under a whore's bed. Cute, huh?"

Completing his ninth circle, Leo was again standing in front of James. He was disgusted. The guy was so scared, he stank. Ritzy James Hamilton couldn't help Leo in Frisco; hell, he couldn't even help himself. Leo's experiment was finished; the DA was finished. Leo knew it as soon as Esmé knocked on his door in the middle of the night. As soon as he saw the Chink driving the car she came in. Esmé's story, before he'd helped her bundle the body of the President up the back stairs of the Palace Hotel, sickened him. Trying to blackmail Harding with a couple of dirty pictures! The creep had no imagination, no staying power, no guts. Esmé Baker was worth ten of him. She'd played Harding's wife like an oboe. The old dame grabbed at Esmé's solution to their mutual problem. The President had never left the hotel. He'd died in his wife's skinny arms. With the help of the private nurse and two Secret Service men, who could doubt it? Who'd want to? Though he'd have to do something about Esmé's not telling him about Hamilton and his little plot with the camera. But not a lot. The redhead was a naughty lady, but she was OK. Leo spat on Charles Mortimer's carpet.

"I don't know how all this is going to come down,

Hamilton, but I ain't gonna be around for it. You're a dead man, Mr. District Attorney, and you can kiss the White House goodbye."

Startled, James stopped drinking long enough to bluster. "What do you mean, Leo? I had nothing to do with Harding, and Blinn was your idea."

Leo looked down at him, blowing tidy smoke rings over his ashen head. "Was he? Prove it. I *make* dead men, Hamilton, I don't work with them. Where's the little Chink? I wanna get out of here."

Before James could ring for Keiko, Keiko appeared.

Leo laughed. "The guy's been listening, ain't you, little man?"

"I listen," retorted Keiko, "I learn."

"Say, you wanna come work for me?"

"I work for missy."

"Missy? You mean that green-eyed broad? Sure you do, little man. Now show me the way out of this mausoleum. It's beginning to smell in here." As Olemi went, he tossed off a couple of little time bombs. "Say goodbye to the wife for me, James. By the way, it's Thursday. You know what I do every Thursday?"

"No."

"I play games on Telegraph Hill."

Left alone, James held his own hand to stop it shaking. What was he going to do now? Going to the office this morning was a mistake. His flat-eyed secretary, Mrs. Heney, was ruder than ever, slamming down papers for him to sign, ignoring his buzzer; even Stringer Bellew made himself scarce. What the hell could they know about anything? Maybe it was in his face. His voice?

The harlot's voice that had served him so often and so well did not serve him now. No one was listening. Not even that squirt, the traitorous Keiko. When he had got back from the mess at the Blue Canary, James had found Lizzie gone; the lock of her door jimmied—from the outside. Taking the stairs three at a time, he'd burst into Keiko's room, snapping on the light.

"Where's Mrs. Hamilton?"

If Keiko had been asleep, he didn't act like it. He sat

up in his monkish bed and, without blinking, stared at James.

"She go."

"Where, you goddam Jap?"

"Chinatown."

"And you let her go!"

"You say she sick, you lied. Missy is owner here."

James strode to the bed, lifted his hand—and Keiko got a grip on his wrist that made him dance with pain.

"You get out. This my room. This missy's house."

Too astonished to do more than get Keiko to let go of his arm, James beat a retreat. James had never had the stomach for combat, and he'd never had the need. His looks, his manner, his voice had always been enough.

He spent the rest of the night without sleep, using his brains. They got him nowhere. Where was there to go? Chase had been in that whore's room with all the rest of them. He'd seen what there was to see. There went his political backing. And the help of Chase's friend, William John Burns, who headed up the Department of Federal Investigation—the guy who was sniffing around the oil leases. James Hamilton was scared. He just might get his ass burned for Teapot Dome after all. But he went to his office anyway. All he had left was bluff.

The first call he got was from Ed Doheny, Jr.

"That was your idea of handling the situation? Your solution? My God, Hamilton, you're an idiot!"

James, holding his end of the receiver, couldn't believe what he was hearing. Ed Junior talking to him like that! The littlest Doheny! Hamilton's world was collapsing faster than he could run.

"My father and I have decided to terminate any relationship we might have had with you, to deny it publicly if necessary. As for your name not appearing on any of those leases, it does now. All of them."

And then the shit had hung up on him. Hung up! James felt like throwing up.

This evening, Leo Olemi's visit was the last straw. James climbed the Stafford mansion's gilt staircase, gripping the glowing glass seashells to steady himself, ignoring Keiko, who ignored him, and went to his private office. Remembering Esmé. Esmé loved him. A woman like Esmé would understand what happened last night. Sometimes a man gets confused. Picking up the phone, he got the operator, gave her a number—then waited. And waited. How many times could he let it ring? A hundred? A thousand? The operator came on. "I'm sorry, sir. There's no answer."

"Let it ring."

"Yes, sir."

And so it rang. Until someone picked up. Hamilton's heart sat on his tongue like a hot coal.

"Esmé?" The harlot voice was eager, pathetic. "Is that you?"

"Yes."

It was Esmé! It was Esmé's cool clear redheaded voice. "It's James."

Like everything else, the line went dead on him. And James sat there, looking at the black receiver. It was Thursday. Esmé lived on Telegraph Hill. What did Olemi mean, play games? What games? With whom?

James picked up the receiver again, but before he gave his father's number to the operator he changed his mind. Why had he wanted to talk to his father? Was he going mad?

Cocaine! He still had the brilliant white dust. James took out his little gold key.

Dowie was writing one of the biggest stories of his life, a story that wasn't just Harding, a story that was Harding *and* Hamilton, Chinatown, and the Blue Canary. Kit saw Harding go up the stairs, but Kit never saw him come down. Not Harding, not Esmé, not James. And though he'd asked after the shoot-out, no one was answering his questions. Not Rose, not Addy, not Li. He'd spent a moment wondering if he'd been hallucinating, going crazy—until he remembered. Fearless had seen him too. But O'Flooty couldn't help. He'd only seen what Kit had seen. Kit could wait. They'd talk, maybe not Li or Addy, but Rose would; she was a sure bet. And then there was Esmé Baker. He'd camp on that broad's doorstep forever if he had to. Meantime Kit had picked himself up, dusted himself down, slapped his hat on his head, stuck a cigarette in his mouth, forgot to light it—and went to work.

Kit's fingers stabbed at the keys of his typewriter, typing out the name James Alexander Hamilton. San Francisco's DA was a goner. The way things finally were, Kit could write what he wanted about Hamilton, what he *knew:* the stuff he learned in Paris—the black marketeering, the medals that had been purchased, not earned, the kids that didn't have to but died anyway, because James, in army supply, had sold the military's morphine to the highest bidder. Bids never came from the guys in the trenches. James in the Arbuckle case, the Buddy Le Blond–Violet Louise rape, dozens of others; his connection to Blinn, to Leo Olemi. Kit was typing so fast his fingers hurt.

Dowie was working in chaos, a vital commotion. Kit liked noise, energy, danger. Just being alive in this wonderful mess was a vote of confidence in the universe. It wasn't every day a president gets killed, or drops dead, or whatever Harding did. Not in San Francisco anyway. San Francisco wasn't like the driven city of New York or the hurly-burly of Chicago, every day another riot, another Broadway flop, another momentous murder, another department store opening. In San Francisco long stretches of sweet time went by, and then, when something happened, it not only happened, it took the world by its gullible news-hungry neck and shook it.

Every phone in the *Examiner's* newsroom was ringing, and when one wasn't ringing, someone was shouting on it. Over at the *Chronicle,* the *Call,* all over the country, things were the same: loud and frantic. Reporters from out-of-town papers were crowding out the office staff, begging for copy, getting in the way; the city editor was having a nervous breakdown at the top of his voice. Two stories, two *big* stories, in one day! He didn't know what to do with himself, so he stood—short, red-faced, and splay-legged—in the middle of the room and made things worse. He screamed at whoever was closest. Kit stuck to his desk.

It didn't help. "Hey you, Dowie! You some kind of

outlaw? What the fuck do you think you're doing, writing a book?"

His editor was on him, breathing in short quick gasps.

Kit, grown confident by a lessening need, smiled sweetly at him. "Why not? What are you paying me for?" He swept his morning copy off the desk, watching it cradle with little sideways flutters to the dingy floor. "You want more lies?"

"Sure," his editor snapped. "This is a newspaper, isn't it? We need all the lies we can get."

Before Dowie could summon a good wisecrack, the editor was off to yell at someone else. Kit could never top him anyway. What can you do with outright honesty? He went back to what the editor had called his book. His book? Why not? He'd done all the running he needed, taken all the notes. On James, he'd been taking notes for years. He *could* write a book. Kit's only problem was the story he was writing. Even as a book, what was he going to do with it? His official stories, one on Harding and the eyewitness report on the Blue Canary, had already gone to press. Neither one referred to the other. This, on the other hand, was his working of the truth, or what he knew of it. People don't want the truth, not this kind of truth. Look at Willie Hearst—he'd proved it. People wanted fireworks and the roar of guns. Who cared why they went off? The sound was enough.

How had Harding really died? That doctor from Stanford said it was apoplexy brought on by overwork. Crap. Kit had his suspicions. Harding wasn't supposed to be in the Blue Canary. The widow was shrilly denying anything other than the "he died quietly in his sleep" version, and the presidential aides were backing her. Though rumors passed through the office with the speed of back-fence gossip, one canceling out the other, they were just that: rumors.

"As the old man says, you writing a book?"

Tad Dorgan was standing over Kit, trying to read his copy off the typewriter. As usual, Tad was under the influence of about twenty-five cents' worth of nickel-a-glass beer.

"Thinking about it."

"Best place to do it. Free typewriter ribbon, free paper, free telephone, and, sometimes, free time."

"But no publisher. No one would touch it."

"Why not? Too dirty?"

"Dirty enough."

"Oh, goody. Let me read it." Tad's fingers grabbed for the page, smearing it with cartoonist's ink.

Kit slapped his hand away. "Not that kind of dirt."

"Oh." Dorgan, disappointed, lost interest. He wandered off into the turmoil.

For the hundredth time that day, Kit's phone rang.

"Kit. This is Dido."

"Dido, I'm busy. Make it fast."

"Dido'll make it fast as you want. I'm leavin' town. Catchin' the eastbound train one o'clock tomorrow, goin' with Louis an' Lil to Chicago an' then New York. You hear me?"

"I hear you."

"You comin' with me?"

"I don't—"

Dido's chocolate voice rose. "What you got here in Frisco, Dowie? Think about that. You spend tonight thinkin' about it. If you're comin', meet me at the station twelve thirty an' bring your music. If you ain't there, honey, I love you, but Dido is sayin' goodbye. Permanent."

"Dido. Give me a—"

But Dido had hung up. The empty hiss in the receiver sucked at his ear. Permanent? Dido saying goodbye?

For the first time since they had died, Kit allowed himself to think about Ike and Chi Mai. About Lizzie pulling away from him and going to Li. What was he still fooling himself for? Lizzie's black flag was still in his heart. The moment Kit saw Blinn and his men bust into the Canary, he knew he loved the dizzy brunette with the dazzling green eyes enough to get his head blown off for her. Kit was in love with her bounce and crazy flash. No thinking about jumping off the stage—he'd been pushed. And all that drinking and talk with Fearless was more bluster; he hadn't got over Lizzie Stafford. Dido knew it, Rose knew it, O'Flooty knew it, and now Kit knew it. And he knew something else. There wasn't any Lizzie; she was lost to him in Chinatown. The only way to save himself was to go with Dido. The *New York World* would hire him; hell, why not? He was the best. And if he wasn't, Hearst had papers everywhere. He'd transfer.

Dido loved him. Dido was cold and Dido was hard, but she loved him. God, it would be nice to let her love him. And, who knew, maybe he loved her too. Jesus Christ, he *did* love her! Not like he loved that crazy girl he'd been watching grow up, but he loved Dido. He couldn't let her go east without him. Life without Dido? Kit had never had a life without Dido. Kit felt a shiver of loss, of a pain that was bigger and emptier than the loss of Lizzie. Women. Damn!

The phone rang again. Kit ignored it, but it kept on ringing. Holy hell! Wouldn't anyone leave him in peace? He had a story—no, dammit, a *book* to write. A book no one would want to print, a book that Washington, or someone else somewhere, would probably kill him for if he tried to publish, but a story he was damn well going to write.

"All right! Who the hell is it, and what do you want?"

"Kit?"

"Elizabeth?"

"Is that you, Kit? I'm sorry if I'm bothering you, you sound so tired."

"No, I'm not tired, just too many phone calls. What do you want?"

"I want to invite you to lunch."

"What, now? It's nine o'clock at night."

"No, Dowie. Not now. Tomorrow. Noon."

Kit gave himself a second to think it over. Noon? That would still give him enough time to meet Dido by twelve thirty.

"Sure. Where?"

"Meet me in Union Square. We'll think about where when you get there. And Kit—"

"What?" Kit was lying; he *was* tired.

"I'm bringing Li. We have something to tell you."

"Fine. I'll be there."

Kit got to hang up this time. He sat there and looked at the phone. Something to tell him? Whatever it was, he didn't want to hear it. They couldn't be thinking of marriage. Chinese weren't allowed to marry whites in this free country. But he wouldn't have to hear it. He'd meet Lizzie and Li to say goodbye. What else was there to say?

## Chapter 30

This then was Lizzie's new world—narrow streets of small shops and yellow faces. Chinese lantern makers stretching varnished cheesecloth over bellying bamboo frames. Merchants and bankers counting on an abacus, tracing accounts with brushes dipped in thick black ink, their tapering fingernails, curled orange, clicking on little balls strung on wire. Repairers of opium pipes using the smallest and finest of drills, files, burnishers. The candlemakers carving tallow into fantastic shapes: dragons, pagodas, gods. Goods from China piled on the sidewalks and Chinese boys darting in and out of the crowd on the milling streets, playing shuttlecock with their heels. Incense drifting from brass bowls on flowered balconies. The odd pluck and whine of strange lutes. An old world tucked away in a new city, a world of tiny bells and tremendous gongs that suited Lizzie's new taste. Perhaps it was an acquired taste but, for Lizzie, easily won.

The reality of others did not bind or attract her; she lived her life in dreams. Once they were the dreams of a rich girl, flirting at society cotillions and hotel teas; now they were oriental fantasies spun on a fragile web. It was easy to dream in Chinatown, to stand at Li Kwan Won's window in a cloth-of-gold mandarin robe, her hair black and sleek and straight. Lizzie's green eyes were foreign and dim with imagining. Whatever was evil here, whatever was sordid and mean and bitter lurking in back alleys or deep in labyrinths under the streets, was as bright in Lizzie Stafford's awakening mind as the wings of silk butterflies, the painted hawk's eyes on tumbling kites, the oil that slicked the skin of gutter puddles.

But Lizzie was not altogether lost in her dreams. Though still wrapped in soft and coddled illusion, she understood one thing very well. She could never marry Li. And a divorce, even in the modern white mayhem of flappers and hip flasks and jazz, was an outrage that San Francisco would not really forgive. Not the San Francisco that had been hers, the San Francisco that could still be hers for the timely turning back. She knew how Gertie Arlington and Neddie Greenway would react, and it made her smile. "Scandalous!" they would say. They'd said it about Aimee Crocker; they would say it about Elizabeth Sian Stafford Hamilton. Divorce James Hamilton to go off with a Chinese? Barely tolerating Aimee, they would shun Lizzie as if she were toxic with exotic disease. But there would be no turning back. She was in love. The darling of Nob Hill had always *been* loved, but what a thing it was *to* love! It gave her a center, a measure to judge the world by. In less than a month after her second wedding anniversary, twenty-seven days exactly, she was beginning to find the white world wanting. It was much too soon to see Chinatown. But just in time to see herself. Close to waking, she couldn't exclude Lizzie from judgment: a quick child with a quick mind, a quick and shallow child. In her dreams she imagined Lizzie's growth. After the siege of Chinatown, the discovery of usefulness she had made on her own doorstep remained directed and powerful. What Li intended to create, Lizzie intended to nurture.

Abruptly, she turned away from the sun shining on Chinatown to the black-lacquered elegance of Li's apartment. It was eleven thirty. She and Li were meeting Kit Dowie for lunch in Union Square at noon.

Li Kwan Won, slim in a black suit, snowy white shirt, and black tie, a gardenia in his buttonhole, tapped a long brown cigarette on his silver case. "Shall I have a man drive us?"

"No, let's not take a car. We'll walk. Let them see us," said Lizzie. "I want everyone to see us."

Li tipped his head and smiled. "In that case, my little rat, outside Chinatown you will not like what you see."

"You're wrong. Nothing could hurt me today. Not today! Little rat?"

"Hasn't Wong Gow told your fortune yet? I'm surprised at his oversight. Lizzie Stafford Hamilton—"

"Please forget the Hamilton."

"—Lizzie Stafford was born in the Chinese Year of the Rat."

"A rat? Good God, Li, how awful."

"Ah, no, not awful. A soft furred creature with bright eyes. Is that an awful description?"

"A soft furred creature with bright eyes is still a rat."

Li laughed. "Then for you we will call it a mouse. The mouse is meant to bring progress, exploration, and insight. As I am a monkey, and you are a rat—"

"A mouse."

"—the combination should be ideal." Li lit his cigarette, lowering his amused face to the match, the gesture making the conclusion of his thought difficult to hear. "Ideal, that is, but for the obvious, which makes it impossible."

No matter if he'd shouted, Lizzie would not have heard. She was slipping off her golden robe, dropping it to the black carpet, then, wearing only a cream silk chemise and silk stockings, stepping over the fallen robe to open the closet Li had given her for her own use. "Since you are wearing black," she said, "I shall wear white."

Lizzie chose a dress of limp light cotton, white court shoes with pearl buttons, and a soft white felt hat with a big brim that folded down at the sides to touch her shoulders. Dressed in two minutes flat, she posed.

"What do you think?"

"That you are lovely."

"I know. Ain't it grand. Shall we go? Not driving, but walking?"

Li stubbed out his cigarette. "As you wish."

If Lizzie had been looking, she would have noticed that he wished not walking but driving, but she wasn't looking.

Arm in arm, Lizzie and Li stepped out onto Grant Avenue. Today the sun was soft, shimmering in a high haze. From Grant they crossed to Stockton, then turned left. From there it was downhill all the way to Union Square.

Her dark head held high, a proud light glinting in her green eyes, Lizzie walked the four blocks from Stockton and California to Union Square, her left arm linked with Li's, her hand on his wrist. With her right, she held on to her white hat. The salty wind blowing off the bay flipped up its drooping brim, tugging the hat from her head. As she walked, her grip on Li's wrist got stronger. Li was right. What she saw on the faces she passed, before *and* after they left Chinatown, she not only didn't like, she loathed. Yellow faces, white faces. Because she was with Li, the yellow faces averted themselves. But not before she caught the look of surprise and firm disapproval. But the white faces! People turned their heads to stare, stopped dead on the sidewalk, or leaned out of their cars, mouths dropping open, some red with anger. As they crossed Post Street in front of the St. Francis Hotel, one man, holding tight to the hand of a little girl, shook his fist. Jostling Lizzie's arm, a smart middle-aged woman in bold blue-and-white checks made her way past them up the hotel's wide steps. Turning her well-groomed head, she gawked at Li, then Lizzie, and gasped. "Oh, my!" The woman flung up her gloved hand as if warding off evil and ducked into the sanctity of the hotel lobby. Though Lizzie kept her chin up, her fierce black brows came together in fury. For those four long blocks, Lizzie chatted, pointing at shop windows—the displays behind shiny glass changing from block to block—talking of Charles Mortimer, of Kit, of money, of change, her heart beating in her throat. She would not pay attention to the faces. She was with Li. Where she belonged. Damn them all.

Li heard the false laughing words but felt the real grip of Lizzie's fingers. Lizzie had the courage to laugh, Li the courage to keep silent. It had been a long time since he had known fear of the *baak gwai lo,* a long time since he had grown used to their smell. Li had never walked through them as his father walked. Like Dido, Li strode. But he could not fool himself. No one here was going to allow them to keep what they had, not the brisk world of the *baak gwai lo,* not the hidden oriental. Li Kwan Won and Lizzie Stafford were shamed in both. Li did not feel fury but knew, instead, understanding. He and Lizzie were breaking the rules; if one man broke rules, what if two men were to do so, or three, or three thousand? What did rules mean, then? To most, rules were belief, and belief reality. Reality was all that kept the demons of chaos chained. Li and Lizzie were slipping the leads of hell. The thought almost made him laugh.

Li caught Lizzie's white hat just before it blew away. He stopped her to put it back on. But what if he took Lizzie away? The nature of belief and reality was the same everywhere, but the rules changed from place to place. Li's pace quickened. Lizzie, not understanding his mood but delighting in the sweet speed, kept up with him.

Life glimmered within Li's reach. It could be done! Sail away with Lizzie, sail west. Why hadn't he thought of it before? Delegate his business interests here in California to Rose St. Lorraine and Addy Chase? That was easily done too. Rose knew what she was doing. She'd been doing it for years before she found him—or he found her. His loud white ghost. Make O Ti Chief Dragon Head of Chinatown? Blue Flag was a good man. He could control and maintain what a more innovative man had created. Li Kwan Won was calling back the little gray birds of death, reining in the flight of the Fire Horse. To travel. To see the country of his ancestors. Not

Canton but Shanghai. Li could carve an empire in Shanghai. In that northern city, whites and Chinese could walk the city's streets with pride. A Chinese could own land in his own name; the whole city, not merely a yellow ghetto, could be his. Li Kwan Won would live with Lizzie Stafford openly as man and wife. Li had never lowered his head, he did not have to lift it now. But his heart? That was another thing. Li paused at the edge of Union Square, bringing Lizzie to a halt beside him.

"What is it?" Lizzie, surprised at his abruptness, looked frightened.

"I love you, white ghost," Li said, and then, in front of the lowering white faces, faces like the three little monkeys—all pretending they did not see or hear or speak—Li kissed Lizzie, pulling her off her feet until only her pearl-buttoned toes touched the ground.

"God, I love you too, yellow man. We will be happy, I swear it."

Lizzie, holding down her hat, ran across Union Square, scattering pigeons. Li, following more slowly, watched as the dark flocks flapped up and then came back down again on the very same spot. Black was draped everywhere, over the balconies, hanging from the windows. The American flags that had hung for almost a week for the visit of President Harding were now at half mast. Impervious, the gray stone monument to Victory stood unnoticed in the middle of the square. In cutaways and a pair of black trousers, the body of Warren Gamaliel was already on its mournful way east, his private railroad car as full of fading bouquets as Rose's white room. By dying, the sad man from Ohio had plunged America into heartfelt gloom but saved himself from the full force of gathering American wrath.

"There's Kit!" called Lizzie, waving the white hat. "Kit! We're over here!"

The crowd in Union Square made way for them, edging away from the sight of the lovely white woman and the young Chinese man. Boys on bicycles, office girls in cloche hats, workers with lunch bags sprawling on the grass, the old on the benches, all blind, deaf, and dumb.

The bells of old St. Mary's began to toll twelve. Lizzie, missing the message of Kit's heavy suitcase, collided with Dowie, spinning him around. "Kit, you came! God, it's good to see you." She had to shout to be heard over the bells.

Three steps behind, Li caught up with them. Unlike Lizzie, Li noticed Kit's suitcase. "You are finally leaving?"

The word "leaving" caught Lizzie's attention. "Leaving? Who's leaving?"

"I am." Kit was in his best suit, a tobacco-colored number with a nipped-in waist. His hat was snappy and his tie was loud. He was standing right next to the curled-back bench he'd spent a good part of Sunday morning sitting on, getting wet and feeling miserable. Behind him, the English chestnut tree flopped its useless leafy hands in the sea breeze. Today, the only real difference for Kit was the sun.

Lizzie looked into Kit's guarded eyes. "Where to?"

"Chicago and then New York."

"When?"

"Now. I've only got a minute, can't make lunch. I came to say goodbye."

Lizzie, unsure of her reaction, tripped over what she thought was her joy for him. The words came out crooked, like her stunned smile. "Why, that's wonderful, Kit. Isn't that wonderful, Li? Kit was made for New York."

"Dido thinks so too."

"You're taking Dido?"

"She's taking me."

"And the newspaper, your job?"

"I quit."

"But Kit, you're a reporter."

"I'm a writer, kid. I'll write books. And who knows? Maybe someday somebody'll buy one." Kit held out his hand to Li. "So long, fella. Wish me luck."

Smiling, Li shook the hand of the boy he'd grown up with. "We are leaving too."

Kit stared at Li.

Lizzie stared at him harder. "We are?"

"Oh, shit," Kit shoved his hat back. "Don't tell me you two are going to New York as well."

"No, not New York," said Li. "Shanghai."

"Shanghai!" Lizzie put her head back and laughed, the long line of her white throat defined in the San Francisco sun, her black hair under the big white hat highlighted blue. "When, Li? When—"

But the words dried on her lips, dried and blew away like burnt paper in a hot wind. Over Li's shoulder, pushing through the sullen crowd that moved around them, a crowd they'd forgotten, she'd seen James. Ashenfaced, blue eyes glinting like chipped ice, Hamilton stepped across the space the people of San Francisco had given to Li and Lizzie and Kit.

They stood there for no more than a second. To Lizzie it was an eternity. All the young men in her life— and Elizabeth Sian Stafford. Way above them loomed Charles Mortimer's monstrous mansion. The hard sun shattered on the glass of Keiko's solarium. Time hadn't slowed, it had stopped. She looked from the strangely set face of her husband—the weak handsome man with bad teeth she'd come to hate—to Kit's sudden mask of dark alarm, and then sought Li's. What she saw in Li Kwan Won's face froze her heart. The beautiful slanted eyes accepted what was about to happen—and some dark mad thing *was* going to happen. My God! Li welcomed it. Some instinct made Lizzie reach for his arm. Li stepped away from her.

"Wong Gow meant me after all," he said. There was pity in his voice. Who did he pity? Who?

With Li's words, time began again, slowly. Picking up speed by the second. But it started like a dream underwater, like a slow dive. This couldn't be happening, couldn't be repeating itself—it had happened before. Two days ago, a week ago, years? The devil doesn't come calling twice, does he? Lizzie turned back to James. And the seconds blurred, went into double-time.

The wind whipped off her white hat, spinning it across Union Square. "No! James!" Lizzie was screaming, but she couldn't hear herself scream. To her own ears it sounded distant, apart, like a fading echo.

The gray gun in James's gray hand came up, pointing at Lizzie, then Kit, coming to rest on Li. Calmly, Li walked toward the gun. And Kit, pushing against solid air, moved in front of Lizzie.

James pulled the trigger, not once, but until the gun emptied. James fired and kept firing until the hammer hit on empty space, making horrid little clicks on steel. Then he threw the gun down and walked away—back into the crowd of white faces, whiter now, stunned by the madness of gunshots shredding a mourning summer's day. In a shameful parody of manners, the crowd opened, making silent way, and then closed behind the district attorney, swallowing Hamilton into itself.

And Li fell. Lizzie pushed past Kit to follow Li down to the green grass of Union Square, holding him, trying to give him life with what was left of her own. From the moment she saw the gun in James's hand until the moment Li lay in her arms, she'd been screaming. And San Francisco heard her scream; people ran toward the shrieks from across the square, from the big hotels and fine restaurants, from the fashionable stores, the flower stalls, the offices, the coffee shops. Everyone heard her but Lizzie. Li's blood, red as the floor of Rose St. Lorraine's Blue Canary had been red, red as Appetite Ike's vest was red, red as the blue blood of Nob Hill, a rich Chi Mai red, blossomed on Lizzie's white dress as she cradled his head.

"Li! Don't die, please!"

Li smiled at her, blood bubbling from between his lips. Slowly, his beautiful blooded mouth formed words. "What does it take to make a man learn? Take my little mouse away, Kit."

"Away?" Lizzie hadn't cried, but her eyes stung as if they'd been dashed with fine white sand.

Li coughed and a great hot gush of fresh blood streamed over Lizzie's hands. With the hem of her white cotton dress she gently wiped his face.

"The Fire Horse took its time," Li whispered. Lizzie had to bend her dark head close to hear. "It came for me a long time ago, I have only been waiting—"

Li's slim body went limp.

"He's gone, Lizzie," whispered Kit, pulling her up.

Her green eyes wild, half mad with dreadful insight, Lizzie twisted on her white heels, pushing Dowie away with bloody hands.

"Leave me alone, Kit! *I* killed him, didn't I? You watched me do it. I killed Li, just like you said I would. Like Rose and Addy said I would. And you all tried to stop me, God, how you tried, but you couldn't. You couldn't—and if you come near me, I'll kill you too!"

Kit had never felt pity for Lizzie Stafford. There was no pity now. There was only love for the poor rich child whose passage into life had cost her so much—had cost them all such a terrible price. "You can't kill me. You can't kill anyone who doesn't want to die."

Gasping for air, Lizzie looked into Kit's eyes. What she saw made her grasp Dowie's neck and push her fierce face against his chest.

Kit lifted her to her feet, brushed the wet black hair from her green eyes.

His arm around her shoulders, Kit Dowie led Lizzie through the curious jostling crowd, her white dress a hateful red flower, her dark head high.

The seven hills of the city shivered.

Sleek and jumpy San Francisco, grand and glittery city, waited, poised for a leap into the vast blue Pacific. Maybe not now, maybe not for a hundred years—but she would jump. What is a hundred years to the patient sea?

# About the Author

The daughter of a nightclub singer and an Iroquois Indian lad, Pamela Longfellow was born in New York City and raised in Northern California, the Carolinas, and Hawaii. She has been a reluctant actress, an unruly model, has cattle-ranched on Montana's Blackfoot Indian Reservation, wandered Europe, and wound up creating a showboat out of a Baltic Trader. She sailed it around England in the media's glare and left it in Bristol. For the moment she lives in Avon, where she is working on her second novel.

# DON'T MISS
## THESE CURRENT
## Bantam Bestsellers

| | | | |
|---|---|---|---|
| ☐ | 28390 | **THE AMATEUR** Robert Littell | $4.95 |
| ☐ | 28525 | **THE DEBRIEFING** Robert Littell | $4.95 |
| ☐ | 28362 | **COREY LANE** Norman Zollinger | $4.50 |
| ☐ | 27636 | **PASSAGE TO QUIVIRA** Norman Zollinger | $4.50 |
| ☐ | 27759 | **RIDER TO CIBOLA** Norman Zollinger | $3.95 |
| ☐ | 27814 | **THIS FAR FROM PARADISE** Philip Shelby | $4.95 |
| ☐ | 27811 | **DOCTORS** Erich Segal | $5.95 |
| ☐ | 28179 | **TREVAYNE** Robert Ludlum | $5.95 |
| ☐ | 27807 | **PARTNERS** John Martel | $4.95 |
| ☐ | 28058 | **EVA LUNA** Isabel Allende | $4.95 |
| ☐ | 27597 | **THE BONFIRE OF THE VANITIES** Tom Wolfe | $5.95 |
| ☐ | 27510 | **THE BUTCHER'S THEATER** Jonathan Kellerman | $4.95 |
| ☐ | 27800 | **THE ICARUS AGENDA** Robert Ludlum | $5.95 |
| ☐ | 27891 | **PEOPLE LIKE US** Dominick Dunne | $4.95 |
| ☐ | 27953 | **TO BE THE BEST** Barbara Taylor Bradford | $5.95 |
| ☐ | 26892 | **THE GREAT SANTINI** Pat Conroy | $4.95 |
| ☐ | 26574 | **SACRED SINS** Nora Roberts | $3.95 |

Buy them at your local bookstore or use this page to order.

## THE LATEST IN BOOKS
## AND AUDIO CASSETTES